# NiKOS KAZANTZAKiS

# THE FRATRICIDES

TRANS-
LATED
FROM
THE
GREEK
BY
ATHENA
GIANAKAS
DALLAS

A TOUCHSTONE BOOK
*Published by Simon & Schuster, Inc.*
NEW YORK

Published by Simon & Schuster, Inc.
Simon & Schuster Building
Rockefeller Center
1230 Avenue of the Americas
New York, New York 10020

TOUCHSTONE and colophon are registered trademarks
of Simon & Schuster, Inc.

Manufactured in the United States of America

10 9 8 7 6 5  4 3 2 1 Pbk.

Library of Congress Cataloging in Publication Data

Kazantzakis, Nikos, 1883-1957.
  The fratricides.

  (Touchstone book)
  Translation of: Aderphophades.
  1. Greece—History—Civil War, 1944-1949—Fiction.
I. Title.
PA5610.K39A653  1984     889'.332     84-27604

ISBN 0-671- 27221-7 Pbk.

I said to the almond tree: "Speak to me of God."
And the almond tree blossomed.

> God Speaks
> Whoever seeks me finds me,
> Whoever finds me knows me,
> Whoever knows me loves me,
> Whoever loves me, I love,
> Whomsoever I love, I kill.
> —SIDNA ALI THE MOSLEM
> (9th century)

# I

THE SUN ROSE in Castello. It had flooded the rooftops and now overflowed, spilling onto the dipping, narrow back streets, pitilessly uncovering the harsh ugliness of the village. Stark and ashen, the houses were barren, stone piled on stone, their doors so low one had to stoop to enter—and within was darkness. The courtyards smelled of horse manure, goat droppings, and the heavy stench of man. Not a single house had a tree in its courtyard, or a songbird in a cage, or a flower-pot in the window, with perhaps a root of basil or a red carnation; everywhere, only stone upon stone. And the souls who lived within these stones were hard and inhospitable. Mountains, houses, people—they were all granite.

Rarely, even in the good years, was the sound of laughter heard in this village; it seemed indecent, an act against nature; the old men would turn and wrinkle their brows, and immediately the laughter would cease. And when the great feast days came—Christmas, Pentecost, Easter—and the people ate a bit more, drank a bit more, and stretched their graceless necks to sing, what a lament it was! Heart-rending, tragic, endless! Trilling mournfully as it passed from one mouth to the other. What ancient terrors, what massacres, it evoked, what slavery, what eternal hunger! Their song revealed, more than their tears could, the incurable trial of their lives, the thousands of years that had passed over them—years full of hunger, of the whip-

7

lash, of death. But they, like cliffweeds, had hooked on to these inhuman gray rocks and would not be torn away. As long as the world endured, these hard-headed people of Epirus would not let go.

Their bodies and their souls were the color and the hardness of stone; they had become one with it, soaked by rain, tanned by the sun, covered by snow; all together, as though they were all people, as though they were all stones. And when a man and a woman left their lonely existences and the priest came to marry them, they had not a single tender word to say, they did not know how. Silently they merged under the rough woolen blankets, with only one thought in mind: to make children—that they might pass on to them these stones, these hills, this hunger.

So many women, so few men! When they marry and the son is planted in the woman's womb, most of the men leave. How else can one survive in this barren wasteland? They go far and are long in returning. "Wide-flung travelers and slow returners" the plaintive song calls them, for they leave their wives behind, alone. And the women wither, and their breasts sag, and hair grows on their upper lip. And when they go to bed at night, to sleep, they are cold.

Their life is an unceasing battle with God, with the winds, with the snow, with death. For this reason the Castellians were not surprised when the killing began, brother against brother. They were not afraid; they did not change their way of life. But what had been simmering slowly within them, mute and unrevealed, now burst out, insolent and free. The primeval passion of man to kill poured from within them. Each had a neighbor, or a friend, or a brother, whom he had hated for years, without reason, often without realizing it. The hatred simmered there, unable to find an outlet. And now, suddenly, they were given rifles and hand grenades; noble flags waved above their heads. The clergy, the army, the press urged them on—to kill their neighbor, their friend, their brother. Only in this manner, they shouted to them, can faith and country be saved! Murder, that most ancient need of man, took on a high mystic meaning. And the chase began—brother hunting brother.

Some of the men put on red hoods and took to the hills.

8

Others barricaded themselves in the village, their eyes glued to the top of Mount Etoraki across the way, where the guerrillas were hiding. With whooping cries the red-hooded ones would storm down the hill, or the black tops would attack from below. And they would pounce on each other, flesh against flesh. And the sweet fratricide would begin. Women with tousled hair dashed from the courtyards and climbed onto the terraces, shouting, to goad the men on. The dogs of the village howled; they ran panting behind their masters, their tongues hanging out as they joined in the hunt; until night came and swallowed up the people.

Only one man stood among them, unarmed and disillusioned, his arms outstretched and empty: Father Yánaros, the village priest. He stood alone, looking to the left and to the right, not knowing which way to turn, constantly asking himself that same agonizing question: "If Christ came down to earth today, whose side would He take? Would He go with the blacks? With the reds? Or would He, too, stand in the middle, with arms outstretched, shouting, 'Brothers, unite! Brothers, unite!' " Father Yánaros, God's representative in Castello, stood in just this manner and called to the people. He cried out, but they passed him by, all of them, the blacks and the reds, jeering and shouting, "Bulgar! Traitor! Bolshevik!"

"Tramp! Fascist! Scoundrel!"

And Father Yánaros would shake his head, dazed, and walk on. "Thank You, Lord," he would murmur. "Thank You for choosing me for this dangerous task. I can endure it, even though I am not loved here. Only don't pull the rope too tightly, Lord. I am a man, not an ox or an angel. I'm only human; how much more can I endure? One of these days I might snap. Forgive me for telling You this, Lord, but at times You seem to forget it, and You ask more of man than of Your angels."

Every morning when Father Yánaros woke up and opened the small window of his cell, he would look out, directly across the way, to the stiff-necked mountain of Etoraki that had no water, no trees, no birds—only rocks; and he would sigh. His thoughts would wander far, back to a sandy shore on the

Black Sea, to the noble village of St. Constantine, where he was born seventy years ago. What peace, what happiness! How well God had cared for that spot! Surely the large icon in the church iconostas, to the left side of Christ, was not an artist's mad fantasy; it was real: St. Constantine, their patron saint, held the village in the palm of his hand, like a nest of eggs, and was about to place it at God's feet.

And when the month of May came, and with it the festival of the saint, what strange intoxication enveloped the town! It was a holy drunkenness, a drunkenness without wine. Everyone forgot his daily cares; they forgot that they were human worms, and sprouted multicolored wings that reached the sky.

"Can man, then, surpass man?" Father Yánaros would ask himself. And he replied: "He can! Yes, he can, but only for an hour, perhaps two hours, perhaps even a whole day; but no longer. This is the meaning of eternity; this is the meaning of the God's Fire that men call Paradise."

Father Yánaros had entered this Paradise many times. Every morning, here in this wild stone village, he recalled those days, and his thoughts wandered back to the Black Sea. There was a holy sect of seven members that took the religious name of "Anastenarides." Father Yánaros was their leader, the Arch-Anastenaris. They performed an ancient ritual, which may have gone back further than Christianity, stemming perhaps from ancient idolatry. He remembered how they would light a huge fire in the center of town. The people would gather around, chanting hymns; the musicians would come with the lyre and the giada; the door of the church would open, and the Anastenarides would appear, barefoot, clutching their "forebears" in their arms: the old icons of St. Constantine and his mother, Saint Helen. But these saints were not depicted in the traditional manner of religious rigidity; they were shown, instead, leaping in mid-air, dancing, with their golden robes tucked and gathered about them.

Until the Anastenarides appeared, the lyre and giada went wild; the clamor would rise to hysteria; people shouted, women fell quivering to the ground. The Anastenarides would proceed hurriedly, one behind the other, with Father Yánaros, neck outstretched, leading the procession, singing wild erotic songs to Death the Doorkeeper, who opens the door for us into eternity. When the flames had consumed the holy wood, and the coals crackled, Father Yánaros would leap into the fire. Behind him followed the whole brotherhood, and the firewalkers would kick at the lighted coals as they began to dance. Father Yánaros scooped up handfuls of the lighted coals as he sang, and threw them at the people as if he were sprinkling the faithful with holy water. What *is* God and eternal life in Paradise? Paradise is this fire, and God is this dance, and they last not just a moment, but forever and ever.

And when they emerged from this holy fire, not a single burn appeared on their feet; not even a hair on their legs had been singed. Their bodies shimmered as though they had emerged from the cool sea on a hot summer day.

All year round the hearts of the villagers were illuminated by the reflection of this holy fire. And love and peace and happiness reigned over the people, and the beasts, and the crops in the fields. The earth was fertile, wheat and cornstalks grew high, olive trees were overladen with the blessed fruit, heaps of melons lay in the fields. Abundant were the gifts of God! Yet this good life did not corrupt the people; the moment their souls became too fat and were in danger of turning into flesh, the holiday of the saint would come again. Once more the huge fires would burn, once more the people would sprout wings.

But suddenly—why? Who was to blame? No great sin had been committed in the village. As always, the villagers fasted during Lent, they ate no meat or fish on Wednesdays and Fridays, they drank no wine on those days, they went to church every Sunday, brought holy bread, prepared kolyva,* confessed, and received communion. Not one wife raised her eyes to look at another man, not one husband raised his eyes to look at another woman. Everyone followed the path of God, everything was going well. And suddenly, as God leaned mercifully over the happy village, He turned His face the other way. Im-

---

* Boiled and prepared wheat that is blessed and distributed at memorial services for the dead.

mediately the village fell into darkness. One morning a heart-rending cry came from the square: "Uproot yourselves! The strong of the earth command. Go! The Greeks to Greece, the Turks to Turkey! Take your children, your wives, your icons, and get out! You have ten days!"

A lament rose throughout the village; the people ran back and forth in confusion, bidding farewell to the walls, the looms, the village spring, the wells. They went down to the seashore and fell on the sand, rolled on the seashells, said good-bye to the sea, and chanted dirges. It is difficult, you see, very difficult, for the soul to tear itself away from familiar soil and familiar waters. One morning, Father Damianos, the older priest, rose at daybreak. He ran through the village alone, without the town crier or Father Yánaros, the younger priest. He ran, from door to door, shouting, "The hour has come! In the name of God, my children, the hour has come!"

From the early hours of dawn, the bells tolled sadly. All night the women had baked bread, the men had hurriedly gathered all they could carry from their homes. Now and then an old woman began to chant a dirge, but the men, swollen-eyed, turned and shouted for her to stop. What good are tears? God said it shall be, so let it be, let's get it over with! But quickly, quickly, before our hearts break, before we fully realize the tragedy. Hurry, friends, lend a hand! Let's bake the bread, let's sack the flour; our journey will be long, so let us take with us our daily essentials: pots, pans, mattresses, holy icons! Do not be afraid, brothers! Our roots are not in earth alone, they spread to the sky and thrive there, too. That is why our race is immortal. Onward then, my children, courage!

The wind was blowing—wintry weather—the waves became wilder, the sky filled with clouds; not a single star was visible. The two priests of the village, old Father Damianos and the black-bearded Father Yánaros, hurried back and forth from the church, gathering the icons, the holy chalice, the silver-bound Bible, the gold-embroidered robes. They paused to bid farewell to the Pancreator who reigned from the dome on which he was painted. Father Damianos gazed wide-eyed at Him. For the first time he noticed how wild He looked, how His lips tightened in anger and scorn, how He held the Bible as if it were a boulder He was about to hurl on the people's heads.

12

Father Damianos shook his head. He was pale, weak, his cheeks were sunken; all that was left of his face were two large eyes; fasting and prayer and love of man had eaten away his body. He looked at the Pancreator with fear; how was it that all these years he had not really seen Him? He turned to Father Yánaros, wanting to ask, "Was He always this wild-looking?" but he was ashamed.

"Father Yánaros," he said finally, "I am very tired. Gather the icons we are to take with us, my son. We will burn the rest —God will forgive us; we will burn them so that the infidels cannot defile them. Gather the ashes that remain and distribute them to the villagers to keep as amulets. And I will go knocking on the doors and shout, 'The hour has come! The hour is here!' "

Dawn began to break. From behind the dark clouds the sun appeared, bald and sickly. A melancholy light licked the village; the doors opened, revealing the blackness within. A few roosters crowed, for the last time, on the manure lying in the courtyard. The stables opened, and out came the oxen, the mules, the donkeys, and behind them the dogs and the people. The village smelled of freshly baked bread.

Father Damianos went from house to house. "God's blessing upon you, my children," he pleaded as he went. "Do not weep, do not curse. It is God's will, and who knows, it may be for our own good. Surely it must be for our own good! He is our Father, would a Father want what is bad for His children? No, never! You will see that the Lord has prepared more fertile fields for us to take root in. Like the Jews, we are moving from the land of the faithless to the land of promise, where milk and honey flow, where the grapevines reach man's height."

On the eve of the festival the people set out in a procession— men, women, and children, all together—and headed toward the small, well-kept cemetery on the outskirts of town, to say good-bye to their ancestors. The weather was melancholy; it had rained the night before, and raindrops were still clinging to the leaves on the olive trees. The earth beneath them was soft and smelled of the rain. Father Damianos walked ahead, wearing his finest vestments with his gold-embroidered stole, carrying the silver-bound Bible in his arms. Behind him followed the crowd, and at the very end walked Father Yánaros,

13

holding the small silver font filled with holy water, and the sprinkler made of thick, bunchy rosemary. They did not chant or cry or speak; they walked, bent and silent. Only once in a while a woman sighed or a deep "Kyrie Eleison" escaped from aged lips. The young mothers had taken out their breasts and were feeding their babies.

They reached the cypress trees; Father Damianos pushed open the gate and entered; the people followed. The dark wooden crosses were soaked from last night's rain, a few lamps burned on the graves, half-faded photographs behind glass testified to the young girls and the handsome young men with curled mustaches who were once alive. The crowd scattered, each finding his beloved grave, the women fell to their knees and kissed the earth. The men, standing, made the sign of the cross and dabbed their eyes with the ends of their shirtsleeves.

Father Damianos paused in the middle of the cemetery, raised his hands and cried, "Fathers, farewell! We are leaving, farewell! The strong of the earth no longer allow us to live beside you, to die and lie down beside you, to become dust again with you. They are uprooting us; a curse upon those who are responsible! A curse upon those who are to blame!"

The people raised their hands to the sky; they raised their voices loudly. "A curse on those who are to blame! A curse on those who are to blame!"

They rolled on the ground, kissed the rain-soaked earth, rubbed it on their foreheads, their cheeks, their necks. Again and again they bent and kissed the soil; they kissed their beloved dead and cried, "Good-bye!"

Father Yánaros walked between the graves and sprinkled holy water over them. Behind him the relatives of the dead cried out, "Good-bye!" "Good-bye, brothers!" "Good-bye, cousins and fathers!" "Forgive us for leaving you at the mercy of the infidels. It is not our fault, may God damn those who are to blame."

Father Damianos knelt on the ground, opened the Holy Bible and began to read from the Gospel of the Resurrection. His voice had suddenly strengthened; it no longer trembled. During the emptying of the church he had taken the Bible from the Holy Altar, opened it, and marked the Gospel of the Crucifixion with a red ribbon. He had decided to read from that, but now, among the beloved dead, he could not bear to leave them saying "My God, my God, why hast Thou forsaken me?" as the final word. He suddenly decided, now, to read the joyful words: "*Christos anesti!*"—"Christ has risen!" He read from the Gospel of the Resurrection and then he let out a loud cry. "Patience, fathers, we will meet again in the Second Coming. Christ has risen! Death is conquered! Death is no more! Man shall be resurrected, so be patient, beloved ancestors. A happy reunion to us all!"

The crowd rose to their feet, the soil from the graves still clinging to their hair and their faces. They took courage, stretched out and joined hands as though they wanted to comfort one another. And almost automatically, they began to dance around the graves, slowly, serenely. And their eyes and their throats were full of tears. They danced quietly, their eyes glued to the wooden crosses, their lips forming the syllables of the blessed names carved there. They looked around anxiously, as though they wanted to pick up the rain-soaked crosses with the photographs and tin wreaths, the cypress trees and the earth, the bones that were buried beneath the earth, and take them along. Take them and leave, tear out their roots and go. They danced quietly, peacefully, and suddenly they lifted their eyes and saw the rainbow—green and red and gold—spreading across the sky, its feet touching the earth. "A good omen, brothers," Father Yánaros cried. "This is the Sash of the Virgin and it has spread over us to comfort and protect us. We raised our hands to the sky, we called to God and He has answered us: 'Go, my children, go, with my blessings,' He replies, 'Go on your way, the Virgin is coming with you—there is Her Holy Sash!' "

Again Father Damianos led the way; the crowd turned for a last look at their dead, but they saw nothing; all eyes had blurred, the world had become a cloud of tears. A frightened cry rose from the living.

"Courage, my children, courage," Father Damianos shouted. "Have faith in God—do not weep." And he wept.

They were patient, controlling their tears until they returned to the village; then they locked themselves inside their homes and began the lament.

Early the next morning they loaded their donkeys and

mules. It was thundering, and a light rain began to fall. They herded the sheep, the goats, the oxen of the village. The housewives lingered on the stoops of their houses, they did not have the heart to tear themselves away. In the church courtyard Father Yánaros had made a pile of all the icons they could not take with them. He made the sign of the cross and set fire to them; the Christs, the Virgins, the Apostles, the Saints all became ashes. Father Yánaros scooped up the remains with a wooden shovel, raised it high, and scattered them to the wind.

They were ready. They made the sign of the cross, fell to the ground, and kissed the earth. They had lived here for thousands of years, generation upon generation; this earth was made up of their ashes, of their sweat and blood. They kissed the soil, dug their nails into it, took handfuls and hid it in their clothing. With forced patience they murmured to themselves, "God is great." "God loves His people." "Whatever God does He does for our good." They steeled their hearts so they would not cry out, but suddenly they could hold back no longer; the first to let out a cry was Father Damianos.

"Good-bye, beloved soil," he cried, "good-bye, fathers!"

His tears fell to the ground, and his beard, his eyebrows, his lips, were covered with mud.

The rain fell in torrents now, making both mud and people one.

Years and years have passed since then, but that black dawn with the mud and the weeping never passes. They took the road to exile—days, nights, weeks—they were cold, hungry. Father Yánaros' wife, a delicate, gently bred woman, could not endure the hardships of the journey; she fell ill and died in her husband's arms. But Father Yánaros did not cry, he lifted his hands to the sky; his lips burned with resentment—resentment and grief—but he controlled himself, he did not utter a sound. He lowered his hands to earth, to the beloved dead body. Alone, he dug a grave on the side of the road, buried her, and went slowly on his way again behind his comrades.

Days, nights, weeks, until one evening they reached the promised land—an empty village recently vacated by the Turks. The two priests blessed the town, they sprinkled holy water over the houses, exorcised the Mohammedans, baptized the town

16

and named it St. Constantine. They made the sign of the cross and entered their new homes. But the village was small, there was not room for two priests; so Father Yánaros took to the road again, with his robes under his arm and a small bundle flung over his shoulder. All that he owned—his two oxen, a few sheep, the clothing and wheat he had brought with him—he gave to the village before he left. Where could he go? What would become of him? He stood in the middle of the road and pondered; he was completely alone, his wife had died, his son—his only son—had left home years ago and had gone wandering from port to port, drifting, threshing the seas, once as a smuggler, once as a captain. Alone, completely alone now, where could Father Yánaros go? He stood there, undecided, in the middle of the road, and night fell. There was not a single light or a door he could knock on to find human warmth. He thought of turning back, but he was ashamed. "All right, Father Yánaros, now let's see what you're made of—heart or mud?" he said to himself. "Get up and walk! Walk and let the road take you where it may. Let God be your guide—He knows." Three days he walked.

On and on he went, no longer questioning where he was going; he knew the Unseen led the way, and Father Yánaros followed with confidence. What joy! he thought, not having to question or fear anything, not allowing the mind to govern, not believing in the visible, but trusting the Unseen and going on!

He came to a brook of clear water and noticed an old man who was bending over the side watching the flowing water with deep concentration. Father Yánaros approached him and leaned over to see what held the old man's attention; he saw nothing except the water.

"What are you looking at, grandfather?" he asked with curiosity.

The old man raised his head and smiled sadly. "At my life flowing and disappearing, son, flowing and disappearing."

"Don't worry, grandfather, it knows where it's going—toward the sea, everyone's life flows toward the sea."

The old man sighed. "Yes, my son, that is why the sea is salty—from the many tears."

17

He turned back to the flowing stream and did not speak again.

He does not believe in God—that is why he fears death, thought Father Yánaros and went on his way. He passed through villages, knocked on doors, they all had their priests, so he went on. He walked with his vestment stole and the Bible under his arm. "Lead the way, Christ," he repeated over and over again, "lead the way, I am following You."

For days now, a tall, snow-capped mountain in the distance came nearer and nearer. Father Yánaros watched with awe as it grew larger; he had never seen a hill with such divine, unearthly serenity. It resembled God the Father, with the snow-white clouds, the snow-white beard, the open arms bent over the green earth with stern kindness. Father Yánaros had entered a ravine; he stopped, dazed—what greenery, what fragrance, what solitude! There were evergreen oaks everywhere, bushes, myrtles, berry trees, and enormous chestnut trees. A holy place, it smelled like church on Holy Saturday. Father Yánaros felt that God commanded him to stop here in this unmarred solitude, after the four days and four nights He had guided him.

The sky had cleared, not a cloud was in sight, the first rays of the sun fell from the sky, and the earth awakened. He went further on; now he could hear the roosters crowing. And suddenly, through the chestnut trees, the sea appeared, sparkling in the distance. From afar the damp wind carried the sweet sound of a wooden bell tolling. Father Yánaros removed his hood, made the sign of the cross and thought, There must be a monastery nearby sounding matins.

He ran, climbed on a small incline, and looked across the way. There, above the sea, wedged in the rocks, was a white multi-storied structure with many doors and windows, with towers and cypress trees. A monk with a spade over his shoulder was walking along the path below. Father Yánaros ran down the incline and signaled the monk as he shouted, "Where am I, holy Father? What do I see there, or am I dreaming?"

The monk stopped. He was young, with a black curly beard, a pointed brown woolen hood, a leather belt, and small eyes that glittered cunningly. His bare feet showed under his gathered robes. He waited a long while before answering; he was looking at Father Yánaros from head to toe.

"Are you a priest?" he said at last. "Where do you come from? What do you want here?"

"Answer my question first," Father Yánaros replied angrily, "and then you can interrogate me."

"Don't get angry, old man!"

"I'm not angry, I'm only asking you, Where am I?"

"Mount Athos," the monk replied, and his eyes twinkled devilishly. "Have you come here to become an ascetic? God help you!"

He lowered the spade from his shoulder and laughed. "If you have a wife, don't bring her here. If you have a female goat or a hen or a ewe, or a bitch, don't bring them either. This is the Garden of the Virgin, no member of the female sex can enter. So think it over!"

Father Yánaros bowed to the ground and prayed. "O immaculate mountain of the God-beloved Virgin," he murmured, "how happy I am to have found you."

The monk watched him, and his eyes, his eyebrows, even his beard laughed.

"Who brought you here?" he said at last, and cupped his hand over his mouth to hide the laughter.

"God," Father Yánaros replied.

"Then lots of luck to you." He snickered and placed the spade back over his shoulder and started off.

He walked awhile, but the devil inside of him nudged him and he stopped. "Don't get yourself in a turmoil, Father," he shouted. "We don't have women here, but we have Nereids, and we manage just as well with them!"

He burst into laughter and disappeared into the myrtles.

"What an ugly way to enter Your garden, my beloved Virgin," Father Yánaros murmured, and his heart tightened. "What gardeners are these You have in Your employ?"

He made the sign of the cross again and entered the Virgin's Garden.

How long he remained on Mount Athos, no one ever knew. He never revealed in what monasteries he had been an ascetic, or why one day he got up and left. Only occasionally he spoke of the Monastery of the Josephian Brothers, where he had remained two years, and learned to paint icons.

There were ten monks, with a glass-enclosed veranda for their

19

workshop. Every week one of them would cook, wash, and sweep, while the other nine, free from daily chores, painted. They painted the cheeks of Christ too red, the saints too well-dressed and too well-nourished. Their cellars were well stocked with food, their brushes were heavy with red paints and their hearts were at peace. Ascetism in this holy place had become relaxation and red paint and luxury.

Life in this monastery appeared just too accommodating to Father Yánaros; this was no holy mountain. He suddenly realized that happiness was a trap of Satan; he was frightened. He yearned to suffer, to hunger, to take the uphill road, to crawl on his knees over the stones, to find God—this should be the meaning of Holy Mountain.

"And so I left," he would say to end the conversation. "I left the comfortable Monastery of the Josephian Brothers, and I went through all twenty monasteries to find the most ascetic one in which to live the monastic life."

"And then, Father?" they would ask.

But he would not reply; he would bite his lip and remain silent for a long while; then he would begin chanting softly, with anger in his voice.

One day, however, he could not remain silent; two monks from a nearby monastery stopped to visit him. Father Yánaros received them in his cell. They smelled of incense and garlic and rancid oil, and the priest had to open his window to clear the air. He would not speak, but the monks were in a mood for conversation. One of them was an old, sly fox, with rosy cheeks and a fat belly and a flowing beard. The other was a young man with a pimply face, a thin beard, treacherous eyes, and a lisp. The older monk crossed his hands over his belly and spoke in a severe tone, as though to reprimand the priest.

"I heard you were at Mount Athos, Father Yánaros. Why did you desert holy solitude and return to the world? May I ask why?"

Father Yánaros' eyes flashed. "Holy solitude?" He clenched his fist as he spoke. "And to do what in holy solitude, your reverence? The monasteries today have become nothing more than beehives full of drones; they don't make honey any more. You

20

call that asceticism? Christianity? Is this what Christ wants? No, no! Today prayer means deeds. To be an ascetic today is to live among the people, to fight, to climb Golgotha with Christ, and to be crucified every day. Every day, not just on Good Friday!"

He tried to stop, but it was too late; his mouth had opened and with it, his heart. He stared at the two monks and shook his head.

"I was ashamed to live alone, desolate, away from the people. No, I did not want that. Try to understand me, Fathers, I was ashamed. I don't want to be a useless stone on the edge of the road. I want to be built into an edifice along with other stones."

"What edifice? I don't understand," lisped the pimply-faced monk.

"What edifice? Greeee, Christianity—how can I explain it? A large edifice—a building, God!"

"That is arrogance," the old monk said as he unglued his folded hands from his belly.

"That," Father Yánaros replied angrily, "that, holy Father, is known as following the pattern of Christ. As you know, Christ remained in the wilderness only forty days. Then He descended from the summit of solitude, He hungered, He pained, He struggled along with the people, and was crucified. What then, is the duty of the true Christian? I say it and I repeat it: to follow the pattern of Christ here on earth."

"And what about us?" lisped the younger man again.

But Father Yánaros did not hear him. He was infuriated, burning with anger. "I have seen a great deal of dishonesty and hypocrisy and lies in both laymen and the clergy. I can be silent no longer! Sometimes—forgive me, Lord—my soul becomes a flaming rod that wants to burn the world, starting with the monasteries."

"What has the world done to you, Father Yánaros, that you should want to burn it? The world is good, it's the work of God."

"It's the work of the devil! It was the work of God once, but no more. Why do your eyes bulge, holy Fathers? Christ roams from door to door, hungry and cold, and not one door, not one heart opens to say to Him, 'Welcome, my Lord, come

21

in!' But then how can you possibly hear Him, how can you possibly see Him? Your eyes, your ears, your hearts are clogged with fat."

"Let us go," the old monk said, nudging the younger monk's knee with his own. "The world has many temptations. We must not listen, we must not look, we will leave. See, Father Yánaros opened his mouth and without realizing it, he blasphemed. Why? Because he is living in man's world—in the kingdom of temptation!"

"Let us go," the young monk echoed in his high-pitched, lisping voice. "The monastery walls are high, and temptation cannot enter."

"Indeed, holy Fathers, for heaven's sake, take extra care." Father Yánaros laughed and the small cell rumbled. "I'm going to tell you a tale which is not a tale. There was once a monastery that had three hundred monks, and each monk had three carts and three horses. One horse was white, the other red, the third, black. Every day they circled the monastery to prevent Satan from entering. In the morning they used the white horses, at noon the red ones, at night, the black. But Satan took the form of Christ and entered."

"Of Christ?" the monks screamed, and slapped their thighs. "Father Yánaros—blasphemy!"

"Yes, the form of Christ!" bellowed Father Yánaros, pounding his fist on the table. "Of Christ, the way you monks have made Him—a hypocrite, an idler, a glutton! You think that that is Christ, and you follow in His footsteps. It suits you well, you hypocrites, you loafers, you parasites!

"But that is not Christ, you poor fools, it is Satan who has taken the form of Christ and entered. I say it and I repeat: the real Christ walks with the people, struggles with them, is crucified with them, is resurrected with them."

"Let's get out of here," snarled the old monk, and mustered all his strength to gather his fat bellies and stand up.

The younger man rushed to his aid; as he helped him from his chair, he turned to Father Yánaros. "I believe you have insulted us, old man," he said with malice in his voice. "The Bishop was right when he said you are a rebel in the church, that you raise your own banner."

22

"Yes, my own banner," Father Yánaros replied, and his eyes flashed, "and do you know who is painted on that banner, holy Father?"

"Who, rebel?"

"Christ, holding a whip! Tell *that* to the Bishop, tell that to the abbot of your monastery. Tell that to all the bishops and all the abbots of the world. Bon voyage, holy Fathers," he said and opened the door, and he was not laughing now.

Father Yánaros remembered with joy the morning he slipped out from Mount Athos without being seen. The sun was shining brightly, like that first day God had created it. The white snow-capped peak smiled, like a rose in the light of dawn. One would have thought God looked down on earth and smiled as He watched this little ant shake the mountain dust from its feet and disappear quickly, quickly among the myrtles and the bushes.

Father Yánaros had felt the cool wind of freedom blowing on his burning forehead several times before, and he had felt great joy. But the joy of this morning was unmatched; the naked branches must feel this way when spring embraces them.

"Today I am born, today I am born," he sang as he leaped over the bushes, and not once did he turn to look back at the monastery, which was now disappearing at the bend of the road.

From village to village, from mountain to mountain, he finally settled in this hill of stones, enthroned himself in Castello. At first it stifled him—there did not seem to be room enough, the place was small, dry. He longed to see a bit of rich soil, a blossoming almond tree, a smile on a human face, a flowing brook. But slowly, as time passed, he learned to love these stones, he learned to pity these people. They were his brothers; on their faces he saw the pain and fear of man. His soul clutched at this wild, rocky earth and sprouted roots. Like the Castellians, Father Yánaros became accustomed to the hardships of this wild life; he went hungry and cold, he had no one to talk to, to unburden his soul to. But he never complained. "This is my post," he would say, "here I will fight."

Until God emptied the seven cups of His wrath over Greece

23

and the fratricide began. The brother-killing broke out and Father Yánaros stood in the middle—with whom to side? They were all his children, all his brothers, on all their faces he saw God's fingerprints. He shouted, "Love, love! Brotherhood!" but his words rolled into an abyss, and from the abyss rose—to the left and to the right—curses and insults: "Bulgar, traitor, bolshevik!"

"Impostor, fascist, scoundrel!"

# 2

THE SNOW on the hilltop had begun to melt, the sun became stronger, the frozen earth began to thaw. The first green blades of grass fearfully pierced the earth. A few humble wildflowers peeped from underneath the stones, anxious to see the sun. Great silent powers were at work beneath the earth. Winter's tombstone lifted—it was the resurrection of Nature. A mild breeze blew, bringing at times the scent of wildflowers from the moss-covered rocks, at times the stench of decaying bodies.

April—Palm Sunday—the Holy Passion was approaching. Tonight, riding a small donkey, Christ would enter heartless Jerusalem, which kills its prophets. "Behold the Bridegroom cometh in the middle of the night," Father Yánaros would chant in a loud voice, welcoming the Saviour who entered man's deathly web, smiling bitterly. And the bell would toll sadly, calling the Christians to church to witness what God had suffered, and what He continues to suffer among men.

It can't be, Father Yánaros thought. I've heard that even the beasts—wolves, jackals, even wild boar—become tame, unknowingly, on these holy days. Warm, compassionate breezes blow; a loud voice rings through the air, full of love, of pain; the beasts do not know who calls, but men know that it is Christ. I wonder why He does not sit on a throne above the clouds. No, He is here on earth, fighting. He, too, feels pain. He, too, faces injustice; He starves and is crucified along with us. All through

25

Holy Week men hear the cry of Jesus in pain—surely their hearts must feel compassion.

These thoughts ran through Father Yánaros' mind early that morning as he stood at the threshold of the church, listening to the village awaken. He felt the doors, the houses, the smokeless chimneys, the narrow village streets, the shouts and curses of men, the crying of hungry children. All this Father Yánaros felt—all this—upon him, within him, just as he felt the veins throbbing in his neck and in his temples, as he felt his nostrils opening and closing and his bones creaking. He was a part of the stones and a part of the people; like the centaurs of legend—half man, half horse—so was Father Yánaros; from the waist down he was the village of Castello. If a house burned, he burned; if a child died, he died; and when he knelt in church before the miraculous icon of the wide-eyed Madonna, the Protectress of Castello, it was not Father Yánaros alone who knelt; behind him he felt the whole village—every house, every soul—kneeling. "I am no longer Yánaros," he would often say to himself in jest, "I am no longer Yánaros—I am Castello."

But as Father Yánaros listened to the town awaken and awakened with it, he heard from the village square nearby the bellowing voice of Kyriákos, the town crier. He seemed to be heralding great news, for doors were banged open, people began to shout, the village was suddenly in an uproar. The old man cocked his hairy ear and listened; and as he heard, his blood boiled. In one great stride he reached the center of the road. A moment of silence—doors and windows opened and closed; women screeched; a dog barked. And then the voice of the crier: "Hear ye, Christians, the Virgin Mother arrives in our village today. A monk, may his blessings fall upon us, brings the Virgin Mary's Holy Sash in its silver case. He will stop at the town square. Hurry, all of you—men, women, children—hurry and worship before the Holy Sash."

Father Yánaros yanked at his whiskers in fury. A curse floated on his lips but was swallowed. "Virgin Mother," he murmured, "forgive me, but I cannot trust these monks. Is this sash really Yours, Virgin Mother?"

Years ago he had bowed and worshiped the Sash on Vatopedi at Mount Athos. It was of brown wool, interwoven with gold

26

thread that had unraveled with the years. The Virgin was a poor woman, and Christ, too, was poor on earth. How, then, could she wear such an expensive sash as this?

Once, at another monastery, they had showed him a child's skull inside a gold box. "It is the skull of St. Kýrikos," the sexton had told him. A few days later, at still another monastery, another box, much larger than the first, was shown to him. "The skull of St. Kýrikos," the vestry-keeper said.

Father Yánaros could not refrain from speaking out: "But the other day they showed me a child's skull and said that *that* was the saint."

"Well," the monk replied, "that one must have been the saint when he was a child."

Father Yánaros was well aware of the trickeries of the monks, and when he worshiped before the Holy Sash at Vatopedi on Mount Athos, he turned to the vestry-keeper, a reverent fat-bellied monk, and asked, "Begging your blessings, holy Father, do you honestly believe this is the real sash of the Virgin Mother?"

The sly monk smiled. "Don't concern yourself too much, Father Yánaros," he replied. "If it's not, it soon *will* be, after a miracle or two."

"Forgive me, Virgin Mother," Father Yánaros murmured again, "but I cannot trust these monks. I want no part of them."

The town crier had paused to catch his breath. Father Yánaros was about to take another stride ahead, but the voice sounded again. With one foot in mid-air, ears cocked, and his body trembling, Father Yánaros listened.

"Hear ye, hear ye, Christians! Come, all those who have sickness in your homes! The holy monk, may his blessings fall upon us, has been given the power and grace of the Virgin to cure the sick. Whether it is illness of the devil's doings, or snakebite, or the evil eye of men." Then, looking up at the road, he shouted with excitement, "There he is—he's arrived!"

And there, from the edge of the road, astride a gray donkey, appeared the fat, jolly monk. He was hatless, and his hair was twisted into a bun behind his head. On both sides of him, loaded on the donkey, were two large baskets full of foodstuffs and bottles. Behind him dragged a gang of children with swollen

27

bellies and spindly legs. Some of them were on crutches; they were all running, fighting to snatch a few beans or peas, or a wormy fig, which the monk took from his wide pockets and tossed here and there as he laughed with glee.

Kyriákos ran, put his arms as best he could around the wide body of the monk, and helped him alight in the center of the square. Men and women had gathered, running to kiss the fat hand of the man from Mount Athos.

"My blessings upon you, my children," he said in a heavy chantlike voice. "My blessings and those of the Virgin Mother. Bring whatever you have as an offering to the Virgin: money, bread, wine, eggs, cheese, wool—whatever you have—bring it and come to pray."

And as he watched the wretched Castellians who hesitated, wondering what they might have to give for the Virgin's grace, the sly fox opened his robe and pulled out a long silver box he had been holding under his arm; he made the sign of the cross three times, raised the box high, and turned it for all to admire.

"Kneel," he ordered. "Here lies the Holy Sash of the Virgin Mary! Hurry to your homes; bring whatever you can, and come to worship! By the way, now that I think of it, how are you getting along with the rebels?"

"We can't hold out any longer, holy Father; we're exhausted."

"Kill them! Kill them! The Virgin Mother commanded me to tell you that you must kill the rebels; they are not humans, they are dogs!"

The crowd scattered to see what they could find to bring as offerings; the monk sat on the stoop outside the coffeehouse, which had been closed for months now. Where would the coffeehouse owner find coffee, sugar, Turkish delights, tobacco for the nargeles?* The monk took out a large blue handkerchief with white dots from under his robes and began to wipe his sweat. He coughed, spat, got up, picked a wormless fig from out of one of his baskets, and began to chew on it. Then he took out a bottle and took a few gulps of raki.

"Which way does the wind blow with your village priest?" the monk asked abruptly of Kyriákos, who stood nearby with

---

* A Turkish water pipe in which tobacco is placed and smoked through a long hoselike funnel.

arms crossed, admiring the holy man. He had not yet been blessed with the sight of an ascetic from Mount Athos, and he could not satisfy his pleasure at this saintly, sweating body with the bun on the head and the flat, infantryman's feet. His nostrils opened hungrily and inhaled the holy stench. Sinking in this ecstasy, Kyriákos did not reply to the question. The monk became impatient.

"I ask you, what kind of man is your village priest? I want to know."

Kyriákos swallowed hard; he looked around in fear of being heard; then he lowered his voice. "How can I tell you, Father? He's a holy terror—a wild man! He can't get along with anybody. Always a sour face—no matter what you do or what you say, he doesn't like it. It's only what *he* says! As if he's holding God by the beard! A holy man, but insufferable! Beware of him, holy Father."

The monk scratched his head. "Best thing then," he said after some thought, "is to have no dealings with him. I must do my work quickly and get out."

He leaned against the wall of the coffeehouse and sighed. "I'm tired, my brother—what's your name?"

"Kyriákos. I'm the town crier, and I'm letting my hair grow so I can become a priest."

"I'm tired, friend Kyriákos," the monk continued. "Her Grace the Virgin has entrusted me with a heavy task. Three months now I've been wandering from town to village, to exhibit Her Holy Sash; look at me, I've gone down to practically skin and bone." As he said this, he touched his paunch and his dewlaps. He made the sign of the cross and closed his eyes.

"I'll take a little cat nap," he said, "just a few minutes until the Christians come to worship. Kyriákos, my boy, keep an eye out lest anyone come near my baskets."

Kyriákos crouched there at the monk's feet, having no heart to leave this holy man sent by God. But just as he began to feel the monk's holiness spread out to him, entering through his eyes, his nostrils, his ears (for the monk had begun to snore), he jumped up, startled. Father Yánaros was standing before him scowling.

"You're not preparing yourself for the priesthood very well,

29

Kyriákos," he said angrily. "Why did you bring him to our village?"

"Who, me?" Poor Kyriákos replied, "He came of his own will, Father!"

"But you're the one shouting his praises."

With his staff, Father Yánaros prodded the monk's large feet. "Eh, holy Father, I have a word to say to you. Wake up!"

The monk opened his egg-shaped eyes, saw the priest, and understood. "Father," he said, "I am happy to see you."

"What do you want in my village?"

"Her Grace the Virgin sent me," the monk replied, and showed the silver box. "I go wherever this takes me."

"Well, Her Grace the Virgin sent me to tell you to leave! Take your box, your baskets, your donkey, your cure-alls, and go!"

"The Virgin Mother . . ."

"Quiet! Do not taint the holy name of the Mother of God. If Her Grace really had sent you, She would have loaded you with wheat and oil and clothing from the Holy Mount, with whatever was left over from the monks, for you to distribute to Her people, who are ragged and barefoot and dying of hunger. You would not be trying to take what little food they have from their mouths. Quiet, I say! I served at Mount Athos, too. I learned your secrets—hypocrites, loafers, church-robbers!" He grabbed him by the arm. "And what are those words you dare to spout, eh? 'Kill them! Kill'? Is that what the Virgin commanded? Is that the reason Her Son entered Jerusalem today, to be crucified? How long will you go on betraying Christ, you Judas?"

He had bent over the monk and was trembling with anger as he whispered, "Judas! Judas!"

While he spoke, the people had begun to gather; silent, bareheaded, their eyes glued with fear upon the silver box on the window sill. Each one held in his hand or in his cap an onion or a handful of wheat or a little wool from his sheep—whatever he had to offer the Virgin. One woman who had nothing took off her kerchief to give; an old man brought an antiquity which he had found while digging in his field one day.

Father Yánaros turned and looked at the crowd, and his heart twisted with pain. "My children," he said, "pray before the Holy Sash, but do not give a grain of wheat to the monk. You are

30

poor, you are hungry; your children are starving; the Virgin has no need of offerings. That She should take from you? God forbid! She gives to you! Why do they call Her Mother of Christianity? Would she watch Her children starve and not reach out a compassionate hand to give them a piece of bread? This holy man here, who came to our village to fill his baskets and depart, saw our poverty. He looked at the hungry children who ran behind him, and his heart ached. Is he not a faithful servant of the Virgin? Does the Virgin Mother not dwell within his heart? What need has he of food and luxuries? Many years ago he turned his back upon the riches of this futile life and went to Mount Athos to become sanctified. And now he feels compassion at our disaster and has reached a decision, God bless him. He is going to distribute among us everything that he has gathered from the villages he passed to get here. Everything in his baskets!"

The crowd let out a cheer at these words—women began to cry. They rushed upon the monk, grabbed his hand and kissed it as tears streamed down their faces. The monk had turned red; he was boiling within, cursing this devil of a priest who had played such a trick to rob him. But what could he do? He was too ashamed to refuse; no, he was not ashamed, he was afraid. The children had already gathered around his donkey, jumping with glee. They had stuck their noses into the baskets, and as they breathed in the smell of figs, their mouths watered.

"Let two people come forward to unload the donkey," Father Yánaros ordered. "Bring the baskets here, and this holy man—sent by God—shall distribute everything to you. But first, let us pray before the Holy Sash."

Before he could finish the sentence, the baskets were unloaded; the women spread out their aprons, the men their caps and their handkerchiefs. The children dug their hands inside the baskets.

"Quiet—quiet," Father Yánaros ordered, and his face shone with pleasure. "First, you must pray and thank the Virgin Mother for sending you this holy man with his baskets."

The monk stood by, moaning; sweat poured from him, and he felt that he would explode any minute. Every so often he threw poisonous looks at the priest—oh, if he could only grab him by his beard and pull it out, hair by hair. For a moment he drew near and whispered in his ear. "You've ruined me," he spat out, and his hot breath scorched Father Yánaros' temples.

Father Yánaros smiled. "Yes, holy Father," he replied in a loud voice for the crowd to hear, "you are so right. There is indeed no greater joy than in giving bread to the hungry. I will say prayers in your name at vespers tonight. By the way, what is your name, holy Father?"

But the monk only groaned with fury. He grabbed the silver box and opened it with a shrug. The frayed sash of brown wool and gold thread was revealed. "Worship!" he said in a dry voice, as though he were saying "Get out of my sight."

Quickly, one after the other, the people bowed and worshiped the holy relic; they were in a hurry; they sensed the baskets behind them, and they were anxious for the worship to end so that they could begin dividing the food. Exhausted and disgusted, the monk fell in a heap on the stoop. They placed first the one basket between his legs, then the other. The priest stood over him to keep order. One by one they came, extending their caps, their aprons, their hands. The monk dug his massive hands into the baskets and handed out his goods, cursing under his breath.

"Damn you, devil-priest! Curse you, devil-priest . . ." He mumbled underneath his breath as he passed out his wealth.

"Not so loud, children!" Father Yánaros said. "The holy man of God is praying."

Each one took his share, kissed the monk's hand, and left, hurrying to his bare hearthstone.

"What joy the Virgin must feel," Father Yánaros kept repeating, "seeing her people emptying Her baskets! What do you say, holy Father?"

But the holy father could stand it no longer. He grabbed the baskets and emptied them on the stones, turning his head the other way so that he would not have to see his possessions disappear.

The crowd fell upon the two piles, and before you could say "Lord have mercy," nothing was left. The monk picked up a fig from the ground, chewed it with fury, and spat it out.

"Kyriákos," the priest ordered, "take the baskets, load them on the donkey, and help the holy man mount. He has done his duty—may God bless him—let him go on his way."

32

Oh, if looks could kill, the monk thought, I'd tear you into little pieces, scoundrel!

Kyriákos brought the donkey to the ledge, put his arms again as best he could around the fat body of the monk, and enthroned him between the two empty baskets.

"Good-bye, good-bye, holy brother," Father Yánaros called to him. "Don't forget to write!"

But the monk was boiling within. He kicked the donkey viciously with his large feet, and without turning once to look back, rode on. When he passed the outskirts of the village and reached the fields where no one could see him, he turned and spat twice toward the village.

"Damn you, devil-priest," he said loudly, "you've torn out my heart!"


Father Yánaros chanted softly, contentedly, as he walked back to the church; he sensed the Virgin beside him, smiling, contented, too, that the Holy Sash had performed its miracle by giving food to the hungry. What did it matter whether this was Her sash or not? For centuries now, countless lips had kissed it, countless eyes had looked at it and wept, countless aching hearts had stood over it. They had filled it with hope and pain, and sanctified it, and it had truly become the Sash of the Virgin. The soul of man has great power, Father Yánaros reflected as he walked, yes, great power! It can take a piece of cloth and make it a banner!

As he stepped across the threshold of the church, he saw a pale-looking soldier sitting on the stone ledge in the courtyard, waiting for him. Father Yánaros had met the boy some time ago and was quite fond of him. A quiet, delicate young man, he always carried a small notebook in his pocket. His blue eyes sparkled with warmth and youth. Last Christmas he had come to confession before communion. A gentle heart, full of tenderness and spiritual desires—he was a student at the time, and he was in love. He kept seeing the girl in his dreams at night, and he felt strong desires for her; this was his greatest sin, and he had come to confess it.

"Welcome, Leonidas!" the priest said, offering his hand. "What's wrong, my son? You look worried."

"I came to kiss your hand, Father," the youth replied, "nothing else."

"Is something worrying you?"

"Yes, but it's probably just growing pains—a windburst, isn't that what you called it last year when I came to confession? The warm wind of youth that opens up the flower buds?"

Father Yánaros stroked the boy's blond head. "A windburst, my son. That wind passed over me, too, once.

"Today it passes over you," he continued, "tomorrow it will pass over your son. Many call it the wind of youth—I call it the wind of God."

He was silent for a moment. "I call everything God," the priest added, and smiled.

The young man swallowed hard; words crept to his lips, but he was ashamed to let them out. Father Yánaros took him by the hand; he leaned over him. "Leonidas, my child," he said, "open your heart to me. I am listening."

The boy's hand trembled within the strong fist of the older man. He could barely control the tears; the words that had crept to his lips had now become sobs.

"Well?" the priest asked, and his grasp tightened to give the boy courage.

"I'm telling the truth, Father, nothing's wrong. Nothing is bothering me—it's just that my heart feels heavy, frightened, as though it foresees a great evil. Can it be that something has happened to her—can the girl I love be ill? Or can it be that Death is hovering over me, over her? I can't quite make it out, so I came to see you. Forgive me, Father, I came to get it off my chest. Already I feel relieved," he said and smiled, but his hand in Father Yánaros' still trembled.

That night, the Castellians gathered within their church to watch Christ entering Jerusalem on the donkey. And the impoverished villagers hurried to spread their clothing on the ground for Him to pass over. The children, with palms in their hands, ran behind Him singing, welcoming Him, for they realized—much more than the wealthy, educated, intelligent ones did—that this humble companion, this barefoot, sad human being was the Saviour of the world. "Behold the Bridegroom cometh in the middle of the night." The church was warm, it smelled of candles and incense; the holy icons, dimly lit, re-sembled ghosts. The church was small and inadequate, but it had room enough for the pain of Christ and the evil of man and the salvation of the world. This small church was Jerusalem, and Father Yánaros held the donkey by its bridle and walked ahead, leading Christ into the holy city that was to kill Him. Already one could hear the sound of the ax felling the tree to be planed and made into a cross. Father Yánaros heard these sounds as though he were the tree, and felt the pain. Surely the Castellians could hear the sounds, too; would their faces soften, he wondered, would their hearts ache for God who is about to be crucified for their sake? And when they leave the church will they look upon all people as brothers? And will they offer their hands to the guerrillas and say to them, "It is a shame for us to fight, brothers, come let us all follow Christ, who is in danger now"?

Father Yánaros fixed his eyes on them; he longed to see a smile, even a little one; to see a light in their eyes, a glow reflected from the passing of Christ. He watched them, watched as the first vigil of Sunday ended, but the faces of the Castellians did not soften. God's passion knocked in vain on their hearts; they would not open them, and Christ remained outside, homeless. Shame and indignation filled Father Yánaros. And when the wake ended and the Castellians turned to leave, Father Yánaros raised his hand and stopped them.

"Wait, Christians," he called, "I have something to say to you."

The villagers scowled. Stamatis and Barba Tassos, two elders of the town, who stood at the entrance of the church selling candles, turned to each other.

"Why doesn't he let us go to our homes?" Stamatis said to Tassos. "I'm sleepy! How about you?"

"If I ever set foot at another one of his wakes again, he can spit in my eye," replied Barba Tassos, and yawned loudly. "I'll never leave the comfort of my bed to come here and stand all these hours again—no sir! I've seen it all, over and over again. I'm fed up!"

Father Yánaros walked to the center of the church. "Listen, my children," he said, "the sky has seven levels and the earth has seven, but still they are not large enough to hold God; yet in man's heart there is room enough for Him. Bear this in mind and do not wound the heart of a single person, for God dwells there. Yet you Castellians, God help you, do nothing but work overtime for Satan, killing your brothers. How long will this go on, cursed men? Shame on you! Have you no pity for God, who enters Jerusalem tonight to be crucified for you? And if you have no pity for Him, if you have no fear of Him, have you at least no fear of hell? You will burn there, brother-killers, you will burn in pitch, forever and ever."

"Tell that to the rebels, priest!" an angry voice replied.

"Tell that to your rebel son," came another voice.

"If only my voice could be heard in the hills, by the guerrillas, and in the valley by the elders, and throughout all the world." Father Yánaros sighed. "But my flock is small, a mere heap of stones—Castello."

The faces of the Castellians remained grim; Father Yánaros pleaded and threatened in vain. God, hell, forever and ever—all this seemed far away to them; their time had not come; when it did, they would see. Lately, because of the guerrillas, they had other problems. Mandras, the first elder of the town, stepped before Father Yánaros, and his sly, sticky eyes were filled with hate.

"Your words may be wise and holy, my priest, but they go into one ear and out the other. Our minds and our reasoning are elsewhere now—on destroying the rebels! Destroying them, my priest, and you talk to us about God! Do you understand, Father Yánaros?"

"I understand, loan shark," Father Yánaros cried angrily. "I understand that Satan is riding herd on all of you."

"And God is riding herd on you," the elder replied, snickering, "so what are you crowing about?"

"We'll talk about that in the other world," threatened Father Yánaros, and shook his finger at them.

"A bird in the hand is worth two in the bush, Father Yánaros," he replied. "We'll discuss it here, in Castello, and since you have a son who is a rebel leader, I suggest that you keep quiet—for your own sake. You asked for it, and I'm telling you."

The Castellians nodded their heads in satisfaction. The elder had said what they had felt all along but lacked the courage to say, God bless him, and they felt relieved now. Some of them laughed, others coughed; they all crept hurriedly toward the door.

Father Yánaros remained alone in church, with Christ and the miraculous Virgin on the iconostas, and the saints.

"My Lord, my Lord," he murmured, "they are crucifying You again!"

# 3

Iт was dawn of Holy Monday; rifles blazed—the people had begun their work early. The guerrillas descended, the soldiers and the Castellians climbed up to meet them; growling, they clashed on the hillside and began with fury to kill and be killed. Father Yánaros left Christ in church—what need did He have of men—and ran to the hill to give last rites to the dying and to help carry the wounded back to the village.

It was a day of God's joy—fresh spring sunlight—the first thorns on the hill had blossomed. The bees, too, had begun their work early that morning; they buzzed around the blossoming thorns and the new thyme, and prepared to make honey. The vultures came, they circled the sky above the people, perched on the rocks, and let out hoarse, impatient cries for the men to hurry and become corpses, so the vultures could fall upon them and begin their work, too. All of God's creation had awakened and was in a hurry.

And the men—one would think they heeded the cries of the vultures—they hurled themselves furiously at one another for the kill! First they fought with guns, then with bayonets, and toward the end, with knives, with fists, with their teeth. The bodies fell, thundering against the rocks. Father Yánaros ran from one dying man to the other, administering communion, closing their eyes, reading the last rites.

"Forgive them, my Lord," he murmured, "forgive both those who kill and those who are killed, or else burn us all, so that we may disgrace You no longer."

38

By noon, Father Yánaros held Leonidas, badly wounded, in his arms. The boy was dying; he opened his eyes, looked at the priest, recognized him, and tried to open his mouth. He wanted to say something, but the blood gushed from his mouth, and his eyes sank. Another soldier ran to him, kneeled and searched the body, found a notebook and took it, slipping it inside his shirt.

"He asked me to give this to the schoolmaster," the soldier explained to the priest, who was watching with surprise. "He had a premonition of his death."

The young man bent over the corpse, kissed it, then grabbed his rifle and rushed screaming toward the hill.

Vassos the soldier had taken a guerrilla alive; he had stuck a knife in his back and knocked him down; they rolled on the ground together, struggling awhile, then Vassos took the belt from his waist and tied the other man's hands. The guerrillas scrambled back up the hill, the soldiers went down to the barracks, the battle was over—the day's work had ended.

Wild from the blood he had seen and the fear he had experienced, Vassos cursed the guerrilla, spat on him, and beat him furiously with the butt of his rifle as they descended the hill. Soft shadows fell over the earth; it had been a scorching day, and now the earth felt cool; it breathed with relief. Blood oozed from the guerrilla's wound, one of his boots was gone, and his wounded leg began to bleed. Vassos stopped, tired from beating the other man; he grabbed him by the arm and pushed him to the ground. The soldiers had gone ahead, they were probably nearing the barracks now.

"I'm going to rest awhile," he said. "Sit there and don't move. Don't move, you poor fool, or I'll kill you."

He knelt behind a rock, took a piece of dry bread from inside his vest and began to chew it—he was hungry. Then he raised his water canteen to his lips—he was thirsty. The guerrilla watched the canteen with longing. Until now he had not uttered a word, but he could keep silent no longer.

"If you're human," he said, "give me a sip, too. I'm burning up."

Vassos looked at him as though for the first time: an ugly boy with a pointed goatee like a jackal's, and small eyes that were filled with terror. He looked at the bound hands full of calluses, the empty cartridge belts across the chest—he must have used up all his bullets. Vassos had grabbed his rifle and slung it over his shoulder beside his own.

"If you're human," the young man repeated, "give me a sip, too, just one sip, I'm burning inside."

Vassos laughed. "Traitor, you sold out Greece and now you ask me for water? Die!" He corked the flask and shook it, laughing, in front of the thirsty man's face.

"Have you no mercy?" the guerrilla sobbed. "Aren't you human?"

"Shut up! I'm human all right, but you're a dog!" He grabbed a stone and threw it at him. "Here's a bone, lick it!"

The wounded man gritted his teeth; he did not speak.

Vassos leaned against the rock and removed his shoes; his burning feet felt cooler now. He looked down at the village; shouting and weeping had broken out in the houses—they were mourning their dead. The sun had set hours ago, the hill had turned purple; from between two rocks the first star of night peeked brightly.

Vassos turned to the guerrilla and nudged him with his bare foot. His eyes lit up—he had thought of a game. "Bark like a dog," he said. "Hey, red one, you're a dog, aren't you? Bark, and I'll give you some water."

The guerrilla jumped up; with startled eyes he looked at the laughing soldier.

"Hey, go on, bark, bark!" he shouted.

The guerrilla caught his breath. He felt a stab of pain from the wound in his back.

Vassos laughed as he began to bark. "Arf, arf! Here's the flask, arf, arf! Bark, damn you!"

"I can't—I'm ashamed," the boy murmured.

"Then die! Have you no mother?"

The young man shuddered; his eyes filled with tears; he craned his neck, looking into the distance—who knows where, perhaps toward home. Then he started to bark—the bark of a dog being whipped—wild, full of pain. He barked and barked and would not stop—the sound echoed on the rocks; the dogs in the village below answered him, all howling at once.

40

Vassos' heart tightened; his laughter stopped short; he had never heard such barking, such pain. He jumped forward and cupped his hand over the man's mouth.

"Stop it," he hissed, "stop it, you! Shut up!"

He grabbed his flask and shoved it between the parched lips. "Drink!"

The wounded man bit the rim hungrily; he drank, drank and came to life, but the tears still flowed.

"That's enough!" The soldier pulled the flask from the other's teeth. He looked at him and for a moment he was moved.

"I embarrassed you, did I?" he said compassionately.

"My mother has no other child," the young man replied.

They both remained silent; Vassos felt a strange weight in his chest. "Who are you?" he asked. "Your hands are full of calluses. What work do you do?"

"I'm a laborer."

"And why did you take up arms? What have you got against Greece?" Anger flared up in him again as he spoke. "What have you got against your country—against religion? Why? Why?" He pushed his face against the other's as he yelled.

"I was working," the young man replied. "I was working and I was hungry. My mother was hungry, too, she was just an old woman. The injustice of it strangled me, and one day at the factory I raised my voice in protest. 'Justice! Justice!' I shouted. 'How long are we going to work and still be hungry?' And everyone—bosses and workers, too—turned on me and threw me out into the street. So I took courage into my own two hands and went to the hills. For there, I had heard, one could fight for justice."

"And did you find justice in the hills, you idiot?"

"No, comrade, not yet. But I found hope."

"What hope?"

"The hope that one day justice will come. She won't come alone, though; she has no feet; we're going to lift her on our shoulders and carry her here."

Vassos bowed his head and fell into deep thought; he was remembering his home and his four sisters, who were left, unmarried, on the shelf. Years and years he had worked as a carpenter to save a little money and get them married. He worked, he

41

worked, and what did he get? A day's meager wages, a day's meager food; nothing was ever left over. And there were four of them; they looked into his eyes with bitterness, with complaint. The first, Aristea, had withered now; her breasts sagged, waiting all these years in vain for a caress to lift them. The hairs on her upper lip became coarse, she was plagued with headaches, she was unable to sleep, and she had become nasty, jumpy, nervous. Often, without reason, she would begin to weep, she would fall to the floor screaming. Their father had died early, before he had the chance to see her married; and Vassos was still just a boy, working in a carpentry shop, hurrying to complete his apprenticeship, to earn more money and set aside her dowry. But he was never able to do it, and Aristea cursed him now; she called him incapable and insensitive; she would pounce on him and scratch him with her nails, then burst into hysteria. The second sister, Kaleroy, spent all her days at the loom weaving things for her hope chest; she withered too, her cheeks were sunken, and a mustache appeared, like Aristea's. At sunset, she would stand at the threshold of their house, primped and dressed in her best, but no one ever turned to look at her. So she would sneak back inside, sit at her loom silently, and weave her linens. Tassoula, the third sister, was clever—a little flirt; her breasts were erect, her eyes never missed a thing, and she looked unashamedly at the men. She went out often and had several girl friends; she also had her eye on the man she wanted—Aristides, a naïve shopkeeper—and she would come and go in front of his little shop swaying her hips. I'm not worried about her, Vassos thought, she's not sitting around waiting to be discovered. No, she's out to get her man, with sword in hand. And the fourth, Drosoula, is very young, still going to school; she says she wants to be a teacher. I'm not worried about her either; it's the older ones I'm thinking of; I must get some money together to get them married and not have them on my conscience. I must, I must! So I can get married, too, to the girl I love, before I lose her. But how can I get married, my God, how can I get married if I don't see them all married first?

He sighed, raised his head, and looked at the prisoner in front of him; he had lowered his head, too, and was also deep in thought.

Vassos turned to kick him, to curse him, to spit on him, to lash out his tensions and find relief; but he changed his mind; his heart seemed to have softened.

"Hey, you poor soul," he said, "you're buried in poverty like me; you're struggling, too, poor fool, and you don't know who to blame; but do you think I do? God blessed the poor with eyes only for beauty's sake."

"But I'm beginning to see, comrade," the guerrilla replied. "I can't make everything out clearly yet, but I'm beginning to see. You'll see one of these days, too; what's your name?"

"Vassos—carpenter from Samos."

"Mine's Yanni, I'm from Volos."

"You have any sisters?"

"No, thank God! I'm an only son and an only child; my father died of drink, and my mother did housework to raise me. She washed clothes in the wealthy homes; now her body's stiff—she can't move at all. Every day she has a relative write me a letter for her, and my heart tears when I read her words. 'Patience, patience, Mother,' I keep answering. 'I think of you every moment, and I'll be home very soon.'" He sighed.

"When," he murmured, continuing, "when? I may never see her again; why, just today, by a hair's breadth, you'd have killed me, Vassos."

The soldier turned crimson; he tried to speak, but what could he say? How could he say it? His mind clouded; he could see the boy's mother, old and paralyzed; he saw his own four spinster sisters; he saw the two pairs of calloused hands, worn from labor that brought no profit; he groaned, a wild anger seized him, and hardly aware of what he was doing, he jumped up, put on his heavy shoes, bent over his prisoner, and untied his hands.

"Go to the devil," he shouted. "Go on!"

"Free?"

"Go on, I tell you!"

A glow came over the young man's face; he offered his hand to the soldier. "Vassos," he said, "my brother . . ."

But the other man did not let him finish. "I said go!" he growled, as though he were in a hurry to get rid of him before he changed his mind.

"Will you give me my rifle?" the guerrilla asked reluctantly.

43

Vassos hesitated; the other man had stretched out his hand anxiously and waited. "Well?" he asked again.

"Take it!"

The young man grabbed the rifle, slung it over his shoulder, turned, and strode toward the hill.

Vassos watched the bent, gasping figure climb the hill—he seemed to be in pain; he noticed his back covered with blood.

"Wait!" he called to the guerrilla. He pulled out a strip of bandage from inside his vest and walked up to the wounded man. Gently he removed his jacket, then his shirt, and bandaged the wound.

"Go on now," he told him, "but hurry before the devil straddles me again!"

Night came, separating the people again; the jackals could be heard in the distance.

Exhausted and out of breath, Father Yánaros reached the stone ledge outside the church and fell in a heap upon it; his heart, his lips, his mind, were filled with poison.

"Lord," he murmured, "I can't go on any longer; I tell You truthfully, I can't! For months and months I've been calling You —why don't You answer me? You have but to spread out Your hand over them, and they will be pacified; why don't You do it? Whatever happens in this world happens because You want it to; why do You want our destruction?"

But no one replied to Father Yánaros' questions. Peace and quiet!—only once in a while came a few sighs and weeping from the homes whose men had been killed; and once in a while the sound of the jackals in the distance that were eating them. Father Yánaros raised his eyes to the sky; silently, for a long while, he watched the stars. The aurora borealis flowed like a river of milk from one end of the sky to the other. This is the real Sash of the Virgin, he thought, all sweetness and silence. Oh, if only the sash would come down to earth and encircle it!

Father Yánaros could not sleep a wink all night; he kept asking God the same questions, and he waited for a reply until it was dawn. At daybreak, an old woman knocked on his door. "Get up, Father," she whimpered. "Get up! Barba Tassos' son is dying; come and give him communion."

He had been wounded yesterday on the hill; Father Yánaros

himself had asked two villagers to bring him back to the village. He loved this boy because he was a handsome, soft-spoken lad whose heart carried a deep compassion for the poor. Many times he would secretly steal bread from his father's house and divide it among the hungry. His name was Socrates, and he came to Father Yánaros' cell often, to learn how to paint; he longed to find an escape from his father's shouts and from the village that smothered and bored him. Slowly, he learned to play with the brush, and soon he was painting saints, or pretty girls that he saw in his dreams—for the only girls he saw when he was awake were dried up from work and poverty.

His mother sat beside the boy, whose heavy breathing came hoarsely now—he was dying. She did not weep; she was used to death, she had seen other children of hers die, too, and nephews and brothers. Death was a frequent visitor to her house, a friend of the family; he came in, chose, took what he wanted, and left; after a little while, he came again. And the old woman watched one by one of them leave, and her home slowly emptying; she had crossed her hands and waited her turn. "Take me," she begged him once, "but don't take Socrates from me." She did not know that Death cannot hear—that he is deaf!

She sat now, watching her son slip away; she held a handkerchief in her hands and waved it over him to chase the flies away. She bent over him and talked to him; she told him what great numbers of men had been killed on the hill so far; she said that he was not to worry, for Father Yánaros would soon arrive to give him communion. She even gave him instructions on what to say to their departed village friends, now that he would go down to Hades and they would gather around him to make inquiries. And the old woman began to remind him which villagers had gotten married, how many children they had born, how the sheep were going to the devil this year and not one was left—the redhoods had eaten them up, God damn them! And that old Mandras had sold Pelagia's house because the poor woman owed him money, and now the unfortunate soul was in the streets. "But don't tell them she came to our door and fell at your father's feet begging him to let her sleep in the stable, or that your father kicked her and put her out. Don't tell them that, my boy."

The dying soldier was gasping now; his eyes were open, but

45

they had begun to get glassy; he could not see. He could not see, he could not hear, but his mother still kept talking as she bent over him, talking so he would know what to say to the departed villagers who would soon gather round to ask many questions.

At this moment, Father Yánaros appeared, and the old woman became silent; she withdrew to a corner, crossed her hands, and watched. Every so often she wiped her long nose on the edge of her sleeve to stop its dripping. Father Yánaros tried to administer communion to the unfortunate soldier, but his throat heaved and sighed, and the body and blood of Jesus, mixed with Socrates' own blood, was vomited up from the wounded lips. The priest stood over him and began to chant from the Funeral Psalm: "With the souls of the departed righteous, O Lord, give rest to the soul of thy servant . . ."

Father Yánaros, too, had become used to death; his eyes were dry, and his voice did not tremble; but he could never forgive Death for selecting the young ones. When the mother saw that it was all over, she made the sign of the cross, kissed the priest's hand, and sat back down beside her son. Suddenly her nostrils caught the smell of food from the kitchen. They must have found mushrooms, she thought, and they're frying them; I'd better go see. She got up and went into the kitchen; Stella, her older daughter, was indeed frying mushrooms; the old woman took a handful, cut herself a piece of bread, and hurried back to her son. She was hungry and sat down beside the body and began to chew, slowly, slowly.

When the hoarse breathing finally stopped, Father Yánaros bent over and put his hand on the boy's heart; it had stopped beating; he rose and spoke quietly. "He's resting now."

Spitting on her two fingers, the mother knelt and touched the earth, rose, and closed the dead boy's eyes. His older sister came in; she took a stone, scratched on it three Greek letters—"Jesus Christ prevails"—and stuffed it in her brother's fist.

"Good-bye," she told him, "good-bye, my Socrates, give my regards to the dead."

"A speedy reunion, my boy," the old woman said; she let out a loud cry and wiped her eyes.

It was night when Father Yánaros returned, weary, from the cemetery; another young man buried, turning to soil and water

46

again. His father, Barba Tassos, the wealthy elder, refused to bring out a bottle of wine and some bread and olives, as was the custom, to pass among the friends and relatives who had attended the funeral. "Isn't the pain of losing my son enough?" he said in reply to his wife's reprimands, "without wasting wine and bread and olives, too? One grief is enough for me!"

Today, again, Father Yánaros' soul had been filled with Death. He spent the nights of this Holy Week walking beside Christ, leading Him one step closer to the grave each time; he spent the days with the people. Oh, if I could only lie down and close my eyes, too, he thought as he walked to his home. If I could only remove the cares of man from my soul, as we remove a soiled shirt! To worry only for the old jackass called Father Yánaros—to feed it all I can so it will have strength, poor thing. But the blessed thing is heavy, very heavy, and the jackass cannot carry the load, it is sure to drop the saddle. Careful now, Father Yánaros—slowly!

He talked to himself as he walked along. Every village door was locked; everywhere there was a deep, heavy silence; the people were tired of crying; they were silent. From the barracks came the sound of the bugle; the sun was setting, the hill had turned purple, but the stars had not appeared yet. A cool breeze blew from the hilltop and, for a moment, Father Yánaros was happy as he felt it on his sweating brow.

But as he approached his house, he stopped abruptly. A small child, withered from hunger, with a swollen green belly lay face down in the middle of the road; it was digging the earth and eating the soil. The priest stood horrified; his eyes filled; he bent toward the child and took it by the hand.

"Get up, my child," he said. "Are you hungry?"

"No. I just finished eating."

"What did you eat?"

The child stretched out its hand and showed him the soil.

"Dirt."

Father Yánaros' blood rushed to his head; he groaned softly, as though a knife turned inside him.

The world is rotten, he thought, rotten and unjust. My God, how can You hold it in Your arms without hurling it down and smashing it into a thousand pieces? So it can become mud

47

again, so You can shape a new world—a better one! Don't You see that this child is hungry? Can't You see it's eating dirt?

He bowed his head, ashamed at his outburst, and continued. "No, my Lord, it's not Your fault," he murmured. "I'm to blame, we are all guilty for this child who eats dirt."

With aching heart he remembered a time he had gone to Istanbul to pay homage to his new Patriarch. An old rabbi friend of his had invited him to visit his home—provided the Christian priest did not consider it a sin. It was the Jewish New Year, and several Jewish actors were to present a short play in conjunction with the great holiday. The rabbi sat beside Father Yánaros, interpreting, and from all that he saw and heard, certain phrases so pierced Father Yánaros' mind that to this day his memory drew forth dripping blood. They had set up a temporary stage in the rabbi's bedroom; the curtain was pulled back, and a pale, skeleton-like man appeared, dragging a child by the hand. From behind the curtain came the sounds of singing and laughter— the holiday tables had been set, and the people were eating, drinking and making merry. Several wealthy, fat-bellied men who sat in the depth of the stage rose to their feet. "The tables are set," they said, "let us go and eat!"

They left, and the pale man with the child remained alone.

"Daddy, let's go home," the child pleaded.

"Why, child? What will we do there?"

"I'm hungry. Let's go home and eat!"

"All right, all right, but listen, my Davey, we have nothing to eat at home."

"Just a little piece of bread."

"Not even a crust, my Davey."

The child became silent. The father stroked its head and leaned over. "Davey, my child, do you know what holiday this is?"

"Yes."

"Tell me, Davey, what did we do today?"

"We prayed, Father."

"Yes; and what did God do, blessed be His name?"

"He forgave us our sins."

"Then since God forgave us our sins, we must be joyful, mustn't we, Davey?"

The child remained silent.

"My little Davey, last year when your mother was alive, we sang a little song at the table; it was a new melody—do you remember it?"

"No."

"Let me remind you—but you'll have to sing along with me."

And the man began to sing in an anguished voice a sad, despairing chant that tore at one's heart. The child sang along with him, and wept.

Father Yánaros wiped his eyes with indignation. He looked around to see if anyone was watching. He controlled himself, but even after all these years, the melody still ripped his heart out. It was as though the thin membrane that covers man's entrails snapped—that tissue formed from the daily cares and the convenient cowardices of men—and this same tortured song broke out, free and uncontrollable. It freed all the terrors drifting within the dark corners of his being—terrors which he had not dared bring out into the light to face. Father Yánaros looked at his guts and the guts of the world and was sickened.

He went back and took the child by the hand again.

"Let's go, child," he said. "I have a piece of bread at home, I will give it to you!"

The child jerked, trying to free its hand from the priest's. "I'm not hungry! I told you, I ate." And it began to cry.

Father Yánaros turned angrily toward the church. "I'm off," he shouted, "I'm off to damn the world before God!"

Father Yánaros entered his home at the side of the church. It was not a house but a cell like the one he had been given at Mount Athos; a table, two stools, a narrow cot on which he slept, and on the wall above the cot, the icon of St. Constantine. He had painted the saint himself, just as he appeared in the icons which the firewalkers held in their arms when they walked over the lighted coals in that distant village near the Black Sea. In this icon, the saint did not wear a royal crown or red robes; his crown was a ring of flames; he was barefoot, and his feet were raised high as he danced on the burning coals.

"St. Constantine was a firewalker," Father Yánaros would say in reply to the startled questions. "Every saint is a firewalker. And so is every honest man in this hell we call life."

But the greatest adornment in the cell was another icon—

49

there on the table beside the Holy Bible—the Second Coming, delicately carved in wood. It was given to Father Yánaros by Father Arsénios, the famous wood carver from the Monastery of St. Anna on Mount Athos, as salvation for his soul. Father Yánaros never tired of standing over it; every day he watched it thoughtfully, and as he looked at it, his heart swelled, he felt a turmoil within, and something inside of him shouted, "No! No!" Father Yánaros never understood who it was or why the voice shouted.

In the center of the icon was Christ, the unsmiling Judge; His hands were outstretched—the right one raised in blessing, the other, with tightened fist, threatening. To His right were the just, thousands of them who had already entered Paradise; they were laughing. To the left, the sinners, thousands of them too; they were crying—what terror appeared on their faces! How their mouths had slanted from the lament! At Christ's feet lay the Virgin Mary, her head raised, her hand outstretched, pointing to the sinners. And Her mouth, half-open, seemed to be crying out, "Mercy, my Son, mercy!"

Father Yánaros bowed and prayed to the Second Coming; and as he watched the Virgin tonight and heard her cry, his voice suddenly rang out: "Dear God, can the Virgin Mother's cry be, in reality, the heart of man crying out?"

He sank on the cot; he did not want to part with the icon—he placed it on his knees and closed his eyes. Sleep was not what he wanted, although he was tired to the point of exhaustion. He closed his eyes to bring the beloved Father Arsénios near, and to feel the glow of that holy day of their first meeting.

It was a sun-drenched winter day when Father Yánaros, a small bundle flung over his shoulder, passed by the grassy, picturesque Monastery of St. Anna. Among the dark green leaves of the orange trees sparkled reddish-purple fruit, all flame on the outside, all honey within. This is what the Will of God is like, he pondered, and his eyes filled with tears; like an orange tree, its fruit all flame and honey! What joy it was, what fragrance, what peace! And the sea, too, that sparkled blue-green, deserted, between the fruit-laden orange trees.

He walked on, and when he came to the first cell, he entered. Inside were four bare white walls; a cluster of quinces hung from a beam on the ceiling; the fruit had begun to rot, and the cell smelled sweetly of quince and cypress wood. A pale, wrinkled monk sat on a stool, carving a piece of wood on his knees. His chest, his face, his soul, were glued upon the wood; the whole world had drowned in the chaos, and all that remained, in this Ark of God, was this monk and this piece of wood—as though God had commanded him to reshape the world.

What softness appeared on his face as he bent, trembling, over his work; Father Yánaros took a step forward; he bent over the monk's shoulder and as he looked, he stifled a cry at what he saw. What miracle was this, what dexterity, what patience, what confidence! There, carved on the cypress wood, was the Second Coming—so real, so alive—with crowds of people, some filled with terror, some with bliss. Christ was in the center, the Virgin at His feet, and an angel at each side sounding the trumpets of the Resurrection.

"Your blessings, Father!" Father Yánaros greeted him loudly. But the monk, engrossed in his creative efforts, did not hear.

Father Yánaros opened his eyes; night had fallen; the flame of the wick burning before the icon of St. Constantine cast a faint light in the long, narrow cell, on the Second Coming still on his knees, on the golden-yellow quinces hanging from the beam. Silence—the village was already asleep; from the narrow window one could see the freshly whitewashed dome of the church softly gleaming, and from the strip of sky that was visible, two stars twinkled.

Father Yánaros closed his eyes again; he returned to Mount Athos, to the cell of Father Arsénios.

What calm, peaceful discussions the two had had; how many days and nights he had stayed with him—they had passed like lightning! Surely this must be how the hours and days and centuries go by in Paradise. The hours passed, and the two souls strolled before God, gurgling like pigeons.

"How can you live like this, Father Arsénios? How do you stand the loneliness?" Father Yánaros asked one day as he watched the sea from among the orange trees and felt the longing to leave, "Have you lived in solitude many years?"

51

"I've been glued to this cell since I was twenty, Father Yánaros," he replied, "like the silkworm in its cocoon. This," he said and pointed to his cell, "is my cocoon."

"And is it large enough to hold you?"

"Yes, it is, because it has a small window, and I can see the sky."

When night came and midnight passed, Father Arsénios would take up his delicate tools with excitement and begin, silently bent over the cypress wood, to carve the holy visions before they could disappear.

One evening, a young monk from the Monastery of Lavra came to bring a message. As the older men sat talking, they heard someone sighing behind them; Father Yánaros turned and saw the young monk crouched, dazed, listening to them.

"Why are you listening to us?" he asked him. "What do you understand of all this?"

"Nothing," the monk replied, "but I ask only one favor of God—to let me listen to your conversations throughout eternity —it would be Paradise!"

Father Yánaros held his breath. Suddenly the urge to leave overcame him—to leave, to take God with him and leave! Here in Castello his soul was crumbling; every day, one by one, its feathers were being plucked. He had fought with the people; he had shouted from the pulpit, from the narrow streets, from anywhere and everywhere; he had shouted so many years now, and what had he accomplished? Did the evil stop? Did it grow less? Did they drop their rifles and stop the killing? Did even one person—at least one person—become a better human being? One woman, one man? No! No one! He must leave! He had to take God with him and leave!

He would go and find Arsénios. Was he still alive, was he still carving out his heart in wood? Oh, to build a cell near him, a cocoon for himself, too, in solitude, to see not orange groves or the sea from a small window, but a piece of sky! And sometimes to go and talk with Father Arsénios in his cell, to talk of the sweet tears that flow from the eyes of men in solitude!

He was the only friend, the only pure and serene conscience he had met on Mount Athos. How many times, here in hell—

in Castello—Arsénios came to the priest's mind and comforted his soul.

As long as such people exist on earth, he thought, the world will not crumble. Father Arsénios is a pillar that holds the world up, above the abyss.

And as he sat there with closed lids, his hands on the carved icon, thinking of his friend and seeing Mount Athos before him like an old holy fresco that is worn out by time and dampness, sleep came and took him. And he had a dream: the trumpets of Judgment Day had sounded; the earth began to shake and rise, and from its depths crept the dead—countless thousands of them, like snails crawling from the soil after the rain, all covered with mud. They dried in the sun, their bones hardened, their flesh tightened, eyes appeared in the empty sockets, sharp teeth wedged back in their mouths, and their bodies filled with soul again. And all of them leaped, panting, and stood up, some to the right, others to the left of Christ, who sat between earth and sky, on a blue, gold-embroidered cushion. And at His feet lay the Virgin, praying.

Christ turned to his right and smiled; and immediately the huge emerald door of Paradise opened wide, and the rose-hued angels with sky-blue wings embraced the just and led them, singing, through flower-bordered paths to the house of God. Then Christ turned to the left and wrinkled his brows; a lament rose, and countless demons with tails and horns held flaming spears and jabbed the sinners as though they were spearing octopuses, preparing them to be tossed into hell. The Virgin heard this lament; She turned; Her heart ached for them.

"My children," She cried, "do not weep, do not shout; my Son is not only just, He is also merciful; do not be afraid!"

And Christ smiled. "My children," He said, "I only meant to frighten you; come, God's heart is great; it holds both the just and the sinners as well—enter, all of you, enter Paradise!"

The demons stopped in surprise; the spears fell from their hands, and they began to weep. "Lord," they howled, "what will become of us now?"

Christ looked at them with compassion; and as He watched them, their horns and their tails fell off; their faces became serene, and curly wings began to grow on their backs.

53

"Enter the House of God," Christ said to them. "The Second Coming does not mean justice—it means mercy."

And as Christ talked, it seems a soft rain began to fall, and everything—the just and the unjust, Paradise and hell and Christ —vanished.

Father Yánaros let out a scream and jumped to his feet.

"O my God," he murmured and made the sign of the cross, "What doors open up for us in sleep, what wings we are given! Lord, we're lost if you keep a record of our dreams, too."

The voices of the night had wakened; in the stillness came the sounds, from afar, of the jackals coming toward Castello.

"Night falls upon us," Father Yánaros murmured, "and the massacre of night begins; now the beasts—birds, mice, caterpillars, jackals—will leap on one another to kill or kiss. God, what kind of world have You created? I cannot understand!"

Suddenly he heard a sound; he jumped up, and in one stride he was at the door; he listened intently; in the darkness, behind the church, he thought he heard the deep moans of a man in pain.

# 4

H E SEIZED his staff and ran outside; the night was warm and sweet, like all nights that follow massacres and battles. It seemed to Father Yánaros that the stars were lower in the skies tonight; they hung like sanctuary lights in God's dark spaces. Thank God for sleep, Father Yánaros thought. It brings us what wakefulness denies. A soft breeze floated within his heart, the sweetness of his dream still dripped, like honey, from his inner being. If only what he had dreamed were true! If only this were the way the Second Coming would be! Mercy! Mercy, not justice! Man, the unfortunate soul, cannot endure justice; he is weak, and sin appears tempting, God's commandments heavy; justice is fine, but it is only for angels—man needs mercy.

Father Yánaros entered the courtyard of the church; it seemed to him that the moans came from there. He leaped over the timeworn graves—priests of the village were buried here according to old custom. Father Yánaros, too, had dug his grave here, with his own hands; he had chiseled letters on a tombstone and painted them red: "Death, I fear you not!" Father Yánaros stood happily for a moment over his grave. "Death, I do not fear you," he murmured, and suddenly he felt free. What does it mean to be free? He who does not fear death is free. Father Yánaros stroked his beard, satisfied. God, he pondered, is there a greater joy than freedom from death? "No," he went on, "no!"

At that moment, still from a distance, came the sound of the

55

moans, more intense now, more painful. Father Yánaros turned from his grave. It must be one of the wounded left behind, he thought, and leaped over the ledge and onto the road. He looked to the right, to the left, as he walked in the darkness. Every so often he would stop to listen. When he passed the edge of the village, he took the path that led to the hill. Suddenly he heard slow, tired footsteps; a stone rolled, someone was coming down the hill.

Father Yánaros ran toward the sound of moaning, stumbling as he felt his way in the darkness. As he fumbled, he heard a low, breathless voice: "Father Yánaros, is that you?"

Straining his neck and moving forward, he perceived the form of a man with hands outstretched, leaning against a rock.

The priest hurried to him; he took his arm and leaned over to look closely at his face. He seemed young, dark, thin—all bones; he appeared wounded; his hands suddenly clutched his chest, and he sighed deeply. Father Yánaros felt the man's chest and pulled back his hand filled with blood.

"Who wounded you?" the priest asked softly, as though it were a great secret.

"You mean who hasn't wounded me!" the young man replied. "Some communist because I'm a Christian! Some Christian because I'm a communist! I couldn't tell who!"

"Come with me; my home is nearby. I'll wash your wound. Are you badly hurt?"

"You're Father Yánaros, aren't you?" the youth asked again.

"Yes, I'm the one people call Father Yánaros; God calls me Sinner—that's my real name. Are you badly hurt?" he asked again.

The youth put his arm over the priest's shoulder and slowly, with the older man's support, they began to walk.

"You know very well," the wounded man replied, "that when a brother wounds you, you are always badly hurt."

They were silent; as they entered the village they could see the whitewashed dome of the church glowing softly. Father Yánaros pushed open the low door alongside the church, and they entered.

"Sit down, my son," the priest said, and helped him to the small cot.

He lit the lamp; its light fell on the pale, embittered, ecstatic face of the young man. Father Yánaros looked at him and drew back in alarm. He had seen this face before, but where, when? In his dreams? The boy wore a monk's robe; a simple cross hung from his neck, and his eyes were large, deep blue, and they looked at the world with astonishment, as though for the first time. The eyes—Father Yánaros had always imagined these to be the eyes of the Angel Gabriel when he came to earth and said to the Virgin: "Hail, Mary, full of Grace!"

And in that moment a flash appeared, illuminating Father Yánaros' mind; now he remembered! Years ago, when the Metropolitan Bishop of Yánnina ordered a painting of the Annunciation, Father Yánaros had painted the Archangel Gabriel in the image of this young monk, with these same deep-blue eyes.

Father Yánaros was frightened for a moment; how mysterious is the soul of man! What strength it has—it can shape and destroy the world! Surely the soul is a flame from God's Fire that falls on hay—the flesh—and sets it afire.

He leaned toward the monk and asked in a trembling voice, "Who are you, my son?"

The wounded man bit his lips. "I'm in pain," he said and closed his eyes.

Father Yánaros felt ashamed—he had neglected the boy's wound to ask questions. Quickly he brought a pitcher of water, opened the man's robe, and carefully washed the wound. Then he took a salve from the shelf, an ointment he had been saving for such emergencies, applied it to the spot, bandaged the wound, and helped the young man lie down. He brought a stool and sat beside him.

The monk relaxed; he opened his eyes, looked at Father Yánaros, and smiled.

"I'm all right; I feel much better now; God bless you," he said and closed his eyes again.

"Do you want to sleep, my son?"

"No, I want to collect my soul, to gain strength, so I can talk to you."

"Rest first; don't tire yourself. I won't question you, not who you are or what you're doing near Castello. I want nothing from you—just rest."

57

"If I'm to rest, I must talk, Father. That's why I came. I have a secret."

"A secret?" Father Yánaros felt disturbed as he looked at the young man. Can he be insane? he thought. Those eyes are like those that see the Invisible; only the insane and the angels have such eyes. "What secret?" he said aloud.

The young man swallowed; he remained silent for a minute, then spoke. "A glass of water," he said, "my throat is dry; forgive me, Father."

He drank and felt refreshed.

"When they shot me, I prayed to God, mustered all my strength to hurry and find you, to tell you this; to entrust you with my secret before I die; for I may die, Father."

"Don't talk like that, my child," Father Yánaros replied and felt an indescribable tenderness for this boy who was fighting with death, who was fighting with God, here, before him.

"Are you afraid of death, Father Yánaros?"

The priest smiled. "No," he replied.

"Well, then?"

Father Yánaros did not reply; what he meant to say was that he feared death only when it took the young men, in the bloom of youth, before they could become ripe, before they could bear fruit; but he did not speak.

"I was afraid of death once, too, Father; when I was younger. But a saintly ascetic said something to me one day, and since then I have made my peace with death."

"What did the ascetic say to you? I'd like to hear it, too."

"He said, 'Death is that point where God touches man.' Father, I feel an invisible hand over me, touching my heart. That's why I'm in a hurry. That's why I gathered all my strength to come and find you, to entrust my secret to you; so it will not die with me."

"Entrust it to me? Why me? I'm seventy years old."

"You are twenty years old, Father Yánaros. I have heard many things about you. Father Arsénios . . ."

The priest sat up with a start. "Who? Father Arsénios? From the Monastery . . . ?"

"Yes, the Monastery of St. Anna, may God rest his soul."

"He died?"

58

"No, he went mad."

"He went mad?"

Father Yánaros' eyes filled with tears.

"He went mad," the monk continued, "from the rigid fasting, from being too saintly, from having too many conversations with God. He could endure it no longer; the trap door opened, and all the hidden demons escaped from within him. He no longer carved Virgins and Christs on wood; he would get up at night, light his lamp, and carve demons and naked women and pigs."

"No, no!" Father Yánaros cried, rising from his stool. "Father Arsénios had no demons within him, only angels dwelled there! Do not taint his memory!"

"Demons and naked women and pigs," the young man repeated. "All of us, Father Yánaros, all of us harbor demons and naked women and pigs within us."

Father Yánaros did not speak; he looked within himself. Walking over to the carving of the Second Coming, he stopped, made the sign of the cross, and bowed to worship. He watched it thoughtfully for a while; for a moment he had forgotten the wounded monk and the secret he supposedly brought; his heart filled with Father Arsénios. "Demons, women, and pigs . . ." he murmured. "Alas, I think this young man is right."

He remembered the day he had asked Father Arsénios what dwelled within a sinner's heart. And he had lowered his eyes and replied in a choked voice, "Why do you ask me, Father Yánaros? Why do you ask me about the heart of a sinner? I have the heart of a virtuous man, and still all the demons dwell within it."

How many years did these demons remain hidden within him—chained by the fear of God? Is that why, with such sleepless agony, he carved the saints? Is that why he had such fear of dreams and refused to sleep? His secret desires could have remained dormant all his life, through deep prayer, and he could have died a saint. But the trap door opened; his mind wandered; and the imprisoned demons revealed themselves.

Sweat poured from Father Yánaros' brow. He felt that he was burning—a great fire—he went to the door, opened it, and stood at the threshold. The night air refreshed him. He remembered his guest, closed the door, and went back to the stool beside the monk.

59

"Tell me more about Father Arsénios," he said. "Don't spare me, tell me everything."

"You feel such pain for one person," the monk said sternly, as though reprimanding him, "why don't you feel as deeply for all men? And I thought . . . and that's why I came."

"I'm a human being," Father Yánaros said stubbornly, "I'm a human being; I'm not an angel yet, you see, and I'm not a beast. A human being . . . I feel pain for even one soul. What happened to Father Arsénios after that? I want to know."

"Gradually his madness increased; he began to walk around undressed through the orange groves; he would fall on the ground screaming hysterically. And one Sunday he walked into church stark naked. Another old ascetic read the blessings to exorcise the demon, but the demon would not leave; the monks beat him unmercifully with their leather belts—blood came out, but not the demon. So they locked him in his cell and brought him only bread and water every morning. He would not touch it; he must have died by now."

"Enough, enough!" Father Yánaros shouted. "Is that your secret?"

"No, it's not, Father Yánaros, but you asked me about Father Arsénios, and I told you," he replied. "I lived in a cell next to his for several months. He sensed all those dark devils within him, and he was anxious to die. To die, before they found the open door to escape. And I am certain that all the while he was carving those saints and angels, his ear was cocked for Death the Deliverer; and he must have heard him in every beat of his heart when Death approached. And he would smile happily then. 'Father Arsénios,' I asked him one day, 'why do you always smile, and why does your face always shine?' 'Why shouldn't I smile, brother Nicódemus,' he replied, 'why shouldn't I smile, when every hour, every moment, I hear Death approaching?' "

The monk's immovable face shone; his voice was calm but filled with controlled pathos; his eyes sparkled as though behind them a huge fire raged. Father Yánaros watched him uneasily; he was leery of the serenity on his face, the calmness of his voice. This soul was a flaming bier that would not burn.

The monk reached out and touched Father Yánaros lightly on the shoulder.

"Listen to Father Arsénios' last words before the demons leaped from within him. 'You're going to die very soon, Brother Nicódemus,' he said to me, 'go find Father Yánaros—I've spoken to you of him so many times—go find him and entrust your secret to him. He can carry it; you cannot. And tell him that I am still alive, that I am still struggling with God above and with the demons below. These are the two millstones that grind me; tell him that.' I bowed, he placed his two hands on my head and blessed me, as though bidding me farewell. Later I understood; he was saying good-bye."

The monk remained silent for a moment; then he looked around the humble cell and smiled. "And I came," he said.

"I came to save you," he added. "Father Arsénios directed me to come and save you."

Father Yánaros smiled bitterly. "To save my body or my soul —which of the two?"

"Both! You know, Father Yánaros, that as long as we live, those two beasts never part company."

"I make them part," the priest said stubbornly.

"That's why you're floundering; that's why you don't know which way to turn. Don't frown, Father Yánaros, I've heard a lot about you. They say you're honest, poor, wild, but good, a brave fighter; you feel compassion for the people—and yet you cannot make up your mind. You're drifting."

"Perhaps it's my duty to drift," retorted the priest, "perhaps that is the post entrusted to me by God; I'm not going to betray it."

"Mercy to the soul that dies before taking a stand—before giving a 'yes' or a 'no,' clearly and honestly," the young man replied. "There was a time when you could be on the other side of the looking glass, Father Yánaros, but bad times have fallen upon us—don't you realize that? You cannot sit back with folded arms."

He was tired of talking; he drank a little water, leaned against the pillow, and remained silent.

Father Yánaros rose; he filled a glass with wine, took two pieces of leftover dry toast, and returned to the young man.

"Here," he said, "you must be hungry, my son. Dip this bread in the wine, so you can have strength to continue."

61

He watched the pale young man with tenderness, then he dipped the bread into the wine and fed him, as a mother feeds her child, as though he were giving him communion, as though the wine and bread were really the body and blood of Christ that would give him strength as they entered his body. A faint color came to the boy's cheeks.

"Thank you, Father," he said, "I feel stronger now. You're stronger, too, Father Yánaros. Can you listen now? Because you are more deeply wounded than I am—remember that!"

"I'm aware of that, but I can stand whatever you have to say; go on."

"You asked me who I am; I'll tell you everything in a little while; I'm anxious to get to the point. I was deacon to a bishop; I was educated, aiming for a bishopric myself. But I saw too many things—my mind opened, I understood. The word of Christ has been degraded, His message upon earth has faded; we only follow the footprints that Satan's feet leave on the mud—Christ's words have been reversed:

Blessed are the deceivers in spirit, for theirs is the kingdom of heaven.
Blessed are the violent, for they shall inherit the earth.
Blessed are they which do hunger and thirst after injustice.
Blessed are the unmerciful.
Blessed are the impure in heart.
Blessed are the warmakers.

These are what we call Christians today."

"I know, I know . . ." growled Father Yánaros. "I know all that, go on!"

"I shook the diocese dust from my feet; I left, and retreated to Mount Athos. But there, too, I found the world's misfortunes in this so-called holy solitude, only meaner, more cunning, because it did not pay to bring them out into the light and let them explode. Did you know that there are three kinds of people, Father Yánaros? Men, women, and monks! All the animosities simmer within the soul of a monk, secretly, without hope. For, as you know, Father, God help the man who lives in solitude with thoughts of the outside world preying on his mind!

So I secluded myself with the profane literature which I had brought with me."

"Literature! So you went into the monastic life dragging all the demons of the world along?"

"You're right, Father, I realized that later; in reality I did not go to the monastery to become an ascetic, but to gather those parts of my soul which had scattered, to discover what stand I should take, and from there to spring forth. For I cannot live without certainty, Father."

"Neither can I, neither can I . . ." sighed Father Yánaros. "That is why I am suffering."

But the young man did not hear him; his eyes and ears were turned within him, looking and listening only to his own heart and soul. Then he continued, hurriedly, because the wound began to hurt again, and he was not certain if he had time to confess everything to the white-haired man before him.

"I cannot live in doubt," he repeated, "and I am tormented. My faith in the representatives of God has faltered, and the pain of men who have been wronged fills me with indignation. To whom shall I turn? To Christ as the Church has degraded Him, or to those who want to shape a new world—a more just world, without Christ? I used to go to church, I fasted, I prayed, I called to God, but I found no relief; God never answered me. I realized in time that prayer is not the way, that neither is retreat; once, they were; they brought the earth to heaven, but no more. Now they alienate us from earth, they do not carry us to heaven—they leave us halfway, in mid-air. 'I must discover a new way,' I told myself, 'I must carve a new path.' But I could not, I could not, and I drifted, disillusioned, like you."

"But I'm not disillusioned," Father Yánaros flared back, angered. "I have a place to stand, my friend—beside Christ— and I'm not worried about what the bishops are doing. Isn't Christ enough for your reverence?"

"Don't get upset, Father," the monk said, touching the priest's knee in a pleading manner. "No, He's not enough, not the way they've degraded Him—with lavish clothes and palaces in which He reigns, eating and drinking the nights away with the nobles of this world! I missed that poor, impoverished Christ, Father, the one who is barefoot, hungry, and wronged,

63

the one met by those two humble students traveling in Emmaus —the Christ of Emmaus—that's the one I searched for and could not find; and that was why my heart ached. Do you understand now, Father Yánaros?"

The priest drew closer to the monk's pallid face; his heart beat loudly. Who is this sudden visitor, he wondered, who sent him to me? God or Satan? Which? I can't tell!

Father Yánaros was torn with the meaning of the monk's words.

"Do you think I'm old and stupid?" he said stubbornly. "You should know that I too have all the torments of youth, although I may be seventy years old. Don't stop! Did you find the Christ you were seeking? How did you find Him? Is that your secret?"

"Now you're going too fast, Father," the young man replied and smiled, "but I . . ."

He did not finish his sentence; he was thirsty again. Father Yánaros brought another cup of water; the monk drank and felt refreshed.

"So I took these profane books," the monk went on, "and went into solitude. 'What are you doing?' the monks would ask me. 'Why is your lamp on all night, Father Nicódemus?' 'I'm praying,' I would reply. 'Can't you pray in the dark?' 'I'm afraid!' Once in a while, I saw Father Arsénios, and we would exchange a few words. He would talk about the wood he was carving and tell me it was not the wood but his soul; and I would speak to him of the barefoot Christ. And suddenly, one night, one blessed night . . ."

"You saw the true light?" Father Yánaros whispered, as he bent over the monk's face.

"How do you know, Father?"

"I see it in your eyes, my son. And then?"

"I did see the true light. And then I came out of my cell. It was Easter, the monks were gathered at the table; they were eating meat, drinking large glasses of wine. I pushed my plate aside, spilled out the wine. 'Get up,' I shouted to them. 'Why are you sitting here with crossed hands while the world is being destroyed? God does not want incense and prayers, He does not want meat. He wants us to walk the straight and narrow path! Let the monastery move like the movable miraculous icons; prayer is not enough today, open the food cellars of the monastery, distribute bread to the poor. Let us share the journey, let us preach the word of Christ: Love! Peace! Justice!' "

"And then?"

"Then two strong monks—Benedict and Abbakoum—grabbed me. They carried me away and locked me in my cell. The next day they chased me from Mount Athos."

Father Yánaros pressed the monk's hand.

"Bless you," he said, "and thank God they did not crucify you. Go on!"

"Don't be frightened, Father Yánaros."

"You think this would frighten me? This is nothing—Christ comes down from the icon and talks to me, and I am not afraid! Go on. And then?"

"Then I took to the hills, Father."

Stunned, Father Yánaros drew back from his seat. "Rebel! Communist!" he shouted.

"You see? You're frightened," the monk said bitterly. "Yes, I saw the true light; I took to the hills and joined the guerrillas."

"But they don't believe in God," the priest shouted. "They've taken Him off His throne and sat themselves on it. You can't shape a world or a government without God. And you went with them! Is this the great secret you came to reveal to me? Then I'd rather flounder and drift forever."

The monk took Father Yánaros' hand and kissed it. "Don't be hasty, Father," he said, "don't be angry with me. Yes, I went with the guerrillas; true, a world without God has no foundations. But a world without justice cannot be governed. Now listen carefully to what I am going to say—to my great secret. It saved me and it will also save you; perhaps it will save many people. It may even save the ideal for which the guerrillas are fighting and dying. Calm your soul, Father Yánaros, be patient, listen to me . . ."

"All right, all right, I'm listening," Father Yánaros replied, and felt the flame of the monk's lips on his hand.

The young man's face turned crimson; his voice, deep and pathetic, came from out of his innermost being; the crucial moment—the most difficult moment in his confession—had arrived.

"Remember," he said softly, "remember the great promise

65

Christ made to His Apostles to console them as they wept, just before He rose to the heavens?"

"But when the Comforter is come, whom I will send unto you from the Father, even the Spirit of truth . . ."

The monk paused, his breath was cut short; he leaned over and looked into Father Yánaros' eyes.

"Do you remember?" he asked again.

"Of course I remember!" Father Yánaros snapped impatiently. "What are you leading up to?"

Again the monk's voice came from the depths of his soul— full of terror, full of contentment; he leaned over and whispered in Father Yánaros' ear. "The Great Comforter has come!"

Father Yánaros jumped back as though a wild beast had suddenly appeared before him.

"He came? Here? On earth?" he shouted.

"Yes, here on earth, in the form of man, with a man's name."

"What is his name?"

The monk leaned over a little more, his lips touching Father Yánaros' large hairy ear.

"Lenin!"

Father Yánaros put his hands to his head and squeezed his temples—he felt that they would burst any moment.

Slowly he raised his head. "Lenin?" he asked finally. "*Lenin?*"

He looked at the monk with horror; the young man had risen, and stood over him smiling, like the Archangel Gabriel.

"Lenin," the monk repeated quietly.

The priest opened his mouth in protest, but the young man put out his hand pleadingly. "Don't hasten to reply, Father," he said. "Hear me out first; I was just as frightened when the light dawned on me—the way your reverence is now. But can't you see, the dawn is always like that. It's a sword that tears out your heart. I was hurt, I rose to defend myself and all that I believed in, until now. But the light slowly cleared my mind, and I finally understood."

Father Yánaros would not let him continue.

"And Lenin is the Great Comforter?" he shouted, and his nostrils flared in anger. "Lenin is going to save us? Lenin?"

"Yes, he is, Father; don't shout; I see that the light has fallen upon you too like a sword. Listen to me; I will speak clearly, quietly, and you will see. I lived with bishops and with monks; I lived alone; I lived with the guerrillas; I made the full circle."

"And you found the Great Comforter among the rebels?" the priest asked sarcastically.

"I found the Comforter among the guerrillas," the monk replied quietly, "but they do not know who sent him and they call him Lenin. They don't even know why he was sent; they think that he came to create a new world, a more just world. But he did not come to create. He came to destroy! To destroy the old world and prepare the way for the One who is coming."

"And who is the One coming?"

"Christ! Because He *will* come—He *will*, Father Yánaros; He'll come and He'll lead the guerrillas. And He won't be crucified again, He won't leave earth this time, to let us fall back into injustices. Earth and heaven, Father Yánaros, will all become one."

"That's what I've been hoping for; that's what I've been waiting for, all my life—for earth and heaven to become one; but I don't know the way, and that's why I am tormented."

"That's why I've come, Father, to show you the way. Forgive me—one so young—trying to guide you; but it's not I who is leading you, it's youth; youth has entered your cell tonight and it beckons you, it cries out, 'Come with us!' "

Father Yánaros bowed his head and groaned softly; his blood whirled, but he did not speak.

The monk leaned over, and Father Yánaros felt his hot breath on the back of his neck, on the lobe of his ear.

"Join us," the monk said in a quiet, seductive voice, "there's only a few of us now; yeast is only a handful at the beginning, but the dough soon rises and becomes bread."

Father Yánaros raised his head. "Did you preach that to the rebels?"

"Not at first; I was silent at first; I was ashamed, afraid to reveal my secret. I lived with them, fought beside them. I killed, too. I fought to destroy whatever I could—just a stone in this world, helping to build the road of God as best I could. I did not speak; I kept my secret within me, even if it tore out my

67

insides. But one day, one early morning, a voice rose from within me. 'These people feel hatred,' it said, 'they kill and are killed; they hope without knowing why. But you know why! Rise and speak to them!' So I did; I stood on a rock, and they gathered around me, about fifty fighters, with their rifles, their bandoliers, their boots, and their beards. I made the sign of the cross before I began to speak; they roared with laughter. I stilled my heart and began, hoping to enlighten them. But before I could say two words, they burst into whistles, curses, and mocking laughter. 'He's been planted here,' they shouted. 'Religion —the opium of the people!' 'Traitor, you've sold us out!' they yelled. 'Get out!' 'Get out!' They beat me mercilessly, and I stumbled away. I went to another hill; it was the same—they chased me from there, too. I went to still another, from hill to hill; always being beaten, cursed, barely managing to escape the traps they set for me. Somehow, God helped me to escape them. But tonight . . ."

Sweat poured from Father Yánaros' brow; he rose and walked over to the small window, leaned his head against the iron bars and felt their coolness. It was a dark night with dark sounds— a gray owl flew quietly by, a jackal on the hill howled softly, satisfied that he had eaten and his stomach was full. Father Yánaros raised his eyes; he saw a strip of sky and three large stars; the moon was high, and the smaller stars had disappeared.

"Well?" the monk asked.

The lamp was low; it was running out of oil, and the wick sputtered. The cell became darker; only the votive lamp burned before the icon of St. Constantine the firewalker, illuminating the dancing feet over the burning coals.

As Father Yánaros watched it, his heart settled back in its place. And as he looked, a weight lifted from his chest; he felt a deep sense of relief.

Laughing, he pointed to the icon. "You're a firewalker, too, Brother Nicódemus," he said. "We're all fish on burning coals, that sing as they sizzle. But are we singing or weeping? I can't quite understand. You call it light, I call it burning coals—it's the same thing."

The monk frowned; he was waiting for an answer, and it seemed that Father Yánaros was only making jest.

"You're not a good man," the monk said, misjudging the

68

priest. "You're not a good man, Father Yánaros, you don't pity the people."

Anger welled up in the priest. "Eh, young man, what do you consider man's greatest virtue? Is it kindness?"

"Yes. Kindness."

"No, it's freedom. Or to be more precise, the struggle for freedom."

"Then why do you preach love?"

"Love is the beginning; it is not the end. I cry 'Love!' because man must begin with that; but when I speak with myself or with God, I do not say 'Love!' but 'The struggle for freedom.' "

"Freedom from love, too?"

Father Yánaros hesitated again; the blood rushed to his head. "Don't ask me!" he shouted.

But he was ashamed at not daring to answer. "From love, too . . ." he added softly.

The monk shuddered; he was frightened. "Then why do you want freedom? For what purpose?"

"Freedom," the priest replied with trembling voice, "freedom has no purpose. And it is not found on this earth. All we can find here is the struggle for freedom. We struggle to obtain the unattainable—that is what separates man from beasts.

"That's enough now," Father Yánaros added, "you've talked and talked—enough! The Comforter! Lenin! The Barefoot Christ! The Rebel-Leader Christ! Muddled words! My brain can't make sense out of all that jumble!"

"Can your heart?"

"Let the heart alone—it's a foolish, fickle thing! Don't involve it in difficult problems; it always goes against logic, anyway, and whoever follows the heart must have a strong constitution. I don't!"

The priest was silent. In a few moments he spoke again. "I'll mention all this to God, and let's see what He says about it!"

"I've already mentioned it to Him," the monk replied, "and He agrees with me."

"God weighs each soul separately," Father Yánaros said, "and He gives to each the suitable reply for its salvation. Let's see what He will say to me, to old Father Yánaros. When I, too, find the road, I swear that I will follow it to the end."

"To freedom!" the monk added teasingly.

69

"To freedom!" Father Yánaros concluded, and felt the sweat pouring from his forehead again. "What I really mean is 'To death'!"

The monk glanced toward the door. "I'm leaving," he said.

Father Yánaros looked at the young man's eyes—they shone, large and deep blue in the half-light. He had placed his left hand over his wound—apparently he was in pain. The priest felt compassion rise in him again—a gentleness, an admiration for this young firewalker before him. This one, he thought, this one should have been my son, not that other.

"Where will you go?"

"I don't know; wherever the road takes me."

"They chase you from the monasteries, they chase you from the hills, they hunt you in the valleys; where will you go?"

"I have an unconquered fortress, Father, and I dwell there."

"What fortress?"

"Christ."

Father Yánaros flushed; he was ashamed at asking such questions—as though he had forgotten Christ.

"Now do you think that I should be afraid?" the monk asked, smiling, as he lifted the door latch.

"No," Father Yánaros replied.

The monk kissed the priest's hand, opened the door, and walked out into the night.

Father Yánaros stood on the threshold of his cell and watched the monk fade and disappear in the darkness. His mind was clear—for a moment there was not a thought in it; he had no urge to sleep. It was Holy Wednesday tonight—there was no vigilance in church—he was free. Carefully he listened to the sound of the monk's footsteps on the stones, slowly fading and finally disappearing.

Suddenly a knife pierced his heart; a frightful suspicion coiled around his brain; he wanted to shout, 'Get thee behind me, Satan!' But his lips were parched and dry. Could this, then, have been Temptation? Father Yánaros knew that Satan took many forms in order to trick man. He had seen him once on Mount Athos in the form of a small, plump boy who roamed outside the monasteries, trying to enter. And another time, here at Castello, in the form of a pretty woman going to the well with a water jug on her shoulder. Gone were the days when

70

Satan appeared before men in his true form—with horns, a tail, and the flames. Men were wiser and slyer now; and, tonight, Satan had entered the cell as a pure God-inspired monk with a cross hanging from his neck.

Confused and angry, Father Yánaros mumbled the monk's words softly. *"Lenin is the Comforter; God sent Lenin, when wickedness broke out in the world, to prepare the way for Christ. How? By destroying this corrupt world. Only in this way can the new path open for the future Christ to come . . ."*

"No, no, I won't accept that!" Father Yánaros shouted in the darkness. "Satan blends truth and lies with great mastery, to trick us. Yes, the world today is wicked and unjust; it has left the hands of God and fallen into the hands of Satan. It must be destroyed, it must! But who will destroy it?"

Beads of sweat poured from the wrinkled brow.

"I can't make heads or tails of all this." He sighed. "I can't! My mind has aged, my flesh has aged, I cannot endure any more; let the pain of the world find a younger man than me."

Mount Athos flashed before him, like a hagiography. The sky above was no longer blue, but golden; below it was the green valley, filled with small white daisies, like stars. And in the star-embroidered greenness rose a white monastery with four towers; and a flag waved from each tower; and an angel was painted on one flag, an eagle on the other, a small white bull on the third, and a lion on the fourth. And in the courtyard of the monastery stood a tree in full blossom, and beneath the tree, an ascetic stood erect with closed eyes, his head raised, listening. And on each flowered branch sat a white bird with a red breast; and all of them had their beaks open in song. The song they sang could be seen on a blue ribbon that unfolded from their beaks, "Solitude . . . solitude . . . solitude . . . solitude." Nothing else.

Father Yánaros crossed his hands and murmured, unknowingly, along with the birds, "Solitude . . . solitude . . . solitude . . . ," and he sighed. What sweetness, what peace, what reconciliation! God comes, you see Him, and He sits beside you like a long-lost father who has just returned from foreign shores laden with gifts.

The priest shut his eyes so that the vision would not disappear. Silence! Silence! A great sweetness! This is what God must be like! This is how man's life should be! Why should we question? Why should we torment ourselves? Isn't God above us? Doesn't He hold the helm of the world? He knows what course we take and where we are going. Man is not God's co-worker, he is the servant; then follow!

But as logic stirred within him, Father Yánaros tossed his head back in anger. "Get thee behind me, Satan," he shouted and spat in the air. "My post is here in Castello, and this is where I will fight, a man among men! The time is gone when man could find salvation in the wilderness. The modern Thevai is the world; courage then, Father Yánaros, God is a fighter, and so is man; then fight beside Him!"

# 5

ᴅAWN CAME; it was Holy Thursday; Christ went from Anna to Kayafas, beaten, cursed, crowned with thorns. The gypsy blacksmiths had already begun to pound the nails for His crucifixion; the angels, too, had begun to look down from the sky at Virtue being crucified on earth. And Gabriel the Archangel sat among them, with folded wings; and his eyes filled with tears. The air was still, melancholy, this Holy Thursday, as if it were the Archangel himself.

Father Yánaros sat on the stone ledge in the courtyard to the right of the church entrance. He had not slept all night; his thoughts were dark; his heart was heavy with a turmoil that would not settle; it felt unclean, imbedded in fat and mud. And with this heart he would not dare approach the icon of Christ on the iconostas, to offer his daily prayers. Sprigs of camomile had begun to grow between the old graves where the bones of the priests of Castello were buried. Father Yánaros sniffed the air and drew in the humble smell of the dead. He looked at his empty grave and, in the faint light, distinguished the red letters carved upon the stone: "Death, I fear you not," but his heart did not leap, either with pride or certainty. This heart of his had become a morsel of flesh filled with blood instead of with God's grace—a piece of flesh that ached and cried out.

"Lord," he murmured, "forgive my heart for calling; this shameless thing does not know what it seeks; but then, how can

73

it possibly know, my Lord? The poor thing is dizzy from stumbling through chaos in its wanderings."

At that moment, a butterfly appeared in the sunlight; it swept earthward and sat upon the camomile branch; it, too, sniffed the remains of the dead; then it fluttered around Father Yánaros' beard. He held his breath for fear of frightening it away; he watched it. A sweet emotion suddenly lifted the weight from Father Yánaros' chest. Of all the birds and beasts, this fearless firewalker loved butterflies the best—in them he placed his faith. It was only when he was once asked that he discovered why. "Because the butterfly was once a worm," he had replied, "a worm that crawled into the earth and emerged a butterfly when spring came. What spring? The Second Coming!"

Father Yánaros moved, and the butterfly was frightened away; the priest felt sad that these two small wings had deserted him, leaving him alone on the ledge in the sun.

For a moment his mind had scattered; the weight that had crushed him the night before was exorcised; he decided to enter the church and prepare the cross for evening. They had brought him wildflowers from Prastova to decorate the crucifix for tonight and the sepulcher for Good Friday. He opened the door of the church and glanced inside; the light entered from the window and fell on the icon of Christ. He could not make out the calm form, the blond beard, the long fingers which held a green sphere—the earth. Quickly he closed the door, as though ashamed to appear in this condition before Him. He sat back down on the ledge.

The sound of footsteps coming from the road broke the stillness; Father Yánaros, glad that now he would have something else to think about, leaned from the outer gate and looked out. A large masculine woman passed by, barefoot, ragged, hairy, loaded down with a bundle of wood. Her badly combed, gray-streaked hair was tied with a wide red ribbon that only a young girl would wear. Behind her ran two children, throwing stones and jeering in singsong fashion, "I want a man, I want him now ! I want a man, I want him now!"

Bent from the weight of her burden, the unfortunate woman pinned her eyes to the ground and remained silent. Father Yánaros shook his head; his heart ached for her.

74

"Poor Polyxeni," he murmured, "your virginity has jolted your mind, and you have become the town's scapegoat. You've stuck a red ribbon in your hair like a wedding banner, you poor soul!"

It was long past midday; the Castellians were all asleep, resting before the long service tonight—the reading of the Twelve Gospels. Not a sound of a human voice could be heard, nor a dog's, nor a bird's; except from time to time a humming noise rising from a few homes—a soft, monotonous, sweet rhythm, like the buzzing of bees; it was the weeping women—mothers, sisters, wives—crying softly, tiredly: their men had been killed the day before yesterday, on Holy Tuesday.

Father Yánaros' heart once again was crushed with agony; the words of last night's unexpected guest leaped in his mind. The more he thought about it, the more certain he was that it had not been a man dressed in monk's robes, the iron cross around his neck. The way he had sighed, so deeply, when he entered the priest's cell, covered with blood; and later, the way he quietly disappeared into the night—surely it was Satan! And the words he spoke—surely only the Antichrist could select them so carefully and speak them so artfully. Father Yánaros desired nothing more desperately, more secretly, in his heart than this: that this unjust world would crumble by the hand of God.

Yánaros turned these thoughts over and over in his mind, and he was confused. They seemed logical, and yet something, someone within him, resisted, refusing to accept them.

"No, no," the voice shouted within him, "this new word that the rebels proclaim cannot be the word of God; if the Comforter were truly their leader, they would not speak with such passion of material things—what to eat, how to divide the loot, how to kill their enemies. Did you ever hear them speak of heaven? Their eyes are turned to the earth: fill all the bellies of the world, they say, and the future will take care of itself. The stomach is their foundation—not the heart, not eternal life! What kind of Comforter, then, is this?"

Father Yánaros sighed; he contemplated for a long while. Often, when he was left alone in the courtyard among the graves, his mind would sink in deep thoughts. He had struggled from this small village, with the brain God had given him, to find an explanation to the mysteries of life and death and the hereafter. And always, he questioned, questioned—and waited for a reply. But today, the monk's words tormented him; he groaned softly on the ledge, and sweat poured from his brow.

"Can it be true? Can it be true?" he murmured. "But if it is, then get up, Father Yánaros, onward! Put on your bandoliers, climb the hill, find the Comforter, and fight alongside him!"

But again the voice leaped within him; it would not let him rise and go.

"No, no," it cried out to him, "don't flare up so easily, Father Yánaros. If the belly is full, will the soul be able to leave it after the sweetness of digestion? The happiness on earth never leads to heaven; happiness is a trap of Satan; earthly paradise is the work of the devil. How many times must I tell you, Father Yánaros? The devil is the leader of the happy, the satisfied, the contented. Christ is the leader of the unfortunate, the restless, the hungry. Beware, Father Yánaros!"

But as he threw his head back, pleased that he had uncovered the trap and had not been fooled by Satan, he recalled a conversation he had had, years ago, in his village, with an old fisherman, on that blessed, distant shore.

It was a bright sunny day in August—like this one—a day that seemed to have come straight from the hand of God. Morning —the sea smelled sweetly, a light breeze blew, two white butterflies with orange spots on their wings chased each other, playing, above the sea shells. Father Yánaros was walking barefoot on the sand; his chest was bare and he was chanting loudly the hymn he loved so well, "Ti Ypermaho"—"To Thee, the Triumphant Leader, do I, Thy city ascribe—thank offerings of victory. For Thou, O Mother of God, hast delivered me from terrors." This hymn had once resounded triumphantly in all the Byzantine churches when the Virgin—the Triumphant Leader —freed the kingdom from the hands of the barbarians. And so, singing as he went, Father Yánaros came upon a humble cottage where two brothers lived. They were happy, inseparable —one was a fisherman, the other a potter. The latter had a potter's wheel, and he mixed mud, tossed it into the wheel, and gave it whatever shape his heart desired. Father Yánaros was tired, so he sat with them to chat awhile; one was mixing the clay while the other was gathering nets to go fishing.

They spoke of the sea, of wars, and of the poor; then of figs—the trees were good this year. Suddenly the fisherman turned to Father Yánaros and said, "Father, I'm going to ask you one thing, and I want you to forgive me. Can you tell me how Christ chose his first disciple?"

Father Yánaros told him all that was in the books, but the old fisherman shook his head and smiled. He leaned toward the priest. "I'm the only one who really knows," he said. "Christ performed many miracles; He spoke many great words, but no one knows them. Don't believe what's in the books; I'll tell you, Father, how He fished for His first disciple—what was his name?"

"Andrew."

"Andrew. There was, imagine, a heavy storm! Wind, fog, huge waves! The fishermen struggled in vain; they were returning with empty nets. Then suddenly, on the shore, behind a rock, what did they see? A fire! And a shadow that moved beside it rose, sat down, and rose again. 'He's cooking something,' one of the hungry fishermen surmised. 'I'd better go and see!' And he ran toward the fire at the edge of the sea."

"It wasn't the sea," Father Yánaros corrected him, "it was a lake—the Lake of Gennesaret."

"What difference does it make?" the old fisherman replied, annoyed. "That's what spoils you educated men. Anyway, he ran toward the fire and found the coals smoldering; scattered around were the remains of fish. But the man had vanished; he called out, not a soul!

"The next day brought an angrier storm. The discouraged fishermen were returning once more with empty nets, when again they saw the fire and the shadow bending over it. The same fisherman as the night before ran to the scene and stopped beside a man who was cooking a row of fish strung through a reed. He was young, about thirty years old, and sunburned.

" 'What are you doing there, friend?'

" 'I'm cooking fish.'

" 'And where did you find them?'

" 'I caught them a little while ago—at sunset.'

" 'But how could you fish in this stormy sea? We haven't caught a thing to eat in two days.'

" 'Because you don't know how to throw the nets; I'll teach you.' The fisherman, as you must have gathered, was Andrew; he fell at the Stranger's feet and said, 'Teacher, I will never leave you again.' That night Andrew told his brother that he had met a man who could catch fish even in the wildest storm. As this story spread, Christ—for that was who He was—gradually gathered His disciples to Him, one by one. At first He taught them how to catch fish, so they would not go hungry. Then He taught them more; and, step by step, unknowingly, they became Christ's Disciples."

Father Yánaros listened open-mouthed to the old man. As the fisherman talked, the priest recalled a picture which he had seen in an old Bible preserved in his church. This holy picture, "The Descent of the Holy Ghost," was one of the many miraculous multicolored miniatures which illustrated the Book. It depicted the Holy Ghost diving, like a hungry seagull, aiming for the Disciples, hooking them from their bellies onto twelve fishhooks. The men struggled to free themselves, but the hooks had sunk deep into their flesh, and the hooks held. As he remembered this illustration, Father Yánaros thought, How perfectly the word of God falls, from the very beginning, and plants itself in the belly of man, slowly rising to grasp his heart and spirit.

The old fisherman looked at Father Yánaros, sensed the priest's admiration, and was pleased.

"That is how God works, Father," he said, "wouldn't you say? You learned people say that God is an Idea—a Rare Thing —who knows what? Others say that He's an old man above the clouds, and they paint Him that way. He's none of these!

"He's a potter's wheel—like this one of my brother's, here. And we are the clay; the wheel turns without stopping; it turns and twists us; it molds and makes us into whatever shape it wants: pitchers, jugs, pots, lamps. Into some of these they pour water, into others, wine and honey; some are for cooking, others for shedding light. That's how God makes people! And if we break, what does He care? He turns, turns, and shapes new pots, and He never looks back—why should He?"

"But what's the point of all this," the priest said, goading the old fisherman, "why should He make me at all? And after He does make me, why should He break me? I don't need that!"

"So what if you don't?" the old man replied in a dry, mocking laugh. "Who asks us, anyway, holy Father?"

Father Yánaros closed his eyes and saw that faraway sunny beach; he heard, so clearly, the words of the old fisherman. Could it be that the illiterate old man was right? Can it be that God, in the very beginning, hooks on to man's guts to root Himself there, and slowly rise? Rise and grasp the heart, then the mind, and later soar above his head? And can these rebels, laying the foundations of a new world, possibly be right? Can they be right in wanting to eat, to quench their hunger first? Roots thrive and spread in the mud before the tree can blossom. What is the purpose of manure? To become honey and sweetness and flesh—to fertilize the fruit! Blessed, then, is the manure—and the bowels of men!

It was in this frame of mind—trapped by Christs and Antichrists—that Kyriákos the town crier found Father Yánaros. Someone was dying again—one of the hostages in the improvised barbed-wire prison—and he must have absolution. The priest rose and stretched his limbs—his knees, his back, all his muscles ached. I've aged, I've gotten old, he thought, I'm old and still I haven't reached a decision. He turned to Kyriákos.

"How much longer, my son," he said, "how much longer?"

"I don't understand what you mean, Father," Kyriákos replied, confused.

"How much longer will we keep crucifying Christ?"

Kyriákos shrugged his shoulders. "Why don't you ask how much longer we're going to keep resurrecting Him? How much longer?"

Father Yánaros did not reply; he entered the sanctuary of the church, picked up the Holy Chalice, and, covering it with the deep red velvet cloth, he set out with it down the road, toward the outskirts of town, to the pit where fifty hostages were imprisoned. The army captain who defended Castello had ordered these old men and women who had husbands or sons fighting with the rebels to be held captive here. The scrawny villagers stood erect, like skeletons, jammed together inside the barbed-wire fence. The women's heads had been shaved, and on the men's foreheads, the word "traitor" had been branded.

Father Yánaros held the Holy Chalice high as he hurried through the narrow streets of Castello. Once again he was on his way to give a dying man communion. It had become a daily procedure—this giving of the body and blood of Christ, this hurrying back and forth to help people face death; often it happened many times in a day. And the men died, and they rested. But there was no rest for Father Yánaros; remembering their last gasping words, recalling their final looks of agony, the dead never stopped dying within him.

As the priest hurried to his destination, the army captain paced up and down with heavy steps outside the barbed-wire enclosure. He was short, thin, sunburned, and had a deep scar on his right cheek. Beneath thorny eyebrows peered a pair of tiny round eyes, like a porcupine's. He paced back and forth, chewing the mustache over his stiff lips, pinning down each of his prisoners with threatening eyebrows and steely eyes while cracking his whip on his old, worn-out boots.

"Traitors," he growled, gnashing his teeth, "traitors, dishonorable dogs that would sell their country!"

A small, mustachioed soldier whispered secretly to the man beside him: "What did I tell you, Abraham? I dreamed of poppies last night, didn't I? We're going to have bloodshed again. What's going to become of us, Levy—tell me!"

Levy, who had a sallow face and hair that fell like corn whiskers, giggled sarcastically through his thin, dry lips. "There's only one hope left for us: Satan! He rules the world today; we're all going to be lighting candles to the devil from now on. What good can we expect from your Christ, who turns the other cheek every time He gets slapped? What good can we expect from our Jehovah, who's never satisfied no matter how many people he devours? No good at all! I say to hell with heaven, and let's worship the horns of Satin instead!"

The Germans had taken Levy from Salonica and sent him to Auschwitz. The Jews were gassed to the sound of music, and Levy was made to stand at the entrance to the gas chambers, playing his violin. Since then, he had only one pleasure—to watch people die.

Panos was shocked to hear such words; he seemed to see Satan, horns and all, standing before him, and he shuddered; he turned to the man next to him for comfort.

"What do you think, Vassos? Did you hear what Abraham said?"

But how could poor Vassos hear anything? His mind and his thoughts were far away, to a barren house and to his four unmarried sisters. His body was bent from work all those years he had tried to save up for their dowries; he had worked, worked, but he had not succeeded in getting even Aristea, the oldest, married.

"What?" he asked the soldier. "I didn't hear you."

The other two soldiers laughed. "The poor brat is thinking of his sister again," they said, and turned to a thin rat-faced boy.

"And how about you, Stratis, aren't you talking? Open up your lips, boy; you haven't said a word for three days."

"I don't want to talk," Stratis growled, "the devil take you all."

"He can't accept his friend Leonidas' death," Levy said, and giggled again. "Eh, poor soul, he's gone, gone! And he'll never come back. Here's to our death, too!"

Stratis remained silent and turned his face the other way to hide the tears. The sergeant approached. "What's all the whispering about, you idiots?" he asked angrily. "The priest is coming to give you communion now, so be quiet!"

"I'm a Jew," murmured Levy, rubbing his hands. "I'm safe!"

From the end of the road Father Yánaros appeared; he held the Holy Chalice in both hands, proudly raised before him as though he were holding a flag, marching off to battle. His head was bare, his graying hair fell on his shoulders, and his boots echoed on the stones like horses' hoofs. He felt a fierce, blind strength flowing from the Holy Chalice into his hands, his arms, and through his whole aged body; the burden made him lurch and stumble over the stones.

As the prisoners recognized the approaching figure, their eyes lit up; all their hopes lay in that Holy Chalice—in the body and blood that it contained. Where else could they find salvation? From men? Until now, men only tortured and killed them; only Christ remained. If He, too, could not bring them salvation, then cursed be the day they were born! Anathema upon the hands that created such a world!

As the priest reached the crowd of prisoners, a pale woman who had been breast feeding her child raised the baby high over the barbed wire.

"Water," she screamed, "in the name of God, water!"

An old man stretched out his bony hands. The army captain stopped. "What do you want?" he growled.

"Freedom," replied the old man in a gasping voice.

"Shut up! Your son is with the traitors!"

"Freedom . . ." the old man murmured again, quietly, pleadingly, as though asking for a piece of bread.

"You're all going to feel the muzzle of my gun," bellowed the captain, who had not yet seen Father Yánaros approaching, "and the first one is going to be that two-faced priest, Yánaros. And then that tubercular schoolteacher, then all of you, all of you! I'm going to clean up this village!"

He turned to the sergeant. "Tomorrow take two of our men and go bring me the schoolteacher; put him and his wife and his child, too, behind the wire."

Father Yánaros stopped; the Holy Chalice trembled in his hands.

"My God," he murmured, "how much longer are you going to surrender your servants to these beasts? Will injustice and pain never end, then, on this earth? When are You going to fortify love, too, my Lord? Now is the time for You to appear! Can't You see? Can't You hear? Have You no pity for these prisoners, these guards, this captain—all of them? Perform Your miracle, my Lord!"

The captain felt heavy breathing behind him and turned to see the stout, square figure of Father Yánaros standing, enraged, before him; the priest's eyes were on fire. The captain frowned, turned his face the other way, and lowered his head; he hated and feared this seventy-year-old wild man of a priest, whose eyes seemed to hurl a silent strength to strike him down; this goat-beard with his chalice, his Bibles, his robes, his hymns, his exorcisms, commanded powerful invisible forces, and the captain, young and brave though he was, feared him. He turned to face the priest, then stamped his foot on the ground.

"Why do you look at me like that, Father Yánaros? Come on, give the man communion and get it over with!"

"Aren't you ashamed? Have you no fear of God, Captain?" the priest said in a low, controlled voice.

The captain tightened his grip and raised the whip as though to strike.

82

But Father Yánaros kept coming closer; now his beard touched the captain's face—it rubbed against it. "You call yourself a man?" The priest's voice was hoarse. "No wonder the world calls you a butcher; and who are these sheep you're slaughtering? Open your eyes and look, you fool! They're your brothers—your brothers!"

"I'm going to see that you're put up against that wall, priest!" bellowed the captain as he grabbed Father Yánaros by the arm and shoved him aside. "Your turn will come soon!"

"Yes it will, Captain; in fact my turn has already come; go ahead and put me up against the wall; I'm ashamed to be living, anyway."

"I'll kill you when I'm ready, and no sooner; now go!"

"I will not go; I will cry out!" He turned to the soldiers, raising high the chalice.

"Enough of this bloodshed, my children," he shouted, "enough!"

The captain leaped at him and grabbed his beard, stifling him.

"Tell that to your son, the traitor, the Bulgar captain!"

Father Yánaros wrenched himself away and turned toward the soldiers. "My children," he shouted again, "do not listen to those who tell you to kill! Lift your heads and cry, "No, we shall not kill!' And have no fear! Whoever believes in the Lord's command is free; whoever believes in the laws of man is a slave. Freedom, freedom, my brethren!"

Raising his whip, the captain darted toward the priest, but Sergeant Mitros, the kind-hearted Roumeliote,* grabbed the old man, pulling him away, only to have the soldiers rush upon him. Father Yánaros fought and struggled to get away.

"Leave me alone," he shouted. "I have no wish to live; let the butcher slaughter me before I curse God!"

"Quiet, old man," the sergeant said softly, "quiet, Father, the sword rules here."

Father Yánaros looked at him with eyes of pain. "You, too?" he said, "you, too, Mitros my boy? How could you stoop to this? How could you have killed those seven women the other day?"

_____
* One who comes from the area of Roumeli near Mt. Olympus.

The sergeant lowered his voice. "May God forgive me," he said. "He understands. I don't do this because I want to. No, I do it because I have to."

"He understands," Father Yánaros interrupted. "God help you, Mitros, you coward; He understands only that the soul is stronger than the body's need—and He does not forgive!"

Father Yánaros jumped up as he heard the rasping breaths of the dying man. He made the sign of the cross. "Forgive me, Lord, forgive me," he said, "I forgot your dying creature." Then he raised high the body and blood of Christ, and descended into the pit.

# 6

WHAT A SAD STATE we're in, pondered Father Yánaros as he walked back to his church. God turned his face the other way, and the earth is in darkness. "An eclipse of God . . . an eclipse of God," he repeated as he strode through the narrow, dirty side streets of the village. Ruins everywhere—doors and walls riddled with bullets, thresholds splattered with blood, hungry dogs sniffing, digging the earth to find the rotting flesh. Father Yánaros tightened his grip on the Holy Chalice; he felt that he was holding God by the hand, leading him through the desolate alleys of Castello, showing him the pain of man.

"Look! Look around You," he said to God. "Forget the heavens, You're not needed up there; we need You here, my Lord, here in Castello—Look! If this cursed brother-killing lasts any longer, we shall destroy ourselves. We're not human any longer, my Lord, our faces have taken on a wild look; we're turning back into beasts. Why, only a few days ago, didn't old Stamatis, that serious-minded elder, grab the ear of Stelianos the merchant and try to bite it off? And the captain! Look at him now! He's not a man any longer—he's a tiger! A tiger seeking blood. How much longer my Lord, how much longer? Your image is gradually slipping away from within us. Instead we see only Satan. Help me, Lord, help me bring Your image back to this little village."

• • •

85

In this world, he thought, you're either a lamb or a wolf. If you're a lamb, you're eaten up; if you're a wolf, you do the eating. My God, is there no third animal, a stronger, kinder one? And a voice inside him replied, "There is, yes, there is, Father Yánaros; be patient. Thousands of years ago it set out to find us, to become human; but it hasn't arrived yet. Are you in a hurry? God is in no hurry, Father Yánaros."

He stopped in front of the barracks—his knees felt weak; a group of small children were gathered around a pile of garbage, digging for leftovers from the soldiers' rations. Their bellies were swollen, their legs spindly; many of them moved about on crutches.

Father Yánaros moved to approach them—but what could he say? They had gone wild; and he had nothing to give them. He stood silently by, watching. And as he watched, with eyes that slowly dimmed, a skinny old woman passed by with quick, long strides; barefoot, tousle-haired, she held a dead child in her arms, a boy of three, wrapped in a torn blanket. Over her shoulder she carried a shovel. She screamed as she walked; her eyes were fierce and they were dry. Father Yánaros recognized her; it was old Areti, the village midwife; the child she held was her grandson. When she saw the priest, a wild laugh contorted her lips.

"It's dead, Father Yánaros," she shouted, "It's gone, too. Go tell that to your Master! You mean to say He didn't have a little piece of bread to give the child? And He's supposed to be the Almighty? And He claims to be the All-Powerful? And He didn't even have a little piece of bread to give this child?"

Father Yánaros did not speak; he looked at the small form that was turning blue, at its swollen belly, its small, skinny neck, its huge bony head. The old woman's mouth twisted; she screamed and she laughed, and her eyes were steeled with hatred of Father Yánaros.

She cried out again: "Tell me, Father Yánaros, what kind of God is this who lets children die of hunger?"

"Be still, be still, Kyra Areti," the priest pleaded. "Do not curse the Lord."

"Why shouldn't I curse Him?" the old woman screeched. "What's there to be afraid of? What can He do to me now?"

She nodded to the dead child. "What else can your God do to me?"

The priest raised his hand over the lifeless body as though to bless it, but the old woman pulled back.

"Don't you touch it!" she cried.

"Where are you taking it, Kyra Areti?"

"To bury it; I'm going to bury it in the field; I have the shovel."

"Bury it without last rites? I'm coming with you."

The old woman's lips foamed. "Last rites? What last rites? Can you bring it back to life? You can't? Then leave me alone, my friend." She squeezed the child tightly to her and with long, quick strides took the road that led to the fields.

Father Yánaros bowed his head and pressed the Holy Chalice against his chest. He wanted to cry out, "Lord, what have You to say to this old woman? What justification can we offer?" But he was afraid, and he remained silent. With bowed head he started off again, down the narrow path to the village and to his church.

A shabby door opened, and a bent old lady stepped out. When she saw the priest, she made the sign of the cross. "God sent him," she murmured. "I'll ask him, he should be able to explain it to me."

She had a son, a redhood in the hills, and he was planning to come down to the village one night, he said, to slaughter the soldiers. Why? What had the soldiers ever done to him? She could not understand. But here was Father Yánaros now, thank God; he would explain everything to her. She stopped in the middle of the road, bowed, and kissed his hand.

"Father," she said, "God sent you to me. Wait, I have something to ask you."

"Speak up, granny, but quickly," the priest replied. "I'm in a hurry."

"Why are they killing each other, Father? Why is my son fighting? He says that he wants to kill the poor soldier boys; why? What did they do to him? I can't sleep, Father; I keep thinking about it and turning it over in my brain; it doesn't make any sense to me."

"You think it makes sense to me, old woman?" the priest re-

87

plied. "I've been asking God to explain it to me, too; I ask and I ask, and I get no reply. I get no reply, my friend, and my soul is in turmoil, not knowing which way to turn. Be patient, we'll see!"

The old woman shook her head; she raised her reedlike arms to the sky, opened her mouth to speak; but what could she say? She turned and slammed the door of her house.

Father Yánaros hurried on; he was breathing heavily, for the air was thick, muggy, reeking of the nauseating stench of rotting flesh. They had buried the dead in shallow graves, and their smell filled the air. You walked through the fields outside the village, and you could see a leg or an arm, or a plucked head sticking out of the ground.

Father Yánaros stopped in front of the smoking ruins of a house; he covered his nose with the palm of his hand as he looked at the rubble. Its owners, old Manoli and Kyra Kallio, his wife, lay underneath the charred remains. The priest knew the old couple well and loved them both. They were paralyzed and so not able to escape when the redhoods entered the village a few days ago. Kind, God-fearing people they were; they had no children and were devoted to each other in their old age. They were the only ones in the village who had a pot of basil in their courtyard, and on summer evenings they would sit on their threshold—this very spot where the priest now stood —and greet the passers-by with a smile. Now there was nothing left of them but the stench.

The priest shook his head. What is the body of man but stench and filth, he thought. How can the soul, which is eternal, stoop to living inside a pit of manure? To hell with the flesh! When you're rid of that, you're rid of the stench—that's why I'm not afraid to die! With a leap, he jumped out of the burning ruins.

"My Lord," he murmured, "what shall I do? Answer me! Help me! Every day I make my report to You; every day I tell You the condition of my village—that we have nothing to eat now, that we are slowly dying; every day at least one soldier deserts and takes to the hills. That cursed son of mine, the red-hoods' captain, keeps sending messages from Mt. Etoraki. 'Surrender! Surrender! Otherwise you will see only fire and the sword! What can we do? What can *I* do? Did You hear Kyra Areti back there cursing? I tell You we can't go on any longer! How can we save the children from starving to death? Tell me what to do, Lord. Guide me, help me! Should I climb the hill and surrender the village peacefully to the rebels to save it from destruction? Or should I just sit back and wait for Your mercy? Alas, we're only human, my Lord; we can't wait any longer; Your mercy is long in coming; most of the times it comes after death, in the other life; but I want it now, in this one!"

He paused a moment, then suddenly, as though coming to a decision, he cried, "Whatever will be, will be!" and he quickened his pace.

He paused a few yards from the church in front of a small house where the tubercular village schoolmaster lay dying. He had been crippled from jails and the whiplash. Father Yánaros loved him because he would bow to no one.

Yánaros had invited him to his cell for a cup of coffee, one Sunday after liturgy, when the schoolmaster was still able to walk. At first he was stiff and silent; he did not like conversations with priests; but slowly, gradually, he gained his confidence and began to speak of Christ as a beloved man, as though he still walked on earth, poor and tubercular, too; traveling through towns and cities, as though His Disciples were scattered about, in factories, or in the earth's bowels digging out coal, or as students or teachers.

"Do you ever see Him? Do you see Him, friend," the priest asked, roused by his words. "How is it that you speak as though you know Him?"

"I do see Him, at times," the schoolmaster replied, smiling.

Father Yánaros made the sign of the cross. "Mercy my Lord," he said, "I don't understand this."

Only after the schoolmaster left, did the priest understand, did he realize that he was speaking of Lenin.

Father Yánaros paused in front of the low shabby door; should he knock? Or should he go away?

Inside, the schoolmaster lay on his bed, watching his wife bend over the fireplace to light the fire; he watched his small son Dimitri, who sat by the hearth with his alphabet book on his lap, spelling words. The child's eyes bulged, and his feet had begun to swell. A black tomcat with orange spots, scrawny and full of sores, had curled beside the fire and purred contentedly. Outside, the dogs barked, doors opened and closed, and from a distance came the sound of boots pounding on the stones. But inside the house there was peace and quiet.

The schoolmaster closed his eyes; this serenity frightened him; he knew that his remaining days were few. He choked back his cough to avoid frightening his wife and secretly spat up blood into a red handkerchief.

He was ill, deathly ill, and he knew this. But this peace was like happiness, and it frightened him. It can't be, he thought, some great tragedy hangs over my home. He looked at his wife, with the black kerchief on her head, silent, sad, old before her time. For years now she had fought poverty and fear and illness. He turned, glued his eyes on his only child, whose feet were swelling from hunger, and the schoolmaster's heart ached. We older ones are condemned, he thought, but will our children, at least, get a chance in life? We fill the ravines and pits with our bodies, to bridge the way for our sons; will they be able to walk over this bridge? Will young Dimitri ever finish reading his alphabet book? Will they let him? Every day they kill women and children in Castello, in Castello and in Greece, in Greece and in all the world. This is the end of the old world; this is the beginning of the new one; and our generation is caught by the two millstones; they grind us—flesh, bones, souls! We are weighed down by that old Chinese curse: "They are damned who live in great epochs!" And what is our duty but to turn this curse into a blessing? It's difficult, very difficult! Oh, proud virtues of man—purity, obstinacy, courage—help us!

The schoolmaster closed his eyes and sank in his thoughts. How many times his heart had filled, how many times it had drained of hope and suffering! Years and years of struggle; years and years of hope; how much longer? He opened his eyes and looked at his son, his wife; he looked at the village and at Greece; his mind spread out and encircled the world—what hopes and agonies were everywhere! Was man always like this, or did his pain increase now, now that the world was crumbling?

He recalled an ancient buried city; the world is exactly like that today—like a buried city; and the schoolmaster shuddered, and felt joy at the same time, as he thought of how the civilized people eat, how they get fat and insolent, how civilizations crumble.

The cellars of Pompeii were full; the women were shameless, sweet-smelling, and barren. The men were merchants and men of letters—shrewd, ironical, tired! All the gods, the whole worthless bunch—Greeks, Africans, Asians—had become one band, gathered in ungoverned and confused misery; faithless, greedy cowards that divided among themselves the consecrated bread and the souls of men as they slyly smiled. The whole city lay at the foot of Vesuvius and laughed, without a care.

The whole world is a Pompeii today, a Pompeii on the verge of eruption. What is the purpose of such a world, with its wretched women and faithless men, with its deceits and its sicknesses? Why should all these sly merchants live? Why should all these coddled children grow up and sit where their parents sat, in the taverns, the theaters, the houses of prostitution? All this dissipation stifled the intellect. Whatever culture those generations had they used up creating a great civilization—ideas, painting, music, science, deeds; but now it has been exhausted; and they are in their last phase—to disappear. Let the barbarians come and open a new path to culture.

The woman rose from the hearth and turned to her husband; every time she saw him engrossed in deep thought, she tried to draw him into conversation. "They tell me that the day before yesterday a monk from Mount Athos came to the village and brought the Sash of the Virgin in a silver case; Aunt Lena next door told me."

The schoolmaster was furious. "Quiet, wife, don't set my blood boiling! Oh, those thieves, those sacrilegious scoundrels! How long is man going to be so blind?"

He broke into a coughing spell, spat on the red handkerchief, and fell back on his pillow again.

"Wife," he said, "we'd better not talk any more, I'm tired." His breathing came in gasps, but in a little while he rallied and sat up in bed.

Eh, comrade Ben Yehounda, he thought. Eh, comrade Ben Yehounda, help!

The schoolmaster closed his eyes; a figure shriveled from

91

hunger and illness and wisdom appeared before his eyes; with thick lips, a humped nose, whiskers growing sparsely on his chin, it motioned slowly in the dark; it would not disappear. It was the obstinate Ben Yehounda, the humble Jew. Every time the schoolmaster lost faith, this impoverished teacher from a small village in the Ukraine came to give him courage. He, too, was poor and tubercular, and dying; but a great idea had entered his mind and hinged itself there: to resurrect the dead language of the Old Testament—the Hebrew language—and to make it the spoken language of all Jews throughout the world. So he began to preach this idea; but the villagers drove him away; he left for Poland, where millions of Jews lived. He had no money, so he walked. He walked and he walked; he stumbled and fell along the way, rose and walked again—for days and nights on end. By the time he reached the Polish border, he could stand on his feet no longer; he fell to the ground, dying. They found him there and rushed him to the hospital; the doctor who examined him shook his head. "You have only two days to live," he said, "three, at the most. If you have any last request, make out your will; you're a teacher, you should know how to do it."

The sick man laughed. "How can I die," he said, "I, who have such an idea?"

"He's insane," the doctors said, and released him from the hospital. Once more he started on his journey. He decided to walk to Jerusalem; to cross all of Europe into Constantinople, to pass through Asia Minor, to enter Syria, to reach Palestine— on foot. He went on; he begged from village to village; wherever he found Jews, he would enter the synagogue and preach his idea; they would only jeer at him, and he would leave again.

Finally, months later, he reached Jerusalem. He knelt on the ground and worshiped; then he entered the Holy City. He found a place to sleep—a cellar—and, losing no time, began to preach. "We must resurrect the sacred language of our fathers; we must speak to God in the tongue of Moses, so that our lips may be blessed as we bring to life the sacred words." But those who heard him only became infuriated; they cursed him and denounced him; they called him traitor, rebel, sacrilegious fool, because he dared to suggest bringing the holy, sacred words of the Old Testament of God into common use, to be tainted by impure mouths. So they drove him away from the synagogues and anathematized anyone who approached him or listened to his words.

But Ben Yehounda, the stubborn, obstinate one, never lost his courage; he shouted, he shouted in the wilderness! He held on to life by the teeth; he would not release his soul before he had completed his task. So he founded a school, married one of his students—a young Jewish girl—so he could have children and teach them to speak their mother tongue, the ancient Hebrew. And then he had a son—but the child was born dumb! "Good for you," they cried, "God is punishing you; this is God's curse; Jehovah has tried you, found you guilty, and condemned you!" But Ben Yehounda would not relent.

"Faith can move mountains!" he cried. "I shall move them!" One day when his son was five years old, a goat chased after the boy; the child was so frightened that his tongue became untied; he ran to his father shouting, "Father, father, a goat, a goat!" And the words were in the sacred language of the Old Testament.

News of the miracle spread far and wide; his followers increased; the idea entered their hearts and settled there; every so often in the streets one could hear the ancient words being resurrected. Years later, through perseverance and courage, the idea finally triumphed. And if you go to Palestine today, you may hear the Jews speaking, haggling, arguing, romancing, lecturing, printing books and newspapers in that ancient resurrected tongue. Ben Yehounda lived forty years from the day the doctors decided he had two or three days to live. And only when he saw the great idea circulating in the streets, like a living man, only then did Ben Yehounda release his soul and allow it to leave his body.

The schoolmaster opened his eyes; his face had a look of serenity. That's what it is to believe! he thought, and if a foolish idea like Yehounda's can finally triumph, imagine what will happen to ours! I can just hear the foundations of earth rumbling. He sighed. Will I live long enough to see this redemption? Will I ever see justice on earth? His whole life passed in a flash before his eyes. As a teacher at Yánnina, they had arrested him

93

and thrown him into prison; hunger, dampness, torture, had crippled his body. He left the prison a wreck of a man and returned to his village to die. Every day, as he fought with death, he remembered Ben Yehounda, and he, too, held his soul by the teeth; he, too, refused to die. And when his friends looked at his pallor, with grave concern, he remembered Ben Yehounda again and would say to them, smiling, "How can I die when I possess such a noble idea? Do not be afraid!"

Suddenly the schoolmaster cocked his ears; someone had stopped outside his door. His wife jumped up, frightened; who could it be? She slipped out, barefoot, into the courtyard, peeked through the crack in the gate, and saw the robe, the beard, and knew who it was; she returned to the house.

"It's Father Yánaros," she said softly. "Shall I let him in?"

"Don't let him in," the schoolmaster replied. "He'll begin talking about God again, and I'm tired of that."

They held their breaths and waited; in a few moments they heard the sound of Father Yánaros' heavy boots fading away.

"What a shame about that man," the schoolteacher mused. "Another good one gone to waste."

He dug his hand under his pillow and brought out a small crumpled notebook which Stratis, the young soldier, had brought him secretly last night. "Leonidas trusted me with this," the young soldier told him. "He told me to give it to you and that you would know who is to have it." Stratis' eyes filled with tears, and he turned, embarrassed, and walked away.

The schoolmaster shook his head. "Another young man gone," he murmured. "What a pity that such a youth could not at least have died for a great idea." Leonidas was a distant relative of his, on his mother's side; she came from the Isle of Naxos. He often came secretly to the house and talked with him. An inexperienced boy, he was in love with a young girl, and he blushed when he spoke of her. She was a student, too, and the first day they met, they ran together through the countryside, jumping about like two newborn kids; the soft, tender blades of grass, and the stones, too, smelled sweetly; the almond trees were in blossom, and the first swallows had arrived. It was noon, the heat of day, and the girl opened her blouse at the throat; a soft breeze blew and between two ancient columns appeared, eternal, the cool sea! How mysterious are these charming sisters—youth, love, and the sea! From the moment he looked between those columns to the sea, holding the hand of this girl who, until yesterday, had been a stranger to him, Leonidas felt his heart and the sea and the grass and eternity join and become one! His life took on new meaning; he looked around him and saw an exciting new world; the butterflies had grown wider than his palm; the earth smelled like warm flesh, and the hills gleamed enticingly, like a woman's loins.

The teacher leafed through the crumbled notebook and his hand trembled as though he were lifting the tombstone of a fresh grave. The handwriting in the notebook was delicate, written on some pages with pen, on others with pencil; here and there the letters were smeared or half erased, as though tears had fallen on them; several pages were spotted with blood.

The schoolmaster raised his head. "Wife," he said, "no matter who knocks on the door, don't open it."

# 7

J ANUARY 23: This morning we discovered the frozen
bodies of three of our men in a ravine. Their feet were sticking
out of the snow, and that's how we came across them. A rebel's
body lay beside the soldiers, frozen, too; he was wearing summer khaki, no sweater, and his feet were bare. He had been
wounded in the legs and had dragged himself over to the soldiers; the four of them were huddled together, their arms around
each other, to keep warm.

JANUARY 29: My dearest, last night I had the strangest, most
irrational dream I've ever seen in my life. I don't know its meaning, but I do know it upset me very much; as though I were
that little fish that was calling out.

It seems that I was far out at sea, and I could hear a little fish
shouting angrily at God. I watched it open and close its mouth;
I could hear no sound, but I knew what it was saying, just as
one understands the mutes. The angry words burst inside my
head; the little fish had raised its jagged, helpless fins and cried
out resentfully to God, "You should give strength to those who
are in the right, and not to those who are unjust! That's the
true meaning of God!" Some larger fish must have wronged the
small one, and she had raised her head to God, complaining.
And God replied to her, but again I could not hear the words,
nor even the voice; all I could see, from time to time, were the
foaming waters churning and whirling over the little fish while

96

she tossed and turned, dazed, in the sea. But during the calm, the fish raised her head again, and I could hear the same words beating inside my head: "You should give strength to those who are in the right, and not to those who are unjust! That's the true meaning of God!"

My beloved Maria, if I stay in these wild hills much longer, I'm afraid I'm going to lose my mind. The only way I keep my sanity is by thinking of you every moment, day and night.


FEBRUARY 1: All day today I was with you, my dearest, all day I sensed your soft, sweet smell, as though an almond tree had blossomed inside of me. Do you remember a year ago to-day? When I first met you? We went on an outing to Sounio to see the Temple of Poseidon; we took bread and oranges, and Homer, with us. The almond trees were in bloom, the ground was covered with soft grass, the newborn kids leaped over the warm earth, and the pine trees smelled like honey—remember? And the sun stood over us and warmed us; he watched with pride as we walked over the rocks like two small, happy insects.

You were wearing a rose-colored blouse and a white velvet beret, and beneath it your hair fell into two long curls that waved like banners in the wind. We walked so quickly—how young we were—it was a virgin world then; how green were the trees, how blue was the sky, filled with love. How old I've grown since then! There was no killing in my life; now the bodies lie in heaps, and I sit on them and my heart has become stone. Remember how we spoke of Homer, and how we were swept up like waves by those immortal verses! What happiness we had; Homer—that sacred text—the Old Testament of our people had suddenly come to life within us. And we could feel the great song entering our hearts, laughing and echoing like the sea. The silver-footed Thetis rose from the depths of the sacred Mediterranean, holding in her hands the new armor for her son; it gleamed, all bronze and gold, with exquisite embellishments—as though it had just come from the hands of God. What designs the lame God had carved on it, in His wise artistry! We held hands and stood there, underneath the pines,

97

in the spring sun of Attica, looking far out to the sea, reciting the immortal lines.

We never tired of it—remember? We could not stop reciting the old man's lines; we watched them flowing, like rivers into the sea. Dear one, life can be so beautiful! So simple and good! And look what we've done with it! I, who stood beside you that unforgettable day, my heart overflowing with love for even the humblest worm. Now look at me, here in the hills of Epirus, a rifle in my hand, killing men! No, no, we have no right to call ourselves human beings; we should be called apemen. We started off as apes, to become men, but we are still halfway. And yet my heart aches with love; it thinks of you, Maria, and it blossoms like the almond tree; it thinks of Homer, and it knows the meaning of man and immortality.

FEBRUARY 2: I woke up this morning, and the almond tree still blossomed within me; my blood flowed in a rhythm, full of joy and sadness and nostalgia; and your name, my Maria, swayed gently to and fro within me, like the seagull on the waves. How I wish that I had time—time and the strength—to set words to that rhythm and make it poetry! A song marched on my lips, and I kept saying, "If they would only leave us alone today, so that I could take pencil and paper."

But the bugle sounded the alarm, and we grabbed our rifles; the rebels were creeping out from Mount Etoraki, where they had been hiding all these months and from where we could not budge them. And again we had to kill and be killed! Now as I'm writing you, it is night; we've just returned, exhausted, blood-ied, a lot of us on both sides killed again, and we've accom-plished nothing—neither we nor they—all that blood spilled in vain.

We feel a great sense of exultation when we read in Homer how men move in battle, how the Achaeans and Trojans are wounded and how they die. Our thoughts take wing, our hearts feel joy to see how this great writer took war and slaughter and turned them into song. It was as though these were not men being killed, but clouds in human form that felt no pain; as though they were fighting playfully in the immortal wind; as though the blood they shed was nothing but the sweet red

98

color of the sunset. In poetry, men and clouds, death and immortality are one. But when war breaks out, here on earth, and the warrior is a tangible body—flesh and bone and hair and soul—what terror, what horror war is, my darling! You go out to fight saying, "I won't degrade myself. I'll remain human even during the slaughter; I don't hate anyone." And I go off to battle with compassion in my heart. But the moment you realize that your life is in danger, that they want to kill you, a dark, hairy thing suddenly leaps from the depths of your inner being—an ancestor that was hidden inside of you whom you did not suspect, and the human face you had disappears, and you seem to have sprouted sharp, pointy teeth, like a gorilla; and your brain becomes a jumble of blood and hair. You scream, "Forward! Attack, men! We've got 'em!" And the cries that come from your lips are not your own; they can't be yours; they're not human cries; and even the apeman disappears, frightened away; and from within you leaps not your father, but your grandfather, the gorilla. Sometimes I am overcome by the desire to kill myself—to save the man within me, to save myself from the beast. But you keep me alive, Maria, and I wait. "Hold on," I say, "one day soon this brother-killing is bound to end." I'll cast off this gorilla skin—the khaki, the boots, the rifle— and I'll take you by the hand, my darling, and we'll go to Sounio together, and we will speak again Homer's immortal lines.

FEBRUARY 11: It's been snowing all day—bitter cold—we're half frozen, and there is no wood for kindling. And at night— every single night—the rebels never let us rest. We watch day break in fear, and we watch night fall in fear. The rifle never leaves our hands; our ears and eyes are on guard every moment —a stone rolls, an animal moves, and we jump up in the darkness and shoot. We are haggard from lack of sleep and from fear. If at least we could be certain that we're fighting for a great ideal!

Our captain's a fierce man, always angry, sour by nature. A dark fate hangs over him; it hates him and pushes him toward the precipice, to his destruction. He senses this and becomes even more fierce; he wants to resist, but he cannot, and he goes on, cursing, toward the unseen abyss. Our captain is like the hero of an ancient tragedy, and I watch him with fear and compassion, as we watch Agamemnon entering his bath, or Oedipus when, frantic and blinded by his fate, he searches for the truth.

And lately, he's not even human! He's a beast. Just recently his wife left him and took to the hills to join the rebels. She had come here at Christmas from Yánnina. What a woman! To us, here on these wild rocks, she was like a miracle; as though it were night and it had suddenly dawned. Here we were, lost in these hills, sleepless, dirty, unshaven, not having seen a woman for so long; she seemed like a Nereid with her blond hair, the beauty mark on her cheek, her slim body, her light walk. And above all, her smell—powder and lavender—that drifted in the air as she passed by!

The captain smiled for the first time, those days, and looked at us as though we were human beings, too. His face had changed; he shaved every day, he dressed better, and his boots were always polished. Even his voice and his walk changed. But she never smiled; every day her face became cloudier, and when she looked our way, her eyes seemed hard and cold and full of hate. And one night she opened the door and took to the hills.

Stratis brought us the news, and that bowlegged fox was bursting with laughter. He came in singing and went around the barracks twittering, "Gone, oh gone is my little bird! And it will never return!" "We're lost!" murmured my friend Vassos. "Now he'll never rest until he gets us all killed! He'll have us in battle day and night." He paused thoughtfully and then turned and whispered to me, so that no one else could hear, "Dying doesn't really bother me, Lenny, I swear it doesn't! As long as I know why I'm dying and for whom I'm dying. But I really don't know. Do you?"

What could I answer him, my dearest, how would I know? That's the great tragedy of it all.

FEBRUARY 12: The alarm sounded at dawn; we surrounded the village so that no one could escape; an order was issued to take hostages all those who had relatives with the rebels—parents, brothers, sisters, wives—and herd them into a deep pit surrounded with barbed wire, on the outskirts of the village.

100

We entered the houses early in the morning and grabbed the old men and women, the wives and sisters. A lament sprang from all the homes; they grabbed on to the doors, the windows, the rims of the wells, and would not let go—they refused to be moved. We struck their hands with our rifle butts, we ripped their shirts and their coats as we tried to pry them loose; a few were wounded until we got them in line and into the pit. At first my heart ached for them; I felt like crying; I couldn't bear to hear their cries and to see the injustice. The older women, the mothers, raised their hands, cursing me. I dragged them by force when all the time I wanted to lean against their withered breasts and cry along with them.

"What did we do?" they cried. "Why are they putting us behind barbed wire? How are we to blame?"

"You're not, you're not to blame," I'd reply. "Come on, let's go."

But slowly, gradually—how strange is this dangerous, dirty animal we call man—slowly I grew ugly. In making the angry gestures, I became angry, too. I beat their hands as they clutched the doors; I grabbed women by the hair and trampled the children with my boots.

FEBRUARY 14: It's been snowing and snowing; the hills are all white, and the houses are huddled under the snow; all the uglinesses of the village are covered, and they have turned into exotic fairy-tale beauties. A snow-covered rag hanging on a line —what beauty! A dead pony completely buried in the snow— such graceful lines! Gentle colors—rose hue at morning, pale blue at noon, purple at dusk! What moonlit calm—what wonder is this world of snow! Oh, Maria my beloved, what joy there would be if there were no war! The two of us would walk over these snow-covered hills, with our heavy boots and heavy sweaters, with woolen caps that cover our ears, and we would come back to a little house at night, where a hot bath would be ready, and a table set with deep bowls of steaming soup, beside a lighted fireplace!

Who was that great world conquerer who, on the hour of his death, sighed and said, "I longed for only three things in my life—a small house, a wife, and a pot of curly-leafed basil; but I

101

never attained them." Life is so strange, my beloved, man actually needs very little to be happy! But he gets lost in his search for false glories and destroys himself. How many times I've longed to throw away my rifle, to get up and leave! To leave and come straight to the door of the small room where you study, my Maria. To touch your hand and feel its warmth in my palm, and not say a word. I think there is no greater happiness than in the touch of a loving hand.

But I can never leave—I would never do that. I'll stay here, with this rifle in my hand, and I'll fight until they tell me to go. Why? Because I'm afraid; afraid and ashamed; and even if I were not afraid, I still would not leave. Those great terrible words: duty, country, heroism, desertion, dishonor, have bound and paralyzed my small, warm, fleshy soul.

FEBRUARY 16: There's only one thing I want to know, my darling, so that I may be able to endure after all that I see and do here; only one thing—why am I fighting? For whom am I fighting? They say we fight to save Greece, we, the Royal Army, the blackhoods as they call us; and that our enemies in the hills—the redhoods—fight to divide and sell Greece. Oh, if I could only be sure! If I only knew! Then all this would be justified—all our atrocities and all the tragedy we spread—killing, burning, leaving people homeless, humiliating them. I would give my life to know. I don't say I would give it gladly—never gladly, because of you, my darling—but with an acceptance, a willingness. I would say, Let me become bones, like my ancestors, since it is written that freedom comes from the bones of its people, as our national anthem proclaims.

I had grabbed a young mother by the neck and kicked her to get her in line; she was the wife of a rebel, and she held a baby in her arms. She turned and looked at me, and never, never as long as I live, will I forget the look in her eyes. No matter what good I ever manage to do in the future, my heart will never find peace again. She did not open her mouth; but I heard a loud cry within me: "Leonidas, aren't you ashamed? How low can you stoop? How low have you stooped!" And my hands were paralyzed at that moment. I spoke softly to her. "I'm ashamed," I whispered. "I'm ashamed, woman, but I'm a

102

soldier, I've lost my freedom, too; I'm not human any more, forgive me!" But the woman did not reply; she raised her head high, her arms tightened around the baby, and she took her place in line. And I thought to myself, If that woman could, she would set fire to the barracks and burn us all. That baby's no longer going to suck milk from its mother's breast; it's going to suck hatred and scorn and revenge; and when it grows up, it, too, will take to the hills—a rebel; and he will finish off whatever his mother and father left undone; we will pay heavily and rightfully for this injustice.

And do you believe it, my darling, somehow this thought comforts me. I've come to the conclusion that the cruelties and injustices we commit will not be in vain—for they wake the soul of the one who has been wronged, they rouse it and set it on fire. All these Castellians could have passed their lives in slavery and stupor; but our beastliness is a good thing; we won't let them rot with patience and cowardice; the slaves that we kick around will rise one day, and all the hills will fall and crush the valleys; and their captain will be—God willing—this baby, held in the arms of this silent, proud mother today.

FEBRUARY 17: War—war and snow! Cold, hunger, vultures! An uneasy silence, then cold again, and hunger and vultures! Patrolling the snow at night, in shifts; one of our men did not return, and we set out to find him; we take hounds and begin the search. Finally we found him, in a crevice, frozen to death, his eyes pecked out—vultures eat the eyes first, you know. And all along the mountain paths are the dead mules and dead horses, killed by cannon, by hunger, by the cold. Vassos said to me today, "I don't pity the men who are killed, we deserve that. It's the poor mules and horses I pity."

FEBRUARY 22: Why am I fighting? For whom am I fighting? Every day my doubts grow and with them, my torment. I've come to the point—though I shudder to admit it—when the only bearable moments in my life here are those inhuman moments when I carry the rifle and hunt men, to kill! Because then I don't have the time or the strength to think of anything; I only fight, like the beasts, to kill so I may not be killed. But

103

the minute that horrible sound dies down, the terrifying question rises before me, like a serpent with a swollen neck. Is it possible that I am fighting to support lies and injustice, to enslave Greece, to save the dishonorable? Is it possible that we are the traitors, the ones who are selling Greece, and can the so-called traitors in the hills be the armed mountaineers and the rebels of 1821? How can I tell justice from injustice, and decide with whom to go, and to which side I should give my life? There is no greater torment, to a fighter, than this doubt.

Today again the captain picked out five young men—five strong, handsome Greeks—and had them shot because they refused to join the national army. Can an ideal that gives birth to such courage, that pays such little heed to death, possibly be a false ideal? This is what I have been asking myself all day. But I can find no answer, for I know very well that I saw this same courage in our own blackhoods when they were brought before the rebels. They had said to our men, when they captured them, "Will you join us and come to the hills?" "No, we will not!" "Then you will be shot!" "Then shoot us! We were born Greeks, we will die Greeks!" So they killed them. And as the shots rang out, the condemned shouted, "Long live Greece! Long live freedom!"

So courage and faith is not the infallible test; but, then, how can I separate the truth from the lies? How many heroes and martyrs have sacrificed themselves for some damned ideal; God has his pure heroes and martyrs; Satan has his pure heroes and martyrs; how can I tell them apart?

MARCH 1: Earth and sky are all one today; you can't distinguish a thing because of the clouds that have gathered and the snow that falls in continuous thick mats. We've been shoveling all morning to clear the paths. There's no war today—the red-hoods have not come down, and we are not going up after them; God has come between us today, and we will rest awhile.

Stratis came by around noon; we were all sitting huddled in a corner of the barracks—Vassos the faithful friend, Panos the simple shepherd, and Levy the Jew. Stratis motioned to us, and we got up. "Come here," he said, "I want to talk to you."

He led the way as we walked outside in a straight line, each one stepping in the snow prints of the man ahead, sinking knee-deep in the snow. He pushed open a door and entered. The house was deserted; we had come here several days ago, and had taken away the old couple who lived here. They were put inside the barbed-wire enclosure—they had two sons that were renowned for their heroism, both of them with the rebels.

We took an ax and chopped up the bunk in the corner of the room for kindling and started a fire. Then we broke up a small couch, and the fire glowed, dancing on the hearth; we huddled around it, close together, spreading out our hands, and drew in the warmth. Our hands and feet thawed, the blood circulated again, our faces shone. We looked at one another— what few things man needs, the poor soul, to make him happy. We spread out our hands toward the fire as though we were praying; as though this fire were the first and most beloved goddess, the great benefactress of man; and the fire seemed to bring us together, like brothers, with her warmth spreading over us like a mother hen.

There were five of us; each one had a different ideal, a different job, a different aim in life; five different worlds: Stratis, a typesetter; Panos, a shepherd; Vassos, a carpenter; Levy, a merchant; and I, a student. And yet, at that moment, embraced by the warmth of that fire, we merged, we became one. Our veins swelled, our hearts swelled; a great, sweet joy filled us— it rose from our feet, there by the hearth, and reached our knees, our stomachs, our hearts, our minds. Panos closed his eyes, drowsily, and fell asleep. Envying him, I lowered my head to sleep, too—I hadn't slept in so many nights—but Stratis nudged me angrily.

"I didn't bring you out here to sleep; open your eyes, you weaklings. I have something important to read to you." He took a letter out of his pocket.

"Men," he said, "I swear to you I don't know how this letter got into my pocket; someone here is a traitor, and he's selling us out. See? It's either the communist newspaper, or red proclamations, or letters. Anyway, I found this in my pocket this morning. I read it and reread it; I don't know what to make of it, so I called you here, you fools, so we could read it together and discuss what it says; unless, of course, we're not men but sheep, who remain silent as they're being led to slaughter. They bleat—baa, baa, baa—which means "Slaughter me, master, so I may be sanctified!"

Levy laughed teasingly and winked his eye at Stratis. "You trickster," he said, "you trying to fool me? A Greek fears only one man in intelligence—the Jew! The Jew fears only one man —the Armenian; you're no Armenian, so you don't fool me that easily. That letter is yours! Watch him men . . ."

"The fox is caught by his own cunning, my friend," Stratis replied, looking at Levy with hatred. "Here, look at the writing, look at the signature!"

Levy took the letter and leaned over the fireplace to scrutinize it. "What? Can this be limping Aleko's?" he cried. "Then he wasn't killed? And all the tears I wasted on him! What a pity!"

Aleko was a brilliant soldier; a cook at Preveza who was also our cook here. He was fat, and he limped, and he had a thick mustache—how many hairs of it we'd swallowed in our soup! He had disappeared over a month ago, and we thought he'd been killed and that the jackals had eaten his carcass. So we divided his belongings—some clothing, socks, sweaters, and four silver spoons he had stolen.

"Is he alive," we all shouted, "is he alive?" "Read on, Stratis." "Where's he writing from?" "What does he say?" "Eh, the limping son of a gun!"

"Who's he writing to?" Levy asked.

"To no one; to all of us," Stratis replied. "It's a circular letter; you'll see, he says so himself. Eh, Panos, wake up, you old shepherd. Cock your ears, all of you!"

Stratis walked over to the fire and began to read, and his voice grew deeper.


Eh, soldiers, you green fools! It's me, the ghost, Aleko the Limper, writing to you. This isn't a plain letter, it's a circular, and I want all of you to read it carefully, because it will open your eyes to the light. It's been over a month since I escaped the slaughterhouse where they've herded you, you poor fools; I'm free, in the hills, with the noble fighters. Don't sit there like idiots, listening to what those evil men tell you; they fill your guts with lies—that we're starving up here, that we're killing the prisoners, that we're befriending the Albanians and the Bulgars. This is the place to be! By the hairs of my mustache—which I fed you all those months—this is where the Greek flag waves! And when we capture a blackhood, he's free to choose. "You want to join us? Then welcome! You want to leave? Good luck to you!" And as for food—"Chicken every Sunday," my friends. God bless the Americans who send you ship-loads of canned meats, tea and sugar and marmalades—which we promptly take away from you during the attacks. If it weren't for the Americans, we'd be in terrible shape. God bless 'em; Uncle Truman knows what he's doing. We hear he's also sending you summer clothing and cannon and automobiles—we can't wait! Summer's coming—time for us to get clothed and armed again. By God, I think of you down there, and my heart aches. How much longer, you idiots, are you going to keep fighting and getting killed? Don't you realize that you've lost the game? That you're the Turks and we're the guerrillas and rebels and that we're the ones fighting for freedom? It's 1821 again, my fellow Turks!

"It's always a few," the captain said to us the other day, "it's always a few that fight for freedom, and those few always conquer the greater number." So for your own good I tell you, leave the herd you've been rounded up in, as I left it—me, the limper. Jump out, come on! Otherwise you're lost, you poor souls. I think of you, one by one, and raise my voice in lament. How is that miserable captain, the butcher? And good old Sergeant Menas, the poor slob with the pig's face? How's our student, Leonidas, who holds his pen and paper and keeps singing like a snail on burning coals while the world burns? How's Abramiko, that devil's disciple? And poor Stratis, that bowlegged half-pint? Eh, you miserable souls, you poor fools, there's still time. Jump out of the graves, come on up to the hills, where you can drink the immortal water. I write you all this —me, Alcko, the lame-footed, fast-footed one, who escaped from the slaughterhouse—me, the cook with the red hood!

107

"That's it," Stratis said as he finished reading. "Now let's talk this over. Let everyone give his opinion—one at a time. If what Aleko says is true . . ."

No one spoke; we were all staring at the fire that had settled and was gasping, dying; and our hearts, which had glowed for a while, were dying with it.

"What is there to discuss, Stratis?" I said to him. "Let's wait until the words settle in our minds first, before we talk."

"Are you afraid?" Stratis asked, with irony in his voice. "Are you afraid they'll catch you and kill you if you try to leave?"

"I'm not afraid of getting killed," I replied, "but I don't want to be killed for nothing. I don't quite know yet on whose side the truth is."

"And you, unanointed one," Stratis said to Levy, "don't you wink at me—I share no secrets with you—speak openly."

"I," Levy said and looked at me mockingly, "I don't give a penny for truth or lies; there's no difference, they're both sluts; they have the same faces. My eyes have seen so much that I hate everything, everything, everything!" He paused and spat in the fire. "There's only one thing I want," he continued, "and that's to stay alive! And I'm alive now, and in my glory, because I'm carrying a rifle and a permit from the authorities to kill! And you know what else I want? I want the war to go on forever—never to end! I don't give a damn who I kill or for what reason."

"You're a fascist," Stratis replied angrily. Levy paled.

"Poor Stratis," he murmured. "How would you understand?" And he spread his hands over the dying fire.

We were silent again. I could tell that Stratis wanted to say something; he looked at us, one by one, but he swallowed his words.

Panos bounded from sleep; he looked at the dying coals, yawned, made the sign of the cross over his mouth, and spoke. "Eh, fellows, now if we only had a pan of cheese pies and then, say, a little jug of honey and a bottle of raki!"

"And if, say, there was no war," Vassos added, sighing, "and no sisters to marry off, and we had just climbed the snow-capped hill simply because we were five friends, five hunters, say, and we were hunting not for men, but for wild boar."

• • •

MARCH 3: There is no greater sadness than being in love and having to part from your beloved; there is no greater joy than being in love and uniting with your beloved. Here, the hours and days and weeks go by, sometimes frantic and full of bloodshed, sometimes weighed down as though they were carrying the dead. And I go on, with time, but my eyes see only you, my love, and I struggle to overcome the separation. I watch the clouds drift toward the north, and I recall the folk songs, the messages and greetings we send with the clouds, the birds, the winds, to the small, warm bodies we love. And the girl sits at her window and watches that cloud; she opens her arms and waits for her beloved to come down to her like the rain.

*Beloved, please become a cloud and a refreshing breeze,*
*Become a gentle gust of rain and fall upon my rooftop.*

MARCH 7: War, still war! The weather is milder now, but instead of our hearts softening, they have become wilder; the rebels come down—we go up—we clash halfway; first with rifles, then with bayonets, then hand to hand. There's nothing more spine-chilling than to feel the body of the man who wants to kill you up against yours; his breath, the foam and saliva from his mouth, his terror merging with yours, and the terrible need to kill him—not because you hate him, but to get him before he gets you. I think there is no greater degradation than killing in fear rather than hate.

I was grappling with a young blond boy; he had no mustache and was barefoot, but wore shin guards like the ancient Achaeans. He had sunk his teeth in the nape of my neck, but I felt no pain at that moment; I had bent and grabbed him by the waist and struggled to throw him down. We did not utter a sound; all we could hear was our gasping breath and the creaking of our bones. How long did we fight? I only remember how my knees were collapsing, exhausted; the blond boy tried to hold me with one hand as he raised his knife with the other. And suddenly he let out a heart-rending cry and fell to the ground at my feet; a knife which had flashed from behind him pierced his back. A friend had come to my rescue—Stratis? Vassos? Panos? I couldn't tell who it was; I only heard a voice say, "Courage, Leonidas!" And I saw the knife gleam; I was on the ground, too, and the blood ran from my shoulder; I was in pain.

When we returned to camp—it was night by that time—Vassos approached me. "Did you see that?" he said. "I fixed him all right; you know, you missed death by the skin of your teeth."

We had taken three prisoners; one was the blond boy with the knife wound in his back; the others were two giants who had entered the battle armed only with clubs, in hopes of getting rifles from the men they would kill. Two other soldiers and I were ordered to guard the prisoners at night. We gave them each a bowl of boiled beans and a piece of dry bread; the two men lunged at the food and ate it like hungry dogs, spreading out on the ground. The blond boy was in pain; he was losing blood; he couldn't eat a thing. I began a conversation with him.

"Where are you from, friend? What's your name?" I asked him.

"From Paramythía in Epirus. I'm Nicolo, the widow's son, if you've heard of me."

"Don't you recognize me?"

"No, comrade, how would I know you?"

"Weren't you and I grappling together earlier this evening, and weren't your teeth sunk in my neck? What did I ever do to you?"

"Me? Why should I have anything against you? I never saw you before—how would I ever know you? What do you have against me?"

"Nothing, nothing . . ."

"Well, then?" he asked, and his eyes grew wide, as though he were just seeing the light. "Well, then, why did we want to kill each other?"

I didn't answer; I went closer. "Does it hurt?" I asked.

"Yes, it does! What's your name?"

"Leonidas."

"It hurts, Leonidas, it hurts a lot; what are they going to do with me now? They going to kill me?"

"Don't worry, Nicolo, we don't kill prisoners, either."

"But suppose they decide to kill me, will you help me, will

110

you defend me, Leonidas? You're the only one I can trust—I don't have anyone else here. Will you defend me? We're friends aren't we, Leonidas?"

"Don't worry, Nicolo, I'll do everything I can," I said and my face flushed with shame.

But what power do I have? How can I, a plain soldier, a student, stand before the captain and demand that they spare Nicolo? I suddenly remembered the dream I wrote you about, the one I had several weeks ago—that little fish that was complaining to God, that was crying out, "You should give strength to those who are in the right, and not to the unjust! That's the true meaning of God!" I see now, alas, that I was that little fish!

MARCH 8: This morning they executed all three of them. As they lined the prisoners up against the wall, the wounded boy turned and looked at me; how will I ever forget that look? He was waiting for me to intervene, to go to the captain and defend him and perhaps save his life. And I just stood there, motionless, silent, trembling from indignation and pain. Nicolo, the widow's son, looked at me with such disappointment and grief that my heart seemed to tear to pieces. I closed my eyes so I would not see him.

The sergeant came around to select the squad for the execution; my knees trembled—what if he chose me? What if he said again, "Come here, Leonidas, my young student-teacher, come get some experience so you won't be afraid of blood!" What would I do? Would I throw the rifle down and shout, "Kill me, too, I can't stand it any longer"? No, no, I wouldn't have had the strength; I would have obeyed, because of you, Maria, because I want to see you again, to touch you again. I've done many cowardly things here, because of you, my beloved; and I've done many heroic things, again, because of you. You're the one who guides my mind and my every deed now.

Thank God, the captain passed me by without calling my name. He chose three others; I closed my eyes as the shots rang out and I heard the three bodies falling with a thump on the snow. I opened my eyes. Nicolo, the widow's son, had rolled over; his blond head was buried in the red snow.

• • •

MARCH 12: I've had a fever for three days now, and all that time my friend Stratis nursed me. I was happy for three days, because I did not know where I was. I had forgotten that they had dragged me into these wild hills to fight, and I thought, in my fever, that I was home in Naxos—my beloved island. And I was not alone; we were together. Stratis tells me I was ranting, that I kept calling your name, that I laughed. It seems we had both received our diplomas, and I had taken you to the island to meet my parents. "This is my wife," I told them, "this is my wife; give us your blessing."

We disembarked at the humble little port; it smelled of rotting lemons and citron, and before we went to my father's home, I took you past the rocks beside the bay, where that stately marble door stood, the only remains of the Temple of Dionysus. When the god of wine kidnaped Ariadne, he brought her here to this rock and they first loved here. We sat on the fallen marble, and I put my arm around your waist. I don't remember what I said to you, I only remember, in my fever, that I felt that I was truly a god. I was overcome with a sweet, godly drunkenness, and I felt that the whole world was sinking, except for this rock which rose above the waves, solid, unmoving, eternal. And both of us were on it, and I was holding you in my arms, and we looked at the calm, wide sea with such happiness. God had come down to earth again, the daughter of King Minos had risen from the soil of Crete. They found themselves embracing on this same rock. Nothing had changed, except their names; Dionysus had become Leonidas, and Ariadne was now Maria.

And later—was it later or that same moment?—we found ourselves in my grandfather's garden in a beautiful little village— Egares—covered with greenery, an hour from the city. My arm was still around your waist, and we walked under the trees. There were so many of them—orange trees, peach trees, apple trees—all laden with fruit. And it was noon, and two butterflies as large as my palm flew by and came and sat on your head and then flew on ahead and led the way, like angels. And every so often they would turn and look our way, to see if we were following; then they would turn back and lead us again.

"Where are they taking us?" you asked, disturbed, and your arm tightened about me.

And I laughed. "Don't you know?" I replied.

"No."

"To Paradise."

For three days and three nights I stayed in Paradise; what happiness that was, what serenity, what gentle, cool relief! Love must be like this—death must be like this.

But my fever dropped today; I opened my eyes, looked around me; soldiers, rifles, bayonets. Stratis was bending over me, watching me with gentle concern.

MARCH 12: I still can't get up, even today; I feel a sweet exhaustion. I can't hold a rifle in my hands yet, let the captain say what he may. The others set out for their work at daybreak; the hillsides echo with rifleshots and mortar. Here and there the litters arrive with the wounded, and the corridor is filled with moans. But I am so sweetly exhausted that all this seems like a dream to me, and it does not weigh upon me. Those around me cry and moan with pain, but I think only of you, my love, of you and poetry. And all day, in this dirty corridor, the four lines of Plato—the verse we loved so much—flutter over my head, Maria my beloved, like those large butterflies I saw in my fever:

> Love, I send a message with this apple,
> Accept it if you will, giving virginity in return;
> Should you refuse, then keep the apple,
> But remember how swiftly beauty fades away.

MARCH 18: A woman with a red kerchief on her head has been sneaking around here lately; she hides and appears, and when we go out to chase her away, she's gone. But every time she's been around, we get word that something has happened—a truck blown up, a bridge demolished, two or three of our soldiers killed. And every night, and sometimes even during the day—around noon—a clear young voice echoes on the hillside. Some young boy, shouting through a megaphone, calls out, "Brothers, unite! Brothers, unite!" Panos, that innocent shepherd, gets terrified; he keeps making the sign of the cross and murmuring, "That's no human voice! It's the trumpet of the Angel. The Second Coming is here!" And we smile halfheartedly and tease him. "Who do you suppose that woman with the red kerchief is, Panos, boy?" we ask him. "It may be the Virgin," he replies, hesitating, and makes the sign of the cross again.

"Does the Virgin kill men, you idiot? Does she carry hand grenades? Does she set dynamite to bridges? What are you trying to tell us, Panos? Don't be a sacrilegious fool."

Panos scratches his head, confused. "How do I know, fellows," he murmurs. "I don't know what to say. She's the Virgin —she has the power to do anything she wants."

"I say she's the devil's mother," Levy adds, to antagonize him.

"She might be at that, it just might be . . ." Panos replies. "Anything's possible. As for me, there's only one thing I'm sure of."

"What's that, old prophet?"

Panos lowers his voice. "That we've all gone to the devil."

Stratis jumps up; he's everywhere, never misses a thing; he needles the soldiers and we call him horsefly, needler, a general alarm.

"Then why don't you join the rebels, stupid?" we shout at him.

"Because the devil's taken them, too," Panos replies.

"And hasn't God taken anybody? Or didn't He get there in time?"

"How could He? He's been sleeping."

We all roared with laughter. "Now be sensible, Panos, does God ever sleep?" I ask him.

"But of course He does; haven't you heard? What have they been teaching you, anyway? Sure He sleeps. And when God sleeps, the devil's wide awake—that's when he gets the chance to do whatever he pleases. Each one does sentry duty; when the devil sleeps, God is awake and He does as He pleases. These days God is sleeping, and that's why the devil's taken us all!"


MARCH 25: A warm breeze is blowing; blades of grass have sprouted in my mind, and I feel anemones blossoming inside of me. Today being our national holiday, the captain made a speech; he hung a map of Greece on the wall of our barracks and, showing us the borders on the north, explained how and why the rebels want to give Northern Epirus and Macedonia to

114

the Albanians and the Slavs. His eyes flashed, and his finger trembled as he pointed to the Greek border. He slammed his palm over Epirus and Macedonia and Thrace, as though he were leading the occupation of those sectors.

"These bits of land," he shouted, "have been plowed for thousands of years with Greek blood and Greek sweat and tears; and they belong to us! We'll never let anyone else have them. Better to die! And that's why, men, we've climbed up to these Epirotic hills and continue to fight; death to the traitors! There will be no mercy for them! It's the firing squad for every rebel that falls into our hands. The end justifies the means, and our end is the salvation of Greece!"

I never did like that man! He's narrow-minded, hard, stubborn; a dark inhuman strength guides him; a beast—wounded and proud—growls within him. Once, a woman caressed this beast; she had spoken a kind word to it and had begun to tame it; but the woman left, and the beast began to growl again with an added wound. But I felt an unexplainable respect for him—respect and fear and compassion. He was courageous, honest, poor; he believed in what he was fighting for; he was ready to die for Greece, at any moment. Under his command you're never certain of staying alive, but you are certain of never being humiliated. Our captain is one of those men—so rare in this world today—who places an ideal above his own personal welfare and happiness; whether that ideal is good, whether it is bad, the important thing is that he will sacrifice his life for it. "Greece is in danger," the captain shouted as he ended his speech. "Greece is calling to us! We must be loyal, all of us, men, together, to save her!" His voice had grown hoarse and a tear had sprung from his small, sunken eyes.

I looked around—many of the soldiers were crying; Vassos kept twisting his mustache, and Panos looked at the map of Greece, as the devout look upon a miraculous icon. Behind me, Stratis coughed loudly—a false, ironic cough—and Levy, yellow, wrinkled, cross-eyed, smiled evilly.

I lay down that night, with the other soldiers, wrapped in my army cape, with my shoes and cartridge belt still on, and holding my rifle. I closed my eyes, but how could I sleep? The captain's right, I thought. The secret is in finding an ideal, raising

115

it above your personal desires, and making it your only aim in life—living and dying for that ideal. Only in this way the actions are ennobled and life takes on meaning; and death becomes immortality in your eyes, because you are certain that you have merged with an immortal soul. You can call this ideal *Country*, you can call it *God*, or *Poetry* or *Freedom* or *Justice*. But only one thing matters: that you believe in this ideal and that you serve it.

Was it not Solomos who said, "Take Greece—or anything else—and seal it within your heart; keep it there, and you will feel the throb of splendor in all its forms"? That "anything else" which Solomos added shows how much this great poet's mind surpassed his time.

I have yet to find that ideal, my dearest, so that I, too, can give my insignificant life to it; I stumble here and there; sometimes poetry stimulates me, other times it's science, then my country. Perhaps this is because I am still too young and immature; perhaps I will never find it; then I'm lost. For man can accomplish nothing worth while or noble on earth if he does not subject his life to a master who is superior to him.

APRIL 1: Early this morning, Stratis ran into the corridor of the barracks, laughing, dancing, and clapping his hands. He let out whooping cries and began to sing:

> "How long, brave men,
> Will we live in the narrow passes,
> Alone, like lions,
> In the hills, among the rocks?"

He ran up and down in a frenzy as he sang, kicking everyone, shoving them to their feet.

"What in hell's wrong with you?" we shouted. "Are you drunk?"

"Drunk? What are you talking about? Where would I find the damn wine for that? I've got great news, you fools! Get up! When you hear this, you'll jump to the ceiling; you'll clap your hands and dance around like dervishes."

All of us hurriedly gathered around him. "Go on, speak up for the love of God, Stratis. What news? Tell us so we can enjoy it, too."

We were hanging on his every word. "You're killing us." "Hurry!" "Speak up, man!"

"Well, just a while ago I went up to the captain's room and stopped outside his door and listened. It was the hour he usually turns on his radio—the one with the batteries he uses to listen to the news. Some devil inside of me kept telling me that something big was happening in Athens; so I cocked my ear, and what do you think I heard? You'll collapse with joy when you hear this!"

"Did the redhoods leave the hills?" one of the men asked.

"Something even better—something better than that!" Stratis shouted. "Anyone else? Panos, my little lamb, you say something!"

"Say what?" The naïve shepherd replied, trying to guess. "We took Argirokastro?"

"No—even better than that, I tell you!" He turned to me. "All right, man of wisdom, you say something!"

"The war's over!" I replied, laughing, but my heart was beating wildly as I said the words.

"That's it! Good for you, my wise Solomon! Friends, the war's over! There was a meeting in Athens; on one side the captains from the hill, on the other, the King, the ministers, and the generals. They shook hands. 'Comrades,' they said, 'why should we go on killing one another this way? We're brothers, are we not? Whether we wear red hoods or black ones, our heads underneath are all Greek heads, are they not? So enough of this massacre; you're courageous men, and we're courageous men; then let us offer our hands in peace and brotherhood!'

"So they shook hands; they signed the treaty; everything began and ended this night; they reconciled. The order has been given for us to return to our homes, for the rebels to come down from the hills and for tables to be set in every village and for wine to be brought out and dancing to take place and for caps to be thrown in the air—red ones and black ones, too. And this very minute that I'm talking to you, Athens is blazing with festivals; bells are ringing, crowds have jammed the streets, the

117

Cathedral is preparing to hold doxology services and the King himself will attend."

All of us fell on Stratis and kissed him, then we screamed and hugged and kissed each other; some cried, some laughed, others danced around; we embraced and shouted, "*Christos anesti,*" "*Alithos anesti!*" "What stupidity, what a curse—to be killing one another all these years." "Long live Greece!"

Stratis threw his cap at the ceiling. "Let's go out, men!" he shouted. "Let's go out and hold a demonstration; let's ring the bell; let's call the priest. Let's take the Holy Bible and rise, all together, in the barracks and give thanks to God."

We streamed outside, took to the roads, all of us singing the national anthem; doors and windows flew open, the Castellians came out. "What's happened, men?"

"The war's over, brothers; the war's dead; it's gone to the devil! Hang out the flags, spread out the blankets on the rooftops, take out the wine barrels and let's drink. The war's over!"

The villagers ran out, making the sign of the cross; women and girls appeared in the doorways, clapping their hands and shouting,

"God be with you, boys!"

Father Yánaros, a robust old man and a real fighter (He was a hero in the Albanian war—his chest is covered with wounds), came out of the church and stood with outstretched arms. "What is this I hear, my children?" the priest cried. "The war has ended?"

"Put on your vestments, Father," Stratis shouted to him, "take the Bible, and let's go out to greet the captain; make a speech so we can shout 'Long Live Greece!' The war is dead, Father, may his bones rot in pitch and tar!"

Stratis began to chant a hymn, mockingly: "Come let us give the final kiss . . ."

The priest made the sign of the cross, and his eyes filled with tears. "Peace, brotherhood! Peace!" his deep voice rang out. "Say it again, men, so it can warm my heart!"

"Peace, brotherhood!" the men shouted in unison. "Put on your vestments, Father Yánaros!"

Mitros caught up with them, panting and out of breath. "Hey, what's going on, men?" he shouted. "What's happened?"

118

"Mitros, my gallant friend, the war's over! Get ready to go back to your warm bed and your sweet little wife."

Mitros opened his mouth; his heart sank. "Talk sense, will you!" he said at last. "You say the damned war's over? Who told you that?"

"The radio!"

Mitros leaped in the air, clapped his hands, and began to dance. "Long live Roumeli!" he shouted. "Join hands, brothers, and let's dance! Death to death!"

Five or six of the soldiers joined hands, broke into song, and danced the *tsamiko* as the priest approached, wearing his gold-embroidered stole and holding the Bible in his arms.

"In the name of God," he said, "this is the true Resurrection. Let us go, my children."

We took the uphill road, and the whole town—men and women—followed us. We knocked on every door as we went, shouting, "Come on, come along!"

I walked beside Stratis, and my thoughts drifted far away, to you, Maria. I was already in Athens, knocking on your door; you opened, looked at me standing on the threshold; your arms stretched out to me, and I bent and kissed your neck, the mole on your cheek. I wanted to speak, but I was choked with emotion. I wanted to tell you so many things, Maria; that we would go to Naxos as I had dreamt in that dream, and receive the blessing of my parents; and the wedding would take place in my grandfather's garden in Egares, under the orange and peach trees. That's what was spinning in my brain as I walked, and my mind flew around you and sat on your hair like a big butterfly.

But suddenly Stratis stopped; he raised his hand. "Wait a minute, men," he shouted, "I have something to say to you!"

We stopped and looked at him.

"It's a lie!" he shouted. "It's a joke! April Fool! And best wishes for the next year, too!" He turned and ran, howling with laughter.

We stood there stunned; our knees buckled. The priest bowed his head and sighed; without a word he took off his stole, wrapped it around the Bible and turned back, toward the church. That stately priest had suddenly become a hunched old man that could barely drag his feet. We scattered silently, and never did the war seem as unbearable to us as it did at that moment. All that happiness suddenly vanished before our eyes—our mothers, our homes, the women we loved—and we were back once more to our dirty barracks and the rifles.

APRIL 3: After the other day's incident our lives have become unbearable; like a streak of lightning, happiness flashed before us, and when we stretched our arms toward it, it vanished. It was apparent that a simple end to our misery could have made us human beings again, but that end never came, and once more we became beasts. Some invisible power, which I cannot name, plays on us, holding us in its fingers, and I still don't know whether that force is blind and senseless or full of vision and wisdom. I've been thinking about that force since the other day, and sometimes I call it fate, sometimes, need; sometimes I call it a blind, evil demon, and sometimes, God. This power governs and turns all; once it uses peace, once war—whichever is more suitable—to serve its purpose. What that purpose is, no one knows. Today it's using war, and woe to him who is not a fighter! I think of this force, and a thousand thoughts spin through my brain; I wonder—whether sightless or all-seeing—is this force Almighty? And if it is omnipotent, how will we be able to resist it? Would it not be more dignified and more practical to co-operate with it, to accept our fate without protesting and enter the war wholeheartedly, body and soul? And thus help, as best we can, to fulfill our intentions? And if, on the other hand, that power is not all-knowing, would it not be wiser to resist it, to set our own goals, those which suit both our hearts and minds, and create a kingdom of man on earth which is more just and more logical than the kingdom of Nature?

Should we submit and co-operate with this terrible force, or should we protest and resist it? My mind stands helpless at these crossroads, not knowing which way to turn; and yet on this decision rests the happiness and the success of man. I believe the ancient Greeks took the first road—the one of harmony—which took them to the miracle of absolute beauty. The Christians took the second path, which led to the mystic glory of love and kindness. Is it possible then, that no matter which path one treads, he can accomplish the miracle of man?

120

My beloved, the deeper my mind delves and the more it leaps from thought to thought, the more it becomes confused and dazed in antitheses. And it cannot find one bit of final logic so it can stop searching and find peace. Yet, I think that if I were with you, if I could touch your hand, I would feel a new strength and all my questions would have very simple, very positive answers. But you're so far away—at the other end of the world—and I stretch out my hand and find nothing to hold on to, and I'm falling; I'm falling, Maria my dearest; I am tortured in so many ways, here in the hills, and I hold the rifle when at that very moment I want to be holding—and I should be holding—your small, warm, beloved hand.

APRIL 7: Sleeplessness, hunger, war! The poor tortured body, how long can it endure? It's not a dry branch or a stone; it's flesh, and if we only had faith, one thing to believe in, we would endure. How did we ever last in those Albanian hills—naked, barefooted, hungry—and still accomplish the miracle that was the Albanian war?

So often I think of our people—those eternally persecuted, long-suffering Greeks—and I am overcome with emotion and compassion and admiration. How many thousands of years we've been fighting, clinging to these stones and the unfertile earth; while the barbarians sweep over us in continuous waves; and still we endure. And not only have we endured, but we have also found the time and the strength to give the world the two most precious gifts: freedom of soul and clearness of mind. We were the first to understand the process of thinking, and through it we brought order to chaos and freed the soul from fear.

And it was not only the barbarians; for thousands of years civil wars have come and gone, staining Greece with blood. Often—though the thought of it is terrifying—often, after such a fratricidal war, our souls soar and create great things. As I am writing this to you, my darling, and pouring out my pain, suddenly a horrible thought tears through my mind. Can it be that this war was necessary so that our souls might take on a new power? Many Greek hearts suffer, fill with rage, gather strength and perseverance from this unholy massacre. And when tempers cool and we are pacified, these very hearts which would

121

have sunk in idleness and mediocrity had war not broken out, will create great things—from indignation and pride; and from their need to forget pain, they transform it into thoughts, into beauty, into deeds. Should this savage war, then, be considered a blessing? Terror overwhelms me at this thought, but what if it is true? What if it is true, my beloved?

APRIL 11: We're waiting for the General's inspection any day now. We're waiting for reinforcements to prepare for a general assault, to rid ourselves at last of these rebels. Our captain tells us that Castello is the key and that whoever takes it opens the door into the valley and down to Yánnina. Sometimes, on a clear day we look through our binoculars and see in the distant mist the mystical city spread along that renowned lake whose deep waters hold the treasures of Ali Pasha and the body of his mistress Euphrosyne.

Some poet passed over this body and made it immortal; another poet passed over another body—Helen's—and made that immortal, too. And Homer, that great patriarch of genius, rises within my inner being; and the desire leaps within me again—like a seed—a desire I have spoken to you about so many times, my beloved, that God may soon bring the day when I can sing of Homer and Helen's reunion. The daughter of Zeus has grown old now; her breasts have sagged, her teeth and her hair have fallen; Menelaus is dead; the valiant men who fought for her sake have either died or aged or become senile, and have forgotten her. And Helen sits sadly, hopelessly, on the slope of the Eurotas, among the oleanders, and meditates on her life. Why was she born? For whom was she born? Her life has gone to waste; it glowed for a moment and immediately died out; soon, everyone will have forgotten her; the coming generation will not even know her name. Was she, then, merely a flower that withered? Was she not a body, destined by Fate, that shook the foundations of the world? A great soul that could not be restrained? Helen walked under the oleanders and sighed. Oh, to leave again, to leave! Some great lover seemed to be sitting on a faraway shore, singing to her, inviting her, enticing her. Oh, to leave again, to escape death; I don't want to die!

She descends the Eurotas slopes and reaches the sea. She undresses and dives into the waves, swimming with great strokes;

122

she is happy, refreshed, the sea is immortal water to her; she lifts her head and drifts toward the east.

And there, on the Ionian seashore, sits a reverent old man on the white shells; a mighty, serene nobleman with a long snow-white beard, like a statue of God; he is blind. With his head erect, he directs his sightless eyes toward Greece. A refreshing breeze drifts by; it is almost daybreak; the old man's senses bloom. "What joy," he murmurs, "what a refreshing breeze, how beautiful the song of the sea is!"

And when he said this, the whole seashore began to sing; the blind old man cocked his ear and felt a sense of harmony swell up within him. He stretched out his hand toward Greece, as though to save someone who was drowning.

And all through the night, Helen drifted, with her head above the waves, and as she approached the Ionian seashore, her hair began to turn crow-black again; her eyebrows tensed like an archer's bow; her withered oft-kissed breasts rose, her lips curled —and when she saw, in the light of dawn, the old man with the outstretched hand, she sensed, for the first time, why she had been born and where she was going.

"Father," she called, "Father!"

And the old man stood up and walked into the sea; his bare feet were cooled by the waves.

"Eleni," he called, "my daughter!" And he opened his arms.

And Helen, virgin, eternally young, eternally rejuvenated, walked into the open arms of immortality.

My beloved, I wonder if I will ever get the chance to compose this ode to Helen? Will I live? Will I survive these hills? Will I ever return to your side? There are days when my heart is filled with dark whisperings; but I have placed my hopes in you, for love conquers death.


APRIL 13: Today, my beloved, I received a letter from my uncle Velissarios, the professor who recently retired from the army. The letter forced me to do a lot of thinking, it also angered me. I am rewriting it to you so that you can see, too, what happens to those who read too much, who preach too much, who overexhaust ideas.

You know my uncle—you saw him one day when we went to

123

his home and found him bent over an open book, smoking his pipe. He talked to us of great problems, of civilization, of God, of war, and as he talked, he cut out paper dolls from a manuscript he had before him—little roosters, sailboats, and clowns—and stood them in a line in front of him and laughed. You remember how wise his words seemed to us, and how they swept us away? Yet, while he talked with such emotion, suddenly he would complete a paper doll and burst into laughter. And we were at a loss—we did not know whether what he spoke was the truth, out of the depths of his wisdom and his pain, or whether he was just mocking us.

That's how I imagine the highest man of every civilization is; he sees everything from such a height that all men look like dirty insects—beetles and ladybugs—and the earth is a mere walnut shell which is tossed and turned by the waves. And from this height, he calmly looks upon the storms of men, and sometimes he laughs, sometimes he nods his head with compassion. But it is a cold, inhuman compassion, which does not condescend to offer its hand to save the walnut shell from sinking.

Many times, when I talked to him of all the things they taught us at the university, he would look at me and smile with a satanic irony. And when I would ask him why he looked at me that way, he would reply, "When you grow up, perhaps you will understand; if I told you now, it would be too soon, you would understand nothing, my words would be futile; but then again you may never understand. I, my young man (that's how he always refers to me mockingly, as "my young man"), I, my young man, see civilizations as a poet sees the clouds rise and swell and fill with rain and wind and lightning; and then a breeze blows, and they change shape, they merge, they part, they redden at sunset. Then a stronger breeze blows, and they disappear. Will you ever be able to see civilizations and people and gods in this way? I doubt it—but try, struggle, reach as far as you can; go forth, my young man, courage!"

Whenever I begin to talk about this uncle of mine (my mother's brother), I can never stop; but this time I *will* stop to let him speak. He knew what he was talking about when he wrote this letter—look with what humor he tosses men and ideas about; but see, also, how, gradually he becomes enraged!

124

My dear nephew Leonidas—greetings, you pseudo-Spartan!

Your last letter revealed that our young genius is infected with an understandable itch, the well-known intellectual restlessness of youth, and you go on creating problems and then struggle to solve them; but you cannot, and you become discouraged, and you blame God and the devil and the mind of man. Then you let out mournful cries, asking me for help. What help can I give you, you poor four-eyed baby lamb from Athens. Attack the problems, my brave fighter, onward! Shout "Aera" as you do when you confront the rebels; lunge against these horrible thorny hedgehogs —the eternal questions; smash your face like all the others have, bleed from the needles, and finally, when you realize that it's not their blood you are tasting in ecstasy, but your own, then, and only then, sign an unconditional surrender and rest. Surrender to a great hedgehog—to a great ideal; there are many, many you know—country, religion, science, art, glory, communism, fascism, equality, brotherhood— you've reached the point of selling yourselves out, my young friends, choose and take! Today there are dozens of great ideals, and yet there are none, because as I've already said, you've reached the point where you are selling yourselves; it's late, the party's over, the prices have dropped, today you can buy a great ideal for peanuts.

When I, too, was young, I remember that an Italian charlatan had come to our island. His name was Carolito; he wore a stovepipe hat and claimed that he could cure all ills. He would stand erect in a cart that was drawn by a patient innocent jackass which he called, for reasons unknown to me, Carolina. And he would hold up his hands filled with bottles and powders and ointments. He cured whatever ailed you; he even extracted teeth and inserted glass eyes; and he also sold wooden hands with hooks, for one-armed people; and wooden legs with springs in them, for one-legged people; and elastic belts for those with abdominal problems. He had magic potions, too, for the lovesick, and a white mouse which selected, with its snout, a little piece of paper which told fortunes in written verse.

125

The mind of man is just another Carolito, my dear nephew; tell it your illness and it will surely find a remedy to cure it; and as I suspect from your other letter, there *is* a remedy for your illness, and it is indeed miraculous. You ask from where we come and where we are going, and what is the purpose of life, and what and how and why? A great illness! But Carolito will give you the answer so you can rest; I know this answer, too, because I am a Carolito, more or less; your remedy then, is—Maria. She will give you a definite answer to all your questions and thus silence you; take at least two or three drops of Maria—as many as you can stand (the more the better)—at night before you go to sleep, and you will rest.

You think I'm joking as I am in the habit of doing, and that I do not condescend to enter into serious discussions with you? You are wrong, my young man! I have never been more serious; this is the superior fruit of all my wisdom. I have no faith in human endurance and in the great ideals which torture young men like the acne of youth. Their blood boils, they are incensed and excited about the beginning and the end of the cosmos, about the purpose of life; and whether the chicken or the egg came first; it's only a skin disease, my young man, nothing else. One morning, as they walk restlessly, engulfed in their great thoughts, they meet a hip-swinging young woman, a round-faced peasant girl, or an anemic Athenian lady, dark or blond or red-haired (there's one for each taste), and they stand with open mouths. And this is the answer—they marry her and calm down.

This, my beloved nephew, is what I have to say in reply to your great idealistic letter. As I told you, I have no faith in men, or in what disturbs them or in their great ideas and ideals. I'm fed up. When I hear a priest preaching love and goodness, I want to vomit; when I hear a politician speak of country and honor and justice, I want to vomit; they have cheapened everything and everyone knows it—those who speak and those who listen; and yet no one dares to rise and spit on them.

I started this letter laughingly, but as I write and recall all that I have seen and heard, I am overcome with disgust

126

and anger. Don't be angry at my lack of faith in your great problems, my young man, forgive me, but they're just a lot of hot air. I am sorry for you, so I send you this prescription; read it whenever you get that intellectual itch, and it will stop, you'll see. They had given me a different remedy, and it failed; so my illness took a turn for the worse, and there is no cure for it now. My soul has become like Carolina, the little jackass—it pulls my mind, the charlatan; and my soul is unconsolable because it knows well the charlatan's tricks and manipulations and it has no faith in him; but nevertheless Carolina continues to pull him, continues to listen to him as he heralds his remedies, and she shakes her naïve head with patience and disgust. Yet I prefer my incurable illness to your cure; I do not condescend to escape, to find security in some great ideal; I walk hatless through the deserted roads, through the winds and the rains and in the terrible storm that has broken out; hatless—neither a black hood nor a red one! Hatless, barefooted, hopeless, and unbending, like King Lear; but not because my daughters deserted me, but because I deserted them. And when I fall in the middle of the road, I would like to die, like Strozzi, my beloved *condottieri*, who died on July 20, 1558 —a holy day. A god-fearing friend of his knelt beside him and clasped his hands pleadingly. "Repent, great sinner," he shouted to him, "repent for all that you have done in your life; you will appear before the Lord soon; make the sign of the cross and invoke the name of Christ."

"What Christ," Strozzi moaned with his dying breath, "what Christ, damn it? I refuse! My holiday has ended."

I would write a lot more, but you are young, and you cannot take it; even what I have written here is too much for you. Good-bye and good health to you! Kill as many of your brothers as you can, you poor fool—it's a dirty job, but you're not to blame. Try, at least, to return home alive, so you can complete your full cycle of life: childish joys, youthful intellectual itches, marriage, suffering, children death. Good night!

Your Uncle Velissarios
*Servus diabolicus Dei*, or, *Servus divinus diaboli* (it's the same thing).

127

APRIL 15: Holy Week! The bell tolls mournfully; we went to church to hear the Passions of Christ. "See the Bridegroom cometh . . ." Father Yánaros gave a sermon; but he quickly became aroused, and, while he had begun by speaking of Christ, he gradually confused Christ with Greece. "It is Greece that suffers," he cried, "Greece that is wounded, that is crucified, to save mankind." We were moved to tears; this priest has a strength that is secret and wild; a deep pain, an unshaken faith, something that is wild and gentle; his eyes and his beard are like those of Moses, and he walks on, passing the desert, but we, the cowards, do not follow him. And as he talked on, we, too, confused the crucified Lord with Greece, with our homes, our lives, the people we love—all that is being lost. In each one's mind Christ changed face and form; at times He became a virgin field and an unpruned vineyard; at other times He was a destroyed herd of sheep or an orphaned home or a bride or a child sucking its mother's breast. Each mourned for that most valuable possession which he could not enjoy; Christ had, in reality, come down to earth and lay dead within us, and we all wept and waited for Him to be resurrected.

I wept, too, my Maria, because I thought of you; to me, Christ had taken on the image of your sweet face, and as I bent to worship Him, I could not hold back the tears.

NOON OF HOLY MONDAY: My dearest, it is warmer today; the sun came out, and my heart fluttered when I saw the first swallow. Spring has reached even these wild hills, my Maria; Christ has risen, like the tender green grass, from the earth; the birds that had left us have returned; soon they will begin building their nests. Like the migrating birds, hope, too, departs, returns, searches, and finds its old nest—the heart of man—and there lays its eggs.

Suddenly today, after all the agony of winter, I feel my heart filling with eggs too; all will go well, my beloved, do not worry; have faith, the buds will blossom, the eggs will hatch, our desires will take form—they will become the home and the son and the song of Helen.

I have faith in the soul—it has wings; it can fly and see the future, much sooner than our eyes. My soul has taken wings tonight, my darling, and it has found you in a little house—our home—with a little human being in your arms who resembles us—our son; have faith, my beloved, all will go well!

EVENING OF HOLY MONDAY:

*Death hovers over my mind today,*
*And I am like the invalid who finds his health again,*
*As though I recovered from a great illness.*

*Death hovers over my mind today,*
*And it resembles the scent of flowers,*
*And I seem to be floating above the storm.*

*Death hovers over my mind today,*
*And it resembles man's longing for his home,*
*After all the long years of imprisonment.*

Here, abruptly, Leonidas' diary stopped. He was killed on Holy Tuesday.

Slowly, the schoolmaster closed the bloodstained notebook; he bent and kissed it, as though he were kissing the dead body of the luckless young man. His eyes were dry, his heart had become stone; life, to him, seemed ill-fated, unjust, heartless, without logic, as though it went stumbling on the earth, not knowing where it was going.

# 8

G OOD FRIDAY: A group of villagers were gathered
in the courtyard of the church exchanging heated words: Stelianos the weaver with the chewed-off ear; Andreas the coppersmith with his thick, dirty hands; Kyriákos the town crier with
his long, unwashed hair; and Panágos the barber of the village,
shoeless, mourning, wearing a black shirt. Scrawny old Mandras
with the small, foxy eyes stood in the center; he was the well-
known landowner and chiseler of the town.

Hadjis, the oldest of the elders, sat on the ledge near the door,
basking in the sun; his joints were swollen, and he moaned with
pain. He had dragged himself to church to see Christ's Bier
and to take back home a handful of myrtle leaves and rosemary
—these he would burn with the incense when his pains became
unbearable, as his grandfathers did to find relief from their
rheumatisms. Who needs doctors? They're only the devil's in-
vention, damn them! The blessed leaves are more effective, and
more practical, too.

Hadjis was a sly one, having experienced much in his youth;
he had been a world-traveler, reaching as far as Athens, even
farther, as far as Beirut; and still farther, to the River Jordan.
He had bathed in the holy waters and become a *hadji.* "It's a
useful thing," he would say to himself, "to become a hadji; people respect you, and it's much easier to fool them." And sure
enough, the very moment he had stepped out of the Jordan, a
brilliant idea struck him. Up until now he had been forced to

130

earn his living shining shoes, being a porter, a smuggler—constantly in danger, barely existing. But now that he had become a hadji, he saw the light. He took all the money he had in his possession, bought some burlap sacks, several lengths of rope, and some wooden poles, and journeyed through the villages and towns of Anatolia. Wherever he went, he set up his tent; he would hang out a sign, a piece of white cloth with thick letters which read, "The Mysteries of Marriage," and then he would stand outside the tent, place two fingers in his mouth, and whistle. The people would gather round, and the sly hadji would make the sign of the cross, climb up on a stool, and begin to shout: "Here, ladies and gentlemen, in this tent, you will witness the mysteries of marriage, the frightening mysteries of marriage, for only one drachma; come now, what's a drachma, ladies and gentlemen? And yet with that one measly little coin you will view the terrifying, horrible mysteries of marriage, and your hair will stand on end. And if it does not, I give you my word of honor as a hadji, a God-fearing man, that I will return your money! Easy now—eh, eh, one at a time now—don't push, there's room for everyone!"

No one would move; Hadjis would whistle again, begin his pitch again, and finally someone would come forth; there was always someone—usually an unmarried man—who would dig into his pocket for that coin so that he, too, could see this great mystery. Hadjis would lift the burlap, and the man would enter; he would look around, rub his eyes, look again, but he would see nothing. Then Hadjis would take him by the arm and say in a sugary tone, "You see, my friend, you don't see a thing, do you? Don't stretch your neck in vain; you won't see anything. But please don't tell anyone when you go out, because you'll be the fool. Tell them instead that you saw many terrible wonders and that from this day forth your life has changed, because now you understand the meaning of women, of marriage, of the world. This is what you must say, so the others can be fooled, too; and they won't make fun of you. Understand? All right, go on your way now so the others can come in."

In this way, Hadjis made a bit of money, returned to Castello, his village, wearing a gold chain across his vest, and soon became an elder. But now he was old—the poor man had aged, he was

131

deaf, half-blind, senile; and now he sat in the courtyard of the church, rubbing his swollen knees, as saliva ran from his toothless mouth.

The others stood over the gravestones arguing. At first they had begun a discussion about last night's vigil service when the Twelve Gospels were read. Old Mandras could not understand why Christ should oppose the Jewish law, since it was handed down by God Himself to Moses, on Mount Sinai. And Andreas insisted that he could not understand why, if Christ were almighty, He did not clap His hands and summon the angels to descend with their swords and slaughter the Jews.

"If it were me," he added, "that's what I'd do—just clap my hands. After all, I'd be God, wouldn't I? So I'd act like a lion, not like a lamb. What do you say, Kyriákos?"

Kyriákos, who for years now had nurtured the desire to become a priest, cleared his throat and scratched his head. It's my duty to speak, he thought, and enlighten them. He had had just a little education, and whenever Father Yánaros was not around, he took courage and expressed his opinions. So in his heavy chantlike voice, he began to speak about Christ; that He, like Kyriákos, was a humble, innocent man with long hair who wanted to become a priest, to spread the word of truth. But the wealthy and the powerful persecuted Him, cursed Him, beat Him, pursued Him; and today, on Good Friday, they were preparing to kill Him.

"You see," old Mandras concluded, "that's what happens to those who speak up!"

Kyriákos looked around him in case Father Yánaros should suddenly appear and, not seeing him, took more courage. Just a few months ago he had found an explanation for Christ's actions, and he felt he had no right to keep this to himself—we must not hide the light under a bushel—so he began to enlighten the villagers.

"Now, for your information, to society, Christ was what we call an irregular verb."

"And what does that mean?" Panágos the barber asked. "Explain yourself, teacher."

"It means that all the people around Him, the Scribes and Pharisees, Anna, Kayafas, were regular verbs; it means that they had the written laws, from the time of their ancestors, and they obeyed these laws. They knew exactly what was good, what was bad, what was honorable, what was dishonorable; for they had the Ten Commandments as their guide. Whoever followed these got on well in society; whoever broke them was a rebel, an upstart against society; and society became angry, confused, and felt its foundations shaken. So it grabbed the irregular verb and said, 'So you refuse to be conjugated like the rest of us, in the regular way? Then down you go!' "

"Ah, so that's how it is," Stelianos said, and rubbed his ear, which still pained him. "But, then, who's right? I'm confused, Kyriákos old friend. Can one person fight the world? Can you take a holy tradition that was handed down from your parents and turn around and say you don't like it? Would it be proper for you to come into my house and say to me, 'I don't like your loom—it's no good,' and then take an ax and hack it to pieces? Why, this loom was handed down to me by my parents and my grandparents; this is the way they taught me to weave and earn my bread, and then you came along . . ."

"Christ is right!" The coppersmith jumped up shouting. "Why not? What are we, stagnated water in a pool? The world moves, it's a living thing, men, it grows; it wore one type of clothing as a baby, but it wears different clothes when it grows up; it discards the diapers and bibs, and puts on trousers. It leaves its mother and father, and builds its own home. And it's only natural. All right, I'm not saying diapers and bibs are no good—but they're for babies. Christ is the first man who realized He was no longer a baby, that the old laws, the bibs and diapers, no longer fit. Do you understand what I mean?"

"Do you understand?" replied the old landowner who had become enraged. "What school taught you that nonsense, or did you learn it all in your tinker shop?"

"Never mind, you old miser, with your money and your farms," the coppersmith answered in an angered breath, "but don't worry, iron bends when it's placed in the fire; and you'll bend, too, you'll see. That, for your information, is what I learned in my tinker shop."

Pleased at hearing this, Kyriákos jumped up. "And that fire is Christ!" he shouted.

"So, that's it," old Mandras said and looked at the copper-smith through narrowed eyes. "Now I see why they call you a bolshevik."

Andreas laughed. "They won't call me a bolshevik any longer; they'll call me an irregular verb! God bless Kyriákos for showing me the light."

Old Hadjis, who still sat on the ledge, looked through dim eyes at his fellow villagers who were shouting and gesturing; he could not understand what the commotion was all about. He could not hear; only a sound reached his brain, like that of turtles fighting and clashing shells.

"What's going on, friends?" he asked every now and then, his saliva running down his chin.

He would be silent, and then again: "What's going on, men?" But no one bothered to reply.

Finally Panágos the barber, tired of listening to him, walked over and boomed in his ear: "They say they want to open up your coffers, old man! Open up your coffers, you hear? They want to see how much money you've got hoarded away."

The old man's arms and legs went limp; his flesh almost jumped out of its skin.

"Eh? Who? Who do you say?" he managed to gasp, and saliva rained on his shirtfront.

"The poor!" the barber shouted in his ear, "the poor people, the hungry, the shoeless!"

The old landowner giggled; his heart settled back in its place.

"The poor?" he replied. "The hell they will! There's a God in heaven!"

The barber leaned over the old man and shouted in his ear again. "But the poor have a God, too, and He's barefooted, too, and He's hungry; and He keeps a record, they say, and marks a red cross alongside the name of every wealthy man. And they say He's marked a red cross beside your name, too, Hadjis!"

The old man began to tremble again; he tried to speak, but his tongue became twisted.

Stelianos, feeling sorry for Hadjis, turned to the barber. "Leave the old man alone before he has a stroke," he said.

Old Mandras was furious. "You lousy barber," he shouted, "who canonizes these blasphemies you spout? Is it the teacher? Or is it that priest with the red cap?"

134

"It's not the teacher, Mandras, nor is it Father Yánaros," the barber replied, and his eyes dimmed. "A three-year-old child told me—a three-year-old child that I saw die of hunger."

"What child, you idiot?"

"My child."

Silence fell over the men. Indeed, just the other day, Panágos' child had died of hunger; months ago Panágos had closed his barber shop because the villagers had no money—they let their hair and beards grow long.

And while everyone remained silent, ashamed, as though they had killed that child themselves, Mathios the coachman arrived, panting and flushed.

"We're going to the devil, thank God!" he shouted happily when he saw his fellow villagers. "They say we're out of ammunition and that the redhoods found it out and will be coming down the hill any moment, to burn us, to slaughter us, to put us out of our misery."

He rubbed his hands with pleasure as he talked.

Poor Mathios, who loved food! He had nothing to eat now; he loved to drink, too, but he had nothing to drink, either; he loved women, but he was poor and ugly, and no woman would even look at him. So he turned against the world: "The devil take it all; since I'm not rich, no one else should be rich; since I have nothing to eat, no one else should have anything to eat, either; that's the real meaning of God and justice."

Old Mandras raised his staff in anger. "Bite your tongue, you dirty barefooted bastard! If God listened to the vultures, no one would be left alive!" he shouted and rushed at Mathios.

But the coppersmith grabbed him by the arm. "The tables turn, Mandras old man," he said. "Don't be angry; the wheel keeps turning, and things go round and round; the poor will become rich, the rich will become poor, and the sword will cut them all down—rich and poor alike. Remember the monk who brought the Holy Sash the other day? Remember what he shouted as he passed the barracks? 'Kill, my children, kill and become sanctified!' That's what he cried; so we kill!"

"The monk said to kill the reds, not the honest people," replied the elder.

Andreas laughed. "Don't worry, my honest friend, I am certain that there is another monk who travels and preaches to the rebels, too, and shouts, 'Kill! Kill the blackhoods, kill the honest people, and you will be sanctified!' So they, too, kill. And so Mathios must be right, the devil's taken all of us."

Mathios could not remain silent. "Eh, my honest friend, I'll tell you an old proverb, but don't take it personally. Satan takes half of all the things that are earned honestly, and he takes all of the things earned dishonestly, including the owner, too! You're going to end up with nothing, because I think the devil will take you very soon, you old chiseler." With that, he turned, and with a leap was out of the courtyard. Hadjis' staff crashed against the wall, crumbling the whitewash.

At that moment, Father Yánaros appeared at the door of his cell. He had heard the shouting in the courtyard, but his mind had been absorbed with the Passions of Christ and the passions of man; he was struggling to find some solution, but could find nothing; and he would look first at the carving of the Second Coming by his martyred friend Arsénios, then at the icon of St. Constantine, the firewalker.

Ah, he thought, if only man could walk on lighted coals and dance over them! Oh, to walk on this earth and not be overcome with despair, with fear, or blasphemy!

He looked at the icon of the firewalker, and as he watched, logic seemed to fortify itself within him. "God is not cool water —no, He's not cool water to be drunk for refreshment; God is fire, and you must walk upon it; not only walk, but—most difficult of all—you must dance on this fire. And the moment you are able to dance on it, the fire will become cool water; but until you reach that point, what a struggle, my Lord, what agony!"

He rose; all morning he had been decorating the Holy Bier with the wildflowers they had brought him from Prastova; he took Christ down from the cross, laid Him on the wildflowers, leaned over, and kissed His bloodied feet, His bloodied hands, His sides from where the white and red paint ran. "There now, be patient, my Son," Father Yánaros told Him. "It's nothing, don't despair. You're God, You will be resurrected; sleep now."

But here, alone in his cell, the voices woke within him, asking questions but receiving no reply; Father Yánaros rose, disturbed. He finally made a decision. "I'll go to church," he said to himself. "I am burdened with heavy cares; I must find out what to do; my village is in danger; my soul is in danger. He must give me an answer—whether to go to the right or to the left—I want a response. In the name of God—a response!"

He made the sign of the cross, and, with head and feet bare, he crossed the threshold of his cell. His face clouded with worry, and the blood rushed to his head.

"The pot's boiling," Stelianos the weaver murmured when he saw Father Yánaros approaching. "Be careful, men!"

They stepped back, making room for him to pass; Father Yánaros did not even turn to look at them; his eyes were focused on God, and in the brilliant light, he could see no one else.

"What news do you have, Father?" asked the coppersmith. "Hasn't the knife cut into the bone yet?"

"I'm going to talk with God; I want no words with men right now."

"Don't go getting us into any more trouble, priest," old Mandras said, looking at Father Yánaros with hatred. "Your eyes are full of treason."

"My eyes are full of dying children; leave me alone."

"I'm not afraid of anyone in this village," the elder said, "except you, Father Yánaros."

"I'm afraid of you, too, Mandras, but for now, forget your own miserable welfare and think of the village."

"My welfare and the welfare of the village are one and the same; what have you plotted this time, Father Yánaros? You put anything that suits you into God's mouth and then you come out in the pulpit and say, 'God told me this, God told me that.' Eh, Father Yánaros, did God tell you that, or did you tell it to God yourself, you impostor?"

"What are they saying, eh? What are they saying?" shrieked old Hadjis, and he rubbed his aching knees.

But no one answered him; all of them had fixed their eyes on the two heads of the village, who were in the midst of this argument.

"A priest is the voice of God on earth," Father Yánaros said and gestured for the elder to step back so he could pass. "Don't chastise yourself, you damned old man! You've done enough to the women and children of this town!"

The old miser opened his mouth to speak, but stopped as the

137

neighing of a horse was heard behind them; they turned to see the captain whipping his gray horse as he rode toward them. Seeing the villagers gathered around the priest, he coiled like a snake ready to spring. The traitor's plotting something, he thought, and he sprang toward them, cracking his whip in the air with fury.

"Bulgars, bolsheviks, traitors!" he snarled, turning his horse first to one side, then to the other; it foamed at the mouth, like its master. Everyone scattered; only Father Yánaros remained by the ledge of the church.

"I'm going to hang you upside down, you scoundrel! Why are you rounding up the people? What are you instigating?"

"I pity you, Captain," Father Yánaros replied in a quiet, austere voice, "I pity you; your heart is filled with poison, and you want to contaminate the world; but there's a God in heaven."

With that he seized the horse's bridle. The captain leaned over, glared at him, and bile rushed to his eyes.

"Scoundrel!" he snarled again and raised his whip.

The priest merely looked at him; his face filled with compassion and bitterness.

"My son," he said softly, "are you still human? Do you ever think of your mother? May I talk to you?"

The captain was confused; the blood drained from his face; a flash of lightning closed his eyes, and everything disappeared; only a humble village house remained, trembling in the air. And at the threshold stood a bent, smiling little old woman brightly dressed in the clothes she had worn as a bride—the clothes she would wear when she died; she was waiting for her son. In the lightning flash the captain saw clearly the wrinkles on her face; he saw her eyes that were filled with such patience and softness, and her withered lips. And suddenly everything disappeared again—the threshold, the house, his elderly mother. The captain opened his eyes and saw Father Yánaros before him.

"What do you want?" he growled. "Didn't I tell you not to look at me like that? Get away from me!"

"My son, if you would only be patient and listen to me," Father Yánaros said and, still holding the bridle, he looked at the captain with compassion.

"Speak up then, what do you want?"

"My son, this is a terrible moment; your whole life will be judged by it. If you are a real man, this moment will prove it; your children and your grandchildren will judge you on how you act now. God will judge you—do you hear me?"

"Go on, go on, I'm listening!"

"Fate has placed in your hands a great strength, here in Castello; you can do whatever you wish—you can take life, you can reduce this village to ashes, you can save it from fire and death; choose! Will you choose?"

"Don't ask me to do that; what are you leading up to?"

"I'm speaking to your heart, if you still have a heart; that's why I asked you if you ever think of your mother."

"Don't remind me of my mother!" the captain shouted, as though he were being knifed. "I don't want you to remind me of my mother!"

"Thank God, you still have a heart, Captain," Father Yánaros said, and a light shone on his face. "You still have a heart; come down and let the two of us sit on the ledge and forget the past, damn it! We must save our village—have you no pity for it? You hold the sword in Castello, and I, the Word of God; get off your horse and let us unite our two great strengths, my son." As he talked, the priest gently stroked the sweating neck of the horse; he looked pleadingly into the captain's eyes.

"Go ahead," he kept saying, "make the sign of the cross and reach a decision . . ."

The sun had begun to set; the wild hills had filled with violets; the first jackals could be heard growling in the distance. A flock of vultures, satiated with food, passed silently over the church; a faint, sharp breeze came from the peak of the hill.

"It's not only Castello, my son," the voice of the priest came again, "it's not only Castello, but all of Greece—the whole world! Christ is in danger. Decide!"

The captain could control himself no longer. "Quiet," he growled. "Christ, Christ! Greece!—Stop it!" His mouth spat out saliva and foam.

"You've begun your exorcisms again, you sacrilegious fool! Lay your cards on the table; you want me to surrender the village to the rebels, eh? Is that what you want? Is that what you

139

want, traitor? Take this!" And he swung his hand down in fury; the whip struck Father Yánaros on the neck and cheek. Growling, the captain jabbed his bloodied spurs into the belly of his horse.

"My child," the priest cried, and his eyes filled with tears, "my child, there's still time to save yourself; there's an abyss before you—wait! Be careful, or you will fall into it!"

"Then let me fall," the captain growled again and turned his horse toward the barracks.

"All right, I've made up my mind, too," Father Yánaros shouted at the horse and rider as he raised his hands to the sky. "God will choose!"

The rider disappeared at the bend of the road, but the sound of the horse, with its bloodied belly, could be heard neighing with pain.

The priest stood motionless and looked at the air that was now becoming misty; he touched his cheek and his neck and only then felt the pain; he looked at his hand—it was covered with blood.

"From now on I expect nothing more of men," he murmured. "But then again, what do I need with men? I have God —I'll go and talk with Him."

# 9

THE CHURCH smelled of incense and wildflowers; the last rays of the sun—red, green, blue—fell on the narrow, stained glass windows of the dome and lit up the Pancreator. Years ago, Father Yánaros himself, lying on his back upon the scaffolding, had painted Him. He had depicted Him, not wild and furious as was the custom, but sad, tormented, pale, like a refugee. "I, too, am a refugee," Father Yánaros had murmured as he painted, "a refugee; they chased me away from my land, away from my peaceful, sweet-blooded Thrace, and I climbed up here, to the wild, Epirotic hills, where I struggle and fight to make the beasts human. Christ is a refugee, on this earth, too, so I will paint Him as one." He took yellow and green paints and he made His cheeks leaner, he curved His lips downward, drew lines on His neck; only around His eyes did he draw long golden rays that illuminated and filled His tormented face with hope. He had Him sitting on a long cushion, embroidered with birds and fish and people, and instead of holding a Bible in His hands, He held a strange, ugly little creature with large wings.

"What does that strange insect represent?" the bishop asked with curiosity one day when he passed through Castello. "Christ usually holds the Holy Bible or a blue sphere—the earth—in His hands; what have you put there? Mercy, my Lord!"

"Look closely, Your Eminence," Father Yánaros replied, annoyed. "Can't you see that it has wings?"

"And what of it? What does that represent?"

141

"The mouse that ate of the body of Christ from the Holy Altar and sprouted wings—a bat!"

"A bat!" the bishop shouted. "Lord have mercy on us; and what does that mean? Aren't you ashamed, Father Yánaros?"

Anger filled the priest. "You mean that Your Eminence still does not understand?" He spoke impatiently. "The Pancreator holds the soul of man in His hand! The mouse is the soul which ate of the body of Christ and sprouted wings."

Father Yánaros strode on, as though he were being chased, and entered the church. He turned the lock, bolted the door, and looked around him with eyes that flashed. In the semidarkness he did not see the black-clothed women who had come earlier in the day from the nearby villages. They had found the door of the church open, and, seeing Christ there on His Bier, they entered, surrounded Him, and began the lament. And slowly, they were carried away—they threw back the black kerchiefs that covered their heads and began to weep for their murdered sons. They were five, the bereaved mothers, and five were the names of Christ today: Stélios and Yánnakos and Márkos and Dimítri and Aristótle.

And suddenly the door rumbled; they saw the priest entering like a cyclone. Frightened, they huddled, dazed, near the pews.

The priest could not see in the darkness; he tripped over the Bier and barely missed falling over with it. But he caught himself in time; he grabbed hold of it, steadied himself against it, and prevented the fall.

"Lord have mercy! The Bier has come to life and wants to run away," murmured Father Yánaros, shuddering. He entered the sanctuary and prayed over a bloodstained rock which lay on the altar. He came out of the Holy Gate and stood before the large icon of Christ at the right of the iconostas. His heart was boiling; for a long while he fought with himself, but the words got jumbled in his larynx and he could not speak. He moaned deeply, slowly, like a small calf. Now, standing before Christ, his anger had ebbed; he was overcome with fear. Father Yánaros made the sign of the cross three times; he bowed in penitence and gathered courage.

"I worship Your passion, my Lord," he cried in a loud voice. "Forgive me; I fear You and tremble at Your strength, but I am only human, and my heart aches. I am a Greek, and You must listen to me; let me shout, let me pour out my pain to You and find relief. Then, kill me; You are the Almighty! I look about, Lord, and study the world which You created; it is not a just world! I say this openly before You! No, it is not just! I study the men You created, supposedly in Your image; I do not understand this. Is this Your image, Lord—are You like these men? So then, is the earth nothing more than a military camp where You have encircled us with barbed wire, which You come to inspect every so often and select the best one of us to kill? What has Greece ever done to You—You ingrate? How can You do such a thing? Why did You not choose Albania or Turkey or Bulgaria? What did these countries ever do for You— what joy have they given You? What great works have they created in Your name? But Greece took You by the hand when You were only a babe, stumbling on the rocks; when You could barely walk the earth; she took You from one end of the earth to the other, like a prince! If it were not for Greece, where would You be? Still among the Jews, drifting and arguing in the synagogues. Greece came along and took You by the hand and out of the synagogues; she painted Your beauty and You became beautiful. She praised Your goodness and You became good; she built palaces for You that reached the skies, and You became a king. And is this her reward now? Have You set out to tear her to pieces with her own hands? Have You no pity for her? Have You no respect for her?"

Father Yánaros was frightened at the sound of his own words; he put his hand to his mouth to seal his unholy lips; he waited in terror as he looked around him at the icons, at the Archangel Michael with the red sandals and the black wings, painted on the door of the sanctuary. "Surely lightning will strike me down now," he murmured. "Would God allow man to be so insolent to Him? My Lord, I am drowning; let me spout a curse so that I will not burst; believe me, there are moments when my brain rattles; stone, wood, the saints, they all take on a new meaning. I look at the icon of the Virgin to the left of the iconostas, and I say, 'This is not the Virgin who sits, so sad and beautiful, with her breast out, feeding You, Lord, this is not the Virgin, it is Greece!' "

Sweat poured from the deeply lined forehead of Father Yánaros; his nostrils sniffed the air; they seemed to yearn for the smell of sulphur—the scent of God.

"Ah, what joy," he murmured, "if only God's Fire would fall and burn me! So that I may believe that God has ears and that He hears me; that I am not shouting in the wilderness, but that my voice rises to the sky, strikes heaven, changes into a lightning bolt, and mercilessly descends upon my shameless head!

"Do you remember that terrible day, my Lord," he cried, "that terrible St. Constantine's day on May twenty-first? Far away in my village, near the Black Sea—the fires were lit in the center of town, and the people trembled around them. God hung from above, and I held the holy icons, our forefathers; I entered the flames barefooted and sang and danced and threw handfuls of burning coals at the people; and the flames, like cool, crystal-clear water, refreshed me; because You were with me, Lord—only You, not the flames, not death, but You! And like crude iron that passes through fire and comes out pure steel, that is how I came away from Your fires, Lord. I felt my whole body, from my head to my toes, turn into a steel sword—an immortal soul—in Your hand! And now I speak to You, and You do not answer; I cry out, and You do not condescend to acknowledge me; but I will cry and shout, until You hear me; that is why You gave me a mouth—not that I may eat, or speak, or kiss, but that I may cry out!"

He turned to the left of the iconostas, to the large miraculous icon of the Virgin, as though he were asking Her to intercede through Her Son. She held the Babe tightly in Her arms and Her eyes, dark, sad, were fixed with fear upon a cross that hung in the air. Her face seemed to have been slashed in two with a knife; one morning, during the liturgy, as Father Yánaros stood at the Holy Gate and prayed for "peace in the world," a loud noise, like a blow striking, sounded from the iconostas; the wooden icon cracked, and the face of the Virgin split in two, from between the eyebrows to the chin. The Christians were terrified; they fell to the floor and waited. "Surely an earthquake will follow," they murmured. "Surely now, lightning will fall upon us and burn us." And after a few days the terrible news arrived: far, far away, at the other end of the world, a fire had fallen from heaven, killing two thousand souls! And immediately, the Virgin, in this small village of Castello, let out her cry; the pain of man had reached Her, and the icon cracked.

"Virgin Mother," Father Yánaros cried, stretching out his hands to the split icon, "You pity the yellow men at the other end of the world; You pity them and yet You do not pity the children of Castello who are dying before Your very eyes? Why do You not plead at the feet of Your Son, that He may put an end to this evil, Virgin Mother?" He turned toward Jesus and waited. Christ looked at him, smiling, but He did not open His mouth to speak. A bee had entered from the open window of the sanctuary and buzzed over the wildflowers on the Bier. Father Yánaros looked about him, dazed; in the center of the church the Bier stood, decorated with myrtle, rosemary, and the wildflowers, and within it, embroidered on expensive silk, lay the dead Christ. It was Good Friday and He awaited the Resurrection serenely, and with certainty. Father Yánaros approached, he leaned over the Bier as though it were in reality the grave of Christ and cried out in a loud, heart-rending voice, "O Greek, my Greek, why do you want to kill your Mother?"

The very soul of Father Yánaros had left his body, had gathered on the tips of his ears, his eyes, his fingers, and waited there. It waited for the miracle. It's bound to happen, he thought. Surely a voice will be heard. Surely God will condescend to reply to man. He waited, he waited; again, nothing. The wind was mute, the Pancreator was deaf, Christ was dead; Father Yánaros was completely alone in the world.

And then his mind became overly arrogant; his anger leaped free of its reins; Father Yánaros raised his hand. "All right, then," he shouted, "there will be no Resurrection! Lie there and wait! You will be resurrected only with Greece, do You hear? Other wise, no Resurrection! There is nothing else I can do, but as a priest, this much power I have and this much I shall do. Even if You lift Your hand and toss me into the bottom of hell along with Judas, even then—and take it from me, Father Yánaros —there will be no Resurrection here in Castello or Chalika or Prastova—no Resurrection in any of these three villages where my vestments empower me."

The blasphemy lingered in the air, and in the curvature be-

145

hind the Holy Altar in the sanctuary, where the Worship of the Angels was illustrated, Father Yánaros heard the painted walls crumbling. He jumped, startled; for a moment he thought that one of the angels had actually moved; the priest turned and, with gathered eyebrows, spoke angrily. "You have nothing to say about it," he shouted. "You're an angel, you cannot feel pain; you are not free to sin; you are imprisoned forever and ever in paradise. But I am human, a warm being that feels pain, that sings, that dies; if I choose to enter Paradise, I will; if I choose not to, I will not; and don't shake your wings at me; don't take out your sword; man is speaking with God—you have no say in this!"

Father Yánaros turned to the icon of Christ; his voice suddenly became strong and joyful. "Lord, only you and I know—not the angels—that we are one. We became one on that holy day in Jerusalem—remember?—it was the evening of the Resurrection; all the races of the world—white, black, yellow—were in church and they waited, with their hearts in their throats, for the Holy Light to descend. The air crackled with electricity; there was fire in every face; the miracle hung over our very heads, like a lightning bolt. Women fainted, men trembled; all eyes were glued upon the Holy Bier on which the heavenly flame would descend. And suddenly lightning flashed in the church, God descended; He leaped upon a group of black men and lit the candles they held; and I, my Lord, was overcome with a godly mania—remember?—I began to shout; what was I shouting? I can't recall the words. I foamed at the mouth, sprouted wings, jumped in the air screaming. The black men grabbed me, lifted me in their arms; I flew over the heads of the people, over the lighted candles; my clothes caught fire; my beard, my hair, my eyebrows were burning, but I was cool and refreshed; I sang the wedding songs of my land. The women screamed, they wrapped me in wet blankets and took me out into the courtyard. The priests took me in, and for three months I fought with God and with Death. I chanted, I clapped my hands; never had I felt such joy and such freedom. The priests shook their heads; they thought I had gone mad, but I felt that the fire which had burned me, which had engulfed me, was You—You, my Lord! 'This is what love means,' I cried, 'this is the way man merges with woman, and God with the soul of man.' Since then, as You well know, we became one, and I have the right to look You in the eye and speak to You with my head held high. I look at my hands, they are Christ; I touch my lips, my chest, my knees, they are all Christ. We both lay upon the Bier among the wildflowers, and we shall not be resurrected as long as this fratricide lasts!"

Father Yánaros was enraged. "Speak to me with human words," he shouted, "so I can understand. You growl, but I am not an animal to understand what You say. You chirp, but I am not a bird; You thunder and flash, but I am not a cloud—I am a man; speak to me in the language of men!"

He was about to open his shameless mouth again; but suddenly his nostrils detected that the air had filled with sulphur; the elderly priest became frightened; he forgot the big words he had spouted and he crouched in fear. "He's coming, He's coming," he murmured, and his knees weakened. "He's coming—there He is!"

At that moment he felt his guts tearing; the lightning bolt had found its mark inside him. He heard a deep, mournful voice and he recognized it; it was the voice of Christ! Christ always speaks from within, from our insides; and He always speaks in that deep, mournful tone. The priest lowered his head to his chest and listened. "Father Yánaros, speak with respect! Father Yánaros, speak with reverence! You came to ask me something; go on then, ask!"

"Ask You, my Lord?" the priest stammered, and trembled. "But You know everything!"

"I know all, but I like to hear the voice of man. Speak!"

"Where, on the soil of Greece, are Your images," Father Yánaros asked, "that I may follow them, my Lord? There, that's what I wanted to ask You! Where are You? Whose side are You on? The blacks'? The reds'? Whose side—so I may join You?"

Sad laughter was heard and again the voice of Christ: "Where am I? You resurrect me every year and you do not know where I am? I am in heaven."

Father Yánaros stamped his foot; anger washed over him again.

"Let heaven alone, Lord, let it be! It's not time for it yet; my soul is still tied to the flesh; I'm still alive; I still work upon the

147

earth; I toil to open the road, I struggle here, on this earth, on this strip of land and sea that is called Greece; on a rock of Greece that is known as Castello. Speak to me of Castello, Lord, of this poor, unfortunate village that You have hung around my neck! Come down to Castello and show me the way; this is the favor I ask of You, no other! Show me the way, Lord!"

Father Yánaros crossed his hands over his open, sweating chest; his voice was now a soft, pleading cry: "My Lord, give me your hand, lead me; should I or should I not turn the village over to the rebels? I listen to the leader on the hill, who wants to bring justice and bread so that the world will not hunger or be wronged, and I take his side. I come down to Castello and I listen to the wild captain shouting of country, religion, and honor, and I take his side, too. I'm confused; there is only one hope for me—You are that hope, my Lord! Give me Your hand, lead me!"

Night had fallen; the moon must have appeared in the sky, for the small window of the sanctuary became softly, sweetly, lit. A gray owl that was perched on the dome of the church sighed, and Father Yánaros' heart suddenly filled with sadness and gentleness.

The voice sounded again, sad and sweet this time. "Father Yánaros, Father Yánaros! I ask one favor of you; do not be frightened."

"Favor of me? Favor of an ant, my Lord? Command!"

"Lead me!"

"Lead You, Lord? But You are all-powerful!"

"Yes, I am all-powerful, but only with the help of man; without you on the earth that I created, I find it difficult to walk— I stumble. I stumble on the stones, the churches, the people. Do not stare like that! Why did I create sharks in the ocean depths that cannot navigate without a little pilot fish to guide them? You are the pilot fish of God; get in front and lead me."

Trembling and wide-eyed, Father Yánaros stared at Christ. Does He mean what He says, or is He merely trying to tempt me? God's words are double-edged—Father Yánaros had known this for many years now—double-edged, double-mouthed, and dangerous; woe to the man who does not obey the word of God; woe to the man who does! Man's mind is confused; God's

148

words open both doors—hell and paradise—and in man's fear, he becomes dazed, he cannot distinguish which door leads to God. Father Yánaros saw both doors open and he struggled, silently, to gain time for his mind to clear and reach a decision. He had fought many times with Satan, many times with God; you can frighten Satan away—you can exorcise him. But God? What can you do to Him?

The priest stared silently at the divine face; he weighed the strange words of God fearfully; what could be their hidden meaning? He pretends not to know—He, the All-Knowing, the All-Powerful! Why? Why? Doesn't He love us? Doesn't He want us? Doesn't He care about man?

Father Yánaros was about to fall at Christ's feet and cry out: "Don't leave me alone; help me!" But he did not get the chance; from within his aged bowels the secret voice came, stern and angry now: "Father Yánaros, are you not ashamed? Why do you ask me for advice? You are free—I made you free! Why do you still cling to me? Stop the penitences; get up, Father Yánaros, take responsibility upon yourself; do not ask advice from anyone; are you not free? Make your own decisions!"

"Lord, freedom is a great burden; how can man hold on to it? It is too heavy, Father."

The voice came again; this time it was soft and sad: "Yes, heavy, my son! Courage!"

His insides closed up again; silence! Father Yánaros raised his head from his chest; a sudden strength rose up from the floor of the church, descended from the dome from where the Pancreator watched, and filled the priest's chest, his insides; this was the first time in all his talks with God that he felt such courage and such certainty.

He placed his palm on his chest. "I take upon myself," he said loudly, as though taking an oath, "I take the responsibility for the salvation or loss of my village, upon myself; I shall decide! You are right, I am free. To be free means that I will accept all the honor or shame—it means that I am human."

He made the sign of the cross, stood on tiptoe, pressed his lips against the face of Christ. "Father," he said, "forgive me for saying too much; anger—that red devil—often saddles me; forgive me and let me ask only one thing of You: help me to

149

speak gently, without anger, without complaint; but, You, too, please look down on this ill-fated earth, look down at her and bless her; she, like Rachel, weeps for her children."

All was serene again. Always, when he spoke with God, sweat would pour from his head; his nostrils would fill with sulphur and fear. He would resist, he would fight, he would become angry with God. But slowly, gradually, he would soften, and reconcile with God; an invisible hand would touch his heart, and his heart would become serene once more.

He bowed in penitence, then murmured contentedly, "We're friends again, thank God, we're friends again! I feel that the Lord is my neighbor again. It is as though a creditor suddenly crossed off my debts; I am relieved!"

# 10

 $\mathfrak{h}$ E PICKED UP his cap from one of the pews and was about to leave, but as he stuffed his hair inside it, a deep sigh was heard in the darkness, and one of the side pews creaked. Father Yánaros was frightened; his hair stood on end; ashamed at his fear, he took a candle from the stand, lit it from the votive lamp which hung in front of the icon of Christ, and walked toward the pew from where the sigh was heard. The candle trembled in his hand, but he took courage and went on. The flame lowered; an old woman who had been clinging to the pew jumped to her feet; and at the same moment, four other women in the nearby pews lifted their pale, wrinkled faces to the light.

"Who are you? What do you want here? Come forward!" Father Yánaros called out and drew back.

The old women rolled off the side pews and fell in a heap on the slate floor, clinging to the edges of the Bier. The priest bent over them and brought the candle to their faces, one by one; what bitterness, what poison-filled lips, how empty their eyes were, empty from the tears!

These are the faces of Greece, Father Yánaros thought, shuddering, these are the mothers . . .

And suddenly, as he watched these five bereaved women, they seemed to be the five great Hellenic mothers—the Roumeliote, the Macedonian, the Epirote, the Moráitian, and the noble mother of the islands.

"What do you want here in Castello?" he asked, disturbed. "Whom do you seek? Who are you?"

151

They all began to talk at once, to scream, to beat their breasts.

"I don't understand a thing! What is all this noise? Speak, one at a time."

The oldest one rose to her knees and stretched her hand out to stop the others; her face was like stone. "Quiet," she said, "I'll speak; I, the oldest."

She turned to the priest. "We are all mothers—our sons are in the war; some are in the valley, others in the hills; all of us have at least one dead. I'm old Chrystal from Chalika. What's happened to you, Father Yánaros, that you don't recognize me? Your mind is somewhere else—still on the blasphemies."

"I was not blaspheming; no, I was not; you should weigh your words; I was not cursing, I was praying. That's how I pray to God—I don't have to give explanations to anyone!"

He walked over to the candlestand and placed the candle on it, then he turned to the old women; his voice had softened now. "I bow my head and worship your pain, mothers of Greece," he said. "Forgive me, my mind took long to return to earth and recognize you. But now it is here, it has left the flaming heavens, where I was talking to the Pancreator, and I welcome all of you, each one separately. Welcome, Kyra Chrystal, bereaved mother from Chalika; welcome Kyra Marigo from Prastova; and you, too, Kyra Christina from Mangano; and your graciousness Kyra Despina from Croustallo; and you, old Zafiro from Chrysopighi. Welcome to the house of the crucified Lord. What do you want? What are your grievances? I'm listening."

"They've taken our homes, Father Yánaros," old Chrystal groaned. "They've chased us out of our villages, both the blackhoods and the redhoods; they're killing our husbands; we wander from cave to cave, hungry, cold—where can we turn? At whose feet should we fall? How will this tragedy end? The villages sent us to ask you, Father; you speak with God; you are the voice of God—his ears, his eyes—here in these wild, dry hills; you should know!"

"Help us, Father!" The others screamed and got up on their knees. "You're the people's last hope."

Father Yánaros paced up and down the church; he stood before the iconostas and looked at Christ, but he did not see Him; his mind drifted far away, over murky waters. Suddenly the

152

church seemed very narrow to him—as though the walls would collapse if he stretched his arms. "God has placed all the heavy burdens on my shoulders," he murmured. "Hold on, poor Father Yánaros!" He bent over the kneeling women; one by one he took them by the hand and helped them to their feet.

"Each one of you," he said, "has a dead man in the courtyard of your house; but I have thousands in mine, thousands, wrapped in black and red flags. No, not in my courtyard, but in my guts; I can't walk any longer—I stumble. And no matter what corpse I look at, I see my face, because they are all my children."

"Help us, Father!" the old women shouted again. "What shall we do? How will this tragedy end? Do you have a way of saving us, Father Yánaros? That's why we came. If God has enlightened you, tell us, so we can go back to those who sent us; we're in a hurry!"

"I'm in a hurry, too!" the priest shouted, and as he said this, he felt the hours passing and realized that he had little time. He had made his decision; yes, he was in a hurry. He looked at the old women, who had taken hold of the Bier and had begun to scream again.

"Get up—let go of the Bier; stand on your own feet! Aren't you tired of weeping? God abhors weeping; man's tears can turn water mills, but they cannot move God. Wipe your eyes, go back to your caves, call a meeting of the people; open your mouths and shout, 'This is what Father Yánaros from Castello advises; there are three roads that can lead us to freedom—God, our nation's leaders, and the people. God is out, and you may as well accept it. He does not interfere in our business; He gave us a brain, He gave us freedom, He washed His hands of us!'

"Does He hate us? Doesn't He want us? Or does He love us so much that He torments us? I don't know; I'm only a man —a sinner; I cannot know the secrets of God. I know only one thing for a fact; that this road is closed—it's a dead end." He was silent; the votive lamps sputtered; the oil was almost gone. Father Yánaros turned—the face of Christ had clouded. A heavy weight fell over the old man's chest, but he did not move toward the sanctuary to get the oil container and refill the lamps.

153

The first old woman tugged at the ends of the priest's robe. "The second road, Father?" she asked. "Advise us, tell us what it is. Explain to us in simple words, so we can understand—we're uneducated women."

"The second road is our nation's leaders, damn them! All of them—all the leaders! I don't make any distinctions. I'm neither a red nor a black; tell them I am Father Yánaros who speaks with God and who would never condescend to worship cowards. And if you were to tear my heart open, you would find Greece there—the whole of Greece—as it is on the maps that hang in the schoolrooms; she lies from one end of my heart to the other, coursing through my blood. Greece! Tell them this, do you hear?"

"We hear, we hear you, Father," the mothers replied. "Go on, and do not be angry with us; the second road?"

"The second road, too, is closed. Not one leader, either red or black, has the whole of Greece in his heart; all of them have her divided—the criminals have cut her in two, as if she were not alive. And each piece has gone mad and wants to eat the other. Kings, politicians, officers, bishops, leaders in the hills, captains in the valley, all of them, all of them have gone mad! They're wild, hungry wolves, and we, the people, are the meat; they see us as meat and they devour us."

He paused again, panting, as though he were climbing a cliff-ridden hill; he sighed.

"Eh, how wonderful it would be," he murmured, "how comforting it would be for me if I also were blinded; I would join the army, too, either right or left, and have thousands of other blinded ones, behind and around me, and I'd be certain that we were on God's side and that our enemies were on the devil's. And I would gloat over the dead Greeks and say, 'Glory to God, there are fewer bolsheviks now.' Or: 'Glory to God, there are fewer fascists now.' But now I stand alone, deserted, and no matter whose corpse I see, my heart aches; because I see a part of Greece rotting."

He was silent again, lost in his thoughts. The veins in his temples and in his neck puffed out, and bloodstained Greece unfolded before his eyes.

But the first woman stretched her hand out again and tugged at his sleeve. "The third road—the third road, Father?"

"What third road? There is no third road! It hasn't opened yet. We have to open it with our labor, pushing onward to make it a road. And who are the 'we'? The people! This road begins with the people, goes ahead with the people, and ends with the people. Many times lightning tears through my mind. 'Who knows,' I say, 'perhaps God is pushing us to the edge of this tragedy to force us to open this third road—whether we want to or not—to save ourselves.' Mothers, I don't know what stand to take, how to judge. But if you ask my heart, it says that this is the reason, this is what God wants. 'Grow up,' He tells us. 'Don't keep hanging from my coattails like children; stand up and walk alone!' "

The old women did not quite understand all that the priest had said, but their hearts calmed down a little; they tied their black kerchiefs tightly; they covered their brows, their chins, their ears, their mouths; they composed themselves for the trip.

But old Kyra Chrystal lingered. The priest's words had warmed her heart, but her mind was still in the dark.

"So?" she said and waited, her eyes on the priest.

"So now the moon will come out; take to the road, call your fellow villagers and tell them what Father Yánaros of Castello advises: Tomorrow, before high noon, all of you, along with your families, gather here in Castello; God has entrusted me with a secret. Whether I understood it or not, we shall see! But no other road exists. Go, with my blessings."

He raised his hand and blessed the five kerchiefed heads; then he unlocked the door.

"With the blessings of God and our country," he said and made the sign of the cross over the heads of the old women.

He stood at the threshold of the church and looked at the mothers, walking one behind the other along the wall, and disappearing. The moon rose from behind the rocky hill; the air smelled of decay.

"Poor Greece," the priest murmured, watching the mothers disappear among the rocks, "poor unfortunate Greece, in her black kerchief."

# II

The moon rose in the sky and descended to earth; the demolished houses of the village shone quietly, happily, as though they were still sheltering the embracing couples. And the jackals had arrived; they wandered through the ruins, licking their chops.

Unable to sleep, two old men who had lost their minds from fear and hunger stumbled, singing, among the rubble. It was an old song, from the days of their youth, which spoke of love and death. Occasionally they would stop, embrace, and burst into laughter.

The moonlight, silent and pale, entered the latticed window of Father Yánaros' cell; it flooded the Second Coming with silver, and on the wall it lit up the crown of flames worn by St. Constantine, and the burning coals beneath his feet; but the saint was invisible.

Father Yánaros sat on the edge of his cot and rested his heavy head against the wall.

"Lord," he murmured, "thank you for this bitter cup you have given me again today; I don't know why You treat those who love You so cruelly, but I have enough faith to believe that whatever You do, You do for our own good, regardless of whether we understand it or not. What audacity for man to want to understand Your actions, Lord! Forgive us; it is not man who questions, my Lord. It is not man, but Satan, who

156

hovers over our heads and questions, questions continuously, incessantly. Our heart does not question, it has faith, it is certain. Night has fallen, it covers the world; another full day, praise God, a very tiring one; I am exhausted. And I still have work to do, difficult work, this night. You said I am free to do as I choose, so, then, I *will* do as I choose; I'm going up to the hill."

He closed his eyes, hoping to sleep, to gather strength before beginning the uphill climb; he waited and waited. But the angel of sleep would not come. Beneath his closed eyelids passed the Passions of Christ together with the passions of man, and suddenly his mind drifted far away, to another Good Friday, a sunlit day when he, with pouch over his shoulder, roamed in search of a nest for his soul. Tall monasteries, like fortresses! Matins, beautiful hymns, monks of all sorts—well-fed, ill-fed, ascetics and hypocrites—the Holy Mount; and on the peak of this mount, God-trodden, touching the sky, the snow-capped Athos.

How he remembered it all! Nothing had faded from his memory; he saw the altar clearly, where the fathers had lined up after matins, to eat a piece of dry bread. A long, narrow hall, the murals peeling on the walls were moldy from time and dampness. The air smelled of boiled cabbage and of sourness.

A swallow entered from the open window and fluttered over the bowed heads of the monks. It recognized each one of them; they were the same monks as last year, a bit older, a bit paler; Manasses, Joachim, Gabriel, Melchizedek, Benedictus—all of them, all of them were there, not a single one was missing. The bird was pleased, and it fluttered gaily, tweeting over the head of the abbot, longing to pluck out a hair of his white beard to strengthen its nest, but as it opened its beak, fear overcame it; it rushed for the open window, toward the light, and disappeared.

Not one monk raised his eyes to look at the bird; over forty of them were crowded at the long, narrow monasterial table, bent and grimacing as they chewed their beans and olives without much appetite. The waiter moved silently about, distributing the wheat bread. Today was Good Friday; the monks sighed as they counted the hours until the Resurrection; when would

157

it come, dear God? A small monk who had climbed high on the pulpit was reading from the Passion Gospels. He was round and pale, and his voice had still not settled at its proper level— no longer a boy's, not yet a man's; he crowed hoarsely: "They climbed, they climbed Golgotha; Christ in the front, bent from the weight of the cross; it was very heavy, you see, the sins of the world had fallen upon it. They climbed, they climbed, and behind them was the Virgin Mary, who beat her breasts and lamented. And others, thousands and thousands of women, mourned after the Virgin Mother; the whole world's mothers, and thousands upon thousands of eyes cried, and lips moaned, and hands raised to the heavens and motioned to the angels to descend. And suddenly there was a great silence, followed by a heart-rending cry that came from the insides of the earth: 'Do not cry, Holy Mother, take courage; take courage, Holy Mother, so the world may take courage, too.' "

The neophyte reader crowed hoarsely as he went on with the terrible plight; and the dawn began to break. The lead dome of the church shone as though it were made of silver, and a large domesticated blackbird perched on the edge of the well and began to whistle the hymn which the monks had taught him. The sound of cackling partridges from the deep ravine rang throughout the monastery.

Father Yánaros, who was seated at the end of the table, raised his eyes; he looked at the monks from one end of the table to the other; his eyebrows knitted in anger. He stretched his neck to observe them, one by one, and he looked at each face with compassion and disgust. They were old and half-witted, cowardly, doubting gluttons. Is that, then, what the holy monastic life did to them? They had all paled and rotted from the dampness; their hands and feet were eaten away, nothing was left but the seven holes in each of their faces—eyes, mouth, nostrils, ears. Or could it be that the Last Supper had come down from the wall where it was painted, peeling from age, and the Apostles now sat, worried and silent, waiting . . . What are they waiting for? Whom are they waiting for? Why are they looking toward the door? Where is Christ?

The smell from the damp ravine floated through the window; the first songbirds awoke, the cocks in the courtyard crowed,

158

and from a distance came the gentle, sweet sound of the cuckoo.

Father Yánaros' temples felt refreshed; he closed his eyes, and that small voice was heard again: "The cursed gypsies have raised their hammers; they were ordered to make three nails, but they made five, and they began to nail Christ to the cross. At the first blow of the hammer, the heavens shook; at the second, angels descended from heaven carrying clean sheets and perfumes and golden jugs of rosewater to wash the wounds; at the third stroke, the Virgin Mother fainted and with her, the world, and darkness fell . . ."

Father Yánaros kept his eyes closed; he felt the pain, as though nails were being hammered into his own hands and feet; he rested his head against the wall on the half-peeled painting of the Last Supper. A white dog with pale blue spots was painted at their feet; the dog was licking a bone. The altar, the monks, the monastery disappeared; Mount Athos disappeared. Father Yánaros stood at the foot of the cross and looked up; he stared, and the blood trickled, and Christ fixed his eyes upon him and smiled.

Father Yánaros let out a cry; he felt faint; this was all that he could remember now. Unable to see the young monk who was reading any longer, he jumped up in terror and stretched out his hand toward the pulpit. "Don't desert Christ on the cross," he shouted. "Hurry and get on to the Resurrection."

He heard voices and confusion outside his cell; people rushed back and forth shouting in the courtyard; many hands began to knock on his door. Father Yánaros opened his eyes, the Holy Mount had disappeared and a crowd had gathered in the road; he could hear his name clearly now. He jumped up, opened the door and as he stood barefoot on the threshold, his hair spilling over his shoulders, he spread out his arms to the right and left, blocking anyone from entering. A large group of men and women had gathered, and their faces glowed wildly in the light of the moon.

"Eh, Father Yánaros," one of them shouted; it sounded like the shrill voice of old man Mandras. "Eh, Father Yánaros, what's all this again? Aren't you going to ring the bell? Go on, open up the church!"

159

"Quiet, quiet! Stop shouting!" the priest replied. "There is no vigil tonight, and there will be no Resurrection tomorrow. Go back to your homes! Christ will lay in His Bier as long as you continue killing one another, fratricides!"

"What's that?" "What's that?" "Mercy on us, Lord!" Frantic voices shouted among the crowd. "Have you ever heard of such a thing in all of Christendom?" "Aren't you afraid of God?"

"Greece is being crucified; you're crucifying her, Iskariotes, and as long as Greece is being crucified, so will Christ. As long as you kill one another, you criminals, He will not rise from the dead. Not in Chalika, or in Prastova, or in Castello; nowhere in these hills where my vestments empower me shall I resurrect Him!"

"So you won't take Christ out of the grave? You'll leave Him like that all year, in the Bier? Well, it's your sin, Father Yánaros—it's your conscience!"

"The sin is mine. I can take it; return to your homes!" Old Mandras pushed through the crowd and stood before the priest; he raised his staff. "You think you can crucify Christ and not resurrect Him?" he said, and foam spat from his mouth.

"I can! I asked and I received permission. Your hands are covered with blood—all of you—go wash them first! Resurrection means clean hands and a clean heart! Christ does not want to be resurrected in Castello, He told me so. He refuses to be resurrected!"

"The bishop will disrobe you for this, you Judas!"

Father Yánaros laughed. "Don't try to frighten me. If the bishop disrobes me, I will merely walk into Paradise without robes."

An old woman screamed, "Don't you worry, you Antichrist, we mothers will gather and resurrect Christ ourselves!"

"Go to your homes," Father Yánaros shouted. "Go!"

He tried to close the door, but old Mandras' staff struck him, and blood spurted from the priest's brow. Kyriákos stooped over and picked up a rock to throw, but he was frightened, and the rock slipped out of his hand.

Curses rose from the people; several black-dressed women threw back their kerchiefs and began to beat their breasts and lament Christ. Father Yánaros wiped the blood from his face; his beard dripped with it.

"Greek fratricides," he shouted, "you want a Resurrection, eh? Do you dare resurrect Christ, you fools? Shame on you!" He slammed the door shut.

"Goat-beard!" "Antichrist!" "Judas!" came the voices, and Kyriákos took courage, grabbed the rock he had dropped, and hurled it at the door.

"Let's go, friends!" Mandras shouted and took the lead. "Let's go to the captain and report this scoundrel!"

One by one the lamps went out inside the houses; the soldiers, lying on their bunks in the barracks, talked softly among themselves, their rifles at their sides. The guards, scattered outside, listened with cocked ears, but the only sound to be heard was a gray owl flying by, or a jackal howling with satisfaction, or a hungry dog barking at the moon which rose sadly over the hill.

The captain, unable to sleep, sat disgruntled, on the threshold of the barracks, smoking one cigarette after another. How could he sleep when the village they had entrusted to him was in danger, when his soldiers deserted every day—one by one; when there was hardly enough food or ammunition left? They had left him, forgotten him here in this wilderness, where he guarded the narrow straits so that the barbarians would not pass. But the barbarians were passing, they were in the village now. Who knows, they may be meeting on the hill, they may even be meeting secretly in the night, too, damn them!

He threw his cigarette down and stamped on it with his worn army boot.

"Fortresses are captured from within," he murmured, "not from without; our enemies are inside. I must clean them out! And first of all that priest; he's too big a bite to chew, the scoundrel, but I'll chew him yet!"

He got up and went for a short walk to feel the cold night wind upon him; on the hilltop the rebels had lit fires; the captain's blood rushed to his head at sight of them; he shook his fist toward the hill.

"Dishonorable ones," he growled, "traitors who sold out your country! I'll get you yet!"

As he said this, a great pain clutched his heart; he remembered the first days he had come to Castello; one morning he had fallen asleep and had dreamed a dream; he dreamt that he

161

lay asleep in the crumbled Chapel of the Forerunner on the side of the hill. And that suddenly, in his sleep, he heard weeping; he opened his eyes, and a woman dressed in black—mourning —stood before him. She was very pretty and very pale, with large eyes, and tears streamed down her cheeks and on her chin.

"Who are you?" he asked, and held out his hands, assuming that she was the Virgin. "Don't you recognize me?" she replied. "Don't you recognize me, my Captain?"

"Who are you?" he asked again and began to tremble.

Her voice came soft and sad. "I am Greece, my son. My people are sending me away. I have nowhere to lay my head, so I came to seek refuge with you, my son."

He screamed and jumped to his feet; tears streamed down his face.

"Mother," he murmured, "don't cry, I won't leave you alone and unprotected; have faith, I will die for your sake!"

From that day, the captain became another man. He had fought in the Great War—once in the Albanian hills, another time on the African sands—one Greek among thousands —a brave fighter among thousands of brave fighters. At first, he was just a plain soldier; but slowly, by daring, he received the stripes of an N.C.O., then the stars of an officer. He became a captain, like many others. But from the night of that dream, he could sleep no more. He felt that Greece no longer stood before him; she was inside him now, calling to him for help. If she is lost, I am to blame, he thought. If she is saved, I will have saved her. And he would leap into battle with fury. Only once, cursed be the day, only once did he forget Greece. He had returned from battle one night and did not find his wife at home; she had taken to the hills to join the rebels.

He spat and turned back—it was midnight now, and he returned to the barracks; cold sweat poured from his brow and from his armpits.

"Forgive me, Mother," he murmured, "I forgot you that day; but we're only human, we poor unfortunates; we love our wives, and we humiliate ourselves because of them."

He sat down, cross-legged, leaned his head against the wall of the barracks, and his thoughts went far, to that village in the hills of Roumeli, to his mother, to the sands of Africa; his mind

162

brought him back to Castello and to Father Yánaros and to his soldiers; it would not let him dwell on his shameless wife who was sleeping with God only knows whom at this hour. But his mind kept going back, again and again, to his wife.

"God damn her, God damn her," he murmured, "the lion fears only one thing—the louse; but I won't let her get me down, no I won't let her!"

He lit a cigarette and leaned back again.

In one of the neighborhoods at the edge of town, near the barracks, a door opened slowly—halfway—and an old woman's head appeared, a red ribbon in her hair. She looked up and down; the lamps were out, the road was deserted; the old woman took courage and stepped out of the door. She was barefooted, a patched shawl was wrapped about her, and she walked, crouching, from wall to wall; every so often she would turn to see if anyone was following her. She crept silently to the barracks and saw the captain, who was now standing up against the wall, deep in thought. Her heart beat wildly; she stopped to catch her breath, and she trembled. The moonlight fell upon her; she was old, all wrinkles, and her large eyes were filled with fire. Her hands were cold, stiff, eaten away by the many clothes she had washed; the whole town taunted her, and the villagers roared with laughter when they met her on the street; so she went out only at night or early dawn. She was Kyra Polyxeni, a servant since childhood in the house of old Mandras. She was in her sixties, and now in her later years she had taken to wearing a red ribbon in her hair. Her long years of virginity had affected her mind; she had dizzy spells and often she would fall screaming to the ground. Not too long ago she had fallen in love with the village butcher, Thanasi, a young man of thirty. Every Saturday night she would put the red ribbon in her hair and linger outside the butcher shop, sighing.

"When will you marry me, Kyr Thanasi?" she would ask every time she caught him alone, "when are we getting married, my dear? I can't stand it any longer." And, to get rid of her, he would answer, "I need a large dowry, my turtledove; we're going to have a lot of children, you know, and children cost money; I want you to live like a queen."

163

"How much of a dowry, Thanasi dear?"

"I want twelve hammocks, six silver censers, and fifty pairs of men's shorts."

"Very well, my treasure, I'll go tell my master." She would return to the house and fall at the feet of old Mandras.

"Master," she would say to him, "take pity on me, give me twelve hammocks, six silver censers, and fifty pairs of men's undershorts so I can marry Kyr Thanasi; otherwise, he says he will not have me."

Old Mandras would laugh. "The son of a bitch wants too much; I can't give you that, Polyxeni. Where would I find fifty pairs of shorts? Let him be." And the poor soul would go back to the butcher. "The master says he can't give me all that. It's too much for him."

"Well, it just wasn't meant to be, my dear; we can't go against Fate, can we?"

"Let's elope!" she would reply, and wiggle her hips.

"All right," he said to her one night when he had had enough of her nagging, "I'll come for you at midnight, and we'll elope. You be ready, now." She went running back to the house, waited for everyone to fall asleep, bathed, washed and combed her hair, changed her clothing, and hid behind the main door and waited. She waited . . . midnight came and left, the dawn broke, but Kyr Thanasi was nowhere in sight! The poor woman fell ill from disillusionment; the dizzy spells increased, her mind dulled, and the years passed. But her heart could not remain idle; she fell in love with Stelianos the weaver. She liked him because he had a deep voice and large ears. One evening she cornered him in church after vespers, when everyone had gone. "Stelianos, my dear," she said, "would you like to marry me?"

"How can I, Polyxeni?" He understood her grief and felt sorry for her. "Can I help it if I'm already married? But my brother Sophocles, the army officer, loves you—I know that for a fact. Wait until he returns to the village, and then he'll marry you."

Sly old Mandras heard of this and he went to Stelianos; together they talked and plotted. And when poor Polyxeni went to Stelianos to ask when her beloved was coming, he told her that he had just received a letter from him. "And what does he say about me, Stelianos, my dear?"

"He says he's coming at Christmas and that he wants only this of you: that you continue to be a good housekeeper and keep cleaning your master's chicken coop, that you do the washings without complaining, and that you take care not to break his dishes; and he also said not to ask Mandras for wages—don't stoop to such a thing—don't forget, you are an officer's woman! You must be proud!"

She waited for Christmas; it came and went. The next Christmas came and went, too, and the years rolled by. Kyra Polyxeni's hair turned white, her breasts sagged, her teeth dropped out, the fuzz on her upper lip thickened. Then the civil war broke out, and the captain came to the village. "My brother Sophocles is here," Stelianos told her. "Go find him and talk things over."

And so, now, every night, the poor woman wraps herself in her patched shawl and when the town is asleep, she steals silently from the house toward the barracks; and when she sees the captain alone, she crawls before him and trembles. Once the captain raised his hand to strike her, and she crossed her hands with happiness. "Hit me, my beloved," she said, "hit me so I can feel your hand upon me."

But tonight, as he suddenly heard her sighing, he became furious. "I'm not in a good mood tonight," he growled, "go away!"

"All right, all right, I'm leaving, my dear," she said obediently, and tightening her hole-ridden shawl about her, she turned back, running from one wall to another, and disappeared.

"I'm going to lose my mind in this place," growled the captain and began to pace back and forth, cursing the rebels, the teacher, Father Yánaros, this idiot woman . . .

"Come here, Mitros," he called to his sergeant, "let's sit down. What do you say about this devil-priest, this Father Yánaros?"

The sergeant wrinkled his face and shrugged his shoulders.

"What can I say, Captain? It's a strange thing; when he's not around, I'm not afraid of him, in fact I can grab him by his beard and pull out the hairs one by one. But the minute he comes in view, 'Get thee behind me, Satan!' My knees buckle. What can that mean? Do you think that what he says is true?

But damn it, if it's true, then the devil has really taken us, sir!"

"What does he say, Mitros? Don't make faces—tell me!"

"He says, 'Christ stands at the right of me; no one can see Him except I, and that's why I'm not afraid of anyone!' Do you think it's true, Captain, sir?"

The captain's anger had mounted. "I think that you're beginning to lose your mind, too, Mitros. It's time to leave here, before we all lose our senses; that's why I called you. Now listen, I don't like Father Yánaros' actions at all. Don't you see him? He's getting a little too dangerous; he talks secretly with the soldiers; every so often he goes into the house of that tubercular teacher, that bolshevik. You mark my words, that impostor is cooking up something with that traitor son of his in the hills. What do you think? Hey, I'm talking to you—where's your mind?"

The sergeant shook his head. "I don't know what to say, Captain. There's one thing I keep trying to push out of my mind, but it just won't go! All this Holy Week it's been eating me up inside—day and night; I'm glad I found you in good spirits tonight so I can ask you; may I, sir?"

"Go on."

"Do you think, sir, that that sash of the Virgin is real?"

The captain shrugged his shoulders. "What do you care, Mitros? Whether it's real or false, it does its job; you heard what that monk shouted when he passed the barracks, didn't you? 'Kill! Kill, and receive the blessings of the Virgin! Kill the red-hoods, and be sanctified!' That's what he cried, bless him! The people hear the voice of God from the lips of the monk and they kill with more fervor; that sash is more effective than a cannon."

"But Father Yánaros says that he is the voice of God, Captain," the sergeant dared to answer, "and yet he preaches completely different things. 'Kill, kill!' shouts the one; 'Don't kill, don't kill!' shouts the other; which of the two is the true voice of God? Or does God have many voices?"

The captain snickered. "Don't be stupid, Mitros," he said, "don't you see what's going on all over the world? Or do you think we're the only ones who have rebels? What do you think they're doing everywhere else on earth? One head dares to rise up and bang! Down it goes! That's what we're going to do, too. That's the meaning of the Holy Sash."

"But for how long, Captain? I don't know what the Russians are doing or the Chinese or the Africans; but there's only a few of us—we're going to be wiped out . . ."

"That's enough talk!" the captain said nervously. "God help us if we start asking questions at this point—we'll all go to the devil! A soldier is supposed to kill and not ask questions. Now go!"

# 12

THE MOON balanced on the peak of the hill; the stars were dimmed by its light, and only a few, the nearer ones, shone in the quiet night. The earth smelled of sulphur and God's presence. Having reached a decision, Father Yánaros hurriedly climbed the difficult uphill road. At intervals an owl hooted sadly and fluttered from rock to rock; Father Yánaros would turn his large head toward it and spit three times in the air, to exorcise any evil that might lie ahead.

He had gathered his patched robe around him and tucked it under his wide leather belt; his legs, bare to the knees, shone in the light of the moon; they were twisted, knotted, like the aged trunks of olive trees. His hat had fallen and pressed against his thorny, still-black eyebrows, and his wild, quick-moving eyes flashed from inside their deep sockets.

He looked around quickly, behind him, ahead of him; Father Yánaros knew these hills well; they were wild hills, all rocks and pebbles. Not a green tree, or grazing sheep, or villages or people; only thorny thyme, wild plants, and pitiful bushes. In the sky were vultures; above them, hawks; and higher, hungry eagles, and still higher—God!

"Poor Greece!" murmured Father Yánaros, shaking his head, toughened by the sun and the rains. "Poor, unfortunate Greece! You're all rock and wilderness and hunger; you're all blood!"

His gaze moved more slowly, more compassionately now, from side to side, from hill to hill, caressing the shoulders of

Greece. Slowly, tenderly, with compassion and pride. And as though she felt the caress, Greece came alive under this loving gaze and shivered from happiness.

He rested his chin on his thick staff, and the old memories came back; his heart swelled, it could hold no more, and it beat against his aged chest to escape. "Where will you go?" the old fighter asked her, as though she were a beloved partridge that he had locked in a cage to listen to her singing. "Where will you go, you little fool? Sit quietly, you're all right here!

"You're all glory and hunger, my poor Greece," he shouted. "From your toes to your head, you're all soul. You must not be destroyed; no, Mother, we will not let you be destroyed!"

He threw back his head, tightened his hold on his staff, and thrust it with might into the ground, as though he were taking an oath. Then he looked about at the bald, deserted hills that were saturated with blood; he looked at the rocks, the cliffs, and he was overcome with divine respect.

"God was born here in these wild hills," he murmured, "the God of Greece—our God, with the evzone skirts, the shin guards, the *tsarouchia*, and our Pancreator was made from these bloodstained rocks. Every nation has its own God; this is our God; this is the one we use—stone of our stone, blood of our blood—pained, a thousand times wounded, stubborn like us, immortal."

He stooped and picked up a black pebble splattered with fresh blood; he kissed it and placed it in the crack of a cliff, as though it were holy bread, so no one would step on it.

He felt the Invisible around him, as hard as the stone, scented like the thyme; the uninhabited hilltops filled with God, and Father Yánaros' heart neighed like a stallion; he was not alone and desolate in the world; all of God was with him; he suddenly felt a supernatural strength in his heart and in his hands; he gained new courage, and the stones began to roll under his boots again.

Other years, on days like tomorrow—Holy Saturday—what a sweet aroma hung over the villages! The ovens were lit, the freshly scrubbed thresholds sparkled, the excited housewives hurried in and out, holding large baskets filled with Easter breads and red eggs, under their arms! What joy it was! How the

169

peasants glowed—how much handsomer they seemed! All year round their faces were like wolves', like pigs'; and on this day their expressions softened; Christ was resurrected within them, and they became people. Father Yánaros would hurry and resurrect Christ at midnight in Castello, then, with his gold-embroidered vestment under his arm, he would immediately make the rounds of the hills; he would speed to the village of Chalika before daybreak, and resurrect Christ there, too, then he would tear away again, and, with the first rays of the sun, panting and sweating, he would reach Prastova! The small chapel sparkled, sun-drenched; the ascetic saints painted on the walls smiled; Christ waited for Father Yánaros and Father Yánaros would bow, worship, and raise Him from the tomb; he would take Him in his arms, slowly, slowly, with gentleness, with pain, as though He were the body of a dead son. He would read the holy exorcisms to bring Him from Hades, he would open the heavy, silver Book of the Gospel, stand on the platform in the churchyard, make his voice deeper and read: "The first day of the week cometh Mary Magdalene early, when it was yet dark, unto the sepulcher, and seeth the stone taken away from the sepulcher." And immediately, from everyone's chest, leaped the cry "Christos anesti!" "Christ has risen!" All the candles would be lit, flooding the area with faint, flickering light; mustaches and eyes and lips and braids glowed; and people fell into each other's arms, kissing and embracing, while Father Yánaros, exhausted and happy, folded his vestment, rolled up his sleeves and turned, leaping with the sun, toward Castello!

His feet suddenly felt heavy; he was tired. He had reached the side of the hill, and he paused at the deserted Chapel of the Forerunner; his mouth filled with bitterness as he looked at the ruins. Several days ago there had been a battle here; bombs had fallen on the desolate chapel. The roof and walls had collapsed; the old Byzantine icons hung in the air.

He climbed over the piles of stone and fallen rafters; he entered, removed his cap, and worshiped the air. The full-length paintings of Christ and the Virgin Mother on the curvature of the sanctuary had crumbled and lay in heaps of paint and asbestos on the altar. Only one wall stood erect—the one depicting the Forerunner, with his yellow bony neck, his twisted beard, the lamb's skin and the reedlike legs. But a bomb had hit the angry prophet in the middle, and his stomach had opened, showing his intestines—plaster and stone and dirt; and these, too, would crumble if a mild breeze blew, or a light rain began to fall, and all that would remain would be the ends of the prophet's feet at the base of the wall and a piece of the River Jordan. Two humble wooden candlestands were still smoking, but the old gold-plated iconostas with the carved filigree grapevine had become ashes.

Anger rose within Father Yánaros as his eyes steeled on the disemboweled Forerunner. "I'd better leave," he said, "I'd better leave, before I begin to blaspheme again; I can't hold on any longer; You are almighty, Lord, and You can control Yourself, but I cannot!"

The blasphemy played on his tongue; he hurriedly climbed over the rubble and went outside. Walking around the north wall, which was still standing, he paused as he discerned thick spots of blood on it. He approached and saw blood and hairs from female braids; here and there the wall was spattered with brains. Father Yánaros' eyes filled with tears; anger consumed him; he wiped his eyes with his wide palms and controlled himself, but he could not take his eyes from the wall.

Only two days ago, here at this deserted chapel, he had listened to their confessions and given them communion. His heart had wavered then, and he tried to leave, but he was ashamed, and he remained to watch their execution. There were seven of them—three old women and four girls. A monk from Mount Athos had turned them in for helping the rebels; they had been caught one night climbing the hill, carrying sackfuls of cheese, bread, heavy stockings, and woolen sweaters, secretly knitted for the rebels during the wintry nights.

The government troops lined them up against the wall. The leader of the squad was Sergeant Mitros, the naïve, goodhearted lad from Roumeli; he was quiet, innocent, and he liked to eat well; his mind was always on his wife and their baby son, far away in a small village near Karpenisi; but on this day his lips had twisted, his eyes filled with blood. They had given him seven women to kill, and his brain had clouded; inside him his heart resisted, and he shouted angrily, to smother its voice.

Mitros turned to the seven women who were lined up against

171

the wall; he let out a cry and Father Yánaros was terrified; that was not his voice, it was an ancient hairy beast that awakened and growled within Mitros' innocent Roumeliotic chest; "Eh, you dirty bolsheviks, I'll take care of you now! Have you anything to say? Hurry!"

"Nothing, nothing, nothing!" replied each one of the three old women.

The fourth, eighteen-year-old Chryssoula, the teacher from Prastova, raised her head; her hair spilled over her naked back, bloody and scarred with whipping.

"I have something to say!"

"Speak up, you slut!"

"*Long live Greece!*"

And at that moment, all seven of them began to sing the Greek national anthem: "From the bones of my ancestors . . ."

But the shots rang out.

The priest made the sign of the cross, approached, and worshiped the splattered remains.

"I don't ask," he murmured, "I don't ask who is justified, and who is not; I don't know—I've lost all sense of reason; I'm old. But my heart cries within. 'One day,' it shouts, 'a new church may be built over these ruins of the Forerunner, for the seven female forerunners!' "

He stood there, lost in thought, for a few minutes; then he bowed, took a piece of charred rock from the ground, and entered. "I shall write their names on the wall," he said.

And he began to write on the whitewashed wall in large, heavy capital letters: PELAGIA, FROSO, ARETI, CHRYSSOULA, KATERINA, MARTHA, DESPINIO.

"What are you smearing on the wall, old man? A memoriam announcement?"

The priest jumped, shaken out of his holy encounter with the seven forerunners; a woman dressed like a nun stood before him; she was tall, big-boned, with proud eyebrows and blond hair that fell, curly and thick, from her black velvet cap; her eyes shimmered in the light of the moon, like those of a tigress. Father Yánaros recognized her as the army captain's wife.

"What do you want here," he asked, "which way are you going?"

"Toward the hill; haven't you heard, old man? I deliver messages to the comrades."

She took a stride and came closer; ironic, her voice rang out. "Do I have your blessings, Father?"

The priest threw up his hand; he raised and lowered it, slapping the air with disgust. "You have my blessings and my curses, all of you—reds and blacks alike! Why did you desert your home and husband, you shameless woman? What devil took you and carried you off?"

The woman burst into laughter. "You call it devil—I call it freedom."

"Freedom without virtue or goodness is of the devil; does freedom mean leaving your husband, burning villages, killing? I don't understand it."

"You've gotten old, Father Yánaros—you've gotten old! The world goes forward, it's gone ahead of you and you can't understand it. I don't have time to talk with you, we have work to do. Good health to you, old man!"

The woman laughed; jumping over the rocks, she began the uphill climb. She stopped a moment, removed her cap, and wiped away the perspiration; her hair spilled over her shoulders.

"Eh, Father Yánaros, make room, it's our turn now," she shouted, and went on her way.

Father Yánaros watched her as she climbed and disappeared from sight. For a moment, he forgot himself. "What strength," he murmured, "what life, what youth! Why do I demand virtue and honor of such a body? Let her get it out of her system first; let her eat up the world and become satiated and have her mouth fill with ashes! Then, virtue and goodness will appear from the ruins."

He recalled the day she had arrived at Castello, last year, to join her husband, the captain. What joy that was, what embracing and kissing in front of the whole village, which had come out to welcome her! The captain had picked her up in his arms, and his angry eyes had softened and filled with tears! Two months went by, three months; but one night when he arrived home from battle, he found the house empty, deserted; his wife had left; she had taken to the hills, joined the rebels; her eyes had seen too much—too much blood, murder, and injustice; she

173

could stand it no longer, so she left, leaving a note behind on the table: "I can't live with you any longer. I'm leaving." And below that, "And stop killing unarmed men and innocent people for revenge."

The captain read the note, reread it, over and over; he did not utter a sound; he only bit his lips and trembled. It was night and he turned to the door to leave, but he stumbled; he fell down, hitting his head on the threshold. He felt no pain and did not rise; he merely shifted to a sitting position, leaned against the wall, and lit a cigarette. It was January, penetratingly cold, but the captain sat with his head tilted back, staring at the heavens with empty eyes. The next morning Mitros found the captain asleep, still leaning against the door, icicles hanging from his mustache.

The captain opened his eyes but did not speak; he rose, pushed away the sergeant's extended hands, and turned toward the church. He entered, locked the door and lit a candle; Mitros, afraid that the captain might kill himself, had followed him and now watched through the keyhole. The captain had placed the candle before the icon of the Virgin and for a long time he looked at its flame, until his eyes clouded with tears. Then he fell upon it and blew it out.

"I don't have a wife any more, Virgin Mother," he shouted. "It was only a lighted candle and now it has gone out." From that day on, his lips were sealed, and darkness fell over his face; his soul became bile, his eyes filled with blood. Only one hope had remained for him—death! And he threw himself in the front line, unsheltered, standing erect in every battle; but he always returned to Castello, alive and discouraged.


When the woman finally disappeared from view, Father Yánaros lifted his hands to the sky. "May God stretch out his hand," he whispered, "over the good and the bad, over the honorable and the dishonorable ones; we're all human beings—idiots and unfortunates—let Him overlook that; we don't know what's going on around us; how many times Satan takes on the face of God to trick us! Our eyes are clay—dirt and tears—how can they distinguish? Take a sponge, Lord, take a sponge and erase!"

174

He felt relieved after these words, as though he had placed the sponge in God's hand and God had begun to erase the sins of man.

He turned toward the seven names he had marked with the charcoal on the wall, made the sign of the cross, and began his upward climb again. He was almost at the peak of Mount Etoraki; the fires which were lit at the rebel positions kept getting brighter; the voices and laughter could be heard clearer now. And the moon had slipped from the middle of the sky and begun its descent.

The rebel voices sounded wilder as he climbed; Father Yánaros could see silhouettes moving quickly in front of the fires, as though they were dancing. The old man's heart began to beat quickly, excitedly, and asked, Should you or shouldn't you? Was his decision right, would it bring freedom? God had left him alone to decide, and he had decided; when he had made up his mind, he was certain that this was the right road to take; but now, as he approached, his knees gave way; new voices rose within him: "They'll trick you, be careful, Father Yánaros; they'll trick you; how can you trust men who do not believe in God?"

The grinding of gravel was heard, and Father Yánaros turned; a wild-faced, sunburned chief shepherd with a crook in his hand had appeared from behind the rocks and faced him. His eyes were small, quick-moving beads, wild and frightened like a beast's; he wore a short goatskin cape, a dirty, round black cap with a worn-out tassel, and his bowed legs were wrapped in torn blue socks. Father Yánaros recognized him.

"Eh, Dimos," he said, gathering his eyebrows, "what are you doing here? Where are you going?"

Dimos looked at him from the side of his sly peasant eyes and remained silent.

"You old goat, why did you desert the village and take to the hill, eh, tell me!" the priest asked.

The shepherd opened his mouth. "What village? There's no more village—it's gone! And the homes? They're gone, too. They pound stakes in the ground, stretch out string. 'This was where my house stood,' they say. 'No, further in,' the neighbors growl; and then and there they fall upon each other, and those who've remained alive are now killing each other."

The shepherd scratched his pointed jackal-like head. He watched the priest guardedly, from the side.

"Go on, get back to your work, Dimos," Father Yánaros said. "Don't mix with either side—left or right—don't become a slave to either. God gave you a free soul—go back to your goats."

"What goats? Do you feel all right, old man? The whole world's collapsing—or don't you know about it? What goats are you talking about? The reds were hungry, so they took half of them, and the blacks took the other half—they were hungry, too. All I'm left with is this staff. So tonight, I'm taking the road uphill."

"With the rebels? What devil has saddled you, Dimos? Speak up. So you want to kill?"

"Yes, I do."

"Why? Why?"

"The leader in the hills will tell me why."

"I'm a leader, too, and I say to you: Don't kill!"

"And let them kill me? Then, kill me, my Aga, so I can go to heaven! This is a cut-and-dried matter—kill or be killed! Better to be the mother of a murderer than the mother of the murdered."

"And why did you choose to go with the rebels? They get killed, too."

"I'm going with the poor and the wronged because I'm poor and wronged myself."

"Who taught you all this foolishness, Dimos? You used to be a goat—you hardly spoke, you only bleated."

"I'm beginning to talk now, Father, what do you think? Did you think I'd go on bleating forever?"

He stepped back, tossed his cape over his right shoulder, and looked mockingly at the priest.

"For your own good, Father," he said—and indeed his voice sounded like the bleating of a goat—"for your own good, you'd better join the dance willingly, otherwise, I'll be damned if they don't force you to join them, and make you like it, too."

He jumped to avoid the swing of the priest's staff, and disappeared behind the rocks.

Father Yánaros cursed himself and began to climb again, his head bowed and his knees weak.

He climbed and climbed, no longer able to think; he had suffered this day. He was only human. He was tired.

Suddenly he seemed to hear the voice of his son, and he was frightened. I'm going to see him now, he thought, shuddering. Any minute now he's going to jump before me, heavy, hairy, with his long arms, and lips filled with laughter and blasphemy. Lord, how did such a demon come from my body? Why did he come to this world? Why did You send him, Lord? What secret message did You entrust him with? I want to curse him, but I'm afraid; I try to give him my blessing, but I'm afraid to do that, too. What manner of beast is this? His parents' home was not big enough for him, and one night he opened the door and disappeared. He circled the world, mingled with women, dipped in sin, denied God, denied his country, even denied his father's name. Here he is Captain Drakos, holding the peak of Etoraki with fire and the sword! And here am I—Lord have mercy on me—about to surrender the village, the soul, the life, the honor of my people, to *him*.

He sighed. Again he heard his heart beating wildly, wanting to escape. At this moment he found it very difficult to be human, to be thrown out of God's bosom as the old eagle suddenly pushes the fledglings from their nest. "Fly if you can, otherwise, be killed!" And the young birds reply, "Father, our wings are not strong enough yet; be patient and wait! Why don't you wait?"

"Don't cling to me, let go—be free!" the eagle replies, and pushes them into the void.

"Yes, Lord, yes, I reproach You," Father Yánaros said. "Why did You arm me with the two-edged sword? Why did You make me free, and then hang the wages of sin around my neck? What joy it would be and what relief if You commanded, if You simply ordered: do *this*; don't do *that*! If I only knew what You want! Oh, to be able to live, to act, to desire, with certainty! Now, all is chaos, and I, the worm, must bring order!"

# 13

WELCOME, Father Yánaros, welcome, you noble warrior!"

Father Yánaros approached slowly; he fingered his beard as he looked around him. Tall, heavy-set men sang as they danced around the fires, bandoliers strung across their chests, rifles slung over their shoulders. And in the lines of dancers, shoulder to shoulder with the men, were young women, red kerchiefs on their heads, carrying bandoliers and rifles like the men. The hilltop was aflame; a great light, a great joy spread out, as though Christ had risen, and the faces of the people reflected the glow.

Father Yánaros stared, and he was carried away by the sight. "What people!" He admired them thoughtfully. "What bodies are these! Lord have mercy! What youth! I don't understand it. Can it be that I have grown old? Can it be that my heart has shriveled up and can no longer feel?"

His gaze took in everything around him—dirty, unshaven, unwashed men with long hair and curly beards—unholy terror! They were from every class: laborers, peasants, teachers, students, shepherds—both men and women. Many young girls had deserted their homes and taken to the hills. Love of danger, of the male breath, desire for freedom, made them put on the rebel cap, comb their hair loose, and set out to share hunger and lice and death with the men. The women cooked, washed, carried off the wounded, bandaged their wounds, took up their rifles, and ran to the attack. Secretly they stole down to the unfreed villages and delivered messages to the secret comrades, exchanged letters, risked their lives unflinchingly. And as the men saw the bravery of these women, how they starved, froze, fought and died, their own courage flared, and they tried to surpass one another.

Father Yánaros watched them with pride as they leaped in dance around the fire, their heads held high.

"Oh, if those unforgettable years would return—those years of youth—that I might toss my shoes off and jump into the flames, spread out my arms to the right and left, and take up the dance again with the angels!"

"Greetings, friends!" Father Yánaros shouted unintentionally and offered his hand.

He came closer; a heavy smell hit his nostrils: roasting lamb and the stench of man's sweat. A chubby young fighter with red shoes and a blond mustache jumped before him. He grabbed the priest from the right, two others grabbed him from the left, and they dragged him to the head of the dance.

"Welcome to Father Yánaros, our handsome friend!" they shouted. "He's come to dance with us, brothers! Come on, gather your robes, Father!" Father Yánaros steadied himself on his staff and stepped back. "Why are you dancing, men?" he shouted. "Let me be; all right, I'll dance, but first tell me why you're dancing. Have you good news? Has the cursed rifle, that mouth of Satan, finally become mute? Have the enemies become friends again? Have they opened their eyes to see that all of us are brothers? Speak up friends; I'm going to burst!"

The fighters laughed. Aleko, the lame army cook, limped forward. "Our brothers in China spilled over the valleys; they walked through the cities, freed millions of people and reached the Yellow River; we heard the news on the radio."

"Who did you say, friends? My ears are ringing from the climb. I didn't hear you. Who did you say?"

"We said the Chinese, priest, the Chinese—our friends, our brothers. Come close, we say; toss the robe away and join in the dance!"

"So now the Chinese are our brothers, too? What do we care what's going on at the other end of the world? Charity begins at home!"

179

"They're our brothers!" the teacher from Chalika piped up, "the Chinese are our brothers. There's no 'other end' of the world any more; charity begins at home, but we're all one home now; all the wronged people are brothers, we have the same father."

"What father?"

"Lenin."

"Not Christ, eh?"

The teacher burst into laughter. "My priest, turn the pages of the Bible, there's a supplement—read the Fifth Gospel—the Holy Gospel 'according to Lenin.' That's where you'll see it! There are no more Greeks and Bulgars and Chinese; we're all brothers. All the cursed and wronged, all who hunger and thirst for justice—yellow, black, white! Open your heart, Father Yánaros, and place them all inside; don't be miserly with your love, lead with the heart!"

Loukas, the leader's adjutant, grabbed Father Yánaros' shoulder. He was a short man with a red, thorny beard, and he wore a black kerchief on his head and a boar's tooth on a leather cord around his neck. "Come on, dance the *zembekiko*, Father," he shouted, "stamp your feet on the earth that's going to claim us all in the end. Easter is near, *Christos anesti!* The *people* have risen from the dead!"

He turned to the other men. "All right men, the hymn!" And at once, all around the fires, the wild, triumphant revised Easter Hymn broke out: "The *people* have risen from the dead! Death has crushed death. . . ."

"You see, Father," the teacher said, "we haven't changed much; we only changed the word 'Christ' to 'the people'—it's the same thing. That's what God is today, anyway—the people!"

"The people are not God," interrupted the priest angrily. "Woe to us if He were that!"

"Woe to us if He were the other," retorted the teacher, "the one who watches children die of hunger and does not lift a finger to help."

"As long as there are starving children there is no God," an angry young woman cried, shaking her fist at the priest as though he were to blame.

Father Yánaros was silent. There was much he could say in defense of God, but he remained silent. Who could fight earthquakes and fires—and youth? He opened his eyes wide and looked at the excited, handsome young men and women, and sweat poured from his brow. He struggled to gather his wits, to see, to understand. Forgive me, God, he thought, can it be that this is a new religion? How did man's heart become so big? before this, it contained only the people of our homes—mothers, fathers, brothers; it was small—small and narrow. At most it took in Yánnina, Epirus; at most, Macedonia, Roumeli, Morea, the islands of Greece, and, further out, Constantinople. It could go no further; but look at it now! Now it has encompassed the world! What is this new attack, my Lord? They tell me to get up and dance for the Chinese, the Hindus, the Africans! I can't! My heart has room only for the Greeks. Can it be that I've aged, I—Father Yánaros who boasted that I was twenty years old and that I'd conquered old age? No, I could never take such a jump now!

Loukas, the wild one, looked at the priest from the corner of his eye, and watched him lean on his staff thoughtfully; he approached him and his voice was mocking. "For your own good, old man, don't come and go between the two sides—both the red and the black bullets can reach you, you know. Make up your mind to join us; you'll have thousands before you to shield you; alone, you're lost."

"No matter what position I take, my friend," Father Yánaros replied, "I don't want anyone to shield me—only God—that's the way I am."

"Ah, Father Yánaros, you'll see that during great danger, this God you speak of will desert you."

"But I will not desert Him!" the priest said and struck his staff against the rocks. "Where can He go! I've got Him by the edge of His robe; I won't let Him go!"

Loukas shrugged his shoulders and laughed. "The robe will tear, it will remain just a rag in your hands; and your ambitious God will have vanished. But why do I waste my time talking to you? I know you, Father Yánaros, you're stubborn as a rock."

The teacher broke into laughter. "You're wasting your words,

181

Loukas," he shouted. "Father Yánaros' soul is like—and forgive me for this—like the bitch my late father kept to guard his sheep."

"A bitch?" one of the women said with curiosity. "Have you no respect, teacher? The old man is a holy man, even if he is not one of us."

"Don't be shocked, comrades; I'll explain, so you can understand. My father was a shepherd; I was only a child, but what I'm about to tell you impressed me greatly, and I never forgot it; we had a white bitch, a real beast, who guarded the few sheep we kept. One night a wolf came into the flock and mated with the bitch. Since that night the dog never barked when the wolf entered. My father would notice the sheep disappearing, first one, then another, yet the bitch was among the flock, and we could not hear her bark. 'What's this mystery,' he said, 'I can't understand it.' One night he took his rifle and set watch; and what did he see? Around midnight he heard the wolf jump into the flock—not a sound from the dog; she only raised her head and wagged her tail. The wolf was about to leap for the sheep when my father fired, and then fell upon the wolf with his ax. He must have been wounded because he ran, howling. Then my father took the club and beat the dog violently. He wanted to kill her but he felt pity; so he opened the door and threw her out. Daylight came. The bitch ran, she ran howling; she climbed the lookout post between the village and the valley and there she stopped. Where could she go? Before her was the wolves' lair, and behind was my father with the club; whichever way she turned, she was lost. Three days and three nights she howled between the wolves and the sheep. Although years have passed, and I'm almost an old man, I still shudder when I remember her howling. The fourth day she was silent; my father went up and found her dead."

"So what, teacher?" a woman asked, "and what do you mean by that?"

"That bitch," the teacher replied, and his voice was bitter—he was not laughing now—"that bitch, comrades, is the soul of Father Yánaros. He howls in the same manner, between the reds and the blacks and he's going to die; pity on his soul!"

Father Yánaros did not say a word, but a knife had slashed his heart; for a moment he was terrified. I'm going to die, he thought. Can the teacher be right? Yes, yes, I'll die howling between the wolves and the sheep. He shuddered; a black whisper of wind raced along his spine.

"Friends," he said, "I'm going to sit down, I'm tired."

He found a rock and huddled on it.

As the dance ended, the fighters knelt around Father Yánaros; some of them took letters from inside their shirts—letters which the captain's wife had distributed to them. Some read them, others asked the teacher for help; and he, kneeling beside them, read their letters to them.

The first who asked the teacher to read his letter for him was Kosmas. Once, a long time ago, he was a settled landowner, and in partnership with an Armenian merchant in Preveza, where they sold fabrics. But the Armenian swindled him and Kosmas became a traveling salesman. When he was a property owner, he hunted down the communists with fury. "The bastards—they want to sell out their country and Christ, too," he would shout. "They want to take my shop and distribute my goods among themselves, I tell you!" But now that he was destitute, he, too, joined the dance of the reds; he wanted to destroy this rotten world and avenge himself with the Armenian. "Whoever is rich, and is a communist, is an idiot," he would say. "Whoever is poor, and is not a communist, is a bigger idiot." Now he called to the teacher and asked him to read his letter.

"Eh, teacher," he said, "if I'd only had you as my partner, I'd never have lost my business."

"But you wouldn't be up here in the hills with us, my friend; you'd be with the blacks in the valley."

"You're right, teacher, to hell with my shop. I just can't get over what happened; but let's stop it now—here's the letter, read it."

The teacher took the letter and read aloud:

"Dear Brother Kosmas: We're all well, thank the Lord, except that all of us are sick—call it hunger, call it malaria. None of the crucifiers—neither the blacks nor the reds—have bothered us yet; but every time there's a knock on the door, our hearts do somersaults. Pardalo, our goat, had kids the other day—three of them—but damn her, they're all male. A short while ago a

183

little old man passed by the village with a white mouse in a cage—he was telling fortunes, but we didn't go. Our mother dreamt that there was a heavy rain, and then the sun came out. We went to the priest so he could explain the dream to us. 'Obviously, a light,' he told us, God bless him, 'a brilliant light—it's a good, blessed dream. Probably Kosmas will return soon; that's the explanation for the sun.' "

"I'm the sun!" Kosmas cried, and burst into laughter. "My poor mother! The old lady thinks about it all day, so she sees it in her dreams."

The teacher went further down the line; he paused and knelt beside a dark-faced giant of a man who was holding a piece of paper in his hand, turning it helplessly as he cursed at not being able to understand what all these black smudges meant. The teacher came and explained it all to him. The letter read:

"You bird-brained oaf—what are you doing up in those hills, leaving me alone in the fields with the goats and the brats? What God-damned people filled your brain with hot air? You write me that you're fighting for freedom—you have rocks in your head, my dear husband. You poor fool, does freedom give you food to eat? Does it come to help me with the chores? Does it clean our house, plow our fields, wash and comb out the lice from our children's heads? You ingrate—is this what you promised me when we were married? I'm a priest's daughter, remember? I was raised in comfort. I'm no peasant girl, don't forget that! I'm not one for heavy chores! Get back here immediately or you'll never see me again. There are plenty of men around, begging me, you know—"

"Enough, God damn her!" the dark-faced one shouted and tore the letter into a thousand pieces.

The teacher laughed. "Don't get sick over it, Dimitri, we've started big things here—the devil with women!" he said and walked on, toward the men who surrounded Father Yánaros, making idle talk.

Two young fighters arrived, sweating and joyful; they wore short shepherds' capes and carried staffs; their hands were covered with blood. They approached and motioned to Loukas.

"Our deepest sympathies," they said laughing.

"Where's the box?" Loukas asked, and put out his hand.

One of the men took out a long silver container from under his cape and handed it to him.

"Alms, Captain Loukas," he said jokingly.

"Don't joke, comrade," Loukas said. "This Holy Sash is going to be our fighting ally; wait and see." He placed two fingers to his mouth and whistled. "Eh, comrade! Eh, Aleko!" he shouted. He turned to the two messengers. "And the clothing?" he asked.

The second man took out a bundle of clothes from under his cape.

"Here," he said, "we left him in his underwear." He spread out a robe, a cap, a belt, two boots, a pair of heavy light-blue socks, and a silver cross on the ground.

"We took his baskets and the mule, too; there were a few figs left in the bottom of the baskets, and we ate them."

"Aleko!" Loukas shouted again.

The men stepped back as smiling, well-fed Aleko the cook limped into sight.

"Present!" Aleko shouted, and stood before Loukas.

"Father Alexander," the second-to-the-leader chided, smiling, "here is your angelic garb—dress quickly! We have a job to do!"

"A monk?" Aleko's eyes bulged, as he took the clothing.

"Dress quickly and don't ask questions!"

Aleko threw off his jacket and trousers, wrapped himself in the robe, pulled the monk's hood over his head, and hung the cross around his neck. He raised his hand, "blessed" the men and the young girls who had gathered around, and roared with laughter.

Loukas held the silver case and tossed it in the air, playing with it as it came down.

"Gather your wits carefully, Father Alexander," he said to Aleko. "I turn over this silver bomb to you—go carefully through all the villages and call out your wares: 'Eh, Christians, the Sash that was worn by the Virgin is here—it is here! It has come to embrace your village, your souls; to rout the black demons, poverty, war, injustice! And the Virgin has a secret message for you: Come to worship, come and hear, all you who believe!' That's what you're to shout, and when the crowd gathers, lean over and whisper to each one, 'The Virgin ordered me to tell you that you will have her blessing if you kill the fascists.

185

They are the black devils—the blackhoods!' That's what you're to say, you understand?"

"I understand; in other words, it's a farce."

"Be very careful, now, and don't laugh; you're a sly one, and that's why I chose you for this job; but this matter calls for the slyness of a monk, because if they even suspect, they'll crucify you, Father Alexander, as they crucified your master."

Father Yánaros stood there, looking and listening, and he choked with anger. This was a different world, without respect, without God, full of youth and heroism and blasphemy. They laugh at the mention of Christ here, and they are prepared to die for justice and freedom. Can these rebels who rise against injustice, can they be—God forgive me—the new Christians, and not know it? And because they do not know it, they blaspheme? But the day will come—it must come—when they will find out. I wonder if Nicódemus, the wounded monk, was right in saying that one day Christ would come to lead these fighters! That He would no longer hold a cross to be crucified with, but a whip to rout the lawless ones, the unjust, the merchants, from the temple of God, from the world!

One by one, Father Yánaros looked at the young men around him, who laughed and cursed and polished their rifles, and he sighed. Ah, if such a God would come down to earth, he thought, how quickly I would wear the rifle belt, even if I am seventy, and I would seize the flag and leap into the assault with them— to scatter the lawless, the unjust, the merchants!

Father Yánaros' mind floated over deep waters; he closed his eyes and listened to the noise around him—the laughter, the crackling fire. Where was he? The moon had just slipped from its zenith and begun to descend. Loukas' first fighter turned, noticed Yánaros—he had forgotten about him—leaned over and nudged him with his foot. "Oh, we forgot about you, Father," he said. "Forgive us, but we had work to do; you see, we had to give a purpose to the Virgin's Sash. He clapped his hands. "Eh, Kokolios!" he shouted.

A wild-haired animal of a man, with two pointed foxlike ears and two crafty eyes, leaped in front of him.

"Present!"

"Where's the leader?"

The animal giggled. "At the lookout post, with the captain's wife."

The others burst into laughter; but the blood rushed to Loukas' head. "Shut up!" he growled.

The animal turned. "Go tell him that his father's here looking for him; he has a message."

"What's he got, you say?"

"A message from Castello—go on now!"

# 14

CAPTAIN DRAKOS slowly crumbled the rock in his fist. He had scrambled atop the high lookout post just a stone's throw from his comrades, and as he crouched there in the moonlight with his neck craned, pondering his black thoughts, he resembled a bear about to spring on his victim.

A flaming, pock-marked face, his head round and thick, full of hair and whiskers—and within it, in flowing waves, were the seas he had drifted upon, the ports where he had anchored, the white, black, yellow, and brown races of men he had seen.

His mind, a dark wine-colored sun, rose from a vast, fertile valley and looked down upon the earth like a hungry lion. At first he could distinguish nothing; the earth had not awakened yet, and her nakedness was covered by the morning mist. But slowly the thin veil moved; lifted by the sun, it became transparent, turned to vapor, and settled over the grass like dew. And one could see the valley flooded with light, and the muddy yellow river, wide as an ocean, crowded with small boats with raised masts—black and orange sails—and the little yellow men who shrieked and jumped like little monkeys on the decks. And suddenly drums and trumpets sounded; the earth began to rumble; millions of yellow feet pounded the stones and the soil as they descended. A song rose in the air from numberless mouths—a wild, joyous, triumphant song that called out to freedom.

They came in increasing waves, singing, from the opposite

sandy slopes, from the green lakes, the distant hills; round, flattened faces made of the mud of the muddy yellow river, with slanted eyes and long braids and turned-down mustaches. The morning sun fell upon them, and their rifles gleamed, and their bayonets, the bronze buttons on their khaki coats and the red and green dragons on their striped flags. They had perched on the long walls; they had crumbled the ancient barriers; they rushed everywhere. They embraced and destroyed thousands of villages; they swept away the old, fatigued noblemen; they raised the well-fed ones from their tables, and sat the hungry down. They covered the walls with huge red flags that had black dragons on them and strange letters that looked like hammers and sickles, and human heads cut off by the sword. And the passers-by lingered and read: "Eat and drink, all you workers of the world—your time has come!"

Men with long braids came from the distant hills, bearing messages. They were barefoot and wore pointed straw hats, and they fell to the ground, screaming and pleading. They all shouted at once in confusion, and one could make out only a few of the archaic words: "Hunger, prison, death!" And the army would go off again, spilling over north and south; Freedom —that armed ghost covered with blood—marched ahead. And behind it, like a tail, the immortal mob: Hunger, Plunder, Fire, Slaughter!

"The air stinks! Who are these people that descend upon us?" asked the velvet-capped nobles from their gold-latticed windows. And in reply, thousands of flaming tongues fell down upon them.

The sun looked at his yellow armies and tried to count them, but they were countless. He smiled, satisfied, and went on. The valley and the wide river disappeared behind him as he rose over jungles, over hot, damp forests that were filled with scorpions and poisonous flowers; the foul-breathed air sparkled with green, pink, and blue wings; the hoarse wind chattered like a parrot; there was a harsh smell of camphor, cinnamon, and nutmeg. The sun was high, and the beasts returned to their lairs, their stomachs full and their mouths dripping blood.

The sun could not bypass the jungle; he reddened angrily and continued on. In the jungle clearings were thousands of men, like armies of ants—Anamites, Malayans, Javanese—with thin-boned joints and flaming eyes that moved stealthily. Motionless, they kept watch; some held hand grenades and rifles; others, daggers bent like scythes. Some carried heavy rods with steel heads or striped flags with laughing lions and white elephants and green snakes painted on them. Generations of them had worked and hungered. Generations of them did no work, but remained silent. Now they had had enough. The sun fell over them, gently caressed their hungry, tormented bodies, and smiled.

One night after work's end, as they knelt, crying softly on the seashore for fear of being heard by their white masters, a strange new god landed on their shores. He began to roll over the pebbles of the seashore, to creep toward them like a huge round scorpion, like a wheel with thousands of slow-moving hands around it that held hammers and sickles. The new god passed heavily over the flogged backs; he walked through the villages, stood in the squares and began to shout. What did he shout? Everyone stood up and wiped his eyes. They watched him with joy and fear, and though they did not understand what he said, their hearts leaped and growled within them. They did not know that a wild beast lay inside; they thought it was a little squirrel that trembled—but in truth, it was the heart of man awakening and growling because it was hungry.

Yes, they stood up and wiped their eyes; they looked around them, and for the first time, saw the hills, the seas, the forests, the fruit on the trees, the water buffalo that rose from the lakes, the birds in the air—all this, all this belonged to them. This was their land, made from the bones and sweat and tears, the very breath of their fathers. They knelt and kissed the earth as though it were their ancestors, as though they were embracing their forefathers. And, shielding their eyes from the sun with their hands, they looked up at their white masters, who sat in the covered terraces, drinking, and smoking aromatic cigars while watching, with glassy blue eyes that narrowed and with mouths that drooled, the fragile Javanese girls, the naked Indonesians, the slender Malayans, who laughed and shrieked and swayed their hips before them.

The bile rushed to their slanted Indonesian and Javanese and

190

Malayan eyes, and at that moment they understood clearly what the new god was saying.

"Get out! Get out!" The cries were heard from one end of the jungle to the other, from one sea to the next. "Get out! Get out! Holland for the Dutch, France for the French, America for the Americans. Out! Out!"

The multi-eyed sun was higher now; he watched his dark-skinned children, heard their shouts and their taunts and, murmuring a blessing to them, smiled and went on.

Now he passed over huge peaks and snow-capped mountains, over sacred slow-moving rivers, over thousands of muddy villages and countless people with thin bodies that were eaten away by hunger, and with large, velvet eyes full of perseverance and forgotten gods. And on the edge of a river, a skeleton-like ascetic turned a prayer wheel. He turned and turned this ancient wheel of fate, and millions of souls gathered around him; and he would speak to them, smile, and fall silent again. Naked, toothless, a mere water snake with arms and legs like St. John the Forerunner—and, armed to the hilt with his soul, he fought a great empire, motionless, there at the edge of the river.

The sun paused above him and illuminated him. Its light went up and down the bald head, the tortured chest, the empty belly, the slender thighs, the skinny legs. What is the soul of man, of real man? the sun pondered. A flame, sadness, joy, an upsurging spring that breaks through the thick skin of earth and rises? Some call it revenge, others call it justice; some call it freedom, others, God; I call it the soul of man! And as long as it can spurt up from the earth, I have faith that my light does not go wasted. How glad I am that I have eyes to see and ears to hear and arms long enough to reach down and embrace the world! What a wasteland, what tragedy if the soul of real men did not exist; and how useless my light would be.

The sun rose higher; it reached the peak of the sky and paused. A desert—sand—the bark of earth steams, inflamed! There is little water here, the wells are dry; the light spills over the rose-violet-colored hills like a waterfall—the only waterfall in this wilderness. Here and there a palm tree, a camel, a glistening snake; a wild, sad cry pierces the air. A hot wind rises and the sand moves; it becomes stormy, like the sea; the spine of

191

earth shivers. And suddenly, in this vast wilderness, tents appear, dark-skinned women, with long, deft fingers stained with henna, mix flour and water. They rub two stones and light small fires; the smoke—man's true banner—rises, and Death is reborn.

Men with white sashes sit nearby, cross-legged, and listen attentively. A peddler has come from distant shores, from the lands of the disbelievers, selling beads and small mirrors and salt and multicolored cloth. He, too, sits cross-legged in the shade of the tent as he tells of the many things that happen far away. He tells of magic machines and of new rifles, of white women and of blond boys. He speaks of the poor and the rich, of starving men who suddenly rise, break down the doors of the rich, and sit down to well-laden tables, lie down on soft beds, mount the iron-winged horses, and spin fantasies in the air.

The Bedouin hearts are set afire as they listen; the eyes bulge and look far out, at the burning winds, toward the west. And the peddler knows that the hour has come; he takes out a notebook from his shirt and reads from it. He says it is the new Koran, the latest message from Allah; it came from far away, from the North, from the new Mecca which is also called Moscow. The Prophet has been reborn; he has taken a new name; he has written a new Koran. He calls to the Arabs again, to his faithful, to gather round him, to plunder the world once more. Haven't you had enough of hunger and scorn and the desert? Go on then, the time has come! Unfurl the Prophet's green flags in the wind! There is only one Allah, and his prophet is Mohammed. Today, Mohammed is called Lenin.

The sun, with his round, innocent face, laughed again. The seed has fallen in the desert now, he thought, and it won't be long before the desert is flowering, too. A hungry beetle, this peddler, so hungry that he goes from flower to flower, from tent to tent, from heart to heart; and his wings are loaded with red seed. God bless you, he added, I'm weary of the face of this old earth. I'm just an old carriage-driver going along the same path without stopping. For years now I've watched the same masters flogging the same backs. Let the wheel turn; let new faces come to light; let the heart move a few paces so that the world may move, too! Go on then, Apostle Beetle, you old peddler, courage! I have seen thousands of beetles like you; they all peddle the same wares, but each gives them different names. You're great storytellers, all of you, and I like you. And men—eternal innocent children that they are—believe your tales; and because the soul of man is mighty, the tales become truth. One century, two centuries, three, four, until finally, wide-eyed, they realize it was only a story and they laugh at it. Then new storytellers come, with other tales, and the people are off again. And that's how my time passes. Health to you, peddler, happy peddling. Now forgive me, but I must be on my way.

Captain Drakos threw his head back and scanned the distance with his eye. He looked at the rocks where he had planted the flag of freedom many months ago. The whole world and all the oceans were gathered upon this hill. All these months, the hill and the people had become one—their fates had merged. He felt that he was a centaur—that from the waist down he was this mountain; he had taken of its wildness and its hardness, and the mountain seemed to have taken on the soul of man. Indeed it had, for as it stretched up to the sky and looked at the valley, it seemed to be calling to the blackhoods below. It felt that it was no longer a hill like the other hills, but a shield of freedom. For months now, men had bloodied their hands on this mountain as they pierced its insides, as they dug nests for their cannon, raised beams, cleared paths. Bombs had covered it with wounds; the stones were burned, and a few thorns and low bushes, which had climbed this far, had become ashes. This hill had drunk of human blood; it had eaten human brains. Its ravines and ditches were sown with human bones. And so it became a ghost; it joined the guerrillas; it fought for freedom. It, too, growled in battle and made threats. And many times it spat flames from its peak as a signal to the other hills.

"All's well, all's well," it murmured sadly, "yet I'm going to explode!"

Angrily, Captain Drakos threw the rock he had been crumbling in his hand; he heard it echoing on the hillside and within him, and then, silence.

"What the hell's wrong with me," he growled. "What is this devil inside of me again, and where is he driving me? He governs my whole life—he, not I! Freedom, they say—bah!

193

What freedom? He's the only free one—the devil within us— he's free, not us! We're only his mule, and he saddles us and goes off. But where's he going?"

Drakos' past life raced quickly before him. He remembered his youth; he had wined and dined; he'd gotten drunk and made love to find forgetfulness; but there was no relief. The devil would rise within him and cry out, "Shame on you, shame on you, beast!" And in order to escape the voice, he went into exile; he became a boatswain on a freighter and lost himself on the seven seas. What a life that was! What excitement! What horror!

Does nothing, then, ever die within us? Can nothing die as long as we are alive? Once more his temples throbbed with the seas he had roamed, with the ship, his comrades, the exotic ports— Alexandria, Suez, Port Said, Colombo, Singapore, Hong Kong —the muddy yellow seas, the yellow women. And once more his nostrils inhaled the nauseating smell of urine and spices and the stench of women's sweating armpits.

He would go ashore freshly shaven, his pitch-black mustache twisted, a cigarette behind his ear. And he would stroll through the secret neighborhoods and select the women he liked. He became acquainted quickly, simply. He would wink his eye at the woman who caught his fancy, or pinch her arm, or look at her and groan gently, like a calf. Love, to him, was like a game he played with his friends when he was a child—leap frog. Five or ten players would bend over, he would spit and rub his palms, step back and jump over them one by one, like lightning, and triumphantly end up on his toes.

What is man's body made of that it can give and receive so much happiness? How is it that lips—a mere bit of flesh—can touch your lips and cause your mind to swerve? Drakos felt a great happiness when his body was pressed against a woman's. During those moments even his soul became flesh, so that it, too, could feel the joy of the tight embrace. And he would return to his ship at dawn, carrying armfuls of bananas and pineapple and silk handkerchiefs dipped in camphor and musk.

On other occasions, Death rode their ship. Drakos would fight him, chase him from the prow where he sat. And the sea would become calm again, and the sailors would put on the pot of steaming meat in the galley. Then bottles of wine would be passed around, and they would eat and drink; they would get drunk and begin to talk of their homes. Each one would pull his yellow, faded photographs from out of his shirt and pass them from hand to hand so the others could admire their wives and children that waited for them back home. But Drakos had no wife or children to show; he kept an old photograph of his father the priest—Father Yánaros—with the robes and the cross on a chain, and the heavy Bible, opened in his arms. He would show it to his friends and roar with laughter. His comrades would take courage and laugh, too. "Health to you, you old handsome goatbeard!" they would shout, and all together they would mockingly chant the funeral service.

What a life that was, filled with smuggling and shame and heroics! Once he had even raised mutiny aboard one of the ships. A storm had come up, and the ship was in danger, while the captain sat drinking in his cabin with two yellow women on his knees. Drakos gathered the crew around him, grabbed the drunken captain, buried him in the hold, and took over the rudder. On another occasion, Japanese pirates attacked them in the middle of the ocean. A wild battle followed; Captain Drakos captured three pirate ships, tied them to the stern of his ship, and towed them to Hong Kong, where he sold them.

And suddenly he had quit everything—ships, smuggling, women. They had reached an Indian port when the telegram came: War in Albania—the cowardly spaghetti-eaters, the sneaks in the night, had entered Greek soil and were tuning their guitars to go down to Yánnina. When he heard this, a voice leaped within him. It was not his voice, it was his father's, his grandfather's. It was an old, old voice, born of freedom and death. When he heard it, he shouted back furiously: "You dare order me to do my duty? I don't need you for that, and I'll show you!"

He hopped on a plane and returned to his country; he put on battle dress, entered the war, fought heroically, and won his stripes. But black days soon fell upon them; the country became infected, it was overrun with boots, guitars, and Bulgarian caps. Drakos took to the hills and fought all these empires, alongside another fifty barefoot, ragged men, until the blessed day came when the winds of God blew over them, and the foreign boots scattered; and the Greeks were left with the Greeks, on their own soil again.

For months he had not washed or shaved or changed shirts. Still smoking from the gunpowder, covered with hair and dirt, he went down to Salonica to celebrate the liberation of his country. He went to a bathhouse and washed, then headed for a barber shop. He changed his shirt and underwear and with his old fellow seamen went to a port tavern. For three days and three nights they drank and sang songs of freedom. On the evening of the fourth day, a middle-aged Jew with thick lips and a crooked nose walked in and sat at their table. They offered him a drink, and then another, and he was soon in a gay mood.

"Eh, my brave young fighters," he said, "with your permission, I will tell you a story. Pay attention, brothers, for, by the God I believe in, whoever understands this will become a new man—a blind man who sees, a heartless man who gains a heart. Joy to him who understands, he'll rise, walk out of this tavern, look around him, and shout, 'It's a miracle! The world has changed!' "

"Go on, you old skinflint, you're killing us with curiosity!" Drakos said and filled the Jew's cup with wine. "Drink so you can think up more stories to tell us."

The old man emptied his cup and began: "One for the money, two for the show, three to get ready, and here we go— good evening! Once upon a time, in the snowy regions of the North there was a land so large that you could walk across it for years and never reach its end. They called it Russia, as you know. In those years, a thousand people, ten thousand people worked, so that one could eat. The thousand and ten thousand went hungry; they were called Russian peasants. And that one person, the one who ate, was called the nobleman. Day and night the noblemen sat before their lighted fireplaces and drank a strong white wine they called vodka; they drank, mellowed, picked up their carbines, stood the peasants in a line, and used them for target practice."

"And the peasants? What did the peasants do?" Drakos shouted, banging his fist on the table. "What about the thousand

196

and ten thousand? All they had to do was breathe on the one and he'd have fallen; if they'd spat on him like this"—and he spat—"they would have drowned him. What kind of fairy tales are you feeding us?"

Drakos puffed and fumed, and spat and banged his fist on the table.

"No, my brave lad," the Jew replied, "they did not breathe or spit on him; they trembled. You see, from grandfather to father they had inherited fear; the fear began the minute they were born, and it did not leave them until they died. They called this fear life. But one day a man came—a giant of a man with slanted eyes, wearing a worker's cap and a worker's shirt. He began to knock on doors like a beggar; he began entering cellars and speaking to the peasants. And what did he tell them? Nothing surprising—things that everyone knew but had forgotten; that they are human beings, that they have souls, that they are hungry; that there exists a thing called freedom and another called justice, and still another called . . ."

The old man lowered his voice so that the tavern-keeper, who had cocked his ear and listened angrily, would not hear him.

"Called what?" the men around him asked, and bent their heads closer to the Jew's lips.

"Revolution," he replied softly and crouched in fear—he sensed the huge hand of the tavern-keeper above him.

"Skinflint! Bolshevik, out! Out!"

He grabbed him by the collar and before the men could intervene, threw him out into the street.

Drakos jumped up; that voice had suddenly leaped within him crying, "The world is dishonest, unjust; it's your duty to save it."

"Me save it? Me, the drunkard? The hairy bear, the liar, the thief, the murderer?"

"You! Yes, you! Get up!"

He rose.

"I'm coming with you," Drakos shouted to the Jew, and hurried outside after him. He took his arm, and they disappeared into the narrow, winding streets.

Tonight, alone in this outpost on Mount Etoraki, Captain

197

Drakos remembered those dangerous days and the flaming nights in out-of-the-way taverns, in the deserted houses and the dark cellars of Salonica. This must be what the catacombs were like, and the first Christians, who were impoverished, hungry, persecuted; their eyes must have burned like this, with love and hate; and this must be how they gathered to decree how they would destroy the old world and build a new one. The comrades were inflamed with joy and anger and certainty. "We're going to save the world," they swore. "We'll save it whether by mouth or the sword!"

Drakos' mind opened; his heart filled with indignation and pain; he took and administered oaths; he gathered comrades, choosing the younger men who thought nothing of life and death, and they all took to the hills. Fate sent him from hill to hill, to these rocks of Epirus. Fire and slaughter! He burned villages and mercilessly killed the elders and fascists. This, he said, is the only way to reach love—through hate! And the other day when he captured Father Laurentios, the monk who had informed on the seven women who were, as a result, shot at the Chapel of the Forerunner, he had no pity for him; Drakos himself took two rafters, nailed them crosswise, made thick nails, and went down to the town one night and crucified the monk, so that the villagers could look at the cross with fear and see how traitors are punished.

"All's well, all's well," he murmured again, "and yet I'm going to burst!" He stretched his limbs so he could breathe easier—he was indeed at the breaking point.

Lately, doubts pierced his heart like daggers; was it possible that this was not the right road? Why should his heart begin to feel this bursting sensation? Why should he want to leave? And where would he go? Where the devil could he go? The very thought infuriated him. No, no, this is the right road; go on, he would shout to gain courage, this is the goal—attack! He shot out blindly to drown this new voice that rose within him. And the other day, when he caught the monk and crucified him with his own hands, both the reds and the blacks were terrified, but he was peaceful for several days. This is the road, he repeated over and over again to convince himself, this is the only road, there is no other; follow it to its end! Listen to no one, onward!

'I'he Lord have mercy on those who weaken and stand in the middle; only at the end, the only salvation is at the end of the road.

From the day this new voice stirred within him, Captain Drakos went wild; he sank deeper and deeper in blood, as though he wanted to destroy all the bridges within him, to reach the end of this road that he had chosen, whether he wanted to or not. It was not the monk he crucified; no, it was that new voice within him; he killed it so it would be silent. But the voice cannot be crucified; you may kill the body, you may cut the throat, but the voice remains; and tonight, again, it rose within Captain Drakos and tore at his chest. "Change the world, you say? Bring freedom and justice, you say? But how can you change the world when you cannot change man? The heart of man? Have we changed, we, the new people? Did we become better men? The hell we did! The small, humble people, yes, but the leaders, God damn them! Look at Loukas, my right-hand man! Jealousy, hatred, spying; ready to put the dagger in my back! The fish begins to stink from the head, as the saying goes."

"Oh, if I only had the power," he muttered and furiously yanked out hairs from his mustache, "if only I had the power to raise my own flag!"

# 15

A SHADOW FELL across the cliff. Captain Drakos turned, startled—a woman dressed in nun's garb stood before him, her blond hair spilling over her shoulders.

His eyebrows gathered. "Where were you?" he asked. "Did you see the leader?"

"I saw your old man the priest while I was climbing up here."

"Never mind my old man, did you see the chief? What news do you bring? Speak up."

"You're to turn everything over to Loukas . . ."

She did not get a chance to finish; Captain Drakos jumped for her throat, but he stopped, picked up a rock, and hurled it with force down the precipice. A sound rose from his throat, like the groan of a bull being stabbed.

"Turn over to *whom?*"

"To Loukas," the woman replied quietly and half closed her eyes to hide her pleasure.

"And may I ask why I'm being relieved?"

"Because you're not acting according to orders; you've been talking, and they found out; now we hear you want to raise your own flag; they don't trust you any more."

She was silent for a moment, then she added, "And besides, they say you're taking too long to capture Castello."

The man's chest shook; the wind shifted at the wild laughter that rang out. But abruptly the laughter stopped, his throat closed; for now he saw the light, at least he thought he saw it.

He took a step; his legs moved slowly, first one, then the other, walking stealthily like a wild beast. He approached the woman and grabbed her by the shoulders.

"Or can it be . . ." he said, out of breath.

He was quiet again; he fixed his eyes into her blue ones, and his breath poured out, hot and impatient, into the nostrils and the mouth of the woman. She tried to turn her face, but he grabbed her by the nape of her neck so she could not move.

"Or can it be . . ." he repeated, and suddenly he tightened his grip, to choke her. "Whore!" he growled, "you played it up to suit you, to suit that half-pint lover of yours; you couldn't wait to be the leader's woman!"

He had grabbed her by the arm now and twisted it; she was in pain, but she bit her lips to keep from crying out. She tried to tear away, but Drakos held her tightly, furiously.

"You cheap whore!" he growled again, "do you think you'll get away with this? You came here and shamed our hill, you bitch; can't you understand that as long as there's a war on, there's no such thing as men and women, only fighting comrades —only brothers and sisters? When the war's over, then you're free to do as you please. But you had to come here now, and dirty us up!"

"It's freedom I'm fighting for, and I'm free; I do as I please!"

"Freedom means doing what the Cause wants you to do, not what you want."

"That's fine for men, but I'm a woman; when I see a man, there's only one thing on my mind—to choose!"

"What do you see in him? He's short, bowlegged, red-haired."

He leaned over her, neighing like a horse, and his beard pricked her cheeks. A thick smell of sour milk and bitter almonds rose from her breast; his nostrils drew it in and he jumped, tore his face away from hers, shoved her aside, and raised his fist; but he stopped, embarrassed, and lowered his hand.

"Get out, you whore! Get out and don't dirty me, too!" he growled. But as she buttoned her robe, he sprang on her, grabbed her by the neck, and bent her backwards.

"Let me go, let me go!" she screamed. "I hate you!"

He moaned over her and sank his teeth in her neck. "I hate you, too; I hate you, too."

201

"Let me go, I loathe you!"

She fought desperately, with her feet, her arms, her nails. The two bodies merged, they separated, their legs entwined; slowly, slowly, with hatred, with nausea, the struggle became an embrace. The heavy unbearable stench from the man's sweating, unwashed, hairy body smothered the woman.

Hate and desire overwhelmed him—a desire to lay her down, to trample her with his boots. He pulled at her robe, tore it away; her white, firm, sweating breast was visible. He reached out and cupped it in his hand; his mind dulled. The woman let out a thin cry; she paled, her eyes rolled back and sank in their whiteness.

"Don't, don't!" she murmured softly now, pleading, and her breasts melted from the sweetness and the pain.

She stretched out her arms, palms open, against the rocks and closed her eyes; she could fight no longer.

For a moment from far away, from the ends of the earth, the woman heard people singing, a dog howling. The veins in her throat and in her thighs swelled and lashed at her like whips, then deep silence, as though the world had crumbled and sank. And the hairy man over her opened and closed his heavy bloodied lips hungrily over the downy, scented body, and he cooed like a male pigeon. And without realizing it, he whispered in a soft, tender voice that was not his own. "My love . . . my love . . ."

How many hours, how many seconds passed? The man and the woman were exhausted; they sat up on the rocks and looked at each other with hate. Suddenly the woman placed her head between her knees; she felt an unbearable nausea come over her whole body, as though she had fallen into a pigsty and could not wash herself clean. The smells poured, drainlike, from her. She took out her handkerchief and furiously began to wipe her mouth, her neck, her breast. The handkerchief filled with blood.

She raised her head, stole a secret glance at the growling man who was pacing back and forth. His thick eyebrows covered his eyes, his huge arms reached down to his knees, and he stepped heavily, clumsily, like a bear.

She wanted to leave but felt a sweet limpness in her body; if she could only close her eyes and sleep awhile!

But the man stood over her, stamping his foot with fury. "You slut!" He spat out the words and kicked her. "I can't stand to look at you any longer; get out! And tell your lover he'll never be the leader."

She jumped to her feet. "Beast!" she screamed. "Pig!"

She covered her bosom, pushed her hair inside the cap, and turned to leave.

At that very moment, from behind the rocks, one of the young fighters appeared. "Captain Drakos," he said, winking his eye knowingly, "your old man, Yánaros the priest, wants you."

Father Yánaros was still standing warming himself by the fire. Shudders passed over his aged thick-boned body; his mind had begun to scold him. "Eh, Father Yánaros," it cried, "oh, tortured, wind-tossed soul, why did you bring me into this pit of lions? Turn back before your son comes, before you're lost!"

But his son appeared at that moment, walking toward him with slow, heavy footsteps. The flames reflected a glow on the younger man's face, with its wide jaw, the black thorny beard, the hooked nose. His long arms reached down to his knees.

Drakos looked around slowly; the men made room for him to pass. Loukas made a move to reach his side, but Drakos looked at him angrily; bile rushed to his eyes; he turned his face away and spat into the fire.

"Where's Father Yánaros?" he asked, and unbuttoned his collar; it was choking him.

"Here I am," the old man replied, and turned from the fire.

His son's lips twisted sarcastically. "Welcome," he growled.

"I'm glad to see you, Captain," Father Yánaros replied. "I have something to say to you."

"I'm listening."

The fighters spread out around them; they held their breaths.

"There must be only the two of us," the old man said.

"I have no secrets from my men, speak freely! What wind brought you here at such an hour?"

"The wind of God; it blew and picked me up and brought me your way. I bring you a message from God; I will say it and leave."

203

"I'm listening."

"Have you no pity for the Greek race? At the rate we're going, we'll soon be extinct; God made only a few of us; if this evil continues, there won't be a head left. The villages are in ruins, the houses are burned, the caves have filled with women and orphans. Mercy, for heaven's sake! Three times you took Castello, three times they took it away from you. All of you, both blacks and reds, have left only ashes behind you. How much longer will this go on? I came to your hilltop tonight to cry out, 'How much longer?' I ask the same of the others. I am a priest, a servant of God, and it is my duty to come and go between the two of you and to shout, 'Love! Love! Brotherhood!' "

Drakos burst into wild laughter. "Love? Brotherhood? Aren't you tired of all that? Is this why you came to our hill? The rifle, that's our answer, the rifle! Go back!"

"I will not go. I said I have something to say to you."

"I'm listening, I'm listening, I tell you, but for your own sake, forget love, forget your gods, face the fact that your cure-alls don't work on us. Speak up, why did you come?"

"To surrender my village—Castello—to you."

Drakos turned to his men. "Bring some raki so Father Yánaros can warm up. He needs strength."

He turned to his father, his voice sarcastic. "Go on, old man," he said, "you made a good start, go on!"

"Don't laugh," the old man replied angrily. "It's not easy to surrender the village, but it's also not easy for you to capture it. Castello is neither in my hands nor in yours. It's in the hands of God and it deserves respect."

A young girl brought a bottle of raki and two glasses; she filled them.

"I have no need of stimulants," Drakos said, refusing the glass which the girl held out to him. "Give it to the old man."

"Nor do I have the need," Father Yánaros replied with annoyance. "And don't rub it in—I'm not an old man."

They were silent for a moment, each looking into the other's eyes. Father and son stalked each other, silently.

"This man is not human, this man is not my son, forgive me, Lord!" the priest cried to himself. "I don't trust him; I cannot turn over the village to him; I will go back."

His son's heart turned over; he looked at his father, and his eyes clouded. What he had suffered as a child—an untamed beast—at his hands! The old man had fought to make him a man! He had hated his father; he had feared him. One night he set fire to his mattress, hoping to burn him, and that same night he jumped over the wall of their courtyard and ran away! He never returned.

"Come on, get it over with!" Drakos spoke roughly, tightening his fist. "And don't think that I need you; I swore that tomorrow we would burn the village!"

Scenes passed before Father Yánaros' eyes: the children that were hungry, the women dressed in mourning, the villages that were burning, the corpses that were rotting in the hills, all of Hellenism that was being annihilated. He looked at the men around the fires; some stood silently by, rooted like trees. Others were like beasts, standing guard because they were hungry, and others like archangels. What shall I do, he wondered, what road should I take? How could these trees and these beasts and these archangels feel my pain?

And as his head rumbled, he heard in his daze the voice of God within him; he recognized it—every time he became confused and his mind was in a turmoil, when thousands of odd voices broke out within his temples, a quiet, clear voice—the voice of God—put everything in order again. And now that Father Yánaros heard that voice again, his knees became steady, he held out his hand and touched the clenched fist of Captain Drakos.

"My child," he said, and his voice trembled now; he knew that thousands of lives depended on this moment.

"My son, must I kneel before you to make you listen? I know that I caused you to suffer a great deal when you were very young, but I did it for your own good. They beat clay, too, you know, to shape it into urns. I may have seemed like a tyrant to you; all right, it's your turn. I, Father Yánaros, who have never condescended to bow before anyone but God, bow and plead with you now. Listen to me, my son, come down to the village tomorrow night; it's Holy Saturday, we will turn over the keys to you, we will celebrate the Resurrection together, we will exchange the kiss of love. But do not kill anyone! Do you hear? Do not kill anyone!"

Captain Drakos placed his hand on his thick beard and raised it over his mouth to hide his laughter. He remained silent.

"Do not harm the village," Father Yánaros continued pleadingly. "You must respect life and the property and honor of men."

"You ask a great deal!"

"I ask a great deal because I also give a great deal! You must not kill anyone—enough of all this!"

"Not kill anyone? Not even that dog, the army captain? Not even that rotten, miserable old Mandras and his sons?"

"No one—no one, they are all my people. I must answer for them at the Second Coming."

"And *I* must answer here on earth at the *First Coming*. I have to answer for my comrades who were killed in the alleys and on the rocks of Castello, Father Yánaros! And don't wrinkle your eyebrows, don't try to frighten me; you think I'm still that boy you used to beat like some dog? Remember how you hung me upside down and whipped the soles of my feet until they bled? So I could become a decent human being, you said! I set fire to your house once, now I'll set fire to your village, too, and I want no bargaining; it's my turn now!"

The village rose in flames before the old man's eyes; he held back his heart so it would not leap out.

"I've sent messages to all the neighboring villages, Captain Drakos; tomorrow at noon the people will gather in front of the church, and we will take over the barracks. We will tie up the captain—most of the soldiers are with us—and then we will signal you. That's what I came to tell you. That's what God ordered me to tell you, have mercy my Captain, swear that you will harm no one."

Drakos looked around at his men. Loukas approached, and as he opened his mouth to offer a word of advice, Drakos covered it with his hand. "I'll make my own decisions," he growled. "I'm the leader here."

He bit his mustache and fell into silence; his face was hard and unmoving, like stone, but slowly, very slowly, a satanic smile spread over his thick lips. He turned to Father Yánaros. "All right," he said, "I won't harm anyone, I'll swear to that."

But the old man shook his head. "What would you swear

to?" he said. "What can someone who does not believe in God swear to?"

"I swear to the idea, the cause—*that* is my God."

"Ideas do not exist, only people who believe in them; for ideas take the form and the body of the men who nurture them."

"My body is large, go on your way, what's been discussed here will be respected."

"May God place his hand upon all this," Father Yánaros said, and made the sign of the cross.

"If God has a hand," Drakos said, and burst into laughter. He turned to his men. "To arms, men! *The people have risen!*"

"*Truly they have risen,* Captain," they shouted back, mocking the Easter Resurrection cry, and the hill echoed with their laughter.

# 16

"Seven times a day God blows upon the reeds and bends them," Father Yánaros muttered out loud as he walked downhill. "What reeds? Men! Blow, then, my Lord, on this ogre, my son, and bend him, too. . . . When he turned past the first rocks and out of the guerrillas' sight, he paused and raised his hands to the sky.

"My Lord," he shouted loudly, so that his voice could reach the sky, "my Lord, how much longer will an Antichrist be the leader of men? How much longer will man look upon man with distrust? The honest men on earth are in danger, and how many are there? Only a few—don't You pity them? Why do You give them love and virtue and humility, and deny them strength? These are the men You should arm, my Lord, these and not the others. The others are wolves; they have teeth, nails, strength. But the sheep? You must arm them, too, my Lord, so they will not be eaten by the wolves. And if You are to appear on earth again, do not appear as a lamb, come as an innocent lion. . . . I weigh and I measure, but I do not understand; why do You torture those who love You so heavily, my Lord?"

Father Yánaros went on his way feeling somewhat relieved after shouting his complaint to God; he was in a hurry to reach Castello. The moon had set and day was breaking; soon the village appeared between the rocks, stone upon stone. Slowly the green and black rooftops of the village became visible, and the chimneys without smoke, and the herds of shacks, sick from the filth, with the church in the center, the house of God, a sad, disillusioned mother—the picture and image of the houses of men. And within the church, Christ, lying on His Bier among the wildflowers, waited today, Holy Saturday, for man to resurrect Him.

Father Yánaros shook his head. "Help us, my Lord," he murmured, "lift Your hand and help us to bring harmony, if You want to see a Resurrection in Castello."

Father Yánaros stole into the village quickly so that he would not be seen; dawn had arrived. He strode quickly across the courtyard, entered the church, and fell in a heap, exhausted, on a bench. His eyelids were heavy, the Bier, the icons, the golden iconostas were spinning, quick as lightning—black, red, gold; he was dizzy; he closed his eyes and immediately he sank into a deep sleep.

The village began to move; it was awakening. A door opened halfway, and a head peeked out; a voice was heard, a dog howled, and again, silence. In a little while, the faltering cry of a hungry baby drifted from some courtyard; it could be heard all over the neighborhood by the puppies, who were hungry, too, and had begun to cry. At the other end of town, the soldiers had awakened and were cleaning their rifles.

How many seconds, how many hours was Father Yánaros drowned in sleep? This was no sleep; the old man had entered the horrible future, and his whole body, from his head to his toes, began to tremble. He dreamt that the sixth seal opened and that he embraced a rock, thinking it was God; and he held it tightly to save himself; and his eyes were bulging as he looked. The sun had become black, and the moon was bloody, and the stars in the sky began to fall to earth, as the rotted fruit drops from wild fig trees when a strong wind blows. And suddenly the darkened skies split open, and seven angels with trumpets came forth.

The first one blew his trumpet, and fire and hail mixed with blood fell on the earth. And one third of the earth and one third of the trees and all the green grass became ashes.

The second angel blew his trumpet, and a mountain of fire fell on the sea, and one third of the seas became blood, and one third of the fish died, and one third of the ships sank.

209

The third angel blew his trumpet, and a flash of fire fell from the sky, and one third of the rivers and springs dried up.

The fourth angel blew his trumpet, and one third of the sun and moon and stars disappeared.

The fifth angel blew his trumpet, and the well of abyss opened, and smoke rose from it; and within the smoke, armies of locusts with poison-filled tails swarmed and stung, like scorpions, whatever living thing had remained. They were like horses trained for war, and their faces were like those of men, and their hair like women's, and their teeth like those of lions, and their voices like the neighing of horses that charge into battle.

A locust saw Father Yánaros behind the large rock he was embracing and leaped upon him. The old man let out a cry and fainted in his sleep; when he regained consciousness, everything —angels and locusts—had disappeared, and Father Yánaros found himself within a large city; the devastated houses were still smoldering; the air was heavy with the stench of corpses; hungry cats and dogs ran through the ruins, and Father Yánaros stood at a crossroad, wondering if he had lost his mind. Once in a while a passer-by would stumble along like a drunk; their bodies were the bodies of men; their faces were those of wild beasts— torn, muddy, bloodied. Standing motionless at the crossroad, Father Yánaros held out his hand like a beggar. "Please, sir," he would ask the wayfarer, "tell me, am I insane? It worries me that I do not know."

"What can I tell you, sir?" the passer-by would answer, without stopping. "You tell me if I'm insane or not! I'm worried, too, for I honestly don't know." He would shake the bloodied mass hanging from his mouth, burst into laughter, and go on his way. And Father Yánaros would still stand at the crossroad motionless, with outstretched hand, waiting in agony for someone else to come along so he could ask again.

"Father Yánaros, eh, Father Yánaros!" He heard someone call him as he stood with outstretched hand, in his sleep. He jumped up, looked around, then walked to the door and out into the yard. No one was there. God pitied me, he thought, and called out my name so I could waken. So I could waken and not see or talk against God's workshop. He went back into the church, dragged himself to the icon of Christ on the iconostas, and stood

210

on tiptoe; he kissed the long-fingered hand that held the green sphere—the world.

"My Lord," he pleaded, "pity us and do not let my dream come true. Peace! Peace! We ask nothing else of You my Lord! Neither wealth and comforts, nor honor and glory; peace! Give us peace, and we will take care of everything else."

He tightened his belt, looked at Christ, and went on: "We have a great deal of work today, my Lord; the salvation or the loss of Castello depends on this day; help us! Don't leave us at this difficult hour, my Lord! Look into the heart of the captain, calm him down; the rebels will come down tonight. Lean over, Lord, and blow into their eyes so they will open them and see that we are all brothers. The heart of man is a jumbled mass of caterpillars; blow on them, my Lord, so they will become butterflies!"

He turned toward the door; at the threshold he paused and looked back at the icon. "Don't play games with us, Lord," he said. "We're human, we can't endure."

He walked outside, and the sun dazzled him; he looked around the churchyard with its few tombstones and paused at his grave: "Wait," he said to it, shaking his finger, "wait until I finish the orders God gave me when He brought me to the world. Don't be in such a hurry."

Small, humble blades of grass had sprung up around the empty grave and between the slates that were laid on the ground; it smelled of spring. The first butterflies had come out of their tombs, testing their untrained wings in the warm air; a golden-green beetle buzzed as it flew wildly, hitting the walls head-on.


"Lord have mercy!" Father Yánaros observed, "the sun is high already; I think I overslept, and any minute now the neighboring villagers will appear; I'd better ring the bell!"

He rose. His bones creaked; his back felt a stab of pain, and for a moment he felt dizzy. The courtyard spun around before him, and he paused for a moment.

"Courage, old mule," he murmured, "hold on; you're passing by a precipice, don't slip." Gently he slapped his heavy-boned body.

A trying day today, he thought. I must have the strength to see it through. He took two strides, grabbed the rope of the bell, and pulled it quickly, stubbornly. He felt that this bell was his real voice. And the church, with its painted saints and demons, with its courtyard and tombstones, was his real body. High in the dome of his head he felt his soul shrieking like a bat in the hands of the Pancreator.

The bell was of bronze and silver and human sound; the wind was warm and scented. Even an infidel would feel that today is Holy Saturday; it smells of Easter, and God, crowned with fresh green grass, rises from the earth!

Every so often Father Yánaros would shield his eyes with his hand and look toward the road to see if the neighboring villagers had set out for Castello. For a moment his face would glow with the Resurrection; for a moment it would cloud thoughtfully; the laughter of the young rebels around their campfire still echoed in his ears. It was as though the whole rebel mountain laughed mockingly while it drove him away. Father Yánaros coiled like a serpent; a cold wind entered his heart. These men have no God, he thought; they fear and respect nothing; they will break their oaths. And the old shepherd trembled now for fear of having opened the gate to the wolf.

Suddenly he was very tired; he let go of the rope, and the bell stopped ringing. He cocked his ears and heard the village doors opening and closing, and human voices approaching. He sat down on the stone ledge and wiped the sweat from his brow. Soon footsteps were heard; someone stopped short in front of the church doors; the old man lifted his head. On the threshold stood a short, stocky man with fat cheeks, a mouth wide as a well, and dirty hair that fell to his shoulders.

"Is that you, Kyriákos?" Father Yánaros asked. "Come in; you're just in time—I need you."

"At your command, Father," the man replied, but made no move from where he stood. "I have a message, a message for your reverence."

"From whom?"

"From the captain, Father. He says he wants you to go to him —he has something to say to you."

"Tell him I have work to do; tell him I don't have two masters—only God."

"Forgive me, Father, but I'm afraid to tell him that. Pity me and go to him."

"I will go when my Master tells me that all is ready, and only then! Tell him that. Eh, you poor soul; Kyriákos my boy, you're preparing yourself for the priesthood in the worst possible way —with fear. To be a priest is to fear no man."

Kyriákos sighed. "I'm afraid of both men and God," he said, "what can I do?"

Father Yánaros felt sorry for this flabby little man, this naïve coward.

"Come here beside me," he ordered, "kneel down."

Kyriákos understood and began to tremble; he knelt and bowed his head. Father Yánaros placed both his wide hands on Kyriákos' head—they were hot, heavy, full of strength; he kept them there, motionless, for a long while. Then he raised his eyes to the sky.

"God of Might," he murmured, "come down and fill this empty wineskin with Your strength. You give strength to an ant, to a mosquito, to a worm; then give strength to this creature, too, to this man. Lord of Strength, give strength to Kyriákos, the town crier of Castello!"

Father Yánaros drew his hands away.

"Get up!" he ordered.

But Kyriákos did not move.

"Again, again, Father; pray again."

Father Yánaros placed his hands on the bowed head again for a long while.

"What do you feel, Kyriákos?" he asked softly.

But Kyriákos did not reply; he felt a sweet warmth, a gentle river, flowing from the hands of the priest—what could it be? Fire, joy, strength? He could not understand it, but he felt his body filling with it.

He grabbed the hand of Father Yánaros and kissed it; then he rose and his face glowed.

"I'm going," he said.

Father Yánaros looked at him with surprise. "Where?"

"To tell the captain that you cannot serve two masters—and that you will go to him when God commands you."

The old man was pleased; he raised his hand. "Go with my blessings," he said. "Do you understand now?"

213

"I understand, Father."

"What do you understand?"

"That I was only an empty wineskin; that now I have been filled; that now I can stand up."

As Father Yánaros watched Kyriákos walking toward the barracks, he noticed that his steps were quick and sure. But, as he watched him, fear and grievance overcame him.

"Ah, man, you poor soul," the priest said loudly, "you can move mountains, perform miracles, and yet you sink in manure, in lethargy and faithlessness! You have God within you; you carry God around with you, and you do not know it! You learn it only on the hour of your death; but then it is too late! Let us who know it roll up our sleeves and let out a cry so they may hear us!"

He grabbed the bell rope again.

"What's happened to Father Yánaros?" "Why is he ringing the bell?" the villagers asked one another with surprise. "Do you suppose that the pigheaded priest has finally decided to proclaim the Resurrection?"

Doors opened and men stepped out, followed by old women wearing kerchiefs over their hair.

"God only knows what he has on his mind again, let's go see!"

The first to appear at the threshold of the church was Andreas the coppersmith, carrying his heavy staff; he grabbed the bell rope in his calloused hand.

"Let it go, Father," he said, "you're tired."

"Good day to you, Andreas," the priest replied, "it's a great day today, we have a lot of work."

"So we're going to have a resurrection after all, eh Father?"

Father Yánaros slapped Andreas' shoulder playfully. "Man first, my son," he said, "man first, then God! Don't be in a hurry."

The priest loved the coppersmith; during difficult moments he always called him to his side. Big and heavy-set, but an honorable man. He had worked in the copper shops of Salonica and become friendly with a Jew who took to indoctrinating him. The Jew would tell Andreas that he was hungry and wronged; Andreas believed him and joined up with other proselytes who gathered at meetings, first in a basement then out in the open in the town squares. They would hold rallies, and Andreas would climb on the Jew's shoulders and make speeches. Their minds would take wing, and they would throw stones, swing clubs, and break up shops. The police would catch them, imprison them, then set them free, whereupon they would start all over again. Until Andreas tired of it all, realized that justice was long in coming, that the rich continued to snatch everything, that the poor continued to be hungry, that women painted their faces, that fat-bellied priests walked around the town square in the company of fools, that the jails were crammed with honest men, the streets with the dishonest. The world would never change! So Andreas returned to his village, to Castello, opened up his own tinker shop, and settled down like a decent man. But how could he escape! The village teacher took him in hand; his mind took wings again, and once more he lost his serenity. He began to dislike the world again, he wanted to form a new one. One day he met Father Yánaros and approached him. "Father," he said, "I don't know what God is, but I know that I am only a coppersmith, a thick head, a thick heart, a piece of rough wood; and yet if I had created the world, I would have done a better job."

The priest laughed. "The world, Andreas, is being formed every day. It's being remodeled every day; don't despair; who knows, perhaps one morning God will call upon you to create the world you have in mind." They both laughed, and from then on they became friends.

The coppersmith took the rope and began to ring the bell with fervor. "I'll even wake the dead," he said laughingly. "It's a great day today for all of us together, the living and the dead!"

He winked slyly at the priest.

"I smell a rat, Father," he said. "Last night I couldn't sleep so I wandered out into the fields. All of a sudden I caught sight of someone climbing the hill; I couldn't make out if it was wearing a dress or a robe."

"It was a robe," the priest said, "it was a robe and inside the robe was an old man, and around his neck hung a village."

"And . . ." the coppersmith added, his tongue twisting, "and . . . did you meet with the you-know-who? Did you come to an agreement?"

"I did."

Andreas let go of the bell; his eyes flashed as he lowered his voice. "Father," he asked, "does this mean the sword will speak?"

"Friendship will speak, Andreas. To the devil with the sword!"

"Oh ho!" the coppersmith cried mockingly, "are you still on that, my priest? You mean you still haven't seen the light? The sword is the only thing that speaks here."

"Love is a sword, Andreas my son; Christ had no other sword but love, and with that he conquered the world."

"Christ would have conquered the world with a reed, or even a feather, but as for us . . . don't weigh everything with the measure of Christ, Father!"

"Christ is within us, Andreas; the measure of Christ is our measure, too; don't humble man so; trust him. Isn't the teacher your friend? Go see him someday, he will explain things to you; the only difference is that he gives the Lord another name. Have you seen him lately? How is he?"

"How else, Father? Day by day he fights with death; but he will not let it put him down. 'How can I die?' he says, 'I have a great ideal.' That's what keeps him alive."

"That's what keeps me alive, too," the priest replied, "that's what keeps the whole world from crumbling; the teacher is right. Give him my regards."

He lowered his voice; he had been speaking to Andreas for some time now, and Andreas listened open-mouthed, with pleasure.

"Fine, agreed, Father," he finally said. "Praise the Lord, you finally got to the meaning of the matter. But if it becomes necessary for the sword to take over, the sword will, so you may as well know it. This world needs pruning, Father Yánaros."

"You're right, my son, the world is a tree and a time comes when the fruitless branches grow wild and destroy the tree; but let's leave the pruning to God."

As the two conversed softly, the villagers moved along the narrow paths of the village, and the churchyard began to fill.

The elders with their caps and their worry-beads, old man Mandras, Stamatis, Uncle Tassos and Hadjis; behind them, like a long tail, came the sons and family men, and the anxious

216

people, with their sunken cheeks, their frightened foxlike eyes, some barefooted, others with torn shoes, all of them in rags; and several old women with black kerchiefs on their heads, and with the endless, half-smothered dirges within their withered breasts. A soft drone rose like a distant lament, like dry branches being lashed by the winds. Two old men and three young women whose minds had broken from fear ran behind the crowd, laughing hysterically. Old Polyxeni, the Mandras maid, was with them. She was barefoot, with a wide red ribbon in her hair; when the fearsome elder saw her, he sent her away with a gesture of his eyebrows.

The sun now slipped over the top of the sky, burning as before the rain. The heated rocks were steaming. Suddenly, from the hillside, came the sound of heavy, slow-marching feet. The stones moved, dogs barked, there was a great clamor, like curses, like crying. Father Yánaros sprang from the threshold, craned his neck and looked out; from the side of the hill appeared bands of men and women from the nearby villages, carrying the church labara. They would merge with other smaller bands who joined them along the way and they swept toward Castello. Five mothers walked ahead clad in mourning, and as they heard the bell ringing, calling out to them, they could not hold back any longer—they burst into dirges. Chrystal, the old woman, threw her black kerchief behind her head and began to unknot her pain; and as her voice broke with fatigue, another woman, from the next path, picked up the tune, beating her breasts, lamenting her son.

Black swirling clouds appeared on the horizon and began to rise; the sun hid for a moment, a small cloud had passed in front of it and the world darkened; the face of peasantry clouded, the villages became frightened and quickened their footsteps.

# 17

Father Yánaros stood on the threshold of the church, and his heart pounded wildly as he watched his people approaching. The blessed hour has come, he thought, the world will be judged by this day. Even if Castello *is* a miserable little village—the world will be judged by today.

Behind the *labara* he could distinguish the men approaching, their tools thrown over their shoulders—picks, hoes, scythes, sifters; they approached silently, with bowed heads. The sun was only halfway across the sky; a strong wind must have blown high above, for the few clouds had scattered. The hills, dipped in light, were gleaming. The vultures watched the people gathering; soon they would all be corpses—the birds were certain of this— and they paused to sharpen their beaks on the rocks. For what man calls war for honor and country, the vultures call a feast! And what man calls a hero, the vultures call tasty meat.

The neighboring villagers arrived; Father Yánaros opened his arms and welcomed them. "Welcome to the house of God, my children; this is the only secure roof, the only impregnable refuge. Come under the wings of Christ, do not be afraid; today will mark the end of all of Christianity's troubles." The courtyard swelled with people; they overflowed into the street. The voices rose, and several black-clad women slowly began the dirges. Old Mandras, his sons, and the other three elders of the village stood in a row before the priest. Behind them, in utter confusion, were the impoverished villagers.

All eyes were raised, watching Father Yánaros and waiting. The sun fell directly on the upturned faces and pitilessly revealed the tear-filled eyes, the sunken cheeks, the wrinkled necks. An old man with eyes swollen from tears raised his staff.

"Eh, Father Yánaros," he shouted, "why did you drag us all here? If you have something to say, say it: We've come to the edge of the cliff; we've eaten everything there is to eat, every bit of grass the hill has shot up. We've shed all the tears that were kept in those sacs behind our eyes. But why do I stand here and talk? Words cannot measure the pain of man!"

His voice cracked; embarrassed, he covered his face with his handkerchief. An old woman untied the scarf from around her head; her white hair flowed over her shoulders. She raised her fist to beat her breasts and begin the lament, but Stelianos the weaver, who stood beside her, grabbed her arm. "We don't want any dirges, Aunt Marióra, so don't beat your breasts—have faith in God."

"I can't stand it any longer, Stelianos, my boy," the old woman screamed, furious that they would not let her chant her lament and unleash her tensions. "No, I can't stand it any longer. Where is the God you speak of? Why doesn't He come to Castello and put the village in order? I want Him here, I want Him now! Stelianos, my son, if God does not help man, what good is He?"

"Father Yánaros is the representative of God in Castello," Kyriákos cried out; he had just returned from the barracks and was still excited. "Quiet," he shouted, "Father Yánaros is going to speak—God is going to speak through the lips of our priest; be patient, Aunt Marióra."

Uncle Thanasi, the medico-philosopher of the village, was infuriated now. He was neat and thin, with a sparse gray beard; he raised his arms in their wide white shirtsleeves and with eyes fixed on Father Yánaros he began to shout. "All I know is that two devils have divided Greece, two devils, curse them! One is red, the other black—neither is a Greek. May God show one up as the liar he is, Father Yánaros, but I think you've set your mind to routing only one of them, and you open the door and let the other in. How are we going to get rid of that one, eh? Who's going to get rid of *him*? When are we going to be free of those two devils, so we can remain masters in our own homes? Damn it, aren't there any Greeks we can leave Greece to?"

Voices rose up from the people. "Quiet!" "Quiet!" "The priest is going to speak."

Father Yánaros made the sign of the cross and leaped upon the stone ledge beside the door of the church.

"Quiet, my children," he shouted, "quiet! I have returned from somewhere very far away, not from the peak of the hill, but from the peak of God. Listen to me, I have an important message for you. I am not the one who speaks, but God. I lay on the slate floor of the church, crying out for God to pity us, that we were being destroyed! I cried, I pleaded, I complained, and for a moment, my mind was jolted with pain. I, the worm, raised my voice to God, threatening! And God pitied me, and a reply came from above. 'Come!' the voice said. 'Where, my Lord?' 'Follow my footsteps wherever they take you!' He stepped before me, and I followed like a puppy; He took the road uphill, and I was close behind. We came to the rebel camp . . ."

"Don't shout; don't raise your fist, Mandras; eh, you! Don't walk out the door! God is speaking, show Him some respect! I am the lips, He is the voice, listen!

"We reached the rebel camp; God paused, opened His mouth, but no one heard Him—no one, only I. He chanted hymns, and I took His words and spoke to the rebels."

Father Yánaros paused for a moment and wiped his sweating brow with the edge of his sleeve. He was inflamed as he spoke; and now, for the first time, he realized that what he was saying to the people was the truth. It happened exactly this way, but he had not realized it before. All this time he had been touching the flames that encircled his body; he knew now that these were not flames—they were God.

"Well," Mandras cried angrily, "never mind the big words, priest, we've had more than enough. What did you discuss with the redhoods? What agreements did you make? I don't trust you, Father Yánaros, you catch fire too easily, be careful you don't burn up our village!"

"Don't burn up our village, Father Yánaros!" "Don't burn up our village!" Voices rose from the crowd—the people had become stormy, they swayed like the sea.

Father Yánaros put up his hand, and the crowd quieted down; again his deep voice rang out.

"It is a holy moment, my children, when the people reach the edge of the precipice, suddenly see it, reach out their hands, and grasp the robes of God. Castello stretched out its hand and it has caught God's robes—salvation is coming!"

"Words, words—nothing but words!" old Mandras shrieked. "Speak clearly, priest! What did you scheme up there with that traitor, your son? Someone go call the captain, we're in danger! Listen to me now, Father Yánaros, weigh the matter carefully before you place the keys of Castello on the tray and surrender them. You hear, Father Yánaros? Do you hear, Castellians and neighbors? That's what I had to say; you heard one, you heard the other—now judge!"

"He's right! Mandras is right!"

"Father Yánaros is right," shouted other voices. "Stop, it's enough!"

Father Yánaros waved his hands and moved his feet, as though dancing on the ledge; he felt God around him, everywhere, like a fire, and he was burning. Whom could he fear now? His soul, all-powerful, leaped within him.

"My children," he cried, "great pain and fear have fallen upon us; rise! We have become a flock of sheep, and each day the butcher selects a few for slaughter; how much longer? Rise up together! This is what God commanded me to tell you: Rise!"

He turned to Kyriákos, who had slowly approached and was looking at him with open mouth and shining eyes.

"Kyriákos, my son," he said, "go into the sanctuary and bring me the Bible that is on the altar; we're going to take it with us."

"We have already risen," shouted the coppersmith, waving his club high over his head. "Onward, friends!"

But old Mandras pushed the crowd aside and turned toward the door. "Those who believe," he shouted, "come with me. Let us go and report to the captain what we heard and all that we saw; Father Yánaros has set a trap for us!"

He reached the threshold of the outer door; behind him were the elders and the sons and several family men; he turned to the people, who moved around, dazed, not knowing which way to turn.

221

"If you believe in Christ, brothers," he shouted, "let no rebel set foot in our village! And as for you, Father Yánaros, we'll settle with you later!"

He walked away quickly, his group behind him, heading for the barracks.

But Father Yánaros only opened his arms to embrace the people; the sunlight fell on his beard and on his hair; he fumed.

"If you believe in Christ, my children, wait," he said, "listen to me! I know for a fact that the rebels had decided to attack our village tonight, Holy Saturday—to enter Castello and burn and slaughter everything, so that not even a stone will remain. There was only one hope—reconciliation! So I went to them and bargained. The fighters will come down, they will not harm anyone; they swore this; they will respect our lives and our honor and our possessions, and we will celebrate the Resurrection together. All of us together, in friendship, in certainty! Blessed be the name of the Lord, my children; Castello will walk ahead to open the road for peace and brotherhood; and who knows the ways of God? Perhaps this humble little village will set in motion the salvation of Greece."

His eyes roamed over the people as his robe fluttered like wings in the wind.

"This very moment that I speak to you, my children," he shouted, "God stands pleased, beside me; none of you can see Him, only I, your priest. Trust me; have faith! Between the two devils—the red and the black—and ahead of them God opens a path and He beckons to us. 'Come,' He says."

The people shuddered; there on the ledge, to the right of the priest, the five mothers saw a shining light and a white tunic and two gleaming eyes.

At that moment, a wild cry rang out; Kyriákos leaped out of the threshold of the church, pale and dazed.

"Brothers," he cried breathlessly, "the Virgin is weeping."

The crowd groaned and ran to Kyriákos, surrounded him, fell over him. He leaned against the wall with foam spouting from his mouth.

"What are you saying, Kyriákos?" the crowd shouted. "Speak up—speak clearly!" "Did you see Her?" "Did you see Her?"

"She's weeping, I saw Her! I went in to get the Bible and as

I approached the altar, I raised my eyes . . . I raised my eyes to pray—and what did I see? Two heavy tears dropping from the eyes of the Virgin Mary! She's weeping, She's weeping! Go and see for yourselves! Don't kill me! Go see for yourselves!"

Father Yánaros jumped from the ledge to hear Kyriákos better; he leaned forward and cleared a path with his elbows to pass and enter the church. He knew Kyriábos was somewhat off. But then, Her Grace *did* perform miracles. Perhaps She felt that Her village was in danger and She wept for it.

"Make room, make room," he shouted, "why are you growling and looking goggle-eyed? She's a mother and She pains for Her children, so She cries. Make room!"

"We want to see!" "To see!" the villagers shrieked. "We want to touch!"

And Chrystal, the old woman, threw off her black kerchief. "Virgin Mother," she screamed, "You're a mother, I'm a mother, too; let me drink your tears so I can be refreshed!"

She screamed at the top of her lungs and fainted. The other old women—her friends Kyra Marigo, Christina, Despina, Zafiro—grabbed her and they, too, began to scream.

By now, Father Yánaros had reached the threshold of the church; he spread out his arms and stopped the people.

"Wait," he ordered, "no one will enter; you'll break my pews, the Bier, the candelabra! Wait, I will go and bring her!"

But the people would not listen; wild cries, shouts, and weeping rose from the crowd.

"The miracle!" "The miracle!" "We want to see the miracle!"

Father Yánaros turned and threw his hands up in the air. "What miracle?" he shouted. "It is no miracle, stop shouting! It would be a miracle if the Virgin saw our pain and hunger and misery and did not cry! Wait, I say, don't shove; eh, Andreas, stand at the door and don't let anyone in!"

Father Yánaros entered; his heart was beating wildly; it was not the first time he had seen a miracle, but he still could not get used to it. He trembled; he would rather see a lion before him—it would have been a thousand times better. Because God stands behind the miracle; God descends from heaven within the miracle, and Father Yánaros had never been able to endure His frightening breath.

He went on, but his knees weakened; now I will see the Virgin, he thought, She will have descended from her icon and She will be standing on the floor, before the iconostas, weeping . . . How should he approach Her, how should he lift Her holy body and take it to the people?

The light flowed through the small window of the sanctuary; the golden Bier gleamed peacefully, and the wildflowers which decorated it smelled with breathtaking sweetness. Out in the courtyard, the crowd rumbled and roared, and stormed in waves to break through Andreas and spill over into the church.

· The wild voices gave Father Yánaros courage, and he walked slowly, hesitatingly, with his eyes fixed on the iconostas. Suddenly he stopped, his breath caught; within the sanctuary, a blue flash cut into the darkness. Father Yánaros' knees buckled; his voice came, choked and stuttering, from his tight, dry lips.

"Mercy, Virgin Mother, mercy! Do not blind me!"

But in a moment, he added, "Let me see you! Let me see you, then let me lose my sight!"

He reached out for support to avoid falling, but he did not catch the pew in time. The roaring crowd had pushed through, trampling Andreas, and spilled into the church. The Bier was crushed beneath their feet; Christ fell to the floor—Kyriákos bent over to pick Him up, but one of the two wooden candelabra fell on him. The blood spurted from Kyriákos' head and dripped from his long, dirty hair, but he felt no pain. He raised his hands toward the iconostas and shouted, "Look, brothers, look; her tears are falling!"

All necks strained; the Virgin had entered everyone's eyes and was crying through them.

All at once the crowd fell to their knees; the slate floor thundered from the weight; and suddenly the light faded. Thunder roared; clouds filled the sky; in the dim light of the church shone the yellow faces of peasantry, with sunken cheeks and huge eyes opened wide; they were not faces, they were skulls; the flesh had melted, showing only the bones.

For a long while there was deep silence; one could hear their hearts beating; and suddenly, a loud indistinguishable noise rose—the people were crying; some rolled on the floor, screaming; others raised their throats in chant, out of tune, hoarse, with mania: "Save your people, Lord . . ."

Kyriákos, his face and neck spattered with blood, burst into wild laughter, then into tears, as though his mind had snapped.

Father Yánaros stood wide-eyed, silently looking at the icon. His heart tightened, his throat clogged, he could not breathe. He took another step forward, closer to the Virgin, stood on tiptoe, pressed his lips on Her eyes and prayed. But immediately he drew back, discouraged; his lips were not wet. I am faithless, he thought. I am an unbeliever and I cannot see. Everyone sees, but I do not.

The grieving mothers untied their black headkerchiefs and rushed toward the icon. As they scrambled before the iconostas, they fought to be the first to stand before the Virgin. Chrystal, the old woman, beat her fists and shrieked at the other women as she went ahead. She wiped the eyes of the Virgin with her kerchief. Then she tied the tears in a knot and hid the kerchief in her bosom.

"Her eyes are filled with tears again!" one of the other old women screamed, and spread her kerchief out to wipe the Virgin's eyes. "Your tears are inexhaustible, Virgin Mother; don't shout, women, don't push, there are tears for everyone."

It was hot; everyone felt they were burning; sweat poured from their necks. The delicately carved iconostas rocked from the people who had fallen against it; already it began to creak. Father Yánaros was afraid it would collapse; he stood on a bench, unhooked the icon and took it in his arms.

"My children," he shouted, "the hour has come. In the name of God, let us go!"

"Let the Virgin go first," the voices shouted. "Let Her go ahead and we will go wherever She takes us!"

"Open, make room, my children, let me pass!" Father Yánaros shouted, and raised the heavy icon as high as he could. "I sense that She is in a hurry!"

"Where are we going, Father?" several old men asked; they had just come to their senses from the holy intoxication; they could hear the bugle sounding from the barracks and they were frightened.

"I'm not taking Her anywhere, my children," the priest replied as he staggered beneath the weight of the icon. "I'm not taking Her anywhere; She's taking me. I swear that She is taking me! Follow!"

He walked out the door; the sun had slipped from the peak of the sky, and black clouds gathered again. Heavy drops of warm rain fell on the face of the Madonna; the tears blended with the raindrops—the Virgin wept steadily now.

Father Yánaros leaned the icon against the door frame; he leaned toward the Virgin's eyes and prayed; his lips and his beard were wet. He no longer asked if these were tears or rain, or if this were a dream. He asked nothing; he felt a great strength flowing from the icon into his arms, his chest, his knees, all of his body. What strength this was, what youth, what flame! He made the sign of the cross. "God forgive me," he murmured, "but if I should open my robe at this moment, I would sprout wings and fly. Who cares about the barracks and the captain and the soldiers and the rebels? Onward!"

He took the Virgin in his arms again and turned his face toward the barracks; behind him stormed the screaming crowd. The icon trembled in the old man's arms; a group of young men rushed at him, grabbed it from his hands, and went ahead. They ran; indeed, they were not carrying the icon, it was carrying them. Soon others rushed up and snatched the icon from the young men's hands. They pushed them aside and ran ahead. And the rain-soaked Virgin, with the deep wound on her face, smiled and labored like a storm-tossed galleon over the rough waves of men. The human sea rushed on, carrying its mistress.

Doors opened, women with disheveled hair appeared; they would look at the tear-soaked Madonna, scream, and join the crowd, moving along with it, crying along with it. The children, swollen—with green bellies, and reedlike legs—rushed along, too, following the crowd, beating their crutches against the rocks.

# 18

IT WAS A WARM April night; the metal of the sky had melted. Gold had been poured over the rocks and thorns and the earth—slowly the shadows fell over the hill. The cloudburst which had broken out for a moment had scattered and passed. It had fallen on the dry grasses, and the earth smelled sweet.

The Virgin shone in the arms of the men; it seemed that the disappearing daylight had found a refuge in the golden halo around Her head and in Her pale, wrinkled cheeks. Beside Her was Father Yánaros, hatless, with his heavy boots and his robe gathered about him, and behind him was a roaring sea—the people.

At a crossroad just before the barracks, Father Yánaros turned and raised his hand; the warlike procession paused.

"My children," he cried, "listen to my voice. We have set out in friendship and in love—not for war. Keep your hands clean—enough of this bloodshed. We have no braggart captain for a leader, we have the Virgin Mary. I lift up my hands and shout: 'Virgin Mother, bring peace and warmth to our hearts! Bring peace and warmth to the hearts of our enemies! Bring peace and warmth to the hearts of the world! It was for this Your Son was crucified.' "

He had not quite finished his words when a wild cry was heard.

"Traitor, bolshevik! I'll kill you!"

227

The army captain jumped before them with fury on his face; his mustache drooped, he was skin and bones, and his eyes were filled with hate. Behind him came the soldiers, and further back was old Mandras with his men. The other three elders—old Stamatis, Uncle Tassos and Hadjis—leaned against the wall of the barracks, biting their tongues, wide-eyed and trembling.

The captain cracked his whip in the air; he took two strides and stood before the crowd; his mouth spat foam.

"What do you dirty villagers want? Where are you going?"

No one replied; only the mothers removed the black kerchiefs from their heads and waved them in the air.

"What do you want?" the captain shouted again. "I'm asking you—answer me! Father Yánaros, are you dumbstruck, you rebel mouthpiece?"

A wild, heavy silence followed; all that was heard was the work tools—the scythes, the hoes, the picks—being lowered from the shoulders of the people.

The sergeant and the soldiers knelt down with raised rifles; they were ready.

Old Mandras' voice rang out. "What are you saving them for, Captain? Shoot! Listen to me—kill the priest, kill him, and the others will scatter to the winds within minutes. Crush the head of the snake, and the rest will die."

"Love, brotherhood!" Father Yánaros tore away from the crowd and shouted. "Love, my children; we do not come for evil, we come in friendship. Do not resist; we are all brothers; spill no more blood; show some respect before the Virgin Mother!"

A pale soldier wearing glasses appeared at the door of the barracks and stood there, confused. Damn this art, he thought, having no heart to step over the threshold, damn the art of killing! The picture of a long, wide field came to his mind—a field on Zante, his island, far, far away, at the other end of the world. It was April, the trees had blossomed, and he sat beneath them with a guitar. But suddenly, the blossoming trees and the guitar disappeared; the angry voice of the sergeant rang out.

"Eh, Nionios! Eh, four-eyes, where's your mind? Get the hell out here—we have work to do!"

"Love, love!" shouted Father Yánaros, and walked toward the

captain, hatless, unarmed, his arms extended as though he were asking for help.

The captain raised his hand. "Fire!" he shouted.

The bullets flew over the heads of the villagers; shame prevented the soldiers from hitting unarmed men. The captain raged with fury.

"Hit them—fire into them!" he screamed again. Then he took out his pistol and emptied it at the crowd.

Stelianos the weaver, who was in front with Father Yánaros, caught a bullet in the forehead and fell over, face down. He had had a hard, tormented life—now he was free. He was pallid and effeminate, with soft hands and a greasy, priestlike voice. His wife, God rest her soul (Lemoni was her name), was the prettiest girl in the village and the best weaver. But she loved to play around, God forgive her, and all the strong, handsome young lads of Castello and of the neighboring villages chased after her. One day Stelianos' friend could hold back no longer; he went to him. "Eh, Stelianos," he said, "all the males of Castello and the surrounding villages are after your wife; she's made a fool of you—throw her out!"

"You think I'm crazy?" he answered. "Everyone's after her and I, who have her, should throw her out?"

But one morning, as she stood combing her hair and singing in front of the window, she fell to the floor—dead! So her husband took over the loom; he began to weave towels, sheets, and nightshirts; then he would load them on his back and go through the villages selling them. No one ever knew why this placid, soft little man suddenly felt that the world was unjust and that it must be destroyed—no one knew how the seed got into him. And if you asked him, he would shrug his shoulders and say, "I don't know . . . exactly how . . . it's just that as I sat weaving all day I fell into thought; and slowly, gradually, I became a bolshevik."

And now the bullet had entered his forehead and the shirts on his loom had remained half finished.

"Aim for the chest!" echoed the voice of the sergeant.

The naïve Roumeliote was kind and gentle, never meaning harm to any man; but when he saw blood, he went wild; perhaps it was from fear.

229

"Damn this miserable art of killing," murmured Nionios again, as the rifle trembled in his hands. "I was made for guitars, not rifles, God damn it!"

But the rest of the soldiers fired as ordered; Mandras and his sons had grabbed rifles from the barracks and joined the ranks.

Moans and groans came from the crowd—five or six bodies fell to the ground. As Kyriákos the town crier opened his mouth to cry out the words that Father Yánaros ordered him to say— "Harmony, understanding! Peace!"—a bullet hit his throat. The blood spurted up, gurgling, and covered his white shirt—his new Easter shirt. And poor Kyriákos opened his arms and fell on the women who were lamenting behind him. He was fat, flabby, his eyes were egg-shaped and his mouth was so large it went from ear to ear. His hair fell dirty and uncombed over his shoulders; since he had made up his mind to become a priest he never washed it, because he had heard that dirt speeded the growth of hair. And now all that dirt was in vain.

Dimitri, the caretaker of the fields in Prastova, groaned like a bull when he saw Kyriákos dead. Kyriákos was his cousin, and he had promised that when he became a priest, he would make Dimitri a sexton in the church, because his work in the fields was tiring, and his feet swelled. And now he lost both his cousin and the comfortable job of church sexton. Fury swept over him; he pulled out the pistol hidden in his belt and aimed at Mandras' sons, who appeared before him, killing young Paul. It was so fast he did not utter a sound—he merely fell, slowly, quietly, to the ground. Just recently he had bought a horse—a black mare with a white spot on its forehead. Paul loved a girl— Uncle Stamatis' granddaughter, Chryssoula—and he would ride back and forth in front of her house. His hair was coal-black and curly, and he let it fall over his forehead and his eyebrows. And just this morning, as he passed by on his horse, she was at the window. The street was deserted, and she threw him a carnation; they had brought it to her from Prastova to decorate the Bier. He caught it in the air and put it behind his ear. It was still there as he lay, sideways, looking at the ground with glassy eyes.

Darkness had fallen; the last light of day which was hiding on the peak of the hill disappeared into the dark blue sky. The wild eyes of peasantry were the only things that shone in the dark wind.

Father Yánaros' eyes filled with tears; he would run pleading to the soldiers, then to his own men: Please, no bloodshed! no bloodshed! But the demons had been let loose, the spilled blood moaned and cried for more blood; soldiers and villagers now fought hand to hand, and the women, too, leaped, with rocks in their hands, which they brought down on the heads of the enemy.

"Fire!" the captain ordered again, and pointed to Father Yánaros, who had been hit on the chin with a rock; blood dripped down his beard.

The captain's rifle was against Father Yánaros' chest, but he did not get a chance to pull the trigger. Andreas seized him, and they both fell to the ground.

"Butcher!" the coppersmith growled as he pulled him down and fell over him. "It's our turn now! We won't always be the sheep; I'll slaughter you!"

The captain mustered all his strength and leaped up, but Andreas still held him by the neck and was now raising his knife.

A heart-rending cry was heard, and a woman wearing a red ribbon on her hair fell on the captain, embracing him.

"Sophocles, my Sophocles," she purred, and began to cry.

Andreas was not able to stop his knife in mid-air; it pierced the woman's heart. She fell to the ground, at the captain's feet, wriggled for a moment, moved her lips, wrapped her arms around the captain's boots, and died.

"The captain's been killed!" The cry rang among the soldiers. "Throw down your arms, men!"

It was Stratis; he threw his rifle away.

But the sergeant leaped to untangle the captain from Andreas. Blood ran from the captain's face and arms; a boulder had hit him in the knee and he could not stand up. Father Yánaros ran and took him in his arms.

"He's mine!" he shouted, and shielded him with his own body.

A loud noise rose up, a wild river broke the dam and overflowed; the hoes and scythes and sickles and picks encircled the few remaining soldiers who resisted; they surrounded Mandras and his group and pinned them against the wall, not letting them move.

The Virgin had stopped at the threshold of the barracks; two

231

old men were holding her; she had her face turned toward the men who were fighting and in the half-light her eyes shone as though they were really filled with tears.

The sergeant and his few men tried to resist, but they were smothered by the villagers; the captain, his head cracked open, rolled on the ground, biting his lips to keep from screaming.

Old Mandras still resisted, jumping against the wall where they had pinned him.

"Surrender, Mandras," Father Yánaros called to him. "Enough of this bloodshed! As God is my witness, I did not want this."

"You killed my son Paul, you scoundrel!" groaned the old man, and wiped the tears that ran from his eyes.

He could control himself no longer and broke out into sobs and laments.

A huge wave fell over them, gathering and rounding them up together, both soldiers and elders, in the large yard of the barracks. Father Yánaros carried in the captain, brought water, washed his wounds and placed him gently in a corner of the yard.

"Don't worry, Captain," he told him, "everything will end well, with the grace of God; whatever happened is over; the evil has come to an end now."

He turned to his own men. "Bring ropes so we can tie them; don't hit them; they're our brothers. They do not know it, but we do; let's tie them up so they will not resist the armistice. And then, tonight, by the soul which I will turn over to God, all of them will be freed. Everyone—every one of them, I swear it!"

The captain raised his bloodied head. "Traitor!" he growled and spat at the priest.

"Since you refuse to be set free peacefully, we'll set you free by force!" the coppersmith said, and tied the ropes around the elders and the soldiers.

# 19

FATHER YÁNAROS entered the church; his heart fluttered; everything he had hoped for, for so long, was beginning to take form. The estranged brothers would reunite in Castello, and Christ would be resurrected in the way He chose—within the hearts of men. Father Yánaros decided he would wake up early tomorrow morning and run through the hills and valleys and the villages, to tell the priests, the elders, all the people, the story of what they had accomplished in Castello, how everything had been resolved peacefully, and how much better and easier was the road of Love. I will become a herald of God, he thought, and shout like St. John the Forerunner in the wilderness. He had shouted and shouted until gradually the stones developed ears, heard him, moved, became friends, and embraced one another; and Christ's church was built.

A sweet turmoil swelled within him; he could see the road opening ahead; he could feel new wings sprouting on his back. Father Yánaros felt rejuvenated; he became twenty years old again. He bowed and worshiped the crucified Saviour on the altar.

"My Lord," he said to Him, "You know that I have never asked a reprieve from death before, but now I ask one favor of You; let me live until I fulfill my task. Then let anything kill me—a sparrow, a pebble, anything!" He floated with joy as he paused before the Holy Gate.

"My children," he said, "be patient; at this very hour, our

233

brothers are descending the hill; we will celebrate the Resurrection with them. The cursed rifle—Satan's voice—is muted. The spirit of the devil is crumbled in *Tartara*. God has triumphed! Now you will see what a Resurrection we will have! The candles will light themselves! Christ will leap from His grave; the Pancreator on the dome above will smile upon us, pleased and satisfied. It is as I have been telling you all this time, and you would not believe it. The soul of man is almighty because it is a breath of God's wind, all-powerful and free. And now, here before us, two roads open: the road to slaughter and the road to love; God left us alone to choose, and we chose the road to love—blessed be the name of the Lord. God is pleased and He beckons to His Son. 'The people have taken the good road; they have seen the true light; come out from the grave, my only Son.'"

Suddenly, as the priest spoke, there came the sound of heavy footsteps, of stones rolling down the hill, and of a drum beating quickly and joyfully. The sounds came closer.

"They're coming!" "They're coming!" shouted several villagers who arrived, panting, at the church. "They're coming, God help us!"

All faces turned toward the door; hearts beat wildly.

Father Yánaros had put on his holiday vestments—the delicately embroidered cloths, the gold-embroidered stole—and in his arms he held the Holy Infant—the heavy, gold-plated Bible.

He stood and waited at the doors of the sanctuary, and his cheeks were flushed with joy. The kiss of love is coming, he thought, and his face glowed.

The redhoods descended; they jumped over the rocks, slipped on the stones, laughed, leaped everywhere—packs of wolves, their eyes gleaming in the darkness.

"When will we come down like this into Yánnina," a voice said, "and Salonica and Athens?"

"And Rome, too—and Paris and London!" A hoarse cry added, "Don't forget that all this is just a rehearsal."

Captain Drakos descended; he was dazed. His mind ran back and forth across his temples like wild prey caught by hunting dogs and ripped apart in the tugging. The words he had exchanged with Loukas ran through his mind again and again. If I were sensible, I would not have spoken, he thought, but I believe in being honest. I speak up and let the chips fall where they may. My head is not steady on my shoulders—one day they will say, "Captain Drakos fell from a cliff, God rest his soul." If I were sensible, I should either have remained silent, or obeyed, or raised my own banner. The first would have been disgraceful; the second, slavery; the third is impossible for me. So all roads are blocked!

Loukas, gruff and embittered, stood beside him. He was short and bowlegged, but in battle he tied a red kerchief around his head, clenched a knife between his teeth, and leaped unafraid. He never looked back to see if anyone was following him, and when he walked out of battle, his clothes dripped blood. He walked beside the leader now, gritting his teeth in anger. They had had an argument, in low tones lest the other men hear them. They tossed words at each other like knives.

"I'm amazed that you joined the party, Captain," said Loukas between his teeth. "In the party one obeys without questions."

"I refuse to free others unless I myself am free," Drakos replied dryly, his lips twisting with bitterness. "Our duty is to bring justice first and then freedom. That's what I did in every village I entered; I cannot remain silent when I see injustice. The first thing I do is to bring order and justice."

"The true communist does not falter when he sees injustice; he accepts it if that injustice helps our cause; everything is for the cause—everything for victory!"

"That's going to be our downfall!" Drakos shot back, infuriated. "That's going to be our downfall. So the end justifies the means, does it? We should go ahead with injustice to reach justice, eh? We should go on with slavery to reach freedom? I hate to say this, but that attitude is going to destroy the cause. It hasn't been very long since I began to realize that if the means we use to reach our goal are dishonest, our cause becomes dishonest. Because the cause is not a piece of fruit that hangs ripe and ready at the end of the road for us to pick; no, no, never! The cause is a fruit that ripens with each deed, that takes the dignity or the vulgarity of each of our deeds. The path we take will give the shape and flavor and taste to the fruit, and fill it

235

with either honey or poison. If we stay on the road we've taken, we're going to the devil and so will the party. I'm giving it to you straight, and I know you're going to pass it on; so tell them and let them knock their heads against the wall. I'm right here, and if they don't like me, let them get rid of me; I won't be the first they've killed for expressing his own opinion; I told you many times and I'll say it again—I'm not afraid to die."

He was silent as he twisted the ends of his mustache.

"Damn it," he growled, "I've never been afraid of life, so why should I fear death?"

Loukas looked mockingly at the captain from the corner of his eye. "You joined the party with your heart full of snakes; you call them questions, I call them snakes. But the true fighter asks no questions; he fights! Only the leaders ask questions and hold discussions and make decisions; we—the others—only take orders and carry them out. That's the only way a struggle is won. One day they asked a Russian communist, 'Have you read Marx?' And he replied, 'No, why should I? Lenin read him!' You understand, Captain? That's why the bolshevik revolution won the victory."

Drakos looked at his first-fighter from the corner of his eye —he drew in his breath.

"Don't play the teacher with me; one thing I know is that blind submission makes slaves."

"You want to raise your own banner then?" the bowlegged fighter asked mockingly.

"I might, I just might; we'll see."

"And with whose support?"

"With my own."

Loukas clenched his fist; his eyes flashed.

"No one should trust you, Captain Drakos; it's not the first time you're revolting; you once threw the captain of your ship into the hold, and took over the wheel."

"And saved the ship! The captain was drunk and would have sunk us all!"

"So you had a taste of mutiny and liked it! But here, Captain, here you'll spit blood!"

"I didn't like it; but I learned to take responsibility without being afraid of threats." He was overcome with fury; the blood

236

rushed to his head and he saw red! "Why are you threatening me?" he growled softly, "why do you look at me and laugh beneath your mustache? You think I don't know? That whore came and brought you the news; but by the hair of my mustache, you'll never be captain here!"

Loukas slowly grasped the dagger underneath his sash.

"Let's walk faster, Captain, before the men hear us." They hurried on, leaving their comrades behind.

Drakos grabbed Loukas' arm. "Put down your hand!" he growled. "The time hasn't come yet! I know that I should kill you now, because you'll kill me the first chance you get, but . . ."

"But what? Are you afraid?"

"But I'm thinking of Castello; let me take Castello and then we can finish our talk, Captain Bowlegs!"

He pulled out his tobacco pouch and turned to Loukas. "We've got time," he said, "here, roll yourself a cigarette."

The men behind caught up to them now.

"This is the way our men should see us," Drakos said softly, "arm in arm. You and I may be digging each other's graves, but these young fighters are pure fire; let's not show them our wretchedness. If the world is saved, they'll have saved it; if it's lost, we—the leaders—will be to blame."

Loukas did not reply, but his eyes had filled with murder; he took the tobacco pouch and slowly began to roll a cigarette.

# 20

THE SKY began to pale, the morning star struggled and slowly faded in the growing light. A sad and gentle smile spread softly over the lonely rocks. A solitary hawk balanced itself in the peak of heaven; it, too, was waiting for the sun to appear and thaw its wings.

In the cool rose-light of dawn came the sound of a bell pealing joyfully—Christ had risen from the dead! The proud fighters entered the village and began to sing. The hymn leaped from their manly chests and rolled over the hillsides; it trod the village like a chieftain with his heavy boots, his bandoliers, his curling mustache. The crowd pushed forward, the doors of the church opened; Father Yánaros came down from the portals of the iconostas, walked toward the great arched gate in the courtyard, holding the heavy silver-bound Bible tightly in his arms. At that very moment the guerrillas, their rifles slung over their shoulders, stepped out of the shadowy side streets into the early light of dawn. They had stopped singing, and walked cautiously; they looked around in apprehension—they trusted no one yet.

The villagers, uneasy now, poured out of the church; they, too, were mistrustful. They saw the rifles gleaming and the eyes glowing in the half-light, and they were frightened. They kept looking back and forth, from the priest to the armed beasts he had brought into the village. The savage guests from the hills came in increasing numbers and filled Castello by the minute. They entered and overflowed the church.

The guerrillas, both men and women, stepped back to make a path for the tall, heavy, fearsome captain who appeared. He raised his fist in greeting: "Welcome, to us!" he shouted.

"Blessed be he who cometh in the name of the Lord!" Father Yánaros replied, and held out the Bible for the captain to kiss.

But Drakos turned to the crowd, stroking his beard, and his voice echoed under the dome of the church.

"We are happy that you have finally seen the light. We bring you justice and order, and soon after, freedom!"

"Not before?" Father Yánaros asked, controlling his turmoil. "After? Not before, Captain?"

"Justice and order first," he said again, and crimson flooded his hairy face. "We must bring order first. Freedom is a strong wine, Father Yánaros, and it can go to one's head. Everyone can't take it, I'll have to choose!"

"May God place His hand," murmured the priest, and threw a secretive, inquiring glance at Christ there on the right of the iconostas. He bit his lips to control himself.

"God is the great Judge—He will decide—we place our trust in Him."

Captain Drakos laughed sarcastically. "We've knocked God off His throne, Father Yánaros, don't you know that yet? Man is sitting on God's throne now. We used to hold Him responsible for all things—right and wrong—but now we are to blame for whatever happens—good or bad. We formed our own government and we take the responsibility."

Father Yánaros groaned; he wanted to cry out, to shout an anathema at this bear who blasphemed, but he held back his heart. He was afraid for the people and he smothered his anger.

These are only words that others put in their mouths, he thought, they only say them to frighten us. But God works within them, even though they do not know it. We must be patient.

"Let us finish the sacrament of giving and receiving the kiss of love; your heart may soften then, Captain."

Father Yánaros began the Holy Liturgy of the Resurrection; never did his voice echo so joyfully, never did his chest shake with such strength, as though Christ were really inside, as though his chest were the tombstone and it was rising to let

Christ out. Christ took on a new meaning: it was man who had been crucified, and died, and now cried out to be resurrected.

Father Yánaros opened the Bible; he held it tightly in his arms as he walked out into the courtyard. Behind him came the rebels; further back the crowd of people holding the unlit candles. The priest climbed upon the stone ledge, raised his voice to shout the holy words of the Resurrection. As he stood there, dressed in silk, with the gold vestment stole, his chest swelled and his throat strained; he looked like a golden rooster who stands in the courtyard to crow for the sun to rise.

The people extended their candles, ready to pounce on Father Yánaros to receive a light. The priest spread his palm on the open Bible; he did not look at it—he knew the words by heart—and his voice resounded triumphantly in the morning wind of spring: "And when the Sabbath was passed, Mary Magdalene . . ."

The rebel leader coughed; Father Yánaros turned and threw him a quick glance. He stood erect, unbending in the center of the courtyard, surrounded by his men, and a triumphant smile spread over his face.

"God help us," murmured Father Yánaros, raising the lighted candles and summoning all his strength as the mournful pleading, the paean of the Resurrection, came from his puffed-out chest: "Christ has risen from the dead!"

The crowd leaped to light their candles from Father Yánaros' flame; Drakos turned to the men beside him, lowered his voice, and gave a command. Ten of them grabbed their rifles and strode toward the outer door. The crowd moved, shaken. A sense of evil passed through the air. He turned to leave, but Father Yánaros stretched out his hand. "Do not go," he said, "I want to talk to you."

The people stopped short, impatiently, as though choking from the rebels' breathing around them. Drakos turned to the priest. "Make it short, priest," he said, "we have work to do."

As he stood on the ledge, Father Yánaros opened his arms wide, turned to the right and to the left, as though he wanted to embrace the villagers who were gathered in the courtyard, the rebels, and all of Castello, all of Greece.

His voice leaped from his chest like joyful bubbling water.

"My children," he cried, "I have been resurrecting Christ for forty years but I have never felt a more joyous, more complete, more heart-filled Resurrection. Because for the first time I realize that Christ and Greece and man's soul are one. And when we say, 'Christ is risen,' it means that Greece is risen, that the soul of man has risen. Only yesterday, on this very hill, brothers were killing brothers. The rocks echoed from the moans and curses. And now—look! Reds and blacks have united in brotherhood and share together their understanding of 'Christ has risen.' This is the true meaning of the Resurrection —this is the true meaning of love. For years now this is what I have waited for; and now it has come. Glory to the Almighty! Captain, the people's eyes are upon you; they await your words; speak to them, this great moment!"

The captain raised his hand. "Go to your homes—go!"

"Is that all you have to say, Captain?" the priest growled angrily. "Is that the way Christ is resurrected? Is that what unity and brotherhood mean?"

"Yes, that's it. We said order and justice must come first. There are enemies of the cause here; I asked to have them brought before me. All of you leave; I will remain here in the courtyard with my men and pass judgment."

The crowd swarmed, pushing and shoving toward the gate; the courtyard soon emptied.

"I will remain here with you, Captain," Father Yánaros said as he folded his vestments—his hands trembled from anger.

Captain Drakos shrugged his shoulders. "Stay and give them last rites," he said, and laughed.

Fury swept over Father Yánaros; his voice came stern and hoarse: "Captain Drakos, the two of us made a bargain. I kept my word and turned over the village to you. Now it's your turn. I gave—now you give! You're the debtor now—I'm staying here to collect."

Enraged at the words, Loukas grabbed the priest by the shoulder. "What are you trying to prove, old man? And what gives you the right to talk to a guerrilla on equal terms? Who's behind you that makes you talk with such assurance?"

"I have God behind me, my son," the older man replied. "I have God behind me, and that's why I talk with such assurance.

241

I have God in front of me, God to the right of me, God to the left of me; I'm encircled by God; all your rifles and all your swords and all your threats will never be able to touch me."

He enthroned himself, alone, on the edge of the stone ledge. As they spoke, the sound of footsteps came from the narrow street, followed by moans, cries, and curses. In a few moments the open gate filled. Old Mandras was at the head, thin and erect, his long neck stretching like a pelican's. Behind him were his three sons and four family men, followed by three of the town elders: Barba Tassos, old Stamatis, and Hadjis. Their faces were drained, their lips drooping, their sashes loose; they were crying. Behind the notables, limping, dragged Mitros the sergeant. He had resisted and the rebels had beaten him. He could barely drag his legs and he was held up by Nionios. Behind them came the other soldiers, torn, ragged, unarmed. At the end, covered with mud and blood was the captain. He had been shot while resisting capture. Blood ran from his wounds. Two fighters held him up. But as they entered the courtyard, he fell to the ground in a heap.

Captain Drakos jumped at sight of the captain. He approached him, craned his neck and looked. The light had now caught the dome of the church and slowly fell over the courtyard; the faces of the men shone and there, among the guerrillas, the light showed the pale, dark-eyed army captain's wife, who stood tight-lipped and bare-necked.

Drakos bent over, watching the captain hungrily, silent for a long while. At last he opened his mouth: "Is it you, Captain? You, sir? What's happened to you?" He turned to his men. "Untie him," he ordered, "cut the ropes! Lift him up." Then he turned to the captain. "You! You've aged, you've rotted away—why is your hair so white?"

The captain bit his mustache with fury; he would not speak. Blood ran from his eyebrow, and a bullet was lodged in his right heel; it must have pierced the bone for he was in great pain. But he gritted his teeth to prevent from crying out.

Drakos watched him with admiration, with compassion, with horror. Was this the raven-mustached, silent, brave warrior whose name resounded throughout the Albanian hills? What a shame, Drakos thought, what a pity that men of such spirit are not on our side! All the virtues should be among our own

242

fighters, all the cowardices and dishonors within the others. But we have many cowards and dishonest ones among us, and the others have many brave men with them. I think that God shuffled the cards wrong and we're all mixed up . . .

"Do you remember me, sir?" he asked. "Look at me closely; don't you remember me?"

The captain wiped the blood from his eyes, turned his face away, and remained silent.

"I served in your company during the Albanian war," Drakos went on. "I had another name then; you were very fond of me and you called me Pirate. When there was a dangerous mission you always called on me. 'Go on, Pirate,' you'd say, 'perform your miracle!' And when you were wounded in both legs during one of the battles, remember, you fell, and the others left you; but I put you on my shoulders, carried you for five hours, and brought you to the hospital. You had put your arms around my neck and said, 'I owe my life to you—I owe my life to you!' And now the wheel's turned—damn it—and we're killing each other."

The captain's knees buckled; he fell to the ground, silent.

"Why did you go with them, Captain?" Drakos continued, and his voice was filled with grief and complaint. "You, a hero, an honorable Greek! Didn't you shed your blood for freedom, in Albania? Why do you betray it now? Why do you fight against it? Come with us—I'll turn my men over to you—I'll serve under your command again. Send me on the difficult missions; we'll fight together again to free our people. Don't you pity the Greeks who are being destroyed? Come, join us!"

Blood rose to the captain's pale cheeks. "Kill me," he murmured at last. "Kill me so I can be free."

He paused a moment and then he added: "If you were my prisoner, traitor, I'd have killed you—so kill me, too. That's all I have to say!"

"I respect you," Drakos replied, and now his voice was filled with mercy and anger. "I respect you and I feel sorry for you, but I'm going to kill you anyway."

"That's the way it should be," the captain replied.

Drakos clenched his fist and turned to his men: "Line them up against the wall," he ordered, "all of them! Captain, can you stand up?"

"Yes, I can," he replied and mustered all his strength to rise,

243

but his knees gave in, and he fell back. Two men ran to help him, but he waved his hand in anger.

"Don't touch me," he growled, "I'll get up alone." He grabbed hold of a stone in the wall, summoned all his strength and stood up. Sweat poured over him, and he turned paler still. He looked around him; below, on the slates of the courtyard sat the guerrillas with crossed legs. On the stone ledge across, sat Drakos with Loukas. At one end Father Yánaros, and at the other . . . The captain's blood whirled, his eyes dulled; black lightning tore through his brain, as he saw that the woman sitting on the other end of the ledge was his wife. Once upon a time he had a wife . . . How quickly fifteen years of happiness had passed—like a flash! It seemed like only yesterday when the two of them had climbed the rocky hills of Roumeli. His elderly mother had stood there at the threshold, dressed in white—her wedding dress, and the same one she would wear when she died. She had waited for them, she waited and waited, since daybreak, and now she cried with joy. The newlyweds began to cry, too, because they were young and it was spring and the ground smelled sweet; and a partridge that was in a cage in the courtyard paced back and forth behind its bars. It watched the new arrivals and cackled sadly, as though she, too, wanted to be married, but her groom was in the hills, and the cage stood between them, preventing their union. So she beat against her prison with her beak and her red feet, trying to escape. "Mother," the bride said, "I want to ask a favor of you. I can't stand to see the partridge imprisoned; give me your permission to open her cage and set her free."

"She's yours, daughter," the old woman replied, "she's yours to do with as you please." And the bride opened the cage, and took the plumed partridge in her palm. She admired her coral legs, the wild, yet gentle, eyes, the puffed-up breast, and quickly she tossed her hand high and released her in the air. "Go on," she told it, "you're free!"

Drakos' voice rang in the air. "Line them up against the wall!" The three elders were crying, spattering saliva and tears on their beards. The soldiers, gathered in a group, were whispering and looking toward the gate; old Mandras spat at Father

Yánaros as he passed in front of him. "Traitor," he said, and spat again.

Father Yánaros rose, walked toward the wall where the men stood in a line at the right and left of Drakos. His heart trembled, but he controlled himself.

"Don't be afraid, my children," the priest cried, "the rebel leader did not come to our village for revenge—he came in friendship. He is a man, a brave lad; he gave his word that he would harm no one—his word of honor—have faith! He only wants to frighten you, and rightly so, because of your resistance to a reconciliation. He wants to scold you and then he'll let you go free—he came for freedom's sake didn't he? Do not fear!"

Old Mandras turned a wild, poisonous look at the priest. "To hell with you, you traitor, you Judas! Do you think they believe in such a thing as honor, you fool?"

Drakos threw his cigarette down and stamped on it with his heavy boot. Then he turned to the captain and to his own men.

"Captain," he said, "you've acted like a man. You have lost Castello, but you have not lost your honor. And those of you who remained—you fought us and killed my men, but it was war, so it's understandable. I take the sponge and wipe all this away; now I offer you my hand, listen to me! Those who decide to put on the rebel cap and fight for freedom are welcome to join us. Those who refuse, die!" He turned to Mandras. "You, old man Mandras, you heartless elder who's taken over the whole village and drained the blood of the poor, I'm not asking you to come along—you, I'm going to kill!"

The old man half closed his small, runny eyes and looked over his shoulder at Captain Drakos. "I made sons and grandsons, I've lived my life, my work is done; I'm not afraid of you, rebel! Only one thing bothers me"—he turned to Father Yánaros—"that I didn't get a chance to skin you alive, you scoundrel!"

Then he turned to his sons. "Do whatever you want. Both honor and dishonor stand before you—choose!"

He turned, lastly, to the young family men. "You family men go with them, you poor souls, save your skins." Then he grabbed his shirt and tore it open, showing the bony, hairy chest. "I'm ready," he said.

245

Father Yánaros stretched his neck, yanked at his beard, and listened; he could not believe his ears. Is this, then, the freedom they bring us? "Surrender and you are free; resist and you die!" If they go back on their word, I will rise and shout; let them put me up against the wall, too. "Onward, Father Yánaros—both redhoods and blackhoods fight you. But don't complain, you want to be free, don't you? Then pay!"

Mitros the sergeant closed his eyes; he could see the little house in the ravine, the oak in the middle of the yard, and in the shade of the tree his wife Margo, with her thick stockings, her embroidered skirt, and the red shoes. He could see her sitting, unbuttoning her blouse, and taking out her breast to feed his son.

He opened his eyes and saw the captain standing before him. "Will you let me go, sir?" he said softly, shamefully, to the captain. "Won't you let me go back to my village, to Roumeli? I want no part of war, damn it! I want no part of it! I wasn't meant to kill . . ."

The captain threw back his head to hear him. "Mitros!" he growled reprimandingly, and his eyebrows arched.

"Captain," Mitros replied, stammering, "command me, sir."

"Aren't you ashamed? Come with me!"

"I'm coming, Captain," the sergeant answered, and at once the hill and the oak tree and his wife and their son disappeared.

The three family men stepped forward. "We're coming with you, Captain Drakos," they said. "Life is too sweet."

Mandras turned his head the other way and spat, but he remained silent.

The three elders—Barba Tassos, old Stamatis, and Hadjis—took a step and staggered; the oldest—Hadjis—spoke up. "Don't you want to take our possessions, Captain Drakos?" he asked, whimpering.

"I don't like haggling," growled the rebel leader, and shoved the three old men back against the wall. "What would I do with you old wrecks? Stand up against the wall!"

Vassos, a soldier with lines in his cheeks, with crooked shoulders, with wide calloused hands, with small sad eyes, stood despairingly, first on one leg, then on the other; he could not come to a decision. Only today he had received a letter from his four sisters, and his heart had filled with poison.

"Captain Drakos," he said, "I have four sisters; I've got to marry them off. Don't kill me."

"Will you join us?"

Vassos swallowed hard. "I'll come."

Three other soldiers from the seven stepped from the wall and came forward. Stratis, the first and most agile, spoke up. "Captain Drakos, we were always on your side. Our rifles were in Castello, but our hearts were in the hills. We'll come with you."

One of the remaining soldiers, Nionios of Zante, spoke. "Captain Drakos," he said, "I'm not coming with you. Not because I don't love life, but because I am ashamed. I'm ashamed to be subjected by force. So kill me."

"If you were ashamed, you'd join us. I pity your wasted youth."

"My dignity as a man does not allow me to be forced into obedience," Nionios replied, and stood up against the wall.

Old Mandras' youngest son, Milton, sighed and looked first at his father, then at the rebel leader, and then at the gate. Oh if he were only a bird, to fly away! He was twenty-five years old and unmarried. All the village girls were his; he loved wine and he played the tambour drum. Every Sunday he would place a flower behind his ear and make the rounds of the neighborhoods. He was chubby, rosy-cheeked, with a lock of hair that bounced over his forehead.

Milton sighed; his mind went to the wine and young women, then to honor and country and to the heroes who sacrificed their lives and became immortal. The poor soldier was dazed; he could not decide which was stronger and more real, which to choose.

Drakos stood before him and watched. "Well?" he asked. "Make up your mind—decide!" The young man bowed his head; his face turned crimson. A cluster of basil that a girl from the village had given him last night still hung over his ear. "I'll join you," he said, and walked away from the wall.

Mandras bowed his head and did not speak.

"The devil take you," his two brothers shouted, and spat at him.

Drakos approached the captain. How can I help him? How can I help him? he thought, and watched him silently. There's nothing I can do, since he's not afraid of death.

He turned to his men who waited with raised rifles. "Ready?" he asked, and raised his hand to give the word. Father Yánaros' eyes bulged as he leaned against the wall; his insides were tearing. Within his fist he felt the hand of the Almighty trembling.

"What is this that trembles? Are You frightened, too?" he said to God, softly. "Are You afraid for me? Courage, my Lord!"

As Captain Drakos raised his hand to give the signal, Father Yánaros jumped up, growling, and walked slowly, heavily, toward the rebel leader. He felt that he had suddenly become one hundred years old; his body had become lead; he felt an unbearable weight on his shoulders. He took two steps, three, and stopped in front of the leader. He did not know what to say; his throat had clogged; he was choking. Finally, with great effort, his lips unsealed. "Are you going to kill them?" he said, and his whole body trembled. Drakos turned and looked at him. The priest's face had become ashen, his mouth slanted, he was breathing with difficulty. "Are you going to kill them?" The old man's voice, short and hoarse, was heard again.

"Yes, death to all who stand in the way of freedom!"

"Those who do not allow others to have their own opinion stand in the way of freedom, too," Father Yánaros reprimanded. "What about the promise you made me? Is this the freedom you bring?"

"Don't meddle in the affairs of this world, old man!" the rebel leader said, exasperated.

"This world and the next world are one; you can win and lose this world, you can win and lose the other, too. I meddle in your affairs because they're my affairs, too, Captain Drakos. I spread my arms over these Christians that you've pushed against the wall and I say to you, "You're not going to kill them! I, Father Yánaros, won't let you kill them!"

"Calm down, old man, for your sake I tell you to calm down! If we let everyone go free now, we're lost; we won't be a nation, we'll be a pack of dogs. Freedom will come in due time, don't rush things; it never comes at the beginning, it always comes last."

"Tyranny, then?" The old man threw his hands in the air and shouted, "Tyranny, force and the whip? Is that how we get freedom? No, no, I won't accept that. I'll rise and shout through all the villages, 'Tyrants, degraders, cursed enemies of the people!' "

"Be quiet! Or I'll stand you up against the wall, too!"

"I was always up against the wall, my boy. I've been expecting the bullet from the moment I saw the truth, so let it come!"

Loukas, who seemed to be sitting on hot coals throughout the scene, could control himself no longer. He jumped up and grabbed the priest by the neck. "Don't shout, priest, you think we respect your black robes? I'll twist your neck, scoundrel!"

"Don't try to frighten me, redhood," the old man replied. "Death only frightens the unbelievers. I believe in God. I'm not afraid of death. I've already dug my grave, there, in front of you, and I've carved on my tombstone the words, 'Death, I fear you not!' "

"I'm going to kill you, you old goat, shut up!" Loukas growled.

Five or six rebels jumped up and encircled the priest, slipping the rifles from their shoulders.

"Kill me, you're welcome to it, my boys. You think that because you carry rifles you carry justice, too? Kill me! You can kill the last free man, but you'll never kill freedom." He walked back to the wall and stood beside the captain.

"Get away from the wall, old man," Drakos said. "And stop talking. Close your mouth, or we'll close it for you."

"My place is here. You cheated me and I cheated the village. I betrayed it. How can I show my face before those people again? I'm anxious to appear before God, to tell Him of my pain, to inform on you and your men, you charlatan! You think you're going to shape the new world, eh? With lies, with slavery, with dishonesty?"

"Father Yánaros, I don't want to ordain you a hero and have you become a ghost," Drakos growled as he grabbed the priest's arm and yanked him away from the wall.

"If you let me live, I'll cry out! If you kill me, I'll cry out! You'll never escape me," the priest said, and as he spoke, the first rays of the sun fell on him and his beard turned a rose hue.

Again Father Yánaros felt the Almighty trembling inside his fist. Anger seized him. "Now, at this crucial moment," he cried within himself, "Now, you are overcome with fear? This is when we need strength; get up, help me save them! You forget that You're not only the crucified Christ, but the resurrected Christ as well! The world has no need of crucified Christs any longer, it needs fighting Christs! Take a lesson from me. Enough of tears and passions, and crucifixions; get up I say, call out for the army of angels to descend; bring justice! Enough they've spit on us, beaten us, made us wear a crown of thorns, crucified us; now it's the turn of the resurrected Christ.

"We want the Second Coming here, here on earth, before we die. Get up, rise!" And a deep sad voice came from the depths of his inner being: "I cannot . . ."

Father Yánaros' hands fell paralyzed. "You cannot? You want to, but You cannot? You are good and just; You love the people, You want to bring justice and freedom and love to the world and You say You cannot?"

The priest's eyes filled. "How sad," he murmured, "so freedom is not almighty, it is not immortal, it, too, is the child of man and it needs him!"

His inner being flooded with bitterness, with compassion, with tenderness; never, never had he loved Christ as he loved Him at this moment. "My child . . ." he murmured, and closed his eyes.

Captain Drakos turned and looked at him; he watched his father's tears running down his cheeks and on his beard. He knew that Father Yánaros was not crying out of fear—he placed little value on his life—he was crying for all men, friends and enemies, blacks and reds. He looked and looked at the old man's tears falling, and suddenly without knowing from where the warm wind of compassion blew, his heart ached for the twelve men who stood waiting against the wall. Their lives hung on one word from him, on one movement of his hand. What should he do? Which was the shortest road to victory? Was it to kill, to kill and bring no end to hate? Or to open his arms, too, like his father, the priest, and conquer hatred through love? He made a move toward the condemned men. "I am keeping my word," he wanted to say, "I bring freedom, you're free!" But his eyes met Loukas' stare, wild and mocking. A demon leaped within him; it was dark, hairy, covered with blood. Drakos raised his hand. "Fire!" he growled in a voice that was not his own.

The rifles cracked, and the twelve bodies fell on the churchyard slates. The captain's body quivered like a fish, then it rolled to a stop at his wife's feet; she shoved it away with her foot.

Father Yánaros let out a cry; for a moment his brain jolted; he turned toward the church, but his mind was reeling, and with it reeled the village and the hill around it, and Greece. Slowly, dragging himself, he moved toward the twelve corpses; he bent over, scooped up a fistful of blood and daubed it on his beard, making it fiery red. He bent over again, took another fistful of blood, and poured it over his head.

"Your blood, my children," he groaned, "your blood is on my hands; I killed you!"

The rebels turned and looked at him, and they laughed.

He went into the church, bowed before the Holy Altar; the blood-spattered rock still lay beside the crucifixion; he worshiped it. Whose blood was on it, a redhood's? a blackhood's? He did not question; he had taken the rock from the hill after one of the first battles. He had placed it on the Holy Altar beside Christ on the cross and before every liturgy, he prayed to it.

He removed his vestment stole, folded it, wrapped it around the Bible, and put it under his arm. He made the sign of the cross as he took his staff from the corner. He felt his heart opening and an inexhaustible river of love spilling out, flowing from Castello to the valleys and the seashores of Greece. Love flowed—it flowed, and Father Yánaros felt relief in his heart.

Who knows, he thought, perhaps Christ entrusted me, the unworthy one, with this great duty. In the name of God, His will be done. He turned to his right.

"Come," he said to the Invisible One. "Let us go!"

He walked out of the church and stood in the middle of the courtyard. "I am leaving," he shouted. "I will do as I said, I will go from village to village and I will shout: 'Brothers, do not believe the reds, do not believe the blacks, unite in brotherhood!' A village without a village idiot is nothing; I will become the village idiot, the lunatic of Greece, and I will go about shouting."

The old man glowed in the morning light; there in the center of the courtyard he looked like a giant with his bloodied beard, with his black, bushy eyebrows, with his heavy staff and large boots.

He turned to Captain Drakos. "I've taken my vestment stole

and the Bible with me, Captain Charlatan. I'm taking with me all the slaughtered battalions and regiments; and all the mothers, murderer, who are dressed in mourning, and all the orphans and all the war's cripples, the lame, the blind, the paralytics, the insane. I'm taking them and going on."

"What are you saving him for, Captain?" shouted Loukas angrily. "Kill him!"

Father Yánaros shrugged his shoulders scornfully. "Do you think that I'm afraid of death? What can that bogeyman do to me? He can take me from this vain life to the eternal one—the poor thing can do nothing more. Death is only a mule; you mount it, and it takes you to eternal life."

He raised his hands to the sky. "If I live," he cried, "if they let me live, I will never crucify You again, I swear; I will never leave You again, unprotected, to the mercy of Anna and Kayafas, my Lord Jesus! You said You hold a dagger—where is it? How long will You go on being crucified? Enough of this! Come down to earth armed, this time. After such pain and bloodshed, I understand man's duty. Virtue!—arm yourself! Christ!—arm yourself! I am going to preach through towns and villages—I am going to preach about the new Christ, the armed Christ!"

He stretched out his hand to the right, to the Invisible One. "Let us be on our way," he said.

The rebels watched him with surprise. "The priest has gone mad." Several of them laughed. "Who's he talking to? Who's he saying 'Let us go' to?"

Father Yánaros raised his hand to Drakos. "Captain Murderer, till we meet again!" And with a steady stride, he was over the threshold.

No one moved; Loukas looked sarcastically at his leader. "He's going to set fires now," he said. "Are you going to let him? Or do you feel sorry for him?"

But Drakos was silent as he watched the old man walk away, tapping his cane on the cobbles. He walked in large strides, his robes fluttering in the wind; his white hair swung over his shoulders as he walked; he was heading for the path to Prastova and he descended hurriedly. The stones dragged under his heavy shoes; beneath his arm, the gold-embroidered stole and the silver Bible gleamed in the rays of the morning sun. The blood of the dead which he had poured over himself had run down his head and dripped on his sunburned nape.

Captain Drakos watched him, and his mind moved far away, to one of the shores of the Black Sea; to a village filled with peace, with Christianity and greenery. This old man had crow-black hair then, and was dark and slender—a handsome priest; how he had stood up to the Turk and defended Christ and Christianity! And when the day came, the holiday of the patron saint who held the village in his palm, how this old man entered those flames and clapped his hands and danced and never condescended to go out into the dangerless wind again!

How Drakos hated him, how he loved him, how he admired him!

And then he had lost sight of him; father and son had separated, and they met in the Albanian war years later. How he had rolled back his robes and climbed the hills, calling to the Virgin! And as he called Her, the soldiers saw Her climbing the rocks, carrying the wounded boys in Her arms. This old man could shape anything he wanted in the air, because he believed, because he pained. And his soul came out of his body and at times became the Virgin, at times St. George the Rider, at times a loud voice that cried, "Christ conquers!" And the inner beings of the soldiers would fill with assault.

Father Yánaros had descended now and was ready to take the path to Prastova; within the still-slanted rays of the sun his shadow fell like a giant on the rose-colored stones and continued on. A little more and he would pass the rocks and disappear behind them.

Loukas jumped over to the middle of the road and raised his rifle.

"Eh, Captain," he called, "now let's see the stuff you're made of! So he's your father: so what? Steel your heart! You have a duty to perform and a report to give. Didn't you hear him? He says he wants to be free!"

Father Yánaros heard the rifle trigger cock behind him; he understood. Reaching to his right, he took Christ by the hand and placed Him in front to shield Him from the bullet.

"Come here, my Son," he said softly, tenderly to Him. "Come, so that they will not hurt You."

Two or three guerrillas came up and stood beside Loukas;

they, too, raised their rifles and took aim as they looked at the captain. Drakos stood by the gate, not speaking, admiring the way his father strode over the rocks, handsome and forceful as an old Archangel.

"Eh, Captain," Loukas called again. "I tell you he's going to set fires—stop him!" He paused for a moment and giggled. "Can it be that you feel sorry for him?"

The captain's blood simmered; the eyes of all his men were fixed upon him, waiting. Loukas laughed again; he winked at his comrades, then turned to his leader.

"Now let's see what you're going to do, Captain," he said, but he did not get a chance to finish.

Drakos raised his hand. "Shoot him!" he commanded in a choked voice, and his eyes filled.

"Eh, priest," Loukas shouted, "eh, Father Yánaros, wait!"

The old man heard the call and turned. His bloodied beard gleamed a deep red in the sun. Loukas pushed aside his comrades and steadied his rifle butt on his shoulder. The bullet caught Father Yánaros in the forehead. The old man opened his arms, and without uttering a sound, fell, face down, on the stones.

# More Outstanding Works by Nikos Kazantzakis